About the Author

Andrew Fuller spent the first 31 years of life in and around Bournemouth. After reading history at King Alfred's College, Winchester he took an MA in Museum & Collection Management at Bournemouth University; then promptly ran away to Cornwall. Today he spends much of time lurking in the past and is almost content.

Some Dreams of Youth

Andrew Fuller

Published 2009 by arima publishing

www.arimapublishing.com

ISBN 978 1 84549 386 8

© Andrew Fuller 2009

Printed and bound in the United Kingdom

Typeset in Garamond 11/14

Swirl is an imprint of arima publishing.

arima publishing
ASK House, Northgate Avenue
Bury St Edmunds, Suffolk IP32 6BB
t: (+44) 01284 700321

www.arimapublishing.com

Contents

The Velvet Marionette

The Velvet Marionette
Prologue

She awoke as her man let out a stifled yelp. Lying face down and sprawled out she quickly became aware of how much of the queen-sized bed she was taking for herself. A smile started at the corner of her lips as she noticed him rubbing his arm.

"Good morning, rough night?" He asked softly.

"Hmm, morning." She stretched out and reached for him. Putting her arm on his chest she drew herself in closer, whilst at all times being careful to make sure that the thin silk sheet still covered their nakedness.

Thin shafts of sunlight edged about the draped windows and the fresh scent from the garden stream trickled into the day bringing with it the delicate hints of elderflower and honeysuckle.

"I feel so tired; I must have travelled miles last night." She whispered, yet despite this she knew it was not the kind of tiredness one could counter with further sleep.

"You haven't been that restless in years." His pale blue eyes meet her deep chocolate brown ones and he squeezed her arm affectionately. "Is there something personal you're trying to tell me?" She responded with a shake of her head. "Because really," he continued in mock indignation "I'm sure I could always find a small, cramped chair somewhere; somewhere I can rest my weary bones without the fear of bruises!" He ran his hand down her exposed arm and under the sheet and across her stomach feeling the delicateness of her soft skin and delving into the rich amber scent that always accompanied her.

She pulled up even tighter to him and leant over him, her chest resting on his, her hair gently brushing his face; neither had to look far for the undeniable love they would always share. She kissed him gently on the lips, a perfect kiss, a kiss that nearly took the life from him.

"I do believe that I have found another possibility." She whispered as her lips passed near his ear. He looked at her with a slight glint in his eye and a smile formed.

"Really, that would be wonderful; it's been years," he gave her another gentle squeeze "are you sure?"

She shook her head tickling his face again with her hair.

"But it is something I must check." He chuckled at the tickling sensation of her hair. She slipped fully on top of him straddling him and pinned his outstretched arms into the softness of the bed, although there was no resistance offered. Gently she flicked her hair across his chest and barely caressed his skin with her breath. "Do you need the Jaguar for a few days?" She asked a short while later when they regained eye-contact.

"No, help yourself, but why not let the train take the strain?"

"I thought I'd drive for a while and see where that leads."

She let his arms go and they held each other in a tight embrace.

"Well that sounds okay; it will give me a little bit of time to do some more on my book."

"It won't take long, no more than a few days I'm sure." She raised herself on her arms above him, then suddenly leaned forward and blew a raspberry on his chest. Before he could respond she had rolled off and stolen the single sheet, lithely wrapping herself in it like a toga before standing at his bedside looking down at his nude form. She raised an eyebrow, but he made no effort to cover himself. "Last one in the bath has to wash the other first!" She whispered provocatively as she darted for the door.

Okay, so maybe getting into the fire engine with her younger sister hadn't been such a great idea after all. Of course she'd really not wanted to and had said so. But her parents had insisted that unless someone went with Toni, her younger sister, then Toni could not go; in the end it saved so much hassle just to get in the bloody thing.

She did not really think that Toni was bothered that much about whether she got to have a ride or not but her father had been embarrassingly insistent that the photographic opportunity should not pass. If he had not been so short, round and thoroughly unable to do anything so public he probably would have got in himself. Of course this would never be admitted yet that's parents for you, so often making their children live their own dreams out for them.

Unfortunately what had started as a bit of annoying, but harmless fun at her school summer fete was now becoming a bit of a nightmare. Not that having to get into the engine with her little sister had been tough enough to endure with so many of her teachers gazing on saying how lovely they looked together and so many of her 'friends' sniggering behind hands. No, what really annoyed her was one over helpful fireman who practically manhandled her into the engine before dumping Toni down upon her lap and a bright yellow helmet uncomfortably onto her head. Plus there were then all the cries from the various firemen about how 'darling' they looked in the back and could they have a copy of the photo to keep in the cab as a lucky memento; god how that had made her father beam with pride if they asked to buy her or swap her for a heard of camels or something; he would probably say yes. She just wanted to take that stupid yellow hat off and fling it to the floor, where hopefully it would smash into a thousand tiny pieces and the bare-footed school ballet troupe would flounce over them and end their pathetic attempts at 'emotional interpretation' for a final time. Okay she was feeling way too bitter now. Still, the thought made her smile inwardly.

They had been the last in a long queue, as apparently was her lot in life, when crackled words had buzzed frantically over the firemen's radio; then before she fully understood what was going on the fire engine was off, the fireman throwing themselves effortlessly into their well practiced action positions, their unwitting captives squashed apparently forgotten in the back.

Any calls that her parents may have made in an attempt to draw the attention of the firemen to their children in the back were drowned out by the wailing sirens so Thomasine clutched Toni tightly and snugly fitted herself into a corner behind the second row of seats against some breathing apparatus.

As she was bashed about she told herself that her parents had probably not called out at all as the fire engine had roared away, no they were probably to busy polishing their pride as the mouths of her teachers and friends hung agog as she and Toni rushed to the scene of the emergency, maybe to serve the community, or maybe to end up on the front page of the local rag; god how her father would beam with pride.

The engine flew around the narrow Penryn streets for several minutes, occasionally it slowed for awkward corners, but most of the time it just hurtled along madly. Toni sat quiet and content, too young to comprehend and apparently quite happy to earwig the muted conversations that emanated from the front. Thomasine looked down at her sister and remembered a time some five years ago.

Thomasine sat in blue denim dungarees; they were decorated across the chest with thin floral embroidery which was perfect for picking at. She wondered why her parents were talking so softly in the kitchen with the door shut. How silly of them to think she would not notice no matter how gently they had done it and didn't they realise that the glass serving hatch, though closed, still allowed a little sound to pass through.

She sat in near silence humming to herself something she had picked up during 'sound and music' a boring hour between maths and lunch spent in the school hall on crossed-legs; she began picking at the shiny patch on the brown cord settee, the result of so many picked noses and secretly wiped fingers.

Her parents came into the backroom, they had something to announce. She listened, a little, though barely heard anything until she realised that they had just told her that she would not be going to the same school as Trudy next term. Was that right? Where they actually asking her for an opinion, or how she felt? She said nothing, just staring at the blank television wishing it would spring to life and take their words away. Instead her silence was taken as acceptance, "Such a good girl, she deserved a chocolate biscuit." As if she ever had a choice in things anyway; the matter was dropped and at ten years old Thomasine's life would never be the same again; and she didn't get that biscuit.

Suddenly the fire engine lurched so violently to the right that she was sure they were on two wheels like in one of those appalling American 1980s TV shows her parents loved, where everyone charges madly and violently about, usually firing guns, yet no one, not even the baddies, ever got hurt. Fortunately the back of the vehicle swung about quickly and suddenly they came to a halt.

The firemen poured out in a collective motion to take charge of whatever situation they would happen across, Thomasine and her sister waited a few seconds and looked at one another before peeking out of the window to see where they were.

The fire engine had travelled several miles from her school and come to a halt on the southern side of town, the haunt of many tourists in the summer months. Here there were few houses for the ground was mostly low and the sea had a tendency to come right in especially in the autumn and spring often causing many undulating sandy bumps to become temporary islands; a heaven for wildlife but horrible if you got caught by the unforgiving tide.

From her elevated position in the fire engine Thomasine could see that where they had stopped was now barely yards from the sea. Across the open countryside before her a pale grey sky frowned upon an encroaching grey-green sea and a few straggling tourists who were being ushered to safety back along the road.

Toni decided that she wanted to get out so they clambered out of hiding place and hopped down; Toni held her older sisters hand tightly as she twisted impatiently about trying to spot her absent parents; understandably she was now getting close to tears. Thomasine quietly listened in to the various conversations going on about her.

Apparently a little further along the beach a section of land, an entire cliff-face actually, had collapsed in upon the rising tide and despite it being the month of May and tourists were beginning to arrive locally, or maybe because they were, the area was to be cordoned off immediately. She thought she might have heard something about people being spotted near some abandoned houses above the fallen cliff-face but her attention was interrupted by the arrival of her parents.

A gust of cool, fresh air filled her lungs; for a moment she thought she could almost hear the words and feel the steps of every person to have visited here mixed in with the breeze. There was a presence in the air that was almost electric. She shivered violently, wanting to hold herself in her own arms; Toni appeared not to notice a thing; was she scared?

Their rusting second-hand hatchback, a far cry from the leather trimmed Mercedes she had enjoyed riding in as a child, squealed to a halt next to the fire engine; its tired mechanics groaned and wheezed, choking and spluttering as they died and she could now see her parents hopping up and down, red-faced and shouting as they were prevented from coming forward by some recently arrived policemen. She heard her father calling for Toni and she vaguely recalled letting her hand go and Toni trotting off. Feeling neither the desire to follow or to move further away Thomasine stayed put. *Go on walk away without me; you'll be sorry later* she thought to herself, hoping they would forget her then feel incredibly guilty later.

She felt an unusual attraction to this place and it annoyed and intrigued her as to why it should be so. Sure she had been to this place before, many times in the past, when she was younger and saw the world through less cynical eyes. In her 'younger days', as she referred to the times pre-senior school, it had been a treat to come and collect shells from amongst the sandy, grass strewn dunes. So many happy memories; but at the same time there was a presence of desolation and loneliness; it was almost like she was hearing the gasping sighs of invisible souls, so unhappy that no one would stop to speak or play with them. She recalled a time when she had been four and collected a discarded yellow crisp packet full of beautiful shells; she left them on a bench they had stopped at on the way back to the car. Her mother had been the first to notice and insisted that dad ran back for them; he had done so grudgingly, but he had actually run. He used to run a lot back then, four or five mornings a week, for fun, now he worked longer hours and never had much time.

For a moment she wondered what had happened to those shells; and how it was that she could remember some things so clearly, yet other events from the same era so little. She had not been back here for a while, excuses came easier the more she made them and it was not as though her parents did not have at least one other child to bring here.

Thomasine watched as her parents each held Toni briefly and engaged in tearful conversation; their words fell well short of her ears. Not that they were far away, a brief jog and she could have been there in seconds, for a moment she nearly did, but then the started to feel embarrassed or was that just an excuse? Suddenly her nose twitched as the rich scent of an unusual perfume floated along with the breeze and the day started to change. She looked about her as the scent grew stronger for a moment then suddenly vanished as quickly as it had arrived; just for a second Thomasine could have sworn she had seen two figures standing atop a high sand-dune now detached from the mainland having been cut-off by the incoming tide. However when she looked more closely there was nothing.

It was rapidly beginning to get darker; there was surely rain soon to be upon the day. Thomasine found herself shivering again as the wind picked up again and she wondered how long she had been standing on the same spot, not moving, or talking, just thinking. The soles of her feet began to itch within her boots *"I'll be treading new ground soon."* She whispered to herself.

Why had no one said anything to her? What was she going to do and where were her parents, had they not even noticed she was missing?

The dark-haired figure on the dune continued to watch Thomasine as her blonde companion bent to the floor and picked up a small sandy coloured shell; standing she held it up to her ear and smiled. "I can hear the sea in this one."

The other figure turned her pale features towards her and looked puzzled for a moment, before allowed a soft smile to appear on her lips; she returned her gaze to the shore.

"Is that her?" Asked the blonde girl, she was answered with a gentle nod. "She looks young."

"Fifteen," spoke the dark haired girl, the first words she had uttered in an age, "younger than is perhaps best, but now is the time."

"Ah fifteen, I vaguely remember," the blonde girl stared across at Thomasine; memories in her eyes "the pain, the heartache…the hormonal unbalance…not to mention the terrifying visions and huge upheaval."

"Of being a teenager?" The dark haired lady queried. "Or, of the way her life is about to change?"

The blonde girl nodded and tucked the shell into a pocket inside her jacket. "Both. I think it is going to rain soon."

"It always rains at the seaside, especially here." The dark haired girl mused.

"Oh yes, I forgot, didn't you say you were here before?"

"A long, long time ago when we came back from Europe after that first trip…this was where we arrived."

"Has it changed much?" The blonde girl asked watching the coastline.

"Not much, well there are more buildings now," she paused for thought then smiled broadly at her blonde companion "and of course there are less people trying to kill me this time."

One

Forgotten

So there she stood, feeling just a little bit silly, not that this really bothered her as it had been a long time since she had felt truly comfortable in any situation. However she did realise that she had better do something apart from just standing around like a spare bridesmaid.

Thomasine or 'The Machine' as some at school took to calling her for her ability to read a book from cover to cover and pay attention in class when everybody else was fooling about tried to think logically. She actually kind of liked the nickname; people might say those things to be cruel and unkind when they were in groups, but she always saw a little flicker of respect in their eyes whenever she passed any of them when they were on their own and that made her feel good; she understood that people often made jokes at they things they secretly liked.

People had recently begun to tell her that she looked like 'that Avril Lavigne' with her slightly gothic clothes, long light-brown hair, big blue eyes and minimal makeup; which was actually kind of flattering in may ways because she knew that lots of the boys fancied Avril; then again surely she had looked like this for ages, well since she had been born anyway, so why did Avril Lavigne not look like her, the great pretender! She did not even care for the music that much, though the choirmaster had noticed the similarities in her and she was sure that he had visions of himself coaching her to Number One stardom and the critical acclaim he might receive. She did not sing anymore and the more people asked her if things were *Complicated* she would ignore them and further more whenever she was looking for a lost…something…NO, she was not looking for her bloody *Sk8ter Boi*!

At fifteen Thomasine was nearing the end of her penultimate year at school and she was getting excited at the thought of going to college, or maybe to put it off for a while and travel to France, or Italy. Although she never really liked any of that fancy food; it was too much like the things that the anorexic girls at school ate in public, before throwing up in secret; just recently she had started to find school restrictive.

Her elder sister was twenty and about to go into her final year at university in Scotland. Thomasine had missed her loads when she had first moved away, but then an autumnal half term holiday had given her the opportunity to go visit and stay with her at her student house. It was an all girl house and everyone there had been really cool and talked and treated her like an adult; even the boyfriends of the girls had shown themselves to be okay, they certainly gave a little hope to the belief that the boys of Thomasine's own age might one day actually become useful members of society and even evolve into something resembling human beings.

But then they were not her sister's boyfriend. She didn't meet him for the first three days; he was barely mentioned until she had overheard her sister having a conversation with him on the telephone. Although only privy to half the conversation Thomasine understood. He was annoyed that he had not been allowed to stay over that week. Slowly it dawned on her how much she was in her sister's way here, a trespasser in another world, one that she was not really ready for just yet. She was grateful to return home a few days later and had never returned.

The beach seemed deserted; the firemen, the police and the tourists had all long gone. It was now very dark and she did not really want to be alone on the seafront all night. Why was it getting dark so quickly; and why had her parents still not returned for her? She had no answers. Just off to her right the gently lapping shore was getting nearer, the beach clinging frantically to the land now just a thinning yellow line that was blown occasionally over land; the taste of salt water was strong on her lips. To her left and behind her the dark open countryside awaited, in front the twinkling lights of the town began to appear and her immediate thought was to go home. But how could she?

She had been standing right here when her parents had chased after her and Toni; or was it just Toni that they sought, for why had they not taken her home as well? She thumped herself on her forehead with the palm of her hand to try and knock that reoccurring thought out. She had hoped they would forget her after all; now they had what was the point in complaining?

Her attention was taken by figures moving in front of her, dark shadows separating themselves from the night and skulking towards her; three of them laughing and joking softly to one another. There was nowhere to hide so she stayed her ground and waited to see if they would say anything to her when they got near.

They walked to within a few feet of her and stopped. She saw them clearly in the rising moonlight, though as yet they had not acknowledged her presence.

They were all female and perhaps all just slightly older than she was. The tallest of them was the same height as Thomasine and looked fabulously glam in ankle-length black lace trousers and the most outrageous twelve inch wide black and red PVC belt; it completely covered her from hips to narrow waist. The buckle was studded with faux, diamonds that grabbed the attention from her multi-slashed black vest with her neon pink underwear visible in various places beneath; she wore a thin baggy black duster and her makeup was 'distressed chic' her eyes smudged with smoky kohl.

The other two were a little shorter, though similarly dressed without actually wearing the same mixture of glam Goth and trash clothes. Apart from their interesting choice of clothes what Thomasine noticed most was the paleness of their skin; she considered herself to be pale yet compared to them she was positively bronzed. However these three girls were truly deathly white, save for their loosely applied makeup that grained in tones of grey and blue, red and green and black.

Thomasine had not gone in a bikini now for almost three years, not since that episode when she was twelve and had been caught out in a suit that would have been a perfect fit a year previously; how could her mother get it so wrong? She let these thoughts run through her mind for a moment and wondered upon the reasoning of girls who would happily flaunt themselves in tiny bikini's, yet consider it quite indecent to be seen in knickers and bra, especially when the bikini's were much more revealing!

She tried not to make it look like she was staring when suddenly she was noticed. There was an awkward moment of silence and although Thomasine was not one hundred percent sure that they would respond to her she spoke.

"You know this area is supposed to be out of bounds tonight?" She remembered how people had been prevented from entering this area, and then felt a little awkward for it was not her position to stop people. However as it seemed there was no one else around and there could have actually been a genuine danger.

The tallest of the girls looked directly at her and spoke.

"Thanks, we hadn't heard that; although it seems pretty normal." She smiled politely and revealed elongated shaped canines; Thomasine's heart quickened and she nibbled the inner of her lower lip. She had wanted a set of fake fangs for ages now and although she had found a supplier in Doncaster and done all the research in finding out the costs, sizing and even obtained a cast of her own teeth, her parents had refused to meet the cost, giving her clothes and electrical gifts far more extravagant in price instead.

"Are you going to the same place as us?" Asked one of the shorter girls, her blond hair neatly cut about her ears, her small piggy nose wriggling as she spoke.

Thomasine shrugged not sure how to commit to a reply.

"You look like you should be," spoke the other short girl pointing at Thomasine's clothing "you'll fit right in and it's not like there's anything better to do out here…if you're on your own that is!"

In unison the three then weaved like smoke on a warm summer breeze about her and moved off into the dark countryside. Thomasine looked down at her clothes. Her parents had politely despaired at her 'summer' choice of ankle length blue velvet skirt over highly polished purple Doc Marten's, cut-off white-ish blouse and blue velvet blazer. She did not really have special clothes to wear for any particular event; to keep such clothes back for special occasions seemed such a waste to her. She turned and began to follow not sure as to their destination, but eager to find out.

The three had not got far. The path they walked had changed from tarmac to compacted grass and dirt and the ground slowly began to rise a little above and away from the gentle wash of the sea. Thomasine caught them up easily and hung just a little back, not keen to catch her skirt, as they walked in single file through a particularly torturous passage of bramble.

They were definitely moving away from the sea now and the ground about them rolled into small hills sprinkled with windswept trees and annoying, almost invisible skirt grabbing foliage. Thomasine was sure that they had passed one or two man-made buildings; abandoned or perhaps not she could not tell; the only light out here was that which reflected from the waxing moon.

After a ten minute walk they found themselves in a wooded copse. It was a small, deep bowl, barely fifteen feet in diameter and the thought, *probably a Second World War bomb hole* Thomasine thought to herself. There was an obviously worn path through the middle and the whole bowl was shrouded by trees and bushes sprouting around the rim. The air was heavy with a damp earthy smell and it appeared that someone had been chopping down trees for here and there for there was a pile of logs, a smattering of sawdust and a small heap of discarded branches spread all over the ground. This spot would make a very atmospheric campfire setting should the opportunity arise. The girls paused for a second and Thomasine could hear movement all around her in the

19

undergrowth; she felt herself tensing, if she had been a dog her hackles would have been well and truly up.

The Goth-clad trio collectively stepped towards a small patch of intensive darkness on the far side of the copse, then bent forward to look into the foliage covered hole. It was actually a small cave roughly hewn into the side of the bowl; there was a bright blue light emanating from somewhere deep within. The three of girls watched and talked conspiratorially to one another as shadows appeared to move inside.

Thomasine edged closer to the girls and in particular the smallest blond girl in an attempt to look over her shoulder. As she caught a glimpse of the figures moving within; *"how strange"* she muttered to herself. She remembered hearing rumours at school about drink and drug fuelled raves taking place in caves on these cliffs. No one was really sure if they took place, although there was one boy, Paul Davis, who had insisted he knew them to be fact for he had been there himself. Few had believed him despite his *space cadet* mannerisms.

Curiously she began to realise that this girl appeared to be vaguely familiar. Thomasine couldn't say exactly where she remembered her from, although school was the most likely probability. There was no name, just a strange familiarity that she could not quite grasp and with that familiarity also a sense of loss or removal, like a memory forbidden to rise. The girl must have sensed Thomasine staring for she turned and smiled; Thomasine returned it and tucked thoughts of identification to the back of her mind as she noticed figures moving amongst the trees.

The three girls returned to the path cutting through the copse and started their journey once more. As they made their way onwards the ground began to crack in seemingly random places producing small holes flooded with light from some underground source. Suddenly people began pulling themselves out from underground and into the evening air leaving the light to flood out from the now widened holes. The two shorter girls departed silently from the taller girl and disappeared off into the darkness, one to the left, one to the right; in the shadows Thomasine heard whispers and giggles as though the girls must be coming into contact with people hidden away in the shadows.

Thomasine stopped walking and looked about; she could feel that she was being watched by someone hidden. To her left she saw movement, a figure, just for a fraction of a second, but then it suddenly vanished out of sight. Intrigued by this she moved a little nearer to the figure's last location. As she got nearer the trees she looked closely and saw in a small gap beyond a stooped elderly man in baggy tweed trousers and crumpled loose fitting white shirt. Initially facing away, he suddenly turned and Thomasine instinctively moved back into the copse afraid that she might have been prying into someone's garden. She could sense him rather than see him coming towards her through the foliage; suddenly a large black cat leapt out from the space where the man should have appeared. It zipped though her legs flicking her skirt with its thick tail and away into the night, releasing a sound akin to a laugh as it did.

She was aware that sometimes the call of a cat could be mistaken for human words. Her first cat Lincoln, had a yowl which sounded so much like a spooky hello; then there was feral Leo, calling for attention whenever he had made an all too frequent kill and most recently Lucy and her need for companionship. Fortunately the black cat had disappeared, although this still left questions without answers.

Thomasine decided to carry on following the tallest girl as she continued to walk along the path; she walked another thirty yards then eventually stopped at a brick wall. The wall was a beautiful warm, dark red colour and formed from bricks that were probably only half the size of regular bricks. They had softly curved edges rather than harsh square ones and the whole wall was covered in copious growths of ivy allowing it to blend perfectly with its surroundings; Thomasine could not tell if it was part of a larger building.

She decided to hang back a few paces behind the other girl as she appeared to be searching for something. She was running her hands over the wall quickly, barely caressing the surface eventually stopping with her hands directly in front of her face. Slowly she started to pull at some of the bricks. They fell away easily to the floor, silently hitting the dirt leaving a rectangular hole in the wall some twelve by eight inches in size. A soft yellowy-orange glow emerged from within and although the hole certainly did not appear to be large enough to allow a person to enter, it was being attempted.

The girl stepped onto the fallen bricks at the base of the wall and leant into the hole she had created; then, surely by some peculiar trick of the light, it began to bend and shape itself about her lithe body allowing her to wriggle her way inside. Thomasine moved closer and watched on amazed as she saw the girl clambering her way along a short tunnel, the whole thing bending and flexing itself to her movements. She was moving quickly, pulling herself forward with the aid of snapped wooden beams that stuck out from the sides of the tunnel at all angles.

Thomasine couldn't believe what she was considering; it was just that the pull of the mysterious interior upon her skin was somehow magnetic. With barely a second thought she grabbed a hold of the wall and stepped as the previous girl had upon the loose bricks on the floor. She continued to watch the girl pulling herself horizontally away from her and silently wished she had spent more time practising in gym class. However once the mouth of the tunnel had opened to accept her she entered easily and began clambering freely, amazed at the sudden strength she felt coursing through her limbs as the tunnel bent and moved with her whims allowing her ever deeper.

Two
Strange guests

The wall must have been a very thick wall for the tunnel continued for such a long time. As Thomasine moved along she studied the wooden struts that poked out and allowed her to move onwards; they where a good handful, rectangular, very dry and stained dark with age. She assumed that they were probably part of the very fabric of the building, although hopefully not a vital part as they were all broken.

Thomasine was trying to understand how this place could possibly exist; eventually she decided someone had fired a cannonball at the building and this must be the path it had left in its wake. As she looked forward and then behind her, the ends of the tunnel appeared to still be the same distances apart as they had when she first entered; however given that the tunnel did not look wide enough to pass through anyway she was willing to go with a little faith and a strong hope that she was making progress. The girl in front vanished from sight; slightly alarmed Thomasine looked behind her and noticed another figure entering the tunnel. Suddenly she found herself involuntarily shuddering and just as quickly expelled.

Thomasine emerged from the hole inside a dreary room painted a dull, sterile yellow, lit only buy a single bare bulb; attempting to gather her bearings she turned quickly upon herself, but there was no visible sign of an entry point. The room was not large, if she tried she was sure that all walls could be touched from this spot; perhaps it was more of a corridor as there were doors to the left and right and nothing else. The muted sounds of conversation could be heard coming from both directions. As she did not know which way the other girl had gone Thomasine decided to go left; opening the door led her into another corridor.

Slowly Thomasine walked onwards trying to pick out words in the distant conversations. The corridor ended in a turn to the right and here she saw a girl of about five with knee length blonde hair standing nervously at a battered wooden doorway. The walls here was old and the red bricks could clearly be seen beneath the cracked plaster; they crumbled at the slightest touch of the child and there must have been damp everywhere for several small ferns had begun to sprout through the floorboards and there was a strong trace of ivy gripping tightly to the wall. The doorway itself was blocked with a flowing floral print curtain in dull chocolate, avocado and sunflower yellow colours; the young child in white vest top and loose, faded rainbow print flannel trousers was peeking about the edges into the darkness beyond.

She was obviously nervous and then having sensed Thomasine looking at her she turned, *'monsters'* she mouthed with great exaggeration, before nearly jumping out of her skin as another blonde girl suddenly leapt out from beyond the curtain with an exaggerated "BOO"! Together they ran off laughing madly leaving Thomasine to regain her composure, glad that there was nobody else about to see her jump so.

Walking slowly Thomasine moved from one yellow room into yet another she finally found the party. This room, though also being yellow was larger but similarly hampered by the same minimalist decoration, which meant nothing on the walls; although this time there were cherry red leather seats fitted against two of the walls and in the corner a series of curved steps, also painted the same pale yellow, disappearing down into the ground.

Thomasine assumed she was in some great house for the rooms had a faded, lived in feeling, though there was no decoration upon any of the walls; no fine fireplaces or ornate coving, everything had been stripped away. Light coursed from the kind of simple glass chandeliers that would have impressed her parents, although to Thomasine they seemed to be far too small and cheap looking to do the job properly.

People were sitting and chatting everywhere. In addition to the red sofas there were a number of very sturdy looking bench's. Some looked hugely expensive and very out of place with eight long legs of cast iron, a back and sides formed from delicate scrolled iron with lots of imagery of eagles and a seat of two-inch thick white marble; she was willing to bet that they did not move them about to often! Others though were most definitely plastic.

Thomasine was met with nothing but polite, interested, but not intrusive, glances, smiles and nods. Every age group from preteen to eighty seemed to be here; the words of the girl she had followed here had proved right, for her clothing did make her fit in nicely; though she wished she had of worn a little more jewellery for everyone seemed quite prepared to display their wealth, or maybe their feelings, in a manner that glittered.

Everyone was drinking from thick glass goblets; red wine by the look of it; and there were empty bottles, with labels written in some indecipherable script, scattered everywhere, there seemed to be nothing else on offer. In front of the various benches and sofas were dozens of small wine tables. They were battered and very old, but also beautiful as the tops seemed to be a single thin slice of highly varnished tree trunk with a narrow cast iron support twisting its way to the floor where is split into three for added stability. None of this furniture matched, she wondered who owned this place, they clearly had taste, but possibly not enough money to buy the nicest, newest things.

Thomasine wrinkled her nose and frowned, unsure as to what to do now, so she moved across the room and sat upon the end section of a tatty red velour sofa; it moulded itself quickly and comfortably to her body; as if it had a memory of having done such a thing many times before; Thomasine's mind began to wander.

She was pushing her dinner of yellow fish, peas and chips about her plate as her father started to read the letter. Mother and father had both completely finished of course, bad manners not to, even Toni who was nearly three was close to finishing; although fish fingers and chips barely compared to the dreaded yellow fish, smoked haddock she believed, now getting ever colder on her own plate; time for a dollop more brown sauce she decided. He read slowly and carefully looking at the audience gathered about him with exaggerated glee as Trudy told her tale of Michaelmass at university.

Thomasine kept on eating, forcing the cold food down; it was still easier to swallow than Trudy's words. They were laced with barely hidden venom and regret; finally she was living an unrestricted life away from the confines of the family home and private education expectations. But mum and dad still cooed at the words unaware that they had built the resentment in their daughter. Toni just ate on regardless.

Snapping back to life she watched people float through the room in blurs and caught fleeting parts of their conversations. Thomasine heard sexual innuendo whispered from between the slightly parted lips of a couple in the distance to her left and haughty female laughter from her right. She leaned over to see that her seat overlooked the stairs and the open drop to the floor below; two elderly pearly queens with glittering clothes and silver hair sat below. They waved and raised their glasses in appreciation, their sparkling jackets and caps catching the light as she nodded a quick response. The sofa shook slightly and Thomasine turned quickly to find that someone had sat down next to her; it was the tall girl that she had followed here. In both hands she held a shot glass filled with red liquid; the girl offered one to her with a smile.

"Here, I bet you've never tasted blood better than this!"

Thomasine took the glass, which was six inches tall and about an inch in diameter. The bottom half was encased in engraved silver whilst the liquid inside came to nearly the top of the glass. She looked at the liquid inside trying not to look shocked at what she had been told; but it did not have the true tang of darkness that blood held.

The liquid smelt fruity like the wine she was sometimes allowed whenever her parents entertained and they had sat down at the dinning table for the very rare occasions of collective entertaining and dining.

"Thanks," Thomasine replied not wanting to appear stupid or out of place "I'll just bet I haven't."

The girl was watching expectantly so Thomasine sipped the liquid; it tasted like wine, a good quality wine, thick and fruity, but wine never the less.

"Nice?" The tall girl asked. "You've tasted blood before of course, but never so sweet?"

Thomasine blushed and remembered how she once, okay twice, or so, had cut herself high on her arm with a small knife she had received in a manicure set from her older sister as a Christmas present two years ago. She had sat at her desk and licked the blood away as more of a dare to herself than anything; one that she had not been able to refuse. It hadn't been so bad, the taste was a little metallic tang nothing more; worse though was the stinging pain in the morning, the brown smears of dried and congealed blood on her arms and lips and the strapping she had worn for 'muscular pain' for the next week to cover the marks which had virtually faded to nothing since. It had not had a lasting appeal to her and was not a thing she thought often of; but she could understand why people did.

When she replied that she had never tasted blood so sweet she was telling the truth; but still she could not shake the deep down fear that once found out she might not be accepted by these people. So were these people the vampyre's she had thought so much about? Thomasine did not believe the portrayals she had seen of vampyre's on television and in books, though she had enjoyed reading Dracula in her English class just over a year ago. The Hollywood remake with its fake accents and way too much blood had just bored her. For weeks after she had been so jealous of Lucy, but that was probably only because of the way the boys had lusted over her; that was so weak.

Thomasine tried to reason with herself; if these people were true vampyre's and she was amongst them did that make her one of them? She had often hoped that maybe she would achieve such a thing, though she was not exactly sure that it would have been like this.

"So this is your first time here right? I don't remember seeing you before." The tall girl held out her hand and Thomasine shook it daintily.

"Tabatha, that's me, Tilly and Tess were the other two you met," she looked over her shoulder expecting them to appear, they did not, "they'll be around, probably chasing some man or something." She said with an oblique wave.

"I'm Thomasine." Thomasine offered kind of hoping that Tabatha was not about to leave her to go and find her friends.

"Of course you are," Tabatha smiled taking Thomasine's free hand, "we so need to go and see someone."

Leaving their half finished glasses they moved off through the building. They passed through a myriad of rooms, all mostly painted in the same mellow yellow, though now Thomasine had decided that it was actually saffron. There were even windows in a few of the rooms, although all had been boarded up and yes, once again, painted saffron; there must have been at least a hundred people tucked away down here; all with friendly faces and all enjoying the evening in their own despotic ways.

Despite most of the rooms looking the same occasionally they came across one that was by contrast very strange and interesting. They walked through one that had all of its walls covered with zebra skins and instead of there being any proper tables to use there were eight battered red drums. These varied in size and made different noises when people put down drinks, or picked them again. Another room was completely devoid of human life and had grey walls with whitewashed wooden floorboards. Hanging from the ceiling, each by four thick ropes where two eight-foot hoops. They hovered about four feet off the ground and upon each of these sat hundreds of candles. They varied in shape, size and colour, some alight and some not; long waxy stalactites dripped everywhere.

Thomasine looked at Tabatha for explanation, but she just shrugged flippantly, appearing not to understand either; but she did explain the cork room. This was one of the final rooms they passed through and its walls, ceilings and floor were all covered in cork panels. Tabatha explained in whispers that cork was rumoured to prevent heart attacks, hence the presence of only old people who apparently never left the room for fear that they might never return to its coveting embrace. There were eight people in the room, all gently rocking in large wooden chairs, where it seemed they had fallen asleep.

Finally they reached a room, which opened into a series of wide steps, upon which sat a large charred Madonna, which Tabatha told her had been rescued from a church that had burnt down, but she could not remember which one. The steps plunged down where they narrowed into a large kite-shaped room that had no other visible exits or entrances. This room differed from the others for it was much more attractively furnished. It appeared homely, certainly lived in, warm and welcoming; there was even the slight scent of perfume or burning incense floating upwards enticing them down. Thomasine often burnt incense at home but there would always be dust and smoke everywhere, not to mention moaning parents. Recently she had taken to only burning them when she was alone in the house, still the lingering smell was a bit of a give away.

They stood at the bottom of the steps for a moment and waited; Tabatha continued to hold Thomasine's hand and still nothing happened. Thomasine turned her head slightly to Tabatha who continued to stare ahead, but only for a second before she inclined her head towards Thomasine.

"Trust me; she will be here," she looked forward again "she just likes to make an impression the first time!" She nodded emphatically deciding that this was the end of the conversation. Thomasine felt the skin in her hands cool.

Across the entrance to the room at the base of the stairs was hung a flower curtain. This offered no real privacy, but it did indicate that they were entering a different arena. It was made from dozens of thin strings threading their way through flowers of purple and white; they looked so real and yet so fresh. Thomasine reached out to touch one and yes they felt real too, but surely that was impossible; they would have to been rethreaded daily!

She peeked through the curtain and saw to her left there was a low gold coloured, though of course it may have actually been gold, table with a marble top. The legs of the table looked oddly shaped, then she twigged; they where made to look like horse legs with dainty hoofs and curling fetlock. It was kind of creepy though, for they were all positioned slightly differently; maybe there were real legs inside, now that sent a shiver down her spine. The table ran along the length of the wall under the stairs and was covered with small bowls of glass and ceramic. They were filled with jewels some of which sparkled, whilst others just sat there dull and dusty, waiting to shine again.

Above the table on the wall was a huge turtle shell, she was shocked and more than a little sickened that people still thought of such things as ornamental.

"Wow," Tabatha exclaimed, "that looks fabulous on the wall doesn't it?"

"Yeah, fabulous," Thomasine replied sarcastically, "it probably looked better on the turtle though!"

There was also a mishmash of fabrics, neckties and handkerchiefs and the like. Satins, lace and velvets of every colour imaginable; even some that appeared to vibrate with colours, through reds to blues and back again, pulsing with the very breath she took and there was the incense. Small sticks burnt in a bronze dish surrounded by dried lavender; the light purple smoke smelt wonderfully invigorating; much nicer she decided than the stuff she had used at home.

Along the wall opposite to this was a long low settee. It was a vibrant orange colour that looked like it might have been high fashion, thirty years ago when it probably resided in the darkest corner of some seedy nightclub; upon the third wall was a large gold mirror. It was roughly rectangular and maybe three feet by four; although the top was bowed outwards. Its frame was lovingly carved in a floral design, as with many things in this place it had seen better days; on either side were candlesticks formed from polished and shaped antlers. Both different, they were blackened and browned with copper fittings and tall orange candles dripped wax in free-flowing rivers because they were not standing exactly perpendicular.

On the final wall at the base of the stairs was a large wooden cabinet, a rickety old affair with large doors at each end and four smaller ones down the middle. Piled high upon the top of this was an odd selection of cushions and two large bowls filled with potatoes. A stuffed red squirrel sat on a wooden shelf just above frozen in a pose as if ready to jump down.

None of the cushions was larger than an average sized handbag though many were much smaller. Assembled from random cloth and jewels, Thomasine briefly wondered what they were stuffed with; she could just imagine them in her bedroom.

"Here we are!" Tabatha said, releasing her grip upon Thomasine's hand.

Thomasine turned to find a feminine figure standing slightly behind her; the girls stepped aside to let her pass.

The figure wore a fitted red dress covered in gold sequins like scales on a fish. It covered every inch of her from ankle to neck and more, for the collar was high, starched and theatrical; gold and red shimmered and spoke gently in rustles as the dress flexed with her movements. Her hair was straight and long, pulled around her ears and down her front it ran well past her waist. It was strange for although Thomasine tried to look straight at her face she could not quite bring it into focus. She knew that it was a silly thought but the woman's face never seemed to be fixed, or exactly in one place.

The figure came to a halt in the centre of the room; she paused for a moment and did not immediately acknowledge their presence. Suddenly she spun about to look upon them, her face smiling and welcoming and strangely familiar. Thomasine's brain chugged into gear as she tried to find a name to go with the face ...*Stephanie Beecham*; that was it, a younger version of the woman her father fancied on television and again the vampyre connection, *Dracula AD 1972*; the likeness was uncanny.

"Who have you bought me?" The women cooed musically. The question was aimed at Tabatha but the lady never removed her smiling eyes from Thomasine.

Tabatha stepped away slightly and turned to face Thomasine. Inside Thomasine winced, okay this was the part where she was found out and these people would turn on her and drink the last drops from her body! Tabatha considered her response.

"New girl; needs a direction I think."

Thomasine silently sighed gratefully.

"Excellent," the woman smiled taking Thomasine's hand, "you like?" She pointed to the pile of cushions. "Pick one, anyone, it does not matter which, just hold one for a while whist I get your measure."

Thomasine smiled inside at the surrealism of the encounter, but still decided to do as asked; what harm could it do?

Looking down at the pile of gorgeous plump cushions she spotted one that particularly took her fancy so she picked it up. Nothing happened, not that she actually thought that it might. The cushion was a soft lilac-purple colour and where it had been neatly sown together small jewels, some plastic, others obviously not, sparked and twinkled in her hands.

The older woman seemed in a trance and hummed a nameless tune to herself, whilst Tabatha had moved across the room and was having a root through the piles of jewellery; eventually she found a particularly vulgar necklace consisting of large blue plastic blobs strung along on a 'chain' of gold coloured plastic. She turned to speak to Thomasine as she modelled the necklace against herself.

"Very nice," Thomasine replied, before adding with a grin "if you worked in a charity shop and had an alcohol problem that effected your judgement!"

"Ow!" Tabatha replied with a look of horror on her face, she clutched her heart in mock pain. "Break it to me gently why don't you." She looked at the necklace again then held it at arms length and dropped it back onto the heap with her nose wrinkled. "Still, girls' got a point."

There was an awkward moments silence before Thomasine decided that she should try to push for some answers. She waved the purple cushion at Tabatha.

"So what's this all about?"

Tabatha shrugged.

"I don't know, this woman just kind of hangs out here and likes to meet people." She rolled her shoulders. "Actually I kind of thought it might freak you out."

"How kind," Thomasine replied tossing the cushion back onto the wooden cupboard where it disappeared into the pile, "is she okay?" She pointed at the lady.

"Probably, she's usually quite quick at getting the measure of people…you must have hidden depths!" Tabatha moved across the room to look in the mirror and spoke without turning, looking at her in the mirror. "So, you ever killed anyone?"

Thomasine's heart skipped a beat.

Tabatha turned to face Thomasine and smiled at her obvious discomfort. Thomasine pondered the question; of course she had never killed anyone, she would have remembered; wouldn't she? Then again maybe she had. Maybe in the past something she had done had caused someone to die, was that same as taking a life?

When she had not sent the money to Africa she had collected with her elder sister Trudy after a sponsored driveway clearances six winters ago, did anyone suffer because of her cheating? She decided to be truthful and replied no.

Tabatha seemed a little deflated.

"Me neither," she admitted shrugging, and then perked up a little, "damn I was kind of hoping that you could tell me what it had been like."

Thomasine was a little confused and almost let her doubts slip.

"But you're a vampyre, I thought they all killed!"

Tabatha rounded on her, indignantly.

"Well, you've never killed either!" Her tone softened and she smiled. "Besides we all know it's about the blood, not the killing. You kill, people notice, they get angry and they hate you and try to stop and control you." She took Thomasine's hand again and squeezed it firmly. "We all, everybody here that is, know what it is like to be different, people hate us and we have to be careful about what we do; you'll see." She turned her attention back to the woman. "Once this is over we'll get on and I can show you the ropes."

Thomasine thought about this for a moment and hoped that by 'ropes' Tabatha was not referring to climbing or anything that might have involved tying up. This was all very strange and Thomasine was keen to keep things moving along.

Tabatha had not yet given up on trying to wake the woman and was busy waving her hands in front of the ladies face. Suddenly she sprang to life making Tabatha jump. The woman let her big brown eyes wander the room for a moment searching; then settled them upon Thomasine.

"Oh there you are; there's such darkness about you that I lost you for a while!" She waved her hand in the air gently as though she was stroking Thomasine's face, though she stood out of reach. "Such darkness," she shook her head "so dark, I stumbled like a babe upon a thorny road signposted with no answers, not even the ones that I set upon their way so I could get back; I could not see a path."

"That's good, right?" Tabatha asked. "A vampyre needs darkness, yes?" She looked from the lady to Thomasine for support.

Thomasine nodded.

"I guess so...I!"

"No." The lady interrupted. "Though not no, or yes, or maybe I don't know what I've seen. I cannot pass a judgement for I cannot see anything either in or out of you; nothing but black." She began spinning on the spot and muttering to herself.

Tabatha seemed disappointed once more, Thomasine hoped that she would not be angry and go stomping off leaving her alone with this woman, who really was starting to freak her out as she continued her rant, but did at least stop spinning.

"There is a point to be remembered, oh yes; the blackness can mean many things!" She whispered the last part conspiratorially. "Either the girl is not a vampyre," she waved at her clothing "which I doubt for she seems so the part." Tabatha stifled a giggle and the woman had to silence her with a hastily raised eyebrow. "Or she is a very special vampyre," she smiled and bowed a little "whose role I cannot tell for the likes of I am not permitted to see such things, or," she raised her hand to prevent Tabatha from interrupting again, "or she simply has failed to fully embrace her vampyric nature and here we can help!"

"So do I get to take her upstairs then and play?" Tabatha asked looping her arm about Thomasine's.

The woman nodded and as if someone had flicked a switch off she instantly lost interest in them; the conversation was over and she flounced off up the stairs leaving Thomasine and Tabatha alone.

Thomasine was kind of sad; she had quite liked what the lady had said about her vampyric nature. It was almost how she would like to describe herself to other people, if anyone could be bothered to actually listen to what she had to say. She did feel like she was ready to fulfil a role; her image and her clothes were just one part of that, just like the teeth were to these other people. Thomasine clenched her hands together and resolved to find out if she really did fit in with these people; she wished she was wearing her favourite rings and velvet gloves.

Odd, she thought, why had that suddenly popped into her mind? The image in her mind was of a small double ram's headed ring and a larger, silver and amber one; also there was a pair of fine midnight-blue velvet gloves with turned up cuffs and simple, pretty floral pattern impressed there. Inwardly she frowned. She did not own such things yet somehow she felt that she should.

"You're far away aren't you?" Tabatha spoke easily; though not directly at her. She stepped away and turned to face her. Thomasine saw that she held her hands together, her fingers intertwined, her fingers now wearing gloves and rings!

"Here, I know they're yours, I wasn't trying to steal them, just picked your pocket and wanted to try them for fit; they were a bad one!"

Thomasine did not argue as she was handed them. She pulled the gloves on, the fit of course was perfect and the rings she then pulled them over the velvet lining, the ram's headed one on the little finger of her right hand and the amber one on the next. She admired them and smiled inwardly and outwardly and thought to herself that all she needed now was her own set of fangs.

"Now all you need are some of these," Tabatha smiled and tapped her canines provocatively "we'll find you some I'm sure."

Thomasine blushed again as her own thoughts had been turned to words, but she felt happier than she had felt for some time. Tabatha started up the stairs and Thomasine quickly trotted after her wondering where and what they were going to play.

Three
Walking

Tabatha led Thomasine back into the maze of saffron corridors and through numerous now sparsely populated. Tabatha told her that many of the people who came here held jobs in the real world and would need to return to them; so as to keep up the impression of being normal.

Thomasine wondered what the time was but only owned two watches; neither of which ever left the house. One lived at her bedside; it was a cheap plastic thing and advertised some cartoon series and had come free in a cereal box. The other hid in her underwear draw; it doubled as a huge black plastic stopwatch worn on a lanyard around the neck. Her parents had bought it for her last birthday when they believed she had become interested in the athletics team; she had gone on about it a lot, though not for any desire of taking part; no the desires had lay completely elsewhere but that had just proved her to be a foolish girl. Because it had been dark earlier she reasoned that it must be getting very late by now; however when they emerged into the world it came as a surprise to discover that it was a bright, sunny day.

The door shut with a firm click; Thomasine turned and found that they were standing on the driveway of an unremarkable 1930's detached house.

"Didn't you used to live around here?" Tabatha asked, shielding her eyes from the sun.

Thomasine considered for a moment and looked about her.

"Well, I don't recognise this place…but there is a certain familiarity."

Tabatha nodded.

"It's probably just this time of night. I don't suppose you've ever been out and about at this late before?"

Thomasine was a bit taken aback; the sun rarely appeared at night.

"I've been up early, very early in fact. When I went to see my sister at university, I got up at half four."

Tabatha frowned, pointing to a watch hidden up the sleeve of her duster.

"Yeah, but it's only eleven thirty in the evening, still early, I guess!"

Thomasine pondered. *How could it be eleven thirty and be bright and sunny; this was just not right at all.* Tabatha must have realised the conflict Thomasine felt.

"Oh I get it; you haven't got your vampyre clock working yet."

"Vampyre clock?" Thomasine frowned. "Was that like a mail away thing, or was I supposed to get it upon joining automatically?"

Tabatha laughed obviously assuming that Thomasine was pulling her leg.

"Well as vampyre's we live our day at night; therefore it's sunny and light at night and dark during the day, or night…if you see what I mean?"

Thomasine was not sure that she did.

"But what about the sun, you know, sizzle, burn, dust gone?"

Tabatha shrugged.

"Doesn't seem to matter, I think it's just one of those myths that boring people like to perpetuate to put us down and make themselves feel safer." She walked off along the driveway and held the painted wooden gate open for Thomasine; the metal hinge squealed and when Thomasine looked to see if anyone had heard she noticed a curtain twitching in the house opposite. Tabatha noticed too and responded with a little wave. "Looks like the natives are restless!"

There was no traffic upon the road, but that was probably not unusual for this time of night or day. "Yeah that's what I thought." Thomasine muttered as her mind began to fill with a strange vision.

Far below the ground burnt widely and she saw people in a smouldering field. Somehow she was high above and it took concentration for her vision to become clearer; she swooped low, so low did she go that she was able to walk amongst the players of this scene but not to be seen by any of them.

The field was not large, perhaps thirty or forty feet-square, but they were near the top of a hill and with the slight slope the view all around was expansive. Thomasine stood in roughly the centre and looked east, away from the faltering sun. To her right a wooden frame had been constructed and at the bottom of this was amassed a pile of bracken, leaves, small branches and twigs. It was possibly the most anorexic pyre that anyone could imagine; not many trees had survived the fires.

Across the field, though mostly congregating near the pyre were two dozen soldiers. She knew that they were soldiers from the leather belts full of weapons, both pointed and percussion, their dark blue uniforms stained with blood, sweat and dust; the many signs of battle.

They looked upon a thin reed mat placed near the proposed pyre where a woman in a sky-blue coloured velvet gown struggled face down. A few feet away a young man in leather trousers and tattered and bloodied white shirt gasped his final breath, his deathly pale face looking up towards the sky. Thomasine was angry. She did not know, or remember ever having met any of these people, but she knew oppression when she saw it and she hated it and wanted to stop it; however no part of her body would move or respond save her eyes, nose and ears.

The soldiers continued to watch and Thomasine could sense the definite tang of fear in the air and it was not only coming from the woman who continued to struggle. The soldiers shuffled silently and looked upon the suffering. They made no attempt to join in, there was no whooping or cat-calling; they were nervous despite the many arms they held. A pale man with a naked torso and ill-fitting blackened leather trousers knelt beside the woman and pushed a short log under her stomach, causing her body to arch slightly. Her arms and legs were spread eagled forward and back, but there was nothing visibly holding them and although she continued to struggle Thomasine could not understand why she was unable to break free.

Having placed the pivot beneath her body the man appeared satisfied and hoisted a battered leather handled axe. He smashed the butt end down upon the base of her spine. The stomach-wrenchingly crack was audible though her screams were thankfully not. He repeated the action again and again; a dozen times in total, then reached to her hips and twisted until he was satisfied that they had indeed been separated from her upper body.

The assembled cast relaxed a little as the dark burgundy blood melted into the sky-blue dress and through to the grass, the ground audibly sighed as it softened and moistened; another wave of fear rushed over the group.

The woman, not yet dead, suddenly found strength and tried to raise herself upon her hands, but there was not quite enough strength there; however whilst the soldiers' attention was focused on the women there was movement elsewhere. The man in the tattered and bloodied shirt, whom Thomasine had assumed was dead, sat up and let loose the most feral sound. He stumbled forward and wrested the woman upwards by the shoulders and without pause sunk his teeth into the pale flesh between neck and bosom.

The woman's eyes flicked towards the heavens and as the soldiers fled the scene in horror Thomasine felt her anger subside. The woman and man collapsed to the ground, indeed so much blood had been spilt that the ground was now quite boggy and they passed easily into it.

Night came but Thomasine was unable to move.

When the day returned Thomasine was very tired and her legs were numb, but invisible hands held her in place. She watched amazed as the ground began to churn upon itself, the brown muddy consistency made it look as if someone with a giant wooden spoon was mixing chocolate cake. Suddenly the man pulled himself free; he smelt all salty and new, like a baby. He reached into the disturbed earth and lifted out the woman who stood on her own two legs, her dress fresh and clean; then for the first time Thomasine was noticed.

This strange couple turned to face her and smiled, both mouthing 'thank you' before simply fading into the ether; she suddenly felt so very dizzy.

Tabatha grabbed her by the shoulder.

"Hello! Earth to Tom; are you going psycho on me?"

Thomasine felt the other girl's eyes burning into hers and struggled to find words to meet the situation; somehow she managed.

"I felt such suffering," then shaking her head she still felt a little wobbly "like I know the pain of death and though it scared me, it did not stop me, or even hurt me, but make me want to carry on."

"Well good for you girl, though you only walked twelve feet and that can hardly be described as suffering…can it?" She looked to Thomasine for closure but found none in her eyes for her thoughts were still elsewhere. "Well I'll tell you what, if this pain rises again let me know and I'll be the one to tell you if it's really the pain of death," she gave an ingratiating smile "okay?"

Thomasine looked at her with sympathy; a girl pretending to be a woman, in a world she did not truly understand; was she such an idol? Thomasine could not make sense of it yet, but something had clicked in the back of her mind. She blanched a smile and switched subject asking what they where going to do now. Tabatha was assured in her answer *we hunt*.

The garden was perfect, a proud and welcoming addition to any English home. A wide manicured lawn was encapsulated by rose bushes and fruit trees; the generous scent of fresh stream water on the warm breeze bought sense to the day as tea was sipped from bone china.

The two ladies from the beach sat in silence on an impossibly ornate ironwork bench with cushions covered in silver sequins for support. In front of them a table covered with lilac lace sat sprinkled with all the refinements tea on the lawn could provide; overhead in the branches of an apple tree candles on glass holders, slivers of lace, velvet, ermine and stainless steel globes moved serenely. Thomasine walked oblivious within touching distance of them upon the pavement. The blonde lady looked in her direction; but not a word was uttered as they continued to wait.

Tabatha and Thomasine walked along identical looking streets for nearly thirty minutes. Eventually they stopped at a cul-de-sac; here the road rose at a steep angle which made the houses, were an unusual mix of styles, appear to loom over them ominously. There were some houses that were detached and quite substantial in size, whilst in between them others were squashed on top of one another, almost as if they had been randomly built over a long period.

Thomasine was beginning to be troubled by this place. She was not ready to say anything to Tabatha yet; there was definitely something wrong here, but could not be sure what it was. It was almost as if she were in a computer game; wandering about a contrived city, she was almost certain that there had to be someone watching, maybe even judging her on performance and ability to achieve defined targets.

The day, or night, grew ever warmer and Thomasine was tempted to remove her jacket; but then that would have meant having to carry it and there were all the issues of loss of arm movement and style etc.

They walked up the centre of the cul-de-sac and stopped in front of one particularly ugly building. It was tall, with a mouldy white and pinky-yellow exterior and bought back memories of being eleven and going with the rest of her class to a town centre supermarket; had that been all the school thought they would ever be capable of achieving for themselves? The tour had been dull and the only thing she could really remember clearly was the ceiling of the fresh fish chiller. It should have been white but a strange substance of a similar icky colour to the house opposite was spread about the protruding ice maker. She had not mentioned it at the time, but later she told her mum; the resulting words were forgotten now, but they had never shopped there again.

The central part of the building stood like some gregarious council-owned castle. Tall and defining, the shadow it cast brought relief from the sun but not from the trepidation she felt. About the central lump were additions built more recently. Those closest to the centre were of the same style, greyish and slug ugly, but as the building broadened out windows no longer matched and there were all manner of doorways in different styles and colours. There where steps; so many steps leading up and about sometimes even disappearing out of sight underground. There was no garden of any sort, just barren places where concrete steps and breeze-blocked walls had yet to be built; building materials, wood, glass and plastics of all sorts where scattered everywhere.

Thomasine gave Tabatha an exceedingly sceptical glance.

"So what is it we are going to do?" She asked feeling that maybe they were going to do something she did not want to; like break in. Not that she would be forced into anything; but she did not want to appear to be the odd woman out.

Thomasine's stomach began to somersault; for a moment she felt excited and not in the slightest bothered about what her parents might be thinking or whether or not they even noticed she was not at home.

She had the habit of disappearing at home, falling into books and music and dreams. She had nearly finished reading the *Malleus Maleficarum*, which to be brutally honest, was not half as exciting as she though it was going to be. Still she had found it in the local library so what did she really expect, they were hardly likely to have any truly controversial works and she was beginning to realise that life, unlike American films and television, was not full of mysterious magic shops full of the most unimaginable delight. However disappointing, the book had given her ideas and a perspective on an era she barely knew existed; besides an anthology of *M. R. James* stories was proving to be most riveting and maybe even persuasive upon her current actions.

Musically her tastes were adroit although her collection was not large and her digital radio was a godsend. She had inherited a box of tapes from her Trudy. There had been about twenty in an old green shoebox she had been told to look for in the cupboard under the stairs, a cliché she often smiled at, but they were now some of her favourite possessions. It had happened last Christmas just after the visit to the student house and for a while Thomasine had loved Trudy for it.

Most were born of the late 80s and early 90s, *The Stone Roses*, *The Inspiral Carpets*, *The Sundays*, *My Bloody Valentine* and so many others, but there were a few from the early 80s; the *Siousix and the Banshees* track *Belladonna* was a particular favourite. She could never quite comprehend why she did not tell her parents she had them. The music was good; lyrically inspiring yet somehow probably not what her parents wanted her to listen to. The less thought about their musical forays made on her behalf the better. That A1 CD for example, for her last birthday; shame it had got stuck under her wardrobe!

Tabatha looked up at the building and was ready to continue.

"Now we make friends." She announced.

"Friends?" Thomasine queried, and then twigged what she had meant. "I'm going to end up knocking on people's doors aren't I?"

Tabatha nodded.

"That's the great plan. It's all very simple, you knock, you smile, you chat…you become friends." She looked away but Thomasine knew she was smiling. "Then when we want them, they're ours."

Thomasine let this run through her mind for a few seconds, talking; friends…sounded a little like distributing *The Watch Tower* to her!

"I'll start over here", Tabatha pointed at the small property next door to the monstrosity "then move about around the street so I'll never be far away, alright?"

Thomasine nodded and forced a smile despite the butterflies in her stomach.

"If I need you, you'll know!"

Tabatha smiled and waved as she wandered off leaving Thomasine to do her bit.

Thomasine walked up the first flight of steps and saw that the path split into four. The first on the right went down to a series of doors. The next on the right and the one on her left looked like they ran around the circumference of the building, whilst the last path in front of her rose to the higher levels; she decided to leave that route to last.

Believing it would be easy to escape if anything went wrong Thomasine trotted down the steps to the lowest level. The steps were grey slabs of concrete placed upon painted yellow breezeblocks. Imposing walls towered on either side and by the time she had reached the doors at the bottom she was about eight foot below ground level making her feel like some serf in a dingy mediaeval prison cell; a general grey/green mould smeared across the walls, coupled with the added stench of moist, rotting wood.

Thomasine stood in front of the doors, being careful to be sure that her skirt did not touch either the walls or the floor, which she had decided, reminded her of the floor in the boy's toilets at school. There had been a summer BBQ and the queue for the ladies had been long and winding; so taking a short cut that Trudy had taught her she marched straight to the boys. No one had apparently noticed, or at least not mentioned it but it was an experience in smell and mess that she had hoped not to repeat.

There were three doors, two green either side of a burgundy; none were inviting. The doors rotted in their frames with the paint peeling and flaking off. Each door had a small letterbox, worn brass locks and a large panel of opaque safety glass; they were numbered one, two and four!

Swallowing her nerves and still not entirely sure what she would say if anyone did answer the door Thomasine tapped briskly on door number one and waited…nothing happened. She turned her attention to door two, again the same result; and then the same with door four. "Okay," Thomasine muttered quietly "not a good start." She wondered what to do and looked about her. It was so dirty down here maybe these houses were actually abandoned; a voice at the back of her mind agreed that this was most likely so whilst maintaining her dignity she left as quickly as possible.

After a brief check to see if Tabatha was in sight Thomasine decided to carry on with her quest to make 'friends'; choosing the next path on her right she walked around the property. The path was an unfinished mix of concrete, gravel and mud still with a breezeblock wall to her left and as she reached the far side of the property, an ever-increasing drop to the ground below; she was glad not to be doing this in the dark for one slip and a girl could easily fall and break a leg, or worse. The path continued to curve onwards for another thirty paces before ending at a white PVC door. Although mostly glass this was not the type that one could see through and evidently someone did live here because there were empty milk bottles awaiting collection. "C'mon, you can do this" Thomasine whispered to herself and tapped firmly on the door. Slightly disappointed nothing happened; she counted to twenty before deciding to move on.

Thomasine went back to her starting point and continued walking around to the other side of the building feeling an unwelcome tingle of déjà vu as she walked. This probably had something to do with the fact that there was still a high wall upon one side and a steep drop on the other. The path continued in a curve around and ended in a PVC doorway that once again blocked the path so she could go no further. But the door had been built the wrong way round. She could see the lock and bolts but the opaque glass was still dark so she could not see through. Wondering who on earth could do something so stupid as to put in a door back to front Thomasine strode up, unlocked the door and pulled it open.

She half expected to be standing where she had a few minutes ago, but instead the door opened into a corridor. A single strip of blue neon light ran down the ceiling away from the door, it ran for as far as she could see, some thirty feet, before vanishing into the darkness that ruled there. The walls were probably whitish, though they glowed faintly blue near the ceiling and less so the further she looked at the floor, which was dark; a trap waiting to happen.

"No friendship can be worth doing this for!" Thomasine muttered as tentatively she prodded forward with her foot. It disappeared into the gloom as if breaking the surface of water and in her mind she was miles away again.

Thomasine was floating over a rustic farmland, she was so high but even here the feelings of loss and the expectations that accompany them where paramount. It was night and catcalls baited the plain, though they were unable to wake the youth and Thomasine was a black cloud waiting, watching. Spotting the lights of a town in the far distance; she changed direction. She floated down and although the journey was going to take a while that was never going to be an issue.

There was a row of houses in front of her; sitting on the edge of a vast black wood. Looking carefully she spied into the back garden of one particularly fine dwelling and there she saw a pure pool. It twinkled serenely in the dark; such a delicious offer; the dark had never shone so. Underlit, the pool glimpsed in and out of sight, but it was not so inviting as the two who frolicked in it.

They were two boys, brothers; sixteen and twelve. Thomasine brushed down through the trees into the undergrowth and nestled amongst them; then they saw her, or rather felt the presence that she had become.

Rising up she watched them as they began to flee, to run for their lives and that excited here. They leapt from the pool and across the garden, then through another and another, in terror, they fled through so many gardens; escape the only thing upon their minds.

Thomasine followed with joy and a song in her heart. Leaping from fence to fence, effortlessly, no rush, she knew that they could never escape. But maybe she wanted them too, or maybe she would rather that at least they would try; she could not decide.

They were loose amongst the woods when they separated and she had to choose. She chose the right path and travelled more than a hundred paces in a second. He turned in terror, twelve years and all and she smiled with such warmth and friendliness before smashing into him, ripping him whole, the parts then vanishing into dust; like a popped balloon, the sum of the parts failing to match the magnificence that the whole had once been. How terribly disappointing! Then there was that tiny scream from the remaining brother. There was no way he could have seen, blood must have told him.

Years passed in seconds and she waited in total darkness, ready and willing to respond to her calling. Around her there had been mutterings of such terrible things for so long now and they believed that they where about to start again. No one had built at this point for years, not since then, the last time and the things that had happened. Now they were building again.

She rose and took to the skies watching. People searched the land, not necessarily for her, just for something, something tangible, something that they could hold onto, an explanation or maybe just someone to blame, a figure to hate; but they could not find her, so they took to hating themselves instead. There were so many people; too many she believed; but they could *never find her. Wherever they trod the evil followed them and things of unmistakable dread rose from the mines deep down below.*

Then a friend went mad, changing at night to his doom, so why had she spared him? Maybe it was his daughter, maybe it was his name, Toby, but the daughter was the new girl at school and she was going to have a tough enough time as it was. Maybe it was because she knew her face all to well and she saw it every time that she opened her eyes. Then there was the knowing and the nagging wondering as to why she could never be.

Breathlessly Thomasine returned to the world; her head pounding with all too real images.

She withdrew her foot and found it partially covered in a viscous, black oil-like liquid. When she placed it back on solid ground a small pool of liquid formed as it all slid so smoothly from her boot; gathering itself into a small pool it somehow then trickled back into the darkness with a tiny splosh!

"Okay, now that was weird!" She muttered to herself, looking around in someway hoping that what had just happened was witnessed by another. Bending down for a closer look revealed nothing, the little light from above failed to reach the floor and for some reason no light from outside illuminated the black floor. For a moment she considered putting her foot back in *better not* she decided.

After waiting a few seconds she shut the door gently, pursed her lips and with a final puzzled glance at the door walked back to the starting point once again; she didn't rush, instead she tried to think through what she had seen and felt. The hatred and wanting to kill had been so real and yet given her such a rush of excitement at the same time; she had really wanted to hurt the brothers. But would she really kill if pushed to it?

There was just one path left to take now; she looked about her to see if Tabatha was visible yet but still she was out of sight. Whatever Thomasine was going to find along this final path she would have to face on her own.

The last steps were particularly steep, but clean, dry and very solid. After a few steps the path turned to the right before then continuing up sharply again; this was then repeated three more times and Thomasine began to feel quite dizzy, possibly she thought from altitude sickness. Thomasine always had a thing about heights. She never really saw it as a phobia, just a kind of intuitive warning system that at least kept her from getting to close to the edge of cliffs. Then there had been that time when she and her family had been going to climb up to the top of Salisbury Cathedral and she had had to stop after the first few flights of steps with a drop of barely forty feet below her. She had never really got on that well with God and so had not wanted to push her luck too far, so she feigned tiredness to return to earth; her parents had gone on without her.

As she got unreasonably higher and was able to look down upon the houses below she began to feel more uncomfortable; *really it hadn't looked this high from the ground.* She was surprised that there had been no more doors and very few windows, in fact this place was beginning to look less and less like a building and more like a nightmare. Walls were built at strange angles in and out of 'the hill', as she was coming to think of it, windows were in odd places, like maybe the hill was full of caves and someone had moved in and blocked up the gaps to make it more homely, it hadn't worked; instead it was as if 'the hill' was constantly giving birth to the most hideous monstrosities.

The walls were mostly white now and Thomasine was sure that she had to be getting near the top, well she better have been because she was starting to get hot and a little bored. One final corner and she stood upon a single flagstone looking down over huge drops on three sides, *whoa steady girl* she told herself as her head swam; fortunately she managed to pull herself together enough to step down a small flight of narrow steps and onto the large flat rooftop.

Four

Tea and toast

Thomasine was not really sure what she would find, though it probably would not have looked like this. With her internal balance still a little out of kilter she looked across the roof which was covered with white shale that crunched happily underfoot as she walked.

At first she kept to the edges of the rooftop. On her right she was able to look down over the road she had just come from; it seemed a lot further away from up here. She walked around the edge not only to see where she had been but also to get a better look over the odd scene that she found on the roof.

Walls of white bricks criss-crossed the roof at random angles and height and in several places small rectangular boxes some two-foot wide and four feet high had been built out of the same white bricks. They were strange because Thomasine had expected them to house air conditioning units but upon inspection she found that they had no openings at all. However the strangest sights had to be the large white spheres that were clustered in two distinct areas, one a group of four and one a group of three.

Each sphere was roughly the size of a beach-ball and stood on short, trunk-like, white pedestal. She moved to the nearest and saw that it was made out of two halves of white plastic. She approached cautiously and almost got within reach when the top half slid up like the visor of a motorbike helmet to reveal a glass bowl within. It was packed with hundreds, maybe even thousands of sweets! They were semi-spherical pound coin sized blobs wrapped in shiny red cellophane; or she thought they were. The hand written label attached bottom centre told her differently.

Lost Souls – *Ready to Eat*

But they looked so tempting shimmering away in the sunlight; she gently placed her hand into the bowl and picked one out. It was cool to the touch and jelly like in its consistency; *"you'll never taster sweeter"* whispered a masculine voice malevolently in her ear causing her to drop the 'soul' back into he bowl as she shuddered. Thomasine took a step back repulsed and the sphere closed. She looked about her carefully, looking for any sign of movement or any way that someone might be watching what she was doing; finding nothing she edged towards the next sphere.

Once again when she was a few steps distant the sphere opened. This time the interior of the sphere was divided into two. On the right a red liquid was being churned by an internal rotor and was full; the left side was blue and only a third full, but was being similarly mixed. It looked like the ice-drinks machines found in many cafés, but this liquid was not an icy slush, it was just a thick, gloopy liquid; it was labelled.

Virgin Souls – RED = *Female* / BLUE = *Male*

Thomasine stifled a chuckle and began to think that it must just be a joke; *must explain why there as red than blue.* Maybe like the whole vampyre thing, the way they called red wine blood and talked about killing. At least she was quite sure it was a joke, these things all had answers.

She quickly walked over to the third sphere in this group and waited with baited breath as it opened up. She almost gagged when she saw the contents and its label.

You

Inside the sphere a black cloud swirled like ink in water, smoke upon the wind; heavy and thick it folded in upon itself constantly moving. Thomasine stood mesmerised and as she looked, finding her eyes glued to the contents. There was more than black, in fact as she looked closer there was very little black at all.

As her vision focused it scanned in tighter and tighter until she felt that she could see the very molecules that each wash of darkness formed. They were not black, or grey, or flat and threatening. Instead they shimmered through every colour of the rainbow, fluctuating a million shades of red, blue, green all sparkling with accents of gold and silver. Suddenly feeling on the verge of losing control she forced her eyes away and took a step backwards; followed by another.

This time the sphere did not close immediately, it just sat there; then following a gap of ten seconds and with an indignant clump, it slammed shut. "Hey", she told herself "there's no way of knowing who the 'You' actually is!"

Thomasine wanted to find out more so began walking across the roof towards the group of four spheres.

She made half the distance before noticing to one side what looked very much like a dinning table built from more white bricks; intrigued Thomasine diverted towards the brick structure. As she got nearer she realised that in addition to the table there where also four brick chairs. It was strange how she had not noticed them previously because she was near where she started her rooftop wander. Momentarily losing sight of the table as she rounded a final stone rectangle she stopped sharply; Thomasine was no longer alone.

Sat at opposite corners of the table where two men; apparently they were taking breakfast! Thomasine found herself holding her breath; they were talking to one another and she was sure still unaware of her presence, barely feet away; she listened.

"Well I say that it's not unusual, you may say that it is wrong, but, I, in my slightly more enlightened position am prepared to take things on a whim; for a while at least." This chap was in his mid-twenties judging by his looks, though possibly in his fifties by his clothing choice of tweed suit, matching waistcoat, starched white shirt and blue tie. As he spoke in his properly clipped English he was spreading pâté upon toast; being careful to prevent crumbs falling anywhere but the china plate on the table in front of him. He wore large glasses which made his face appear thinner than it probably was, his chin was absent and his nose positively rampant.

"Well, *I*," said the other man who was dressed in a similarly coloured shirt and tie but with a grey sleeveless pullover "stand by my view. See how she gapes and gawps, barely congruent as to her intensions or purpose. I'll wager she's never even done it…" The first chap almost choked on his toast and the second snorted his contempt. "Done the deed, you know, embraced her role." He wiped his chin and dropped the remaining pieces of the toast that he was eating onto his plate.

"Oh, do grow up old chap, we all know they fail, happens all the time; just another want-to-be."

"I believe the term today is wannabe!" The other guy retorted.

Thomasine knew they where talking about her and deciding that she had been standing for long enough she sat herself uninvited next to the chap wearing glasses and opposite the other. They paid her no attention.

The chap with the glasses spoke again.

"I have a feeling that she will do the trick, sort out the order, finally cut out the boring," he turned and smiled broadly at Thomasine though still not speaking to her, "I think this will finally bring a sense of closure." He offered Thomasine a soldier of plain toast, which she accepted, surprising even herself.

"Well, she could at least say thank you; such rudeness!" The other chap lent over the table to Thomasine and waved his toast at her. "Don't you think?" He asked.

"Thanks, for the toast, not the lecture." She replied.

"Ah splendid, see I told you so!" Glasses guy nodded appreciatively at her and gave the other man the evil eye. "If he," glasses guy pointed at the other man "could keep his mouth shut for more than thirty seconds he might see her potential."

"She still won't see," the other guy replied "I told him we should not rely on a girl, but oh he would just be so insistent."

"You want to watch it," glasses man said tapping the side of his head knowledgeably "knows all, sees all…"

"Does bugger all!" Thomasine was shocked at what she had said, but it had shut the two bickering men up; she shrugged her shoulders. "So who are we talking about?" She asked, and then took a nibble of the toast; it was very good, cold but just the right consistency being softness in the middle whilst crunchy on both sides.

The two men remained silent with their attention firmly on their toast. She considered stealing a bit more toast from one of their plates to try and get their attention but then she saw the door. In that last stone rectangle she had passed there was a door of lightly stained wood; it was slightly ajar. There was a moment of uncomfortable silence because the two men had noticed that she had seen the door.

"So what's through there?" Thomasine asked.

The chap with the glasses was looking directly at the door.

"Well I have to say that I have never seen that door, open or not before. Then again, I have never seen you before; so maybe you should go through."

Thomasine rose from her chair.

"Okay…oh by the way, sitting on those stone chairs is definitely not good for your posture," she walked to the door "or your arse!" The two men looked at each other with shocked expressions upon their faces and began eating again.

Stepping through the door Thomasine found herself at the top of a spiral staircase. She was at the top of a huge polygonal interior, the entire building that she had traipsed about appeared to be one vast hollow space. The smooth walls where criss-crossed with thin metal supports from the top right to the bottom holding them in place. The floor was not too far below so she started out down the winding path.

Round and round she went getting ever faster all the time even though she was unsure why; eventually, feeling quite dizzy she stumbled onto the floor below. Holding onto the rails at the bottom until her head had settled she took stock of the situation; people were watching her. Fortunately they seemed to be more embarrassed about her presence than she was.

The staircase ended on a rough dirt floor, which slanted substantially from left too right. Upon the wall in this lower area was a battered and rusty clock-face. It was far too large to have ever been intended for this purpose but there was no way of telling where it had come from originally.

The centre of the room was reasonably flat and here she spied two sofas. *God this is turning into a bad night at blind date* she thought as looked at the couples sitting on each.

She walked towards the nearest sofa where there where two girls whispering to each other. They were both dressed simply in pale silk gowns, possibly even night-wear; often the same thing. Their skin was pale, Thomasine believed the correct term was translucent and was unwilling to admit to herself that had never used the word in conversation. Their feet were bare with the toenails painted alternate red and purple; from the nails trails of metallic sequins ran and gathered themselves at the ankle where they then turned to painted shades of silver, gold and green and worked their way up the girls' legs until they disappeared out of sight at around knee height. As one they both turned to face her; their faces were filled with worry and that troubled Thomasine.

They continued to whisper to one another and Thomasine was unable to hear what was being said. The worry was foremost in those large clear-blue eyes below their delicate blonde hair. Tentatively she took a step towards them, just a step but they instinctively flinched away; like she thought, *terrified*. She really wanted to talk to them but was worried it might exacerbate their agitation.

She turned to her left and looked to the other sofa where the next couple sat. They clutched hands, looking worried and confused; they were silent. Their large clear-blue eyes spoke volumes; possibly most about their relationship to the other two people.

"Hi," Thomasine muttered with what she hoped was friendly little wave. "What doing in here?" She aimed the question at the girls, but they responded by trembling slightly and occasionally casting eyes across to the other people here. Thomasine understood.

"So, you are family!" She said a little embarrassed. "Nice place," she offered suddenly struggling for words, "have you lived here long?" She was met by silence and that annoyed her. Thomasine was doing her best to be civil, though really she had little idea how to help. "So you're obviously family, right?" She allowed a slight tone of anger into her voice, it worked and she got a response from the couple she had decided where the parents.

They both wore plain flannel shirts and trousers that resembled pyjamas and their hands where entwined; as where those of the girls. Thomasine found it slightly unnerving that their actions were so similar. She took a step in the 'parents' direction; they raised their hands in defence as though they feared attack.

"No, please; we're just a family trying to get by." Said the man.

His sentiments were reflected in the eyes of the woman. There was a palpable taste of fear in the air. It excited and reviled Thomasine in equal measure; though she could not explain why. She was not happy with this situation having always tried to be a balanced and friendly person, even in the face of extreme adversity; there was something about this situation that just seemed sick to her.

"No one is going to get hurt," Thomasine reassured them, "just tell me what you are scared of? Maybe I'll be able to help." She offered with a smile.

The two girls spoke in unison, a rather gaunt and haunting monotone lilt.

"They told us we were different, the first of our kind, but we failed to fulfil our role; now we must stay here until we might be allowed to leave."

Thomasine mulled this over for a moment.

"Who are 'they' and what made you different?" She asked and she expected a reply. The girls both looked to their parents, who looked back seemingly unwilling to respond.

"Two men." Was the girls' hushed reply.

"They weren't eating toast were they?" Thomasine interrupted; all four just looked at her as if she was daft. "Never mind." She muttered.

"They came and told us that as vampyre's we had to do more to gather friends, but we just wanted to be left alone, to live the way we wanted too…"

"And now they are alone; or at least they should be." A familiar voice cut the air from behind. Tabatha, Tilly and Tess were standing on the last three steps of the staircase watching the scene. Thomasine had no idea how long they had been there, nor what part they were playing in any of this but with an increasing level of annoyance she rounded on the girls.

"Is it a punishment?" Thomasine demanded to know.

"Yes," Tabatha replied, "we all follow the instructions given to us; they didn't."

"You can't just go round arbitrarily dictating how people should be; you don't have that right." Thomasine argued.

"You stupid cow, you know nothing." Tabatha sneered as she took a step forward, Tilly and Tess remained a pace behind ever fulfilling the minion role. "You're just another wannabe; you have no opinion, no voice and no vampyric future!"

Thomasine was hurt by what Tabatha was saying. For a while she had thought of her as a possible friend but she was damned if she was going to let anyone dictate to her. Keeping her voice low and level she took a step toward Tabatha.

"So what now, you think to hold me here too?"

"We could, if we wish, it's not like there's anyone on the outside who'll mind." She smiled sickly, god Thomasine wanted to rip that from her face; as with her thought the smile folded to a frown.

Thomasine felt a little tingle running from her spine, though her stomach and out through every inch of her body; the sense of fear rising about her tasted like a slight electric charge as she realised; Tabatha was not as sure of herself as she was letting on.

"I think you people should leave." Thomasine turned to the four people seated on the two sofas; they did not move. She stared at them hard and felt a guttural urge to growl violently; somehow she kept it in. They must have sensed her anger for they gathered themselves together and stepped away towards the wall at the lowest corner of this strange prison.

Tabatha stamped her foot causing a little puff of dust to rise and charged towards Thomasine, her eyes now shrouded in black angry shadow.

"Remember I told you that I would be the one to tell you about pain, you can't ever leave here." She screamed angrily.

A calming voice told Thomasine not to worry or be scared. Although she had never been a fighter or trained to defend herself the thoughts and impulses were suddenly in her body. A blueprint for survival existed and instinctively she felt and saw every movement and knew the outcome before the events had taken place.

When Tabatha reached for her she was barely inches away; calmly Thomasine held out her hand, the fingers instantly winding their way about Tabatha's thin neck bringing her to an instant, shuddering halt; her feet scraped for purchase on the dirt. Thomasine would have liked to see into her own eyes for whatever Tabatha saw there terrified her.

"Why not, I can always walk." She whispered calmly in response to her last words and for a moment enjoyed the realisation in Tabatha's eyes; then she threw her as easily as if she was tossing a small doll across her bedroom. She flew like some human-mutant bird, flapping madly like that *freak* from the banned film, clucking and barking like a demented chicken to try and avert the impending crash she was about to have against the wall of the dome. She sailed over the heads of the four from the sofas and passed straight through the wall. Thomasine hoped that a body shaped hole would be left, but alas no, it was just a big hole.

Quickly Thomasine looked to see if Tilly and Tess were about to intervene; they were nowhere to be seen.

"Well?" She walked towards the group as the huge prison began to tremble and shake. "Are you coming?"

Thomasine had stepped through the wall with the other four people just behind her, however as she emerged on the other side she found herself standing alone in the middle of a familiar suburban street. There was no sign of the building she had just been in, or the cul-de-sac; it was as if it had never existed. She could feel the strange power inside here settling down; it did not vanish, she could still feel it trickling through her muscles and she liked it. Thomasine was not sure if she was a killer, or a vampyre; but she knew that she should try to find answers; her only option was to return to the rooms where this strange night, or day, had begun what seemed such a long time ago.

Thomasine found the path back to the house easily; she felt sure that there was some kind of imbedded map in her body guiding her and it worked perfectly. Although hardly recognising any of her surroundings she quickly found the correct street. The door to the house was open and she quickly walked though finding herself back in those saffron corridors; a few people where still present; none made eye contact. Thomasine ignored them as she knew who she wanted to see.

Thomasine stopped once as she found herself in a small anteroom near the top of the stairs leading to the woman's lair; the air was heavy with a vaguely familiar scent. The room was quite small and the only item of furniture inside was a black table. Upon this a smashed cobalt idol sat upon a carved copper tray. Next to it were four vases. The first was amber and contained fire, whilst the second was blood red and held rhubarb. Next to this was a white vase holding daisies and a forth was transparent and contained catkins. She waited a second to see if anything would happen; it did not. *Whatever*, she thought, and quickly turned and continued on her way; the smell however lingered in her nostrils.

Finally she arrived back in the lowest level where the strange women had made her hold a cushion and talked nonsense. *What are the chances of actually getting any real answers* she wondered?

The woman was sitting eyes closed in a round wicker chair, surrounded by companions; silent companions. Thomasine remembered reading about these during one of the many break-times she had spent alone. They were slightly less than life-size and consisted of human profiles painted onto a flat wooden board. She had never seen any before, save within the pages of that book and they were slightly spooky in appearance for despite being two dimensional their eyes appeared to follow her. There must have been at least two dozen; children, maids, fine gentlemen in fancy wigs and soldiers…she recognised those especially.

"Welcome back," the woman spoke gently and without surprise, "people rarely come back here; I cannot possibly think why?"

"To you or this place?" Thomasine pondered as she watched the figures.

Instantly the woman's face changed into one full of horror. Her face twisted and contorted, the mouth became a black void filled with rotting teeth, her nose appeared to sink into her skin, the eyes reddened and bulged forth as if something inside was trying to escape. Emitting a hideous scream and releasing a stream of spittle down her chin she leapt forward in her chair, coming within inches of reaching Thomasine before baulking. Thomasine was busy examining the floral basque, made from dead flowers, pink lacy cloak trimmed with pink fur and huge flower the women wore in her hair. Thomasine looked briefly at the monstrous face and felt repulsed but not scared so she stood her ground and waited; the woman realising she was not having any effect slunk back into her chair; her face returning to normal.

"You want to know if you're a vampyre?" There was moment of silence and the women looked away sheepishly. "I still do not know."

"And what of Tabatha, Tilly, Tess and the family, what happened to them?" Thomasine asked, the woman turned back to face her but her eyes where closed.

"Well someone threw Tabatha through a wall," she opened one eye to look at Thomasine and then closed it. "So she's dead; Tilly and Tess never existed, they were just projections created by Tabatha. As for the others…they have returned to their previous state; out of my sight."

"And Tabatha was a vampyre?"

The women nodded, but replied ambiguously "Maybe; although she might have been a projection of someone else."

"What do you mean?"

"You'll work it out soon enough. As with so many things in this and every other world there are varying degrees of everything. Just because you have two vampyre's together in a room it does not mean that they will think and act in a similar manner. As with human…some are good, some do bad; some just do nothing."

Thomasine pursed her lips and wondered what next. She was not really any better off information wise, but she did feel different and she felt as though she was getting somewhere and that had to be positive.

"I think I must look elsewhere." She said more to herself than the woman.

"Well you are only fifteen," the woman smiled and raised her hands, "no offence, but maybe you still have things to learn."

School, Thomasine had forgotten such things existed. How much time had passed, had she been missed? What would they say when she returned to school? She didn't know; but she knew that she would learn something more about herself if she returned. Making her way back through the maze of passages once again she found herself on the sunny suburban street; now to go left or right?

55

Five
New friends

Thomasine stood in a place of sand so pale that in places it was almost bleached white. The sun shone from so very high above in a sky so blue, such a blue that if she had not seen it for herself she would not have believed that such a colour could have ever existed. She was standing in a place where steam engines came to die. There was no indication as to how they got here; the few tracks that were visible had disengaged from any larger system decades ago. There was an air of death and desperation; and not just from the machinery.

She saw nothing moving, nothing truly alive; yet somehow there was a sense that all was not gone; all the memories lingered. Orange and brown were now the colours of the season. Despite this the harsh elements of the desert could not quite erase the tales that these huge beasts might yet have to tell; if only there was someone to hear them.

These souls had travelled forever; they had never known a beginning or an end, just a brief transition period between one time and another. Thomasine felt a tug on her soul; she had to be away; their tales were tempting, but they would have to wait a little longer to be told.

Next Thomasine found herself walking with her hand firmly clasped by her mother as they walked together along Oswald Road towards her primary school. It was a walk she must have made a thousand times. She had first come here when she was even younger, when her mother would collect her from the prep school a few streets away before then going on to collect Trudy. Later as Trudy had moved on to day boarding it was Thomasine who came here to learn.

Thomasine and her mother walked slowly and in silence as they made there way amongst a parade of other similar couples; young mother's with children ever eager to escape at their sides. Down the narrow street they walked, choked with cars, both parked and those trying to weave their way through the organised melee. There was no off-road parking for the small houses here, the pavements were not wide and they were very uneven, especially for feet as small as eight-year olds.

Within five minutes they found there way to the front gate. Not that there actually was a gate, just a break in the wire fence between a concrete post and the garden-wall of a neighbouring house. Thomasine said goodbye to her mother then trotted up the path, which wound about a small metal barrier meant to keep children off the grass; it rarely worked. She passed the workshops where boys from the senior school made noises in metal and wood and ran to her friends who welcomed here and they danced and played as parents and younger siblings watched on, some of the adults smoked, some where happy, some sad but only one of the watchers had an inkling as to the nature of the dark clouds that floated apparently invisible above their children.

Thomasine watched the younger version of herself giggling and joking with her friends and briefly she thought she might cry for the memories of happier, carefree times. Fortunately the feeling quickly passed over as the scene began to change before her eyes. The darkness above swirled away to nothing, leaving only clear blue sky.

It had been thirty minutes since she had left the saffron corridors and whilst the road she had walked was unfamiliar its outcome had been as surprising as everything else in the last few hours.

The watching kith and kin melted into the ether, as did the shouts and cries from the brightly clad children, all scrubbed fresh and ready for every possibility that life may throw at them; so what had changed? Nothing, she decided. The scene in front of her had moved on. The school remained the same, as did the houses and buildings surrounding it but more people had arrived upon the scene.

On the grassy area just inside the 'gate', which now actually was a tall black gate, ten people milled about, sometimes approaching the gate as if to escape, only to pull back when they found themselves stared upon by the group of people on the pavement side of the gate. They either stood still or rummaged in wooden baskets filled with leaves and toadstools. Occasionally they would pull forth their hands to reveal rotting apples and horse chestnuts, which were thrown with disdain onto the grass amongst the children. Thomasine stepped away from her vantage point by a telephone pole to the left of the scene and walked nearer the action.

The ten people inside the fenced off area sometimes vanished and more people appeared to take their place, in time they too would vanish to be replaced by others. These people were all unusual in someway; either being overweight, too tall, too short, one had a large nose, whilst another wore a beautiful 1950's style dress that was fitted tight to her waist then blossomed outwards. Her hair was jet-black and long, falling over her shoulders to her waist and her face was obscured by a pig mask; only her dark brown eyes could be seen mournfully looking out. Whatever 'defect' they may have held that prevented them from being the perfect vision of normality became accentuated whenever they went near the gate.

The whole class was lined in alphabetical order outside the Headmasters office. Thomasine checked her watch and pinched herself to make sure this was real; it was. At ten thirty on a Friday morning they should have been in a maths class; they weren't, so all was good with the world.

The office was situated next to reception in between the two large halls. One was usually for assembly but was currently coping with a first year class sitting bored as they watched The French Connection on a large roll down screen; whilst the other was for gym. Here non-athletic girls struggled to dodge the large green ball that was thrown with unnatural ferocity by members of the netball team. How the girls in the queue giggled as another gangly sprat received bruises that would last a fortnight; unfortunately they were also well aware that next time in P.E. it might be them on the receiving end.

As there were classes in both halls the crocodile of chattering girls wound its way from the small bench outside the office, past reception and out into the quadrangle, a strange open place of cracked flagstones and rickety benches wedged between the rows of classes where girls were allowed to spend their breaks so long as they did in virtual silence. The crab-faced woman with the bright red hair in reception glared at each of them in turn as they waited near the office door, each having to spend approximately two minutes in the Head's presence; then back to class. As she waited her turn Thomasine looked into the large trophy cabinet and at the tarnished contents within. None had been won any more recently than the early 1980s and did not appear to have been polished much since.

As Thomasine neared the door, she realised that some of the girls were taking longer than two minutes; was that a good thing and would she be one of them if it was?

"Come in!" It was her turn now.

"Sit please!" Without looking up Mr North gave his instructions and began to fiddle with his notes. There was silence and Thomasine took a moment to examine the room, realising that after nearly four years at this school she had never actually been in here before.

Mr North was definitely 'old school', rumour had it that he was to retire next year, his thinning combed-over grey hair and slightly yellowing skin at home in his bespoke pin-stripe suit. There was no computer, in fact no technology at all in this room except the off-white telephone, which incredibly still had a revolving dial on it. There was a bookcase with three shelves of books packed tightly together; most were fiction she believed; Thomasine thought that being in charge led to there being lots of free time. There was a small radiator attached to the white wall by the window, a rubber plant and on the wall behind the desk two photo's; one of the whole school population from 1977 and one of the queen, probably of a similar vintage. He looked up.

"Ah Thomasine," his pointed nose and round wire glasses adding to an illusion of aloofness, however he did smile and seemed genuine. "Our very own prep school girl, how are you finding things?"

Without waiting for a reply his nose was back into his pile of notes and Thomasine struggled for words that might make a difference. "Yes, yes, good hmmm…excellent projections," he looked up "well there is nothing here to indicate that you will not be getting anything but a good handful of 'C's, or more, to set you upon your way to college, hmm?"

Thomasine nodded and offered a half smile.

"Excellent, any thoughts as to a career path?" He looked back at his notes and the thing that stuck most in her mind was the lack of attention that was being paid to any answer that she might give.

"Yes, yes, good hmm, excellent projections" he looked up and for the first time Thomasine noticed the paleness of those blue eyes, for some reason the image of a Finnish fisherman came to her mind; strange. "Well there is nothing here to indicate that you will not be getting anything but a really good handful of 'C's, or more, to set you upon your way to college, hmm?"

Thomasine nodded again and to her disdain felt herself reddening; had he not just almost repeated himself word for word?

"Excellent: any thoughts as to a career path?" Yet once again his attention was drawn away and down to his notes before an answer could be given. Thomasine realised that he was just repeating himself, she wondered if he was like this with all the girls, one hundred and fifty to see in a day probably did get a bit confusing for him.

"Well I would like to be a teacher, of history," no response came, just more notes being scribbled "maybe even head teacher!"

No response still; then.

"Your teachers and I have had a rethink on your tutoring and decided to drop you from the following top sets." He drew a deep breath and she feared the inevitable.

"These would be Maths, English Language, English Literature and Advanced Level Science." He pronounced clearly. "You are going to get the grades required even without the extra tuition, so there will be the opportunity for someone less fortunate than you to be given the chance to improve." He finally looked up and smiled so warmly all the arguments in her head melted away.

"Have a great summer holiday and we will be looking forward to that final push in the autumn; okay?"

Thomasine rose from her seat and left the room her mind in turmoil. Ignoring the remainder of her class she swept left and through the assembly hall and class 1PB's attempts to transpose The French Connection into playtime drama suitable for an audience of eleven year olds.

Wow and how did she feel inside? The silent corridors and low hubbub from the many occupied rooms dulled her senses as she made her way back to class. Annoyance, that he had not paid her much attention, yes; angry, that he was allowing her to be dropped from top-set classes, yes; happy, that they were dropping her top-set classes, yes; at least they acknowledged her intelligence; but also positive that he thought she would achieve her aims. And she would.

The group of people on the pavement stood saying nothing, they didn't have too; they just looked on almost lacking opinion or ability to communicate in words, but when a girl who was too tall began getting near to escaping she suddenly grew even taller, then she backed away sobbing into the prison; for that is surely what it was. This continued over and over again with different people, as each approached the gate they changed their physical aspect in some grotesque form. Then Thomasine noticed that there actually was no lock upon the gate, and truthfully nobody had been nasty to these kids; so why did they react this way? Was the fear of being bullied, threatened, or being treated like an outcast worse than it really was?

As these thoughts crossed her mind everyone on both sides of the gate stopped moving and all turned as one to look at her. As they stared she felt their feelings slamming into her like bricks through tissue. Hatred, anger, envy, pain, suffering, wanting, needing, love and loss barely did she manage to remain standing as so much familiarity hit her and though she really wanted to, she refused to cry. Suddenly she realised that there was a small hand within hers, she looked down to see her little sister Toni in her prettiest party dress all greens and pinks and covered in lace and bows; oh how Thomasine had hated having to wear it as a child.

"Can we go now; I don't want to be late for Toby's party!" Her voice was soft and slightly pleading, her eyes were also on the people staring back.

"Of course," Thomasine replied, "being late would never do at all."

She turned on the spot, for Toby lived just a short walk away; however the instant they turned the two found themselves standing upon his doorstep. *I could get used to this* Thomasine told herself. Toni let go and pushed her way through the door shutting it quietly behind her; evidently Thomasine was not invited so she stood on the doorstep a moment waiting to see if anything was going to happen.

She vowed to wait ten minutes and then if nothing happened she would knock and… well, then she would just have to make something up. Ultimately she had waited nearly twenty minutes when a small blue vintage van pulled up outside the house; expectantly she watched as two men emerged.

The intricately painted sign on the side of the van proclaimed that they were *The Gold Men - procurers of the finest jewellery'*; they bustled past her to the front door and onwards, arguing as they went. From what she heard they were here to provide everyone with jewellery as a memento to some great coming-of-age event, they were late and not at all happy about being here; not in the slightest. Thomasine fumbled with the rings on her fingers and wondered what to do.

"You thought it was going to be cherry and walnut!" A gentle Scottish voice spoke musically from behind her. Thomasine whirled about to see that two women had appeared on the pavement beside her.

One was slightly taller than Thomasine and quite thin; although not supermodel thin. Her hair was long and blonde, almost white and she had big beautiful blue eyes. She wore a smart white blouse and green velvet skirt that disappeared to the floor. Her hands were clasped in front of her and her little diamond and silver rings sparkled in the sunlight. She wore a jacket that matched her skirt and to Thomasine she appeared every bit the perfect Victorian lady. The women nodded her head forward as a greeting, or maybe to indicate that she was the one who had spoken. Next to her was perhaps the most beautiful woman Thomasine had ever seen, not that she considered things that way, but she did appreciate a person who could present himself or herself so perfectly.

This lady was taller by about six inches than Thomasine. She had neatly cropped dark hair and fair skin, with brown almond shaped eyes that men must have simply drowned in their droves in. She wore a black velvet dress that fitted her body perfectly. Every inch of skin was covered except her hands and face, which was framed by the addition of a high collar under-shirt which was buttoned with a large ruby on a silver or platinum mount. She smiled warmly and spoke through perfect teeth so softly her lips barely moved though her voice was strong and soothing.

"But it turned out to be foxglove and lentil and the taste was, well, quite disgraceful!"

"Huh?" Was all Thomasine managed in response as her brain raced.

The taller woman spoke again politely.

"The birthday cake you had when you went to Toby's house for his fifth birthday."

The memory came back to her. Now Thomasine was very confused.

"Toby…like the jug." The dark haired girl mused.

"But surely not with those ears?" The blonde girl added.

"He's got the clothes, but nowhere to wear them!" The other girl returned.

"Who are you?" Thomasine asked, her head almost spinning as she tried to keep up with the conversation. "And how do you know that?"

"Forgive me," the darker haired girl spoke, "I am Cara," she held out her hand and Thomasine took it gently; the skin was smooth and cool. "And this is my companion Beatrice, Bea as she is known by her friends." Thomasine took her hand; it felt the same as Cara's, Bea smiled. When she touched them both she could sense no malice or fear within them. It was as if they were perfectly content and ease with their world; she envied that. Cara continued.

"And you are Thomasine; I find it prudent to be aware of the people about me and I have met so many wonderful and interesting people by doing so. I know you want to walk with us; I could hear your cry a lifetime away."

"You're vampyre's aren't you?" Thomasine asked, knowing the answer even before they both nodded. "Just like Tabatha…"

"No," Cara interrupted, "Tabatha was not a vampyre. I have, in all my two centuries of living known only twenty, all of whom are my friends."

"Oh," Thomasine mouthed, "you're two-hundred years old? You look good." She hoped that she did not sound sarcastic because she did not mean to be.

"Thank you, but just a little over two-hundred actually, still it's a girls' prerogative to lie!" Cara smiled warmly as Thomasine giggled, then continued. "Whilst I consider myself to be a Regency girl at heart, Bea here is a Victorian lady, but all my friends come from different periods, still, they do not hold themselves by a particular style of taste; it must be of their own choosing."

"So am I a vampyre?" Thomasine asked. "How do you know if you are?"

"Well personally I was born this way, although the term vampyre is a worldly one, which we choose to accept rather than hold as our modus operandi if you will." She turned to her friend. "Bea here and my other friends all accepted my gift at some point in their life after their birth, but they none-the-less are just the same as I."

"And I..." Thomasine trailed off feeling herself deflate. Here where the kind of people she had dreamed about being with. Could it possible happen, everything had been so strange, maybe a dream, would this be any different? She remembered Tabatha and the feelings she had felt so recently and wondered.

Bea spoke.

"We saw you with your younger sister when your parents chased after that noisy fire engine." Thomasine remembered how she thought she had seen people watching her. "Your parents were very concerned for her safety; they love her greatly, as they have love for their daughters all."

"Sure." Thomasine muttered, her eyes looking at the ground. Cara rebuked her gently.

"Do not judge them too harshly; you may desire to return to them."

Thomasine ran this thought through her mind and concluded that she was even more confused about her current position than she was when with Tabatha.

"How come I did not see you then, and why did they turn and leave me, why did they not see me and call for my return?" She asked.

Cara was patient to explain.

"You did not see us because you did not occupy our world then; but you felt us. We exist within the world and interact with it as we choose. We saw you and what you might become...and now here you are; there is a way back, should you choose. But you will only get one choice and that decision will be soon. As for your parents...well, for the moment their memories of you have been taken, but it is not permanent; yet."

"So, we were hoping you might join us on a little trip." Bea said; her accent musical as she glanced toward Cara. "Will you? Right foot forward, for luck."

Both of the girls smiled warmly and Thomasine made her choice. She nodded and looked at the two of them in their beautiful clothes.

"Well...so long as you don't mind me coming with and I'm not getting in the way...okay."

Six

Tea for three

As they walked Thomasine's new friends explained that they were going to a museum to pick something up. They were amusingly vague about which museum and what exactly they were going too collect and Thomasine was keen to find out more.

"Well," said Thomasine as she recognised the streets "as we seem to be in Truro I guess it must be The Royal Cornwall Museum."

"Almost," said Cara "not actually *The* Royal Cornwall Museum, but The *Other* Royal Cornwall Museum."

"But there is only the one Royal Cornwall Museum…isn't there?"

Bea smiled and Cara gave her a sly wink and told her to wait and see.

Thomasine felt a real sense of affinity with the two ladies, *sometime you will just feel comfortable with someone* she told herself and this was the first occasion that it had ever been true. Okay she accepted that they were much older than her, although they did not act like they were *that* much older. They kept the conversation light and open-ended. Bea mentioned her youth in nineteenth century Scotland and briefly how she had met Cara, who really had saved her from a fate worse than death and Cara talked a little about herself and her fiancé. Thomasine was listening of course, but inside her brain was filling with questions; like watching a film and wanting to know what happens at the end, she resisted the urge to ask the questions just as she would resist the pressing of the fast forward button.

Thomasine did ask about their looks and how they kept them for so long. She had assumed that like it said in so many books that a person stayed the same as they where when they became a vampyre; however Cara was keen to point out that this was only partly true. Apparently they retained the image held when they had accepted their 'vampyre' nature, which was not the same thing as becoming a vampyre.

Without a watch it was hard to tell exactly how long the journey had taken, but by the time they reached the classical revival museum it distinctly felt to Thomasine as late afternoon. Thomasine asked about how night and day affected them as she had not been convinced by Tabatha's explanation and she was right to be sceptical. Cara told her that whilst daylight did not affect them, night and day and the vampyre perception of them remained the same.

Turning of the main high street they walked a little further then stopped outside the Royal Cornwall Museum. Thomasine looked up at it and frowned, it had been a while since her last visit and it still looked just as she remembered; a place full of odd collections where bored kids could disappear easily and snog. Then she noticed that her two new companions were looking across the road; Thomasine did likewise. Performing a perfect comical double-take she saw that on the opposite side of the road to the Royal Cornwall Museum was an exact replica.

"What the hell...?" She stammered and performed another double-take. "I don't remember seeing that before!" She looked above the entrance and noticed that this 'new' replica was actually called The *Other* Royal Cornwall Museum. Cara caught Thomasine's eye and opened her mouth to say something else but before anything came out she stopped and smiled, her eyes seemed to sparkle at Thomasine's amazement as she shook her head and began walking towards the door.

Thomasine joined them as they swept through the large marble framed doors with bay trees wither side. Bea explained there where to prevent strikes by lightening and neutralise the effects of witches; Thomasine just nodded and agreed and acted like she already knew that. Above the door was the motto *'Be good or be gone'*; she and Bea held back as Cara approached the reception desk which was round and built of some ancient wood that Thomasine thought was probably now protected; how the past allows us such misdemeanours. At a distance all is acceptable, like old fur coats, elephant feet umbrella stands or tortoise shell jewellery; the crimes have been committed and destroying or hiding the objects away was not going to change anything. Thomasine had long understood that history should not be judged from a moral stance by those in the present.

There were two men behind the desk and neither was in a hurry to talk to Cara, but too her credit she waited patiently. Presently she was noticed by one of the men, an exceedingly wide man of about sixty years with all of his hair on his face and none on the top of his head.

Cara slipped words to him and called for his colleague; she stood silently whilst they whispered to each other rapidly then moved to their computer. It was obvious to Thomasine that neither was proficient in its command. Eventually the wide man came back to Cara muttering words and shaking his head; Cara remained patent. Shortly the conversation stopped and the man left the desk and disappeared off into the bowels of the museum,

Cara returned to Bea and Thomasine.

"All is not well?" Bea noted.

Cara smiled gently.

"Apparently it is *'not on their computer'*; though they assure me that they will find them, it just might take a little time."

Bea nodded, her eyes scanning the rest of the reception area.

"Shall we take tea whilst we wait?" She turned to Thomasine. "Tea?"

Thomasine agreed and they moved through to the tearoom.

The tearoom was panelled in wood and Cara told her that in the past it had been a library. She led them to an ancient looking round table in the corner where a window overlooked the vast museum gardens and the wall behind them was decorated with images of the museums construction. All three picked a paper menu from the centre of the table and skimmed through it; it was full of teas that Thomasine had heard about, but never tried. Whenever she had a hot drink at home it tended to have originated in a glass jar from the supermarket and was labelled simply either tea, coffee or hot chocolate. Fortunately each named type of tea had an accompanying description and she ended up plumping for a *Lady Grey*.

Cara and Bea both consented to her choice and mulled over the selection of cakes on offer. They all had fancy names, presumably for things that were quite simple and the prices where not listed so where probably quite extortionate; Thomasine's rule of shopping #one; if it has no price, it's either free or you can't afford it! Thomasine cautiously pressed the inside of her jacket with her arm as she leant forward to check she had bought her wallet, she had; but she couldn't remember how much she had left in it.

Cara and Bea finished their musings and placed their menu's back in the little stands at the centre of the table; then the strangest thing happened. Within seconds a waitress arrived at the table with a silver trolley. Not a word was exchanged as she placed delicate bone china cups on beautifully painted saucers in front of each girl and a silver pot of tea between them. Then onto the table she placed a silver cake stand piled with the most magnificently tempting selection.

Just as Thomasine was beginning to get comfortable with her surroundings the scene began to change. The walls of the tearoom melted away to be replaced by a series of small shops and the table they were sitting at became a much simpler affair formed from chipboard and spindly metal legs. The tea items vanished and instead glasses of cola, crisps and sweets appeared in front of them and then she noticed that Cara and Bea had changed too. Thomasine looked at her clothing, school uniform; then she recognised where she was.

Thomasine remembered all the times that she and her friends Tania and Tracy had come here after school. Tania was a highly intelligent swot, with big funky glasses and a quirky sense of humour. She was always at the top of the top set regardless of the subject, yet she displayed a beguiling ability to be completely unaware as to how she achieved such things and completely above all forms of comment whether positive or negative from her peers. Tracy on the other hand was thin, blonde, beautiful and totally dotty. She had a weakness for boys and them for her; although this did include not actually being able to hold onto one for more than a week. She was convinced that all men where attracted to her bottom and displayed it often in skin-tight pants or short skirts.

Thomasine could not actually remember the name of this café, maybe it never even had one, but she knew where it was, on the corner of Brassy Road, near the Victoria Church. The sun was out and they were enjoying a few hours together before they would each have to return to their homes for dinner.

The road was quite which was unusual for this time of day when a strange yellow and orange bus rolled slowly passed them; Thomasine instantly decided that there was something distinctly creepy about it even though it was old in style, curvy and kind of cute in a way modern busses never are. The three girls tried not to pay it any special interest, because that is what normal people would do and they didn't want to be seen like them. However it became more difficult to ignore as the sounds of cheery music, singing and clapping began emanating from within.

The bus stopped opposite them and the three girls found themselves having to look as a small crowd of interested bystanders began to gather. Whoever was on the bus obviously had to carry everything they travelled with them for many of the windows in the bus were open and various items of damp clothing were hanging out attempting to catch a few drying rays of sun.

Eventually from the bus stepped a man; he was about forty with sleek silver hair and a slightly orange complexion. He wore smart black chinos, highly polished brown shoes and tight black t-shirt that did his lean body perfect justice. He walked over to Tracy and began to chat, Thomasine could not actually here the words he said, but Tracy was being polite, talking back and smiling as she did. As if by magic he produced a thin yellow ice-lolly from behind his back. The ice began to quickly melt as he offered it to Tracy with several drips falling onto the table in front of where she sat. Thomasine's stomach was doing somersaults of warning about this person and she mouthed her fears, though the words where silent to her ears; apparently her friends did not believe her for both looked at her as if she was plainly daft.

The feeling of dread rose and Thomasine was ashamed to find herself unwittingly getting up from the chair and beginning to back away from the table and her friends. She turned away as she walked but the feelings did not subside; so she looked back. The man was following her, his eyes glowed a vibrant red; from his trouser pocket he pulled a silver pistol...he aimed and fired it at her.

Thomasine reacted quickly, throwing herself to the ground as the bullet moved so very slowly. He missed, but now stood over her, feet away his breath was sickly sweet with the scent of vanilla; white spittle sat at the corners of his mouth.

"Next time!" He muttered before fading into the air.

Thomasine put her hand to her throat and felt something wet there, blood, she really had only just been missed by the bullet.

As quickly as the tearoom scene had vanished it now returned; Cara was picking up the teapot and beginning to pour into each of the cups. There was milk, cream, sugar and honey in small pots. Once finished she then handed each a fine china plate from the bottom of the cake stand.

"First choice?" Cara offered. Thomasine was about to reach for the stand; but stopped her hand going to her throat, her eyes blinking at the surroundings. Had they maybe never changed at all? She swallowed a gasp and tried to focus.

"We did not order these, but they were what we wanted..."

"How is it done?" Cara interrupted; winking subtly. "Answers always come, and sometimes half the fun is in the waiting for them."

Thomasine soaked in the inviting scent of fresh tea and tried not to look as if she had just been shot as she pulled her jacket straight.

"So how come I've been to the Royal Cornwall loads of times and never noticed this place before?"

"Sometimes buildings move." Cara replied, her face a picture of honesty.

"Buildings can't move...can they?" Thomasine asked her eyes wide at the possibilities of what Cara said.

"Well imagine how bored you might be if you stayed in the same place for hundreds of years!" Cara explained with a little shrug of her shoulders.

Thomasine looked about her and wondered if she should say anything else.

Bea and Cara both smiled and Thomasine felt another tickle of warmth inside her; like she was with sisters. She was happy for it, she felt more relaxed than she had in a long while; there was a heady sense of control emanating from the two ladies and it was completely different to how she had felt when hanging out with Tabatha.

Enjoying their tea as they sat for over an hour in the tearoom; Thomasine found herself consuming two cakes and three cups of tea, but only because that matched what the others had done. Obviously figure-watching was not too high on the priority list when one was a vampyre! Cara and Bea talked about their pasts a little more. Thomasine was never truly convinced that they told her everything about themselves, but then why should they? They were pleasant and polite, taking interest in her favourite music, which apparently they had quite a taste for themselves and they didn't ask any awkward questions about her life or her feelings about anything contentious.

Cara explained that they were here to collect three pots, which had been deposited in this place some one hundred and forty years ago; on the understanding that they could be used for display but should be returned when requested. Evidently they were not on display and their current location unknown. Neither Cara nor Bea seemed particularly worried by this in fact they almost seemed to expect it and were perfectly willing to wait for them to be found. Still if you were immortal and time and people travelled on a different plane it was understandable. Bea suggested a tour of the museum whilst they waited and both Thomasine and Cara agreed whole-heartedly.

They walked the long dark corridors of the museum. Thomasine often heard people before she saw them, a cough or squeak of shoe upon the polished marble floor was occasionally audible and it was only after this happened twice that she realised just how silently they were walking; well Bea and Cara were, they must have had the softest footfalls ever though Thomasine's own heavy boots were most percussive. Their movements were almost unnatural, so gentle and graceful in fact that she found herself trying to imitate them.

They passed walls filled with paintings and labels so small Thomasine could not read them all. Fortunately Cara in particular but also Bea, displayed an amazing depth of knowledge and explained who people where and even told her anecdotes that Thomasine would never have otherwise known.

Whilst Bea continued to wander, Thomasine found herself pausing by a painting with Cara at her side. The portrait was a subject from the twenties, a woman with an hour-glass figure and hair that fell in waves to her shoulders.

"You love art don't you?" Cara asked her eyes now removed from the painting and upon Thomasine.

"Some," she replied "not modern stuff...though...I do like the stuff that Vettriano produces."

"Oh yes, I simply adore *The Singing Butler.*"

Thomasine waited for a moment, then turned and caught her eye.

"Sorry, I don't know any of their names." She replied, biting her lip.

"You know, the one with couple dancing on the beach, as the maid and butler hold umbrella's against the elements!"

Thomasine broke into a huge smile.

"So that's what it's called. I love that, I have a picture of that taken from a Sunday supplement on the cover of my geography book."

"I know," Cara replied placing her arm on Thomasine's, "you must view my copy of *Lovers and other Strangers*, some of his lesser known, darker work...fascinating."

"I love the way that you want to know what is going on outside the frame of the picture...where have the people come from, where are they going; how did they get there...." Thomasine looked to Cara who nodded.

There were no cases of objects to start with for objects were large and placed in small recreations of the places where once they might have originally been found, a kitchen, a dinning-hall or salon or such. Cara smiled and stopped as they reached a nineteenth century gentleman's study.

"Oh look," she exclaimed, "we have a pair of torchéres just like these at home." She stepped about the guide-rope and walked right up to them. She invited Thomasine to come closer; Thomasine hesitated for a second as she glanced around trying to spot any hidden cameras but still gave in to temptation.

The torchéres were six and a half feet tall and hugely decorative ornaments with large square feet and twisting bodies rising to a plinth. Cara told her that it was hollow at the top and one would put scented oil in then when turned on they would heat up and provide a pleasant scent for dinner parties or quiet evenings alone. Thomasine looked to the floor and saw the remains of cable running from the base, any plug long gone as the internal electrics where quite improper for this modern time. Cara showed her the hidden bakelite button on the copper body; she pressed it and was surprised when suddenly the whole thing shuddered slightly and began to emit a truly awful smell akin to roasted wet dog.

Cara pressed the button again and the smell began to dissipate, although not very quickly. "I do believe it needs a good clean!" She said as they stepped away from the area to see Bea who had moved onto the next display.

"But it wasn't plugged in! Was it?" Thomasine asked.

"No," Cara replied, "be especially careful what you touch here. There is a lot of fun to be had, but also danger."

They rejoined Bea, who winced as she noted the canine smell they bought with them; Thomasine's stomach was doing lots of little summersaults. This was beginning to be the best museum trip ever!

At the furthest end of the museum they found the remnants of the interior of a church. Cara explained that it was from a small village many miles away that had been raised to the ground nearly two hundred years ago. What was here in the museum was as close a reconstruction as they had managed with what remained and without any photos of the interior. There was the larger part of one wall and most of the alter end, part of the tower above and one side of pews. The three girls took seats with Bea sat on her own on one pew, whilst Cara directed Thomasine to sit with her a few aisles back.

They sat in silence for a few moments and then Bea spoke.

"I remember these seats especially." She reached down between her legs under the chair and felt for something there. "Ah yes, my father and brother would put their hats here, all the men did back then, the women kept theirs on their laps."

Thomasine felt down under her chair and yes Bea was right there was a strange metal frame there, she never would have guessed its purpose. Could it be that Bea really had personal experience of this place? Bea pointed to part of the wall above the remnants of a broken stained glass window and rose from her chair waiving for Cara and Thomasine to follow suit.

"Maidens Garlands," she shook her head slightly, "I forgot these were here, or assumed they were lost."

Thomasine looked up to see the Maidens Garlands, which where rough paper crowns covered in paper rosettes. Their once bright colours still slightly visible, few were marked with a name; Bea explained more.

"They were made and placed upon the coffins of young girls who had died before marriage."

"Hence Maiden." Said Cara; Bea raised an eyebrow smiling coyly.

"Well I was good most of the time, so maybe more *Maiden* metaphorically rather than literally!" She winked provocatively and Thomasine instantly knew exactly what she meant; so did that mean that Bea was dead? If she was a vampyre was that likely, or not? Thomasine was not sure. "The secret was discretion," Bea continued "a talent now sadly lacking in most." She turned to Cara and rolled her eyes, raised an eyebrow and smiled with a suggestive secret. "Besides…pot, kettle, black…is there not someone here who slept with their future fiancé on the first night that they met?"

Cara blushed, just a little, but took Bea's words in the good natured way in which they were intended, though she quickly explained to Thomasine how she and her future man had been forced to spend the night together in a carriage after their train had broken down. Apparently he had been the perfect gentleman and they had been together almost ever since.

They began to make their way back towards reception along the other side of the museum pausing occasionally to look at interesting exhibits; ultimately they came upon a large archway. It was tall and vaulted and Thomasine realised that it looked quite out of place here; really it would have been more at home in a cathedral. Beyond the arch there was a series of marble steps that were so wide that the three of them could easily walk up them side by side. The marble had thin blue veins running throughout and no matter how hard she tried Thomasine just could not get the image of stilton cheese out of her mind.

The stairs went up thirteen steps before turning right and continuing up for a further thirteen; then they turned right again and once more there where thirteen before they found themselves on a wide landing facing a set of huge wooden doors inlaid with a delicate leather floral pattern. All the time they walked up the stairs they had found themselves overlooked by mediaeval scenes of hunting, jousting and other courtly pursuits for the walls were covered in a huge tapestry that hung from the vaulted ceiling high above. The colours were vibrant and there appeared to be gold and silver thread woven through the fabric, but whilst it looked in such fine condition it did have a kind of funky smell that made you not want to hang about it for too long.

The landing was empty save for a waist-high wooden plinth, upon which sat a bust of Saint Columba, whom Cara explained was responsible for the Book of

Kells of which Thomasine was familiar with from a school trip to Dublin two years previously. Next to the bust was an open ledger recording all the names of the people that wished to enter; Bea was pushing the doors without luck whilst Cara and Thomasine had gone to examine the ledger. In firm red printed letters across the top of each page was the order SIGN BEFORE ENTRY and the ledger itself was quarter-full with signatures. Written by each name was a date and although the writing of the names was in a scrawl that was virtually illegible, the dates where. The last entry was dated as the 7th June 1967, whilst the earliest was, if the ledger was to be believed, dated from some time in 1493.

Various inks and writing styles had been employed over the many years and it was then Thomasine noticed that that there was no pen.

"Do you have a pen?" Thomasine asked Bea as she came over to see what the others were looking at, but whilst Bea shook her head Cara began flipping through the pages.

"I think that what is required is a mental, rather than physical mark." She pondered out loud, finally reaching the last page with names on; now there were three new signatures. Thomasine was forced to suppress the embarrassment she felt for whilst the first and second new signatures, 'Lady Cara Manton' and 'Beatrice Beadle', where written in a fine flowing fountain-penned script, her own 'Thomasine Westall' had been written in what could only have been biro; still it was definitely her signature. Suddenly the doors gave a slight click and turning the three found them open a few inches. Cara stood between them as Bea and Thomasine pushed open the doors and they stepped into another world.

The floor of highly polished oak shimmered as light cascaded from a hidden source somewhere high above; at first just about twenty feet in front of them was visible but as they stepped further down this path more lights came on and areas they had passed were returned to darkness.

Rows of books ran from the central isle off into the blacked-out distance and although not everything was in sight it was quite clear to Thomasine that this place was far to large to have existed above the museum; but how could she argue when there were just so any books to be read? Each of the rows of books was about six feet wide and fifteen shelves in height, far too high to read the spines let alone lift the books down. Above this was a landing and further rows of books identical to the ones below could be seen. White marble busts were placed on carved wooden plinths at the end of each row, which was blocked by a burgundy velvet rope, but Thomasine knew that this was not going to stop them.

"Ooh books," Cara muttered to herself as they walked, Bea grinned happily and Thomasine, well, she never knew that such a place like this existed here in town, if she had she would have come here sooner and often; in fact she may never have left. Thomasine looked to Bea as she spoke.

"Some people, they say, claim that a person's fortune in the short term or for a particular venture can be dictated by the random opening of a book and the reading of the first lines found there." Bea looked from Thomasine to the room in front of her.

"Please tell me we have a little time to spend her?" Thomasine asked.

Cara wrinkled her nose and appeared to be thinking over the possibilities, but her sparkling eyes gave her away. She nodded and the three of them separated and began wandering through the library.

The library was not organised like a modern one and that was perhaps best for the books for the most part were not suited to a modern library; few people would ever appreciate them. It was divided into sections: autobiography (including Diaries, journals and Letters); Biography (individual and collective); Essays, *Belles Lettres* and Literary Criticism; Fiction; History (including Oratory and Rhetoric); Philosophy and Religion; Poetry and Poetic Drama; Prose Drama; Social and Political Science and Travel and Topography.

Thomasine intended to head straight for history, her favourite subject, but got distracted on route and ended up in the fiction section. The smell was fantastic, that book scent, the age and the knowledge, the sweat of creating such things and the world that they might lead her into. She came across original copies of works by all three Bronte sisters; a translation of *Arabian Nights* complete with images that made her blush and look over her shoulder to check she wasn't being watched, Sheridan Le Fanu's *In a Glass Darkly*, but her favourite was *Morte D'Arthur* by Sir Thomas Mallory a 1484 version. The cover was leather so strong and firm, to the touch it seemed barely days old. The pages where well thumbed but not badly yellowed or fragile and she turned each page gently, so sad that she could not read the Mediæval Latin, her history classes strangely yet to cover such topics; then an incredible thing happened. Gazing upon a page where an illumination dripped in glimpse of lapis lazuli and gold the words started to blur. Thomasine held the book in one hand and rubbed her eyes firmly then allowed them to refocus on the text; she must have been more tired that she thought. But surely it was true the words so inaccessible moments before flowed and shaped themselves languidly and there, yes it was true, they settled and she could read it all.

She flicked a few pages; then stopped and wondered, what if? She closed the book and put it back in its proper place and selected another *The Golden Asse of Apuleius* by William Adlington. It sounded interesting and turned out to have been produced in 1566, once again every word was legible and suddenly she was so happy.

Thomasine left the fiction section and moved through to history thirsty for the possibilities that were surely so real. As she went she saw both Cara and Bea each buried in a book. Whoever had constructed this library clearly had a fine taste and plenty of money. But the books were not all similarly bound and the more she looked up and down the rows of books the more she noticed. There where more recent books as well as old ones, some were well read, others less so; this really was the most eclectic collection. In the history section there were books with fabulously coloured spines in a glass cabinet. Tentatively she tried the doors and they opened. The names on the spines where written in languages she did not know. Certainly not Latin; though something in her mind hinted...Eastern Europe. She focused on the words for a moment in the hope that they would reform into something that she could understand but this time she was to be disappointed.

She selected a book with a fine purple and green spine and what appeared to be an engraving of a sheep on the front. The title made no sense so she opened the book near the back. She flicked through it slowly looking at words and diagrams she did not understand, but she tried. On one page she read the end of a piece of text, muttering the strange words in the way she thought they might have been spoken.

The text was part of something larger and as she turned over the page she found that what she had just read was the end of a longer piece of text. As her eyes flicked across the words she felt a strange power building; a strange sense of something unworldly pulling her eyes inwards, something she was not sure of. The power grew and Thomasine realised she could not release her eyes of the pages but from deep within she found the strength to slam the book shut and just in time!

The book exploded with a hugely elaborate POP sending Thomasine to the floor. Smoke and paper tatters poured around her and smothered her in an avalanche of Himalayan proportion. As she laid there a trifle stunned a hand reached out and lifted Thomasine off her bottom where she sat amongst small pieces of paper on a slightly smoking floor; there was a rich sulphur smell in the air. Her ears where ringing and she feared that she might be about to receive a telling off of biblical proportions; fortunately the cool hand belonged to Cara; she was blank-faced, though this broke quickly into a warm smile and half chuckle.

"I told you to be careful about what you touched!"

"I was," Thomasine replied, "I think it might have been something I read?"

Cara picked up the remnants of the books cover and read it out loud.

"Practical humours and Misdemeanours, a fine book, though not if you receive one as a gift."

"Huh?" Thomasine responded dusting paper off herself as Cara explained.

"It is a joke book, not like one you would be familiar with, but one young men of the late sixteenth and early seventeenth centuries would often sneak into the libraries of their tutors or fathers. These men would eventually notice this book that should not have been there and they would read out some of the text and then…"

"Boom!" Thomasine added.

"Sometimes," Cara frowned and dropped the remnants to the floor, "sometimes the effects were a lot more… permanent." Her face broke into a wide smile; she gave Thomasine a big hug and Thomasine understood an affection she had never known before and returned the hug. They released one another and Thomasine noticed that Cara was carrying two books.

"What have you got?" She asked.

"A book of *Hugh Latimer's Sermons*, printed in 1551 and a copy of *Utopia* by Sir Thomas Moore, 1516 an undisputed classic that I have not read since I was a child and I just cannot seem to find my copy."

"Are you taking them?" Thomasine asked.

"Of course," Cara seemed surprised by her question.

"But won't anyone mind?" Thomasine looked fondly at the rows of books and wished she owned so many of them.

"Oh," Cara exclaimed, "I thought you knew."

"Knew what?" Asked Bea; reappearing at Cara's side.

"That this is a Library of Lost Books," Cara explained to Thomasine. "Have you ever read a book then parted from it, only to realise a desire to reread it later in life?"

Thomasine considered this for a moment. Of course there were books just like this in the back of her mind. Strange books that she could not remember the name of from infant school, right through to her copies of *The Famous Five*, that had strangely vanished and either gone to a car boot sale or to her younger sister.

"Yes there probably are books I would like to read again, but there is usually a reason why they are gone; they don't go anywhere in particular," she looked at their faces and suddenly felt a pang of doubt about what she said, "do they?"

"Books are very special things," Cara explained, "whenever a person reads one a little bit of themselves goes into the book, I do not know how, or why, but if that little bit is special the book will always belong to them and should they ever be parted from that book it will end up in a place like this. Believe me when I say that there are thousands of places like this all over the world; if only people realised."

Bea waited patiently for Cara to finish then caught her eye and nodded towards the stairs. "They're ready."

Cara led them across the library toward the front of the building. They made their way to an alcove Thomasine had not noticed before; it was small and dark and framed with Hellenic columns. Cara reached to one side of the alcove and felt for something hidden. Then there was a soft sliding sound and the back of the alcove swung away. She explained that this museum used to be serviced by small Greek citizens that had come with a larger part of the collection. They had lived in the museum and cleaned and provided it with everything that it might need. Thomasine looked about her but Bea added that they might never be seen.

They passed through the alcove and along a narrow tunnel which emerged onto a small plinth some forty feet above the ground floor. There was no barrier to prevent a fall but Cara and Bea didn't seem bothered; they walked from the plinth onto a marble walkway and across to the top of a large column. The roof was just above her head and Thomasine, whom certainly had no head for heights, concentrated hard before making her way safely across the three-foot wide walkway to stand on the column top, which in itself was only about six feet square, aside her friends.

Columns of black silk flowed from the roof and fell, wrapping themselves about the column to an area of highly padded seating below. For a moment the thought crossed Thomasine's mind that if she did fall she should aim for one of them and hopefully she might bounce to safety.

"Do you want to go first?" Cara placed her hand on Thomasine's hip "You don't have to…"

"Down?" Thomasine asked; she was so reassured and vibrant with what had happened in the library that she was willing to try anything; she wanted to go first. She grabbed the black silk and stepped from the plinth. For a moment she felt nothing and that feeling was amazing. Then gravity took hold and she fell, her stomach leapt from where it should have been to her mouth and she wound down at a steady speed to land with a soft thump on the padded cushions below. As she floated down she saw a side of the museum she might never witness again and though she had trusted her life to luck and whim of that silken fall she was feeling fantastic.

Thomasine stood on a padded silken settee, bouncing slightly, feeling naughty and exhilarated. She gazed up to see Cara looking down.

"Catch!" She shouted as she dropped her books and they fell straight into Thomasine's grasp as gently as falling feathers. Thomasine breathed a sigh of relief then Cara came down, winding about the column slowly and landed softly next to Thomasine. She let the silk go but the weight of the two of them having used it must have caused it to break and gently it fell, unwinding itself from the column as it went and landing on top of them.

Together they fought there way out from under the silk and looked to the top of the column for Bea who was not to be seen. Suddenly from the left, behind the padded sofas Bea appeared from a previously hidden black alcove.

"Staircase," she indicated over her shoulder, "well hidden, especially from the people working here, and judging by the dust not used for many years." She showed her fingers and the layer of grime she had collected before wiping them clean on a tissue.

The three gathered together, with Thomasine handing back the books Cara had dropped to her and made their way to the front desk.

Seven
Moving on

They stood before the desk and waited for the man there to look up, which after a minute or so he did; smiling graciously at their presence he picked up three rotund blue and white porcelain pots from the floor behind the counter and placed them one at a time onto the counter in. They were each about two-foot tall and at least three-feet round at the widest point; each was toped with a matching lid embedded with the number 4 elaborately shaped in green.

"Now I can see why you invited me along!" Thomasine said without thinking as she saw the three pots and the three of them.

"Oh no," Cara pointed out, "there are about a dozen to bring home in total, so we shall have to return, you are not just here as a carry-all."

Thomasine blushed and deep inside knew that and hoped that Cara was not offended by what she said. One of the men that worked here ran to the desk and whispered something to the other man behind the desk frantically. Thomasine heard something about a silk curtain having fallen from the ceiling. Exchanging a knowing glance the three girls each took a pot, which Thomasine was pleased to find was remarkably light, almost nonexistent even and they left the museum.

Walking back down the steps into the fresh air and the early evening Thomasine suddenly felt a twinge of panic. The street was different; evidently what Cara had said was true and the building had decided to move again. Questions bounced about in her head. What actually was she doing? Where was she going?

"So, where to now?" Thomasine casually asked as they walked along the pavement. To her left there was a castle in ruins in a grassy square and some of the magnificent old walls had strange carvings and small wooden doors that led to who knew where. Across the quiet road were shops whose neon lights were starting to imprint themselves upon the gathering gloom.

Cara talked about trains and a return to the seaside, but Thomasine thought that they were already near the coast; then again they weren't in Truro any more. She reassessed. Whilst she had recognised her old school, Toby's house and the museum which had been in Truro, the streets she now walked where quite unknown to her; though they did remind her of London.

The three of them chatted idly as they walked; if they did have a train to catch they apparently had time to burn. Thomasine was paying attention to what was being said rather than where she was going.

At first she did not notice that the pavement was narrowing. This continued for a while until she noticed that her hip was bumping into the wall, then she realised that she was walking on a slightly raised stone ledge running alongside the pavement. She saw that Cara and Bea were walking in single file behind her also on the ledge so she carried on. The stone ledge subsequently changed to white plastic, then to red and she found that on her right she was no longer looking into the windows of shops but she was walking past a large neon sign that buzzed slightly in the air and stated that the building was known as the bulC ocilaC…or as she realised in reverse the *Calico Club*. Its front was created from huge slices of white and red plastic making it look not unlike a giant deckchair. She was very impressed by its boldness and was rather surprised that it should exist at all as it was kind of 'in your face'.

Thomasine flicked her eyes to the other side of the road to see if there was anything as interesting over there and was rather surprised to find herself overlooking rooftops.

She looked down to the road; it really was an awfully long way down. She gulped in a deep breath, tried to take a steadying step and fell. She reasoned to herself that she was so worried about taking the wrong step that she may have actually made herself fall. She fell down vertically her stomach remained absolutely calm and surprisingly she was looking about her and not at the ground.

Without the grasp of a silken wrap the fall was so terribly quick.

She shuddered a little as she landed on her feet still clutching the pot because she was terribly worried that it might smash, which when you are falling to your death is a slightly strange thing to do; Thomasine gasped in what she thought might be her last breath.

Mentally she gave herself a quick once-over still not moving from the spot. *Feet?* Yes, two, toes all working. *Legs?* Yes, two, flexing okay, knees intact. *Pelvis?* Yep, still there, she rotated her hips and there was no pain. *Back and arms?* Yes still there, apparently intact. *Heart?* She held the pot in one hand and put her hand on her chest, it beat remarkably calmly.

Maybe she had imagined the whole thing. Thomasine turned to see where she had just been and no she had not imagined it. The *Calico Club* was a huge nightclub, but once may have been something quite different. Wide steps rose to a small door and there may well have been stone columns underneath the neon plastic exterior. The top of the building was pointed and looked very much like some grand Roman-esque building and up there, running about the top, was the ledge she must have tumbled from. Cara and Bea were still up there looking down; they both waved then continued to walk across.

Thomasine looked along the street and noticed how strange it was, each end was much higher and here in the middle the road dipped exceptionally; almost as if this grand building was so heavy the road had sagged over the years down into the ground. She trotted along with her ceramic pot and arrived at the top of the hill as Cara and Bea were stepping of the stone ledge back onto the pavement and was practically hoping up and down ready to fire of questions; however Cara and Bea were ready.

""Did you know," Cara asked, "that in the Zhengzhov region of China, monks from the Shaolin Temple are able to perform incredible acts simply through the power of concentration?"

"These include," Bea added, "running horizontally along walls for more than twenty feet and surviving substantial drops."

Thomasine stopped what she was about to say, rolled her eyes and reconsidered her questions.

"Okay, I get it, don't ask about how I just fell so far and remained intact, as is your pot," she waved it Cara who smiled, "I gather that I, we…I really am not that sure what I want to say…but you know?" Bea gave her a little hug, being careful not to drop her pot.

"We do know you know, we have both been through this and realise that it is a little strange."

Thomasine struggled to control her emotion and felt tears beginning to whelm up within her; was the situation going to overtake her? She so hoped not. Cara came forward and hugged her too. Thomasine found herself enveloped in their perfume, so warm and enriching; she was amazed at how a scent could trigger such a welcoming feeling.

That triggered another thought and the memory of lost days. Once again she wondered how long she had gone, how long it had been since she had slept or eaten properly, cakes not included. Time held no meaning anymore, but did that mean that she was always going to be fifteen? She realised that it could have benefits of course. Her looks would never go, but would anyone ever treat her like an adult no matter how old she got. Then what of marriage, or heaven forbid kids, definitely no plans on that front for a long time; but would she always have to date teenage boys? If she always looked fifteen her chances on the dating front were limited.

Her mind and gaze had wandered and she refocused on the world she found Cara and Bea looking at her waiting.

"We have both had those feelings too." Cara spoke gently, Thomasine blushed; *did they know what she was thinking?* She wondered

"That is to say that we all worry and wonder if we are taking the right path and during that time strange things seem to happen and you will reflect and mull over the past, present and future."

Thomasine took a breath and smiled weakly but not crying.

"Then we go onwards." She said and the others nodded. As they walked on a short man in his 50s with receding hair and a women of a similar age with an abundance approached.

"Fantastic pots!" He enthused not actually paying the three girls any mind at all; his words directed to his female companion.

"Yes," she agreed, "definitely old."

"Yes, old," he agreed.

"Very old." The woman said enthusiastically.

"But fantastic?" He asked looking at the pot in Thomasine's hands closely.

"Fantastic." The women agreed attempting to reach for it. Thomasine pulled the pot out of her reach, the woman frowned, and looked to Cara, then Bea, both were stifling giggles.

"But would you say fantastically old?" She asked, spying the pot in Bea's hands and making a beeline for it.

"Or old and fantastic?" Cara interrupted.

The man and woman stopped speaking and looked indignantly at the three girls, ignoring their pots; suddenly they turned on the spot and began walking away. As they walked off they discussed prison diets and how bright they are on the inside, though Thomasine thought she heard something about curries or cherries.

They walked only a little further to the lobby of a beautiful Art Deco hotel. Tall angular windows frowned down upon the entrance which was shaped in a geometric square design dripping with chrome and coloured glass. There were gentlemen on the door in long burgundy coats, with plenty of gold brocade and flat caps. Through the doors they walked, opened for them as they where and Thomasine felt like a proper lady. Then she looked at her clothes and those of Cara and Bea. Now *they* were proper ladies and she felt such an imitator and vowed to redress the issue as soon as possible.

Cara led them through the magnificent lobby, across the marble floor to a lift caged within decorative floral ironwork; Thomasine half expected them to be challenged but when they were not she assumed that the girls must have rooms here. However this was not the case for once all three of them were inside Cara pressed the button for the basement and with seconds they had descended into virtual darkness.

Still they had not finished though for now Cara led them past baskets of laundry and noisy boilers, through a myriad of corridors until they came to a large black door. Behind the door was a tunnel heading into the ground. It was so steep. Going down the walls were cream and green, smoke and grease tainted the air whilst the walls and floor were gloomy and wet. They slipped and slid as they went, giggling as they did, then Bea must have slipped completely for one moment she was standing on Thomasine's right side then suddenly she wasn't. With a whoop of delight she skidded away from them on her bottom as gravity took hold and the grease did its worse.

"She can be such a child at times." Cara mused, a distance in her eyes. They could still here Bea giggling even though she was far out of sight and they continued to walk carefully after her.

Several minutes later they reached the bottom of the tunnel to find Bea waiting, twisting her skirt about so she could try and look at her bottom.

"Does this look as icky as it feels?" She asked turning around so the others could see her very grim and greasy looking posterior.

"Well it is difficult to say, without touching," Cara was being sarcastic as she kept a straight face, "but yes!"

Thomasine stifled a small giggle and Bea frowned at her jokingly.

"Well I don't care!" She announced. "It was fun. And besides I can always change on the train."

From where they stood the path branched in opposite directions and for the first time Thomasine heard the sound of trains nearby. They were not the sorts of sounds you might expect to hear though; the screech of brakes, the shouting of platform staff, commuters and the electric sounds of a massaged voice over a loudspeaker system; no these sounds were proper railways sounds. The chuffing of steam and whistle of guards she remembered them from a school trip on the Watercress Line in Hampshire, made more interesting by the fact that nearly everyone else but her had hated the stiflingly hot day and smelly trains full of smelly old people who 'remembered the old days'.

Cara directed them down the left-hand path and they walked a short way before arriving on a platform. There stood a magnificent green steam engine trailing a fleet of matching carriages. They were still underground and the air was a little smoky, but Thomasine could see light at the end of the tunnel not so very far away.

Plastered on the wall was a tired poster that proclaimed all families could not head for Birmingham; but Thomasine did not understand this and refused to bring up the matter with the others for fear of looking stupid.

They walked away from the engine and along the platform, which was completely devoid of people. But Thomasine could hear people talking, speaking, shouting and whispering; there where male and female voices, young and old, bitter and sweet and she became a little frightened as the words buzzed about her ears like dreamy bumble bees on a summer's eve. She hugged the pot tightly and carried on walking, glad that Bea was on one side of her and Cara on the other and looked at the carriages as they passed and watched the figures inside moving like blurred shadows. Finally after walking the full length of the train they reached the last carriage and Thomasine had noticed that each had been branded with a *M. R.* monogram.

"So is this like one of those restoration lines, like the Watercress Line?" Thomasine asked.

"I remember the Watercress Line when it actually went somewhere." Cara replied distantly. "But no, this is no restoration line; the train continues to travel the same tracks that it always did."

Thomasine wondered about this for a moment as a guard suddenly appeared from thin air and opened the carriage door for them. He was immaculately dressed in the way that no guard would ever be today when strikes over colours worn are the norm and passengers are just another inconvenience of the job.

"So what does M. R. mean on the carriage, it's printed on every one…is it Midlands Railway or something?" Thomasine asked.

"Close," Cara replied, "it's Manton Railway actually; my fathers'."

"Your father owns a railway! Wow he must be mega rich."

Cara paused, as she was about to enter the train after Bea.

"Yes I suppose he probably was, but money was never the issue for him, it was the process of doing…the creating and building that drove him."

"I'm sorry." Thomasine spoke and Cara turned to her smiling.

"There is no need, he passed away a long time ago and I am very proud of what he achieved no matter how little people remember of it today." She placed her arm on Thomasine's shoulder and looked her in the eye. "In your era, I do not mean you personally but the era in which you find yourself, death is such an ugly thing, a time for sorrow, of mourning and gloom. But this is so frequently a selfish act. People die and yes there probably is some call for sadness, because they will be missed, but if you remember someone and feel sad I think that is disrespectful to everything that they achieved. The person has died, yes, but no matter who they where, or what they achieved they left some kind of impression upon the world and that is what must be cherished."

Thomasine was thinking and realised Cara was waiting for a response, her arm still on her shoulder, her eyes searching.

"When my grandfather was ill for so long in that home and death was inevitable the whole family was so sad."

"Certain topics that cannot be broached in conversation?" Cara asked.

"Yeah," Thomasine smiled as she remembered, "but my memories of him are all of the slightly younger man who used to make spinning tops for me in his shed and playing with me and Trudy in his garden in the summer."

Bea poked her head out of the door and Cara turned to the guard thanking him as she handed over three tickets; nodding he disappeared into the ether.

"I tell you I heard it again." The old man wheezed as he stamped along the black corridor, shadows dancing an informal jig against the wall, his neon vest ablaze via torchlight.

"I didn't," spoke a younger man from just behind him "and I can't believe you're making me come down here, no one's been here for years."

"You'd have heard it if you hadn't been thinking about that bit of skirt from earlier, you're embarrassing sometimes."

The younger man shrugged.

"Maybe; got a great butchers of her bap's though…nipples like red rivets!"

He was cut of by the unmistakable wheeze of a steam engine getting underway.

"See; I told you!" The elder man hurried along calling for the other to follow; he did so grudgingly.

They stomped along the corridor for a few more seconds before halting as their way forward was barred by a large iron gate that possibly had not been opened since Dr Beeching had ordered it shut.

"No way forward, see," the younger man seemed satisfied that he was proved right "there is no way anyone could get down here let alone a whole train! Honestly you're madness must be rubbing off on me."

The older man said nothing, instead he shone his torch through the grill but the dark shadows stayed just out of reach. He swept it about and spied a steep tunnel to the left. They both looked up and noted the grease and dirt.

"Up here?" Asked the younger man.

"No," mused the older "old maintenance shaft I think, doesn't look like nobody's been here for years."

"Kind of like I was saying ten minutes ago." Muttered the younger man and he started to leave.

The old man chanced his arm once more through the grill, leaning on it he got the shock of his life as a shrill whistle sounded from beyond and he was caught by a blast of steam from days gone by; the memories of the past as familiar as his last meal. Then there was silence.

The younger man had stopped, startled and struggled to keep his voice steady.

"I'm going for a cuppa; would you care to join me?"

The older man turned wide eyed, he smelt slightly of smoke.

"I do believe that I might."

They returned to the surface in half the time of the descent and never spoke of the tunnel again.

Eight
Ride a rocking horse

Thomasine expectations were high as she entered the carriage and she was not to be disappointed. The floor was covered thickly in a lovely squishy green carpet and the walls, apart from the windows, were panelled in a deep, rich wood whilst the seats were huge and upholstered in vibrant green leather. From the ceiling ornate brass gas fuelled lanterns hissed softly as they cast light softly downwards.

The carriage had been divided by a wooden wall in what Thomasine assumed was roughly half; in this half there were four blocks of green leather seats; the three of them were alone. Bea was standing by the second row of seats, her pot was in the block next to it; the train rocked gently and the journey was underway sending shadows from the swaying lamps bending and stretching in time with its movements.

Cara and Thomasine joined Bea.

"I'm going to change these things." Bea pointed to her clothes. "How about you Thomasine, fancy a change of clothing?"

Thomasine smiled immensely at the offer.

"I'd love too, I feel like I've been in these clothes for years... but I didn't bring a change."

"No matter," Cara said, smiling from her seat as she nodded to the far end of the carriage." I am positively sure that we can find something you will like."

"I could not... impose." Thomasine spoke; blushing a little yet again at her new found friend's generosity.

"The clothes were made to be worn, yet mostly they just hang about and that does seem such a terrible waste, does it not?"

"Well since you put it like that, ok." Thomasine beamed hopeful of what she would find as Bea led her through to the next section of the train. The inside was as amazing as she hoped it would be. The windows were covered with green velvet screens and the gaslights made Thomasine imagine that she was backstage in the dressing rooms of some grand theatre. To her left and right built-in wardrobes were filled with gorgeous dresses, the like of which Thomasine had only ever dreamt about, whilst opposite there was a wardrobe filled with more contemporary clothes.

"What do you fancy?" Bea asked, obviously not feeling shy or nervous as she removed her jacket then undid the buttons of her skirt letting it fall to the floor. She hung the jacket on an empty hanger and placed it into one of the wardrobes, whilst her skirt she picked up and placed into an oval wicker basket; her legs were blemish free and as pale as the rest of skin.

Thomasine looked at the rows of dress.

"I'm not sure," she answered truthfully, "these clothes are so beautiful, but I'm not sure that they're practical for what might come."

"Good point," Bea said as she selected an identical skirt to the one she had been wearing and slipped into it. "There is no rush though, try a few things on and see what feels comfortable, personally I find many of the clothes that Cara likes far too heavy. Then again some of the others swear by twentieth century clobber and I just cannot get to grip with that either."

There was a moment of silence as Thomasine tried to come to term with the huge range of clothing and the fact that she might have to strip in front of a person she did not know. Fortunately that was solved as Bea, now redressed in fresh clothing, excused herself and left the room, telling Thomasine to take her time and to repeat her view that she should try on a few things. She also told her to place her own clothes in the basket and they would then be cleaned and ready for whenever they were next required.

Thomasine was alone in a fabulous playhouse and she struggled to know where to begin. *So many clothes yet so little girl* she pondered. She picked items randomly at first and held them to her body whilst looking at her reflection in a full-length mirror she found inside one of the wardrobes. None looked right and she knew that she would have to try on a few more things; not least because this might be the only opportunity she ever got in her life to try on such beautiful and fantastic clothing.

She took off her jacket and shirt and noted a certain sweaty twang about them, an unfriendly smell that was not too extreme but also none too pleasant. She removed her skirt and looked at it. It was covered with a thin layer of dust and grime; she folded everything neatly and placed it in the wicker basket and wondered what to try on first.

She spent the next hour trying on so many items of clothing. Yet nothing was right, nothing made her feel… happy. Someone knocked gently on the door.

"Thomasine," Cara called "if you want to freshen yourself up go through the far door, okay?"

Thomasine looked and saw that there was a narrow door tucked into the corner of the opposite wardrobe; there must have been yet a further part to this carriage. She called her thanks back to Cara and moved on through to the next section.

This part of the carriage was not large, maybe only six foot square at best. The walls were still covered with that same wood but there were no windows at all. There was a single light above, a small leather-backed chair in one corner and what looked like a copper bird cage in the centre of the room. She walked around it for a moment puzzled then realised that it was a shower, of sorts, though she had never seen one quite so antiquated as this. She reached inside to the ornate daisy-style handle and twisted it; warm, beautiful warm water caressed onto her skin from above and she struggled to prevent herself from diving straight in.

Instinctively she checked about her; but who was going to be watching? Still her friends had often told tales of pervy shopkeepers who hid secret cameras in the changing booths that tempted young girls in with their offers of low priced clothing. She thumped her head with the palm of her hand, in a mock attempt to dislodge these brainless thoughts. Still with another careful look over her shoulder she went naked and bathed.

Selecting a particularly fine raspberry scented soap from a pile in a small brass tray in the shower she relaxed and felt herself drifting away. The water was constant and soothing; easing out little twinges and pains she had collected over the last few days. The smell reminded her of summer puddings and dawn scents, of her bedroom and despite the warmth she shivered. Momentarily the images of Tabatha and her friends flitted through her mind the images not quite at ease with her memories of the events that had taken place. Was she a bad person for standing up to her? Thomasine was unsure and resolved herself to speak with Cara about it when the chance presented itself. Her mind eased, she relaxed and was away.

Thomasine's bedroom was dark. She did not feel like she had just woken up and the fact that she was dressed supported this, yet she was uncomfortable; something in the bedroom made her feel unwelcome. She could make out the shapes of her flat-pack wardrobe, chest of draws and desk; she had wanted real wood but her parents could not afford it just now. Next to her bed sat the metal MEN AT WORK sign that she had told her friends she had stolen on a night out, the reality being the rather less grand truth that someone else had stolen it, probably on a drunken escapade and dumped it in her front garden one night.

The room still smelt faintly of the decorating that had recently finished after eight years of waiting for her father to get around to it. She had wasted no time in plastering, rather neatly, the walls with posters snipped from music magazines of bands she did not know, but kind of looked cool; but that had failed to get any response or disapproval from her parents so she had taken them down and kept them in a well-thumbed scrapbook, constantly reappraising her own image. Korn, Cradle of Filth, Blink 182, Placebo and more all influenced her; she knew that a Goth lifestyle would set her as different from the majority at her school, but the irony of shopping for alternative clothing at high-street retailers had not failed to pass her by.

Her vision was blotchy, being that it was made up of the inconsistent parts of light blobs of yellow, blue and red that would not quite conjoin to produce a definitive image. She could just make out her stereo glowing faintly on her chest of draws; its blue faceplate appeared to swirl hypnotically whilst the green standby button tore into the night furiously. There was something moving here and it wasn't her.

She could not see them clearly, but there was definitely something hiding in the shadows, darting about, backwards and forwards always just slightly out of sight. Then they attacked. There must have been about half a dozen of them, pulling, nipping at her clothing but especially at any patch of bare skin. Thomasine could not tell what they looked like, only that they were smaller than she was and silent, so very silent. She swung about madly battering them away as best she could and doing fairly well for the longer the attack went on the less they managed to get near to her and then suddenly they were gone.

Thomasine waited in silence in her room. She wanted to leave this place for she could still feel their presence hiding at what they probably thought was the edge of her senses. She muttered under her breath for help and she was obliged. A figure in black, a little taller than she, but whose visage was invisible appeared at her side. The figure held out a thin pale hand and offered a small metal pillbox. The voice that accompanied this action was familiar; Tabatha.

"Problem cure-alls?" She shook the box and the pills inside rolled about gently. "Take one and you'll be invincible, they'll never touch you again."

Thomasine looked into the box and watched as the pills strangely fluctuated in colour as they rolled from blue to pink, to yellow, very tempting. She reached in a pulled one out. Her fingers trembled and tickled as the pill seemed to excite at her touch and fluctuated faster, though now through purples and rubies.

"You do not find the answer to your problems in the swallow of a pill." She flicked the pill across the room and away into the darkness.

Tabatha tutted. "How about this?" The pillbox in her hand changed into a small manicure set and from it she pulled a very sharp knife.

"No." Thomasine stuttered as her arm began to throb in anticipation. "I don't need that."

"Then you'll face your demons alone!" Tabatha spat.

Tabatha vanished into the shadows as the demons returned but this time Thomasine was in no mood to be drawn into a fight. She concentrated hard as they approached her, feeling strong and knowing that she was not truly alone she faded slightly and the demons passed right through her.

They swung about, their actions ever more manic but still silent, yet there was nothing for any of them to grab hold of. Still they refused to leave though and she was sure that she remained in this situation for hours and now tiredness was coming. Her concentration was weakening and she really wanted to be away from here; if only she could remember where she should have been; she was scared now and she started to become solid again, the brushes of demon touch becoming more common. There was loud knock on a door somewhere that was not here.

"Thomasine," there was a further knock and Cara spoke again, "Thomasine are you still awake?"

"Erm, yes, I'm awake." Thomasine mustered shivering again despite the warmth as she checked to make sure she really wasn't in her bedroom.

"You will be positively prune-like if you stay in there much longer."

Thomasine looked down at her fingers they were wrinkled, her feet too, but the heady scent of soap and the warmth of the water made it all seem okay.

"How long have I been in here?" She asked, expecting an answer that was less than the reply.

"An hour, you are more than welcome to stay longer but I have found some beautiful clothes; why don't you come and try them and join us for a drink?"

"Of course," she replied, almost falling out of the shower "be there in five minutes."

"No rush."

Thomasine grabbed a huge soft towel and wrapped herself tightly in it; she grabbed her underwear from the floor where she had thrown it and moved back through to the dressing room to see what Cara had found for her to wear.

A mannequin had appeared from somewhere and on it were clothes. She looked at the full-length buttoned velvet coat and wondered what was underneath. Carefully she undid the beautiful buttons which were silver and ornately enamelled with a fine crest, she gasped as she saw the clothes underneath. There was a soft knock at the door.

"Would you like a hand; the buttons on the back are a little trying? It was Cara once more. Thomasine lifted the black coat and looked to the back of the red top and saw that it was buttoned fully top to bottom and probably a girl could only fasten it if she was a contortionist.

"Yes please." She replied and Cara entered.

"Do you like this?" Cara asked.

"Very much, it's gorgeous…" Thomasine hesitated, "I'm not sure I should wear such things, I shall be afraid that I might ruin it."

"Oh don't worry about that, you'll find clothes like this much tougher than their modern counterparts, though I do believe there are miniskirts and the like somewhere in here; if you would prefer?" Thomasine's look of horror spoke volumes and they both smiled.

Cara directed Thomasine behind a wide silk screen covered with Chinese prints. Here she found a cream silk camisole and matching silk shorts. She emerged to find Cara had placed the skirt over the mirror and unbuttoned the top. Now Thomasine saw that it was a sleeveless affair with a high neck in beautiful deep red and pink brocade. Cara placed it on her then fastened it quickly; it fitted her perfectly as it extenuated her shape as it fell to her hips. The skirt then went on, but it was just a tiny bit too long, Thomasine looked to Cara a little disappointed, but she pointed out that it was of course the perfect length from waist to floor when she wore shoes.

Putting on her Doc Martens she looked at her image in the mirror. *Wow*, she thought and Cara backed her on this view. She had never felt more beautiful, her clothes feeling such a part of her new life.

"Here," Cara said and Thomasine found her reaching about her neck, "this is a birthday gift for you."

"My birthday?"

"I know it is a bit early, but why wait?"

About her neck Thomasine found a necklace of amber, diamond and jet. It was long so Cara wrapped it about her neck twice, even then it still fell to Thomasine's stomach, but it looked good and Cara insisted that it went with the outfit. Thomasine was very grateful and told her plenty of times, but Cara just smiled telling her again that clothes were made to be worn.

"You're like the sister I never had," Thomasine told Cara, who smiled politely, making eye-contact in the mirror as she stood slightly behind her.

"You have two sisters, they can never be replaced."

"No," Thomasine asserted, "I do not want to replace them, or forget them, it's just that in my dreams, if you like, you are the sister I never had."

"Well for that then I am grateful." Cara smiled broadly. Her eyes shifted away from Thomasine her thoughts and memories temporarily far away. "I never had a sister, or a brother, or mother," she moved her gaze back as Thomasine was about to speak, "not that I am sad for this. No, there was father and myself and then, just when I thought I might go insane, I met the most wonderful man."

"And everything was wonderful?" Thomasine mused.

"Oh no," Cara added with ease, "there was the whole part of my awakening to the vampyre life, then when my fiancé died so soon after I met him, my pact with death and then the return of my fiancé nearly one hundred and eighty years after I lost him."

They remade eye contact in the mirror and Cara must have sensed the questions that Thomasine had bombing through her mind.

"I will explain more as we go on; will you give me that opportunity?"

"Of course," Thomasine turned smiling and gave Cara a sudden little hug, "I have seen and touched and done things that I have only ever dreamt about. I'm not sure that I could ever return to my old life now; the school, the mundane existence."

"Schooling is important, "Cara added with a smile as she helped Thomasine brush her hair into shape with a fine bone-handled brush, "but often not as important as learning things through experience."

Thomasine admired her finished appearance in the mirror and so liked the way she was looking that she chose not to put on the black velvet coat for now.

They moved back through to the first part of the carriage and Thomasine found that Bea had pulled all the velvet curtains across the windows which gave the carriage a lovely snug feeling. They took seats next to Bea where there were glasses of warming red wine waiting. Thomasine sniffed it carefully before she tasted it, *just checking* she reminded herself.

Bea commented on how nice Thomasine looked in the clothes, making her blush in response. They talked idly for an hour about the place that they were going. From what Cara said they were returning to Cornwall, although the exact place was not named. Cara described it as quite a floral town, with pleasant parks and a beautiful seafront. Thomasine of course wondered again why they were going, but the reply was an obtuse nod to the blue and white pots they had carried and the promise that she might have fun and find herself at home, or at the very least learn something and for this she was willing to travel.

After the wine they separated to different booths to rest. Thomasine was happy to do so for she had not slept for an age. She watched as Bea and Cara fell effortlessly under the spell of Morpheus, almost like cats, as if they had not a care in the world. Thomasine was not sure that she wanted to sleep in case she missed something, or maybe creased her new clothing. But eventually she could not refuse and she fell into a refreshing dreamless void ready for the next day.

The train had stopped and as someone had pulled open the curtains the sun beamed in through the many windows. As Thomasine awoke so did the others; stretching the night away and ready to face whatever might come. They collected themselves together and found fresh tea in a delicate silver pot and china cups waiting for them. Thomasine did not know how this had got here and she did not ask, it tasted refreshing, Lady Grey again, unless she was very much mistaken.

There was toast, currant buns, with jam, marmalade and butter in silver dishes and even a small china plate with biscuits, which at least Bea did not think it so un-lady-like to dunk in her tea.

Once they were adequately refreshed they left the train and found themselves upon a simple platform with an attractive station, looking very rural and old fashioned. The only other person visible was a guard with a small iron trolley. Cara called to him and gave him instructions to take the pots to an address Thomasine could not hear and then they were free to wander.

The station itself could have been one of the recreated scenes in the museum; it was quite literally a perfect example of how Thomasine imagined it would have looked like back in the 1930s. They passed through the neat waiting room with its little ticket office and refreshment hatch offering tea, coffee and Bovril; everything clean, tidy and even smelling pleasant. The station had been built upon a quiet country lane, Thomasine half expected horses and carts to be parked outside on a dirt track, but the road was tarmac, although there was no traffic upon it. Judging by the dried manure in the road though it was clear that horses did use this way, but there were also thin tyre tracks through it, not that she examined it any great detail. They walked a little way and the quiet road found its way to a busier thoroughfare. Here all manner of vehicles, young and old, merged into a continuous stream.

Thomasine noticed the growing cloud of smog above. Fortunately this did not last long for as they appeared to be entering the outskirts of the town, passing over a wide stone bridge, Cara directed them down some steps. These wound around and about one of the stone legs of the bridge before arriving on the grassy park floor below.

The floor beneath the bridge was a contrast of shadow and light but nothing could hide the strangest sight that now faced them; rocking horses, lots of them.

At first Thomasine was not completely sure that what she was seeing was real and the other girls seemed similarly confused. The grass was a beautiful summer green and undulated slightly as it was interspersed with small groups of bushes, trees and even a small stone fountain, or maybe a wishing well, she could not be completely sure. Sprinkled over the grassy area was a scattered stream of dead leaves. Thomasine pointed this out but Bea said that they were not dead, but rather dried, and therefore someone had placed them here deliberately. Throughout this sprinkling of leaves were a variety of rocking horses. They ranged in size from pony to fully-grown adult and their condition varied hugely; some were beautiful painted and shone in a fabulously pristine condition, whilst others were tired and did not invite a touch let alone play.

There appeared to no one watching and Cara and Bea passed mischievous glances before walking across the grass towards a pair of fine adult sized horses that stood side by side, their heads, tails and legs as if in full flight. Thomasine reluctantly followed watching carefully about her. She was sure that they were entering some kind of contemporary art exhibit and therefore probably being monitored.

Cara and Bea each mounted a horse, tucking their skirts under them and began riding them back and forth in an ever-quickening, maddening way. Thomasine walked to them and as they eventually slowed themselves spoke.

"Shouldn't ladies like you be riding side-saddle?" She asked, knowing that she herself never would.

"They only did that in books," Bea pointed out, adding, "it's much more fun this way." Cara gave her *a look* and Bea added. "Oh yes, and horses are a lot easier to control this way too."

Eventually they released their charges back to the open field and continued upon their way.

Through the quite park, the town never far about them they passed through tree filled groves and warm picnic areas. Groups of students, both English and foreign enjoyed the day playing football, drinking, picnicking and snuggling up together; no one paid the three of them any heed.

The park continued onwards and a small stream bubbled up from underground and the rock-strewn path was a joy to follow. The park was cut across at two points by bridges and Cara told Thomasine that the first was called the Seven- Handed Old man on account that it was squat and there were seven wide arches of thick and heavy iron, whilst the second was called The Bone Fingered Bridge, for it was exceedingly tall and constructed from beautifully engraved cream marble and yes there were five stands to it, one being much shorter than the others.

The gardens eventually gave way to a large stone Art Deco pavilion and beyond that a short promenade led towards the seafront and a picturesque fishing commune huddled into the safe embrace of frightening granite cliffs. Here houses were built upon houses and there were no proper roads just tiny alleyways that led to who knew where. In the harbour the water was low and the boats that where in found themselves fixed firmly into the wet sand that had appeared from beneath the vanishing tide.

They walked anticlockwise around the small harbour, past the old RNLI launching station, now a museum and masses of smelly lobster pots drying in the sun. As she looked back towards the town Thomasine could see that the houses on the cliffs were built in distinct eras. The eldest nearest the centre, then the Victorian's came and built holiday villas higher on the cliffs, with better views high above the smelly sorts below. Then there were the council houses from the 1950s and 60s and now so many new builds were blossoming amongst their elder counterparts. Homes so out of place they should have been reserved for new towns. However the city-types that came here never cared if they were out of place; they rarely mingled with the locals.

They walked as far as they could along the harbour wall and out to a small lighthouse built upon the end. The sea was calm and huge black rocks could be seen poking out of the water; Thomasine was sure that this place must have been a difficult but grateful sanctuary during a storm. She wondered briefly of all the lives that may have been lost here.

Bea pointed out towards a series of rocks that ran from the cliffs out into the sea about half a mile away. There was something small and black on top of it.

"Do you see?" She asked. Thomasine nodded. "And that other one, over there?" She pointed further down the coast to another rock, this time on its own, upon which was a something else that was black.

"What are they?" She asked.

"Reminders." Cara whispered.

"Of what?" Thomasine puzzled before the others spoke again.

"Of man's weakness," Bea replied, she pointed to the single rock. "That was an iron watchtower, a place where smugglers would wait and lay down their plans and that one," she pointed to the other, "was their ship."

"We left them there as a warning to others!" Cara spoke softly and was looking at Thomasine when she turned her head around in shock at what she had said.

"You have a thing against smugglers?" She asked.

"Oh no," Bea replied, "but when they turned their interests into matters that should not have concerned them measures had to be taken."

Thomasine considered this. What did they mean about *'matters that should not have concerned them'*? Should it matter to her, or was it simply their right to defend their own?

"So why are we here? It is very beautiful and all, but there is more...isn't there."

Cara nodded, her eyes flicking from Thomasine to the sea and back again.

"You are here because there is someone you must meet, that is tomorrow, but also you are learning all the time and what you have seen and heard and what you will see and hear will effect your final decision."

"Oh." Thomasine managed. Cara took her by the shoulder and gave her a little squeeze, and then Bea did similarly. "Why do I get the impression that you are going to leave me now?"

"Not just yet," Cara replied "but I must be sure that you fully understand our world and what might await you."

Quickly Thomasine responded.

"I do, I think, but there is still a lot I want to understand that I do not at the moment."

Cara looked to Bea and then they both looked to Thomasine and smiled warmly as if some unspoken agreement had been made. They started to walk back in the direction that they had come and Cara spoke.

"Then we shall rest for a while at *The Sailors Harvest* and ready ourselves for the party tonight."

Nine

In the inn

Slowly the girls retraced their steps back along the harbour wall. Thomasine was excited about the prospect of going to a party with Cara and Bea and she was sure that if the events of the last few days were anything to go by, it would be the most magical experience. They walked until they came to a seafood restaurant and the first of a series of small alleyways that led them on a weaving path inland. Narrow lane followed narrow lane and she hoped that they might find time to return here later for some of the shops that were tucked away seemed quite interesting.

There were the usual bars, restaurants and run of the mill gift shops that one always finds on the coast as well as number of trendy surfing shops. However amongst all this she did see at least two shops with cluttered windows selling antiques and other curios. She felt a strange compulsion to buy presents for her family, like she was on a daytrip and would be expected to bring home souvenirs. Thomasine realised that this was a strange and found the feeling unsettling; she hoped they would pass quickly.

Eventually the lanes led to a wider pedestrian precinct and here chromed tables and chairs from several restaurants filled the centre. Many of the seats were taken and their seemed to be good business taking place, despite the tension in the air. There was a malaise that before now Thomasine believed she might have missed yet now was acutely aware off.

A group of young men were noisily drinking and throwing food, threatening all with an aura of ignorance and vileness that made Thomasine feel incredibly angry and sick at the same time; she shivered as the feeling slipped through her, leaving an oily sensation in its wake.

They had only just entered the area but Bea and Cara had stopped, their eyes taking in the scene in an instant before they then began walking again, this time straight at the group of boys. Thomasine had come to an abrupt halt too and watched as she was sure she had seen a glint of malice in the other girl's eyes. She followed a step behind, nervous as too what might be about to unfold; she had never been one for confrontation even at the best of times. Why she was nervous she could not tell; was it because they were three girls, facing six or seven boys? Maybe it was the fact that one of them was actually quite cute, in a Charlie from *Busted* kind of way, although that mono-eyebrow thing was so…yuck. Maybe it was that she feared for the boys for she felt deep down that if Cara and Bea were ever really annoyed they were the kind of girls who were likely to be proactive.

As they approached the strangest thing happened. They had closed to about ten feet when they stopped again, Thomasine held her breath anxiously and was amazed at what she saw. The boys all fell silent and as one returned to their own table, dragging chairs that had been knocked over back into place; then once seated, they fondled drinks cautiously and all cast their eyes downwards towards the table; silence covered the area and the girls started walking again, still towards the boys. They passed within a foot and Cara uttered a single word as they passed "Slepe!" and the boys fell, their eyes closed, into the deepest slumber.

By the time the three of them had reached the other side of the pedestrianised zone Thomasine dared to cast a glance back and found to her delight that the atmosphere had completely changed. Families talked and joked loudly, whilst children ran about and restaurant employees worked with smiles upon their faces; and through all this the group of boys slept, ignored completely by everyone else present. Thomasine tugged Cara's coat and they all stopped, Cara and Bea turned to face her questions.

"How did you do that?"

Cara smiled a little and raised an eyebrow.

"It just is."

Thomasine looked back towards the boys then at Cara.

"How long will it last?"

"Until the restaurant manager wants to go home, and in anticipation of your next question no, they do not come to harm or know of what happened," she looked to the sky and noted the sun was starting to hide itself amongst the rooftops, "we are nearly there and the party will not wait, ready?"

Thomasine nodded and they continued on their way.

They passed through more tiny alleyways until eventually they stopped at an ancient wooden doorway; above this hung a wooden board with a portrait of a fisherman surrounded by gold painted upon it, *The Sailors Harvest* no doubt. Bea opened the door and in they went.

Its smell was familiar and Thomasine was reminded of the museum for walking in here was like they had stepped back several hundred years.

"Are they open?" Thomasine asked in all innocence.

"They never shut." Bea replied.

The inside was all low ceilings, knotted black wood and granite floors with an air that reeked of strong beer. The atmosphere was intoxicating, helped by the fact that the bar was unusual for there were no gaudy plastic optics or vibrant neon for the beer sponsorship signs; Cara continuing to lead them onwards.

The stairs were barely wide enough for them to pass singularly and they were virtually vertical so steep was the climb, each step being at least twelve inches in height and extraordinarily narrow in width. Finally they arrived on the third floor and here leading from the narrow corridor, where the wooden floor undulated and creaked mysteriously, there were three doors, two on one side and one on the other. It was only now that Thomasine realised just what a strange shape this building was. It was almost as if the other buildings were trying to force this one out, like it did not belong and it was being squeezed out of existence by its neighbours.

Cara allocated each of them a room and they separated though not before she told them to think 20's, Thomasine wondered what she might have to wear, her clothes that she had obtained form Cara were fine, but certainly not 1920's, 1820's possibly but Bea whispered to her that wardrobes had been prepared and to not worry.

They separated and Thomasine quickly found herself facing a wardrobe the like of which she had not seen outside her drama classes inside a room straight out of *Treasure Island.* The room was not large, certainly smaller than her bedroom at home with a small leaded window, rickety looking bed and several pieces of furniture. From the low ceiling beams hung a wooden candelabrum complete with real candles, which were already lit and in the fireplace a fire had been prepared.

On the simple dressing table was a pile of pristine looking magazines from the 1920s and she quickly took off her clothes and placed them across the back of the small chair that came with the table. She flicked through the magazines and as she did she began to rummage through the wardrobe. She identified several pictures of girls in the magazines that she thought were quite attractive, and then looked for matching clothes. The choice was varied for whilst the flat-chest, boyish, look was popular it would not really sit well on her; fortunately there were some styles that were designed to accentuate a figure.

After just ten minutes she had a collected a considerable pile of clothing and she turned to her bed for contemplation; how could she chose? However whilst sitting on the bed one thing led to another and tiredness crept up from nowhere. The mantle clock above the fire said that it was two hours until it was time to leave so she settled down for a nap.

Thomasine dreamt so often that she had come to think of it as her second existence and in this one she was walking the narrow streets of this town. She considered that as humans spend approximately a third of their lives asleep and often dreaming was a more pleasurable experience than living then the land of sleep was just as important as the 'real world'. She walked and whilst the streets did appear very similar to those of the village she was staying they were actually a lot more complex than she remembered and without the others to guide her she quickly found herself lost. As she stopped and looked about the streets she had just walked down simply vanished and buildings began shifting locations unhelpfully.

She had stopped by a building which was notable for several reasons but she thought that her attention may have been drawn to it building in particular because it had been painted a pale duck-egg blue where as all the other buildings were white or beige or some other fairly neutral colour.

From pavement level there were four floors of sash windows above ground and a basement below, the basement windows poked just above the pavement so anyone passing could see in. She moved closer to the building and knelt down. Inside there were lots of neat display cases packed with miniature tools, lanterns and rigging from ships, lifebuoys and a picture of a sailor standing proudly in his waterproofs on the deck of a small sailing vessel. Thomasine knew little about boats, but she thought from its size that the man was probably a solo sailor. Her interest grabbed she wanted to see more so she went through the door, then down a series of steps into the basement; there was little room to manoeuvre.

Upon the wall to her left there were floor to ceiling shelves packed with books on sailing. Strange how she knew instinctively that they were about sailing without at first actually looking clearly at any of them; even when she did the words on the spines would not focus; she just knew. Looking further she saw long low cabinets running through the centre of the room filled with parts of a ship. There must have been about two hundred in all, ranging from inch-long pieces of tatty sail to a two-foot length of fibreglass hull, with the name 'Juicy Julia' painted on it; all had been meticulously labelled. On the far side of the room she saw a tall glass cabinet in which there were just a couple of items; she moved closer.

The cabinet was white on the inside to extenuate the starkness of the display and was empty save for two items. The first was the front page from the Herald, apparently a local newspaper. There was a repeat image of the man standing on the boat, under the headline 'Dead Tide Claims Another', but the accompanying text was illegible. Next to this was a small silver and enamel medal complete with burgundy ribbon set into a dark blue velour lined case. Thomasine did not know for what the medal had been awarded because there were no labels for guidance.

"That," said a masculine voice "is my legacy!" Thomasine calmly turned to face the owner of the voice, a man a clear foot taller than her, dressed in a simple black suit she recognised him from the photo. "I travelled the world in that boat," he pointed to the cabinet of bits and pieces, "and this is all there is to remember me by." He walked about the room and Thomasine watched him and listened as he grumbled.

"I sailed the seven seas, journeyed to distant places you can barely imagine and look how they treat me. Everything I had is gone, just my books saved and only then because they were in storage…do you know they never even found my body!" He looked at her and she shook her head. "You see! You stand here but you probably don't even know why? He moved to stand next to her and she responded.

"Was the driving force behind what you did simply to be remembered?" Thomasine enquired. The man's face changed to one of surprise and then one of anger.

"How dare you question me, how dare you stand in my memorial and disrespect me so."

Thomasine was unapologetic and measured in her response.

"I will offer you the respect you deserve, not the respect you think you deserve…I do not know you from Adam, but it appears to me that somebody thought enough of you to remember and isn't that everything?"

His anger turned to a frown as he considered.

"But it seems so little and beside what would you know, you're not even dead yet!"

"Is that supposed to matter?" Thomasine asked. "Whether I am alive or dead, whether people remember or forget me it doesn't matter, as long as I, within myself am happy with the life I led."

"Ah, but what of your family and friends, do you not care what they will think of you when you are longer about?"

"Not really," she replied, "I'll be kind of dead and therefore beyond the whole worrying about what anybody is thinking thing."

A wicked grin trickled across his lips.

"I said, when you were no longer about, not that you would be dead. The two are quite distinctly different."

"If I were, no longer about, I might well be of a mind that wonders what people think of me, but that's human nature and ultimately I can't change the way people think; so let them get on with it."

"Everyone is concerned with image, even you, in your beautiful new clothes, are concerned about how you look, even when people cannot see you!"

"A friend once told me, that in every conversation between two people there are in fact six people present. There is the person you are, the person you would like to be seen as and then the person that the other person sees you as."

The man simply smiled and Thomasine awoke.

The last remains of the day filtered upon the distant skyline above the rooftops and through her open window, Thomasine was a little warm but not uncomfortably so, for she wore only the silk under garments taken from the train. It was very quiet and she considered reaching out for one of the magazines on the dressing table; but it was just a little too far. Then she remembered; the party.

Instantly she was up, had she slept right through? Had Cara and Bea simply left her in the land of Nod? Heart beating rapidly she put her ear to the wall and was thankful to hear Bea moving in the room next door; she checked the clock, fifteen minutes until the agreed meeting time. Calming herself she washed herself quickly in the china bowl provided, then selected an appropriate dress, an above the knee number in silver and pale blue silk with a soft white cotton jacket; the overt paleness of her skin was further accentuated by a thin silver chain dotted with silver pebbles. There was a knock at the door and Thomasine quickly opened it to let both Bea and Cara in.

They looked stunning. Bea wore a cream dress with matching corsage, a simple pink feather cape and a huge necklace of pearl and diamond, whilst Cara was dressed in a floor length white silk dress with a fluffy white feather shrug. Cara helped Thomasine to fix her hair up into an appropriate style as Thomasine was rather scared to see the mess it was in after her sleep.

"Your hair looks like the aelf's have been through it." Cara commented as she helped shape it.

"Aelf's?" Thomasine gave her a puzzled look in the mirror. "There are aelf's here, screwing with my hair…that's friendly!"

"Actually it is rather," Bea commented from the bed where she sat waiting "if they did not like you they could have done a lot worse. It is just there way of showing interest."

Thomasine tried to look about her as Cara worked away and wondered what else there might be hiding in her room.

"Do not let her scare you," Cara gave Bea a wistful look over her shoulder "if the aelf's know you are not out to hurt them they never hurt you...ninety percent of the time."

"Ninety percent of the time?" Thomasine repeated wide-eyed.

"Well...eighty...roughly." Cara smiled at her in the mirror; Thomasine was not quite sure how seriously to take her; but she was still watchful.

When Cara was finished with her Thomasine found that Bea had pulled her a perfect pair of shoes from under the bed and some complimentary jewellery for her necklace in the form of huge opal and platinum broach from a secret compartment at the back of the wardrobe.

Now they were ready and Cara led them down the tight stairs, Thomasine was grateful for the rope hand rail, but such was the grace of the others they managed without. Downstairs they found candles blazing and a warm fire on the hearth but nobody about, though someone hummed from behind the scenes.

Outside the inn they walked toward a beautiful silver Rolls Royce, it was perfect, or as perfect as Thomasine would assume for attending a 1920s party. Cara took the drivers seat whilst Bea opened the rear door for Thomasine and she bounced her way in with Bea joining her. The interior was fabulous real wood, leather and fine smells; it was hard to believe this car was at least eighty years old.

"She's been restored beautifully; have you had her long?" Thomasine asked.

"Since new," Cara replied her eyes visible in the dashboard-mounted rear view mirror "but she has never been restored, I just look after her." She patted the dashboard and talked more to herself than the others. "Though I am sure I should use her a little more." She pressed the starter and the car purred into life.

Ten

Another party

Cara steered the large vehicle with ease through the narrow streets and across several squares where people were drinking and eating, though strangely not paying any attention to this magnificent car that passed them by. They made there way out of town and along the coast. The number of houses soon disappeared to be replaced by dark open fields. They were travelling up steeper roads as the cliffs grew ever more sheer affording incredible views over the calm sea.

The car was slowing in places as it struggled up the inclines. Cara was clearly a lady who took great care of her possessions for she never over-revved the engine and they always managed to make the next turn. Suddenly they reached a peak and in the back of the car Thomasine believed that they were about to fall over the cliff. However in reality the road dived downwards sharply in upon itself and at the same cautious pace the car made its way down equally steep roads. Finally Cara steered them down a service road which should have been blocked by an angry looking steel barrier, somehow it had been left raised and they made their way into an area where the local council stored their beach cleaning equipment, deck chairs and such like. The area was slightly set back from the wide beach, nestled in the protective embrace of sandstone cliffs there was an obvious path leading to the beach.

Cara stopped the car and Thomasine looked at the quiet, empty coast.

"A beach party, cool," she muttered looking at the window. "So where is everyone else?"

"The party is not here," Cara explained "we just need to pause here for a while so you can see Mr Morphus, then we will go onto the party."

"Mr Morphus? What a strange name."

"It is an old name," Bea explained "it's been in these parts for years."

"Is this Mr Morphus a vampyre then?"

"No," replied Cara softly her eyes scanning the beach "but I do believe that you will find him interesting."

They got out and made their way along the path towards the beach. The air was acrid with the salt from the sea, but also something else, something Thomasine could not quite put her finger, or rather her nose on; like old flowers or the smell that would often inhabit the air after her grandmother had buzzed through a room; that old person smell. Wisely she chose not too mention this to the others, knowing as she did just how old they were she did not want to offend.

They stopped short of the beach and rested against a wire mesh fence that had seen many better days. Everyone looked towards the sea. At first Thomasine saw nothing but beach and calm sea; she heard nothing but the soothing wash of the waves and felt the cool air pass through the few patches of stringy grass that inhabited this place. Then through the gloom the strangest thing came into sight and Thomasine found herself gripping the fence fiercely as she struggled to understand.

Maybe it was just the way that her eyes had now become adjusted to the gloom, maybe something more, for now she could see the strangest items upon the beach. There was a tall wardrobe, a decorative iron four-poster bed, various items from a kitchen, including the sink and a washboard. Across the wooden breakwaters various furnishings were draped. There looked to be silks and velvets, lace and linen, all once fine and bright items now made tardy and old by time and the forces of nature.

She looked to the others for explanations, but they simply shushed her and told her not to disturb him as suddenly he appeared from within the wardrobe and they listened for a while to Mr Morphus's thoughts.

"Stupid pine cones, always hiding in the most obscene places...wouldn't have had it happened if old George had never died, could never get a thing right. Stupid women couldn't run a brothel in a brewery that one," he strutted to the sea and loudly broke wind "stupid foreigner...he was always the one to turn too, smelt like chicken, which is strange because I was sure that it said salmon on the wall of the butcher's, though he would not know, that one...bloody foreigner, Nancy...Nancy...coming here from the land of the Jocks, fiends, sell moose to the goose and turn his mothers grave to Cook if he thought it would make a farthing. Nancy, Nancy...where the bloody hell are you?" He spent a moment spinning on the spot, digging himself a small hole, Thomasine knew he would get dizzy and fall over just before it happened. "Ah there you," but no one had come to him "I was taking the dog for a walk but got lost for a while, what's for supper?" Suddenly he thundered back across the beach in their direction but stopped ten yards short and instead diverted his attention to a partially sinking chaise-lounge, which was now little more than kindling; he tripped over it, breaking one of the legs. He did not notice. "Those pesky kids always leaving their toys about the house, I'll send them to Timbuktu for a shilling a shot; that should settle their lots."

He was busy emptying the contents of a chest of draws onto the beach when as she watched it seemed to Thomasine that despite his insane ramblings his main issue was with his furniture, he really could not decide where to put it all. Cara moved from the far side of Bea to stand next to Thomasine and in hushed tones she started to weave his tale.

"In the mid-nineteenth century this man, Mr Morphus, had been the wealthiest banker in London and this had bought him a large estate with a magnificent mansion." She pointed along the beach and Thomasine stood in awe at the massive ruins that now dominated the skyline to her right.

"Where did that come from?" She asked, looking to Cara for an answer. "That was definitely not there a minute ago…was it?"

"It was," Cara assured her "and it has been for sometime, but people no longer remember the tragedy, so no longer see the house." She returned her attention to Mr Morphus.

"Such a vain man, so rich not only in monetary terms but also spiritually with a fine wife and nine blessed children and so many servants…but when tragedy came he alone escaped and rescued the few items that remained in the ruins."

"All his family and servants died," Thomasine looked to the madman wandering on the beach and felt pangs of sorrow for him "life can be so cruel." She muttered.

Bea joined in the conversation.

"But so can humans, it was his penny-pinching over substandard materials and bullying hatred for the workers that led to the poor standard of work in the house."

"And his choice to watch from the shore as the building blew, a ball of flame so violent the screams of the dying barely escaped, "Cara added "such was the hatred for him it was two weeks before anyone would dare venture up here. They believed that he had simply returned to London with his retinue, he always bought everything with him from London and had very little to do with the people nearby."

"Sounds familiar." Thomasine muttered.

"But the sons and daughters of locals who were employed here were eventually missed but all they found was ruins of building and man." Cara pointed to a series of graves now illuminated by the moonlight. "They buried their own dead then left him to his own devices, he barely noticed, instead he continued to rearrange his so precious furniture…and so here he remains."

They all fell silent for a moment and watched as he moved about his furniture, each lost in their own thoughts. Thomasine's mind was in turmoil. At first she had felt such sorrow for him, but now she thought that this may have been misplaced. Why where they showing her this place? Bea cleared her throat audibly and she signalled to Cara as Mr Morphus was beginning to remove his clothing and heading for a large safe which had been placed on its back and filled with seawater like a bath; quickly they returned to the car.

"So what do you think?" Cara asked Thomasine.

"I'm not sure," she replied "why is he still here, I mean how can he still be after so much time has passed?"

"Why, you mean, does he still exist here and no one notices?" Thomasine nodded and stopped walking; Cara turned to her. "I do not think I ever believed in god or heaven and hell, in anything really apart from the reality of death; but even in this there are exceptions."

"Vampyre's, like yourself you mean?"

Cara nodded.

"But apart from the few of us who can never die, there are thousands of these little bubbles of the past interacting with the present."

Thomasine just considered this for a moment, but it still did not explain why he continued to exist.

"When I first saw his madness and you told me his tale of loss I felt great sadness for him, but then when you say he caused his own downfall and so much pain for those about him…I felt that like, maybe he deserves everything he gets."

"And you think that being judgemental makes you a bad person?" Cara asked watching her closely.

"Does it? Is it for me to judge?"

Cara shrugged and placed her arm through Thomasine's

"We all do, but it is important to remember that although we are privileged to see the past, we cannot change it; though we might have had a part to play in it." She paused for a moment. "Maybe he does not really exist here at all, maybe he and the others that are like him are just memories kept alive by the few of us who see."

"Like ghosts?" Thomasine wondered.

"Some might say." Cara replied.

The journey in the car began again and they moved inland away from the coast where the sky was clear; twinkling stars and blooming moon allowing quite a perspective over the lush countryside. The inside of the car seemed darker than a normal vehicle; well this was no normal vehicle. On the dashboard the four dials glowed with a creepy green iridescence and the headlight beams were gentle in the darkness, allowing a view along the road of about thirty meters; they had not passed another vehicle so far. Occasionally they would pass through junctions equipped with strange signposts, all white with small black lettering studded with reflectors, but Thomasine recognised none of the towns or villages named.

After about ten minutes of silence Bea opened a small compartment hidden between the two front seats, its interior lit by the creepy green iridescence. Inside Thomasine saw a selection of drinks and glasses on ice. Pulling forth a bottle of champagne Bea opened the window and unleashed the cork. The ride in the Rolls Royce was so smooth that she was able to pour the sparkling liquid into the glasses as they sat on a purpose built shelf that slipped out from under the cabinet.

Placing the half empty bottle back into the ice filled cabinet she handed a glass to Thomasine and another to Cara in the front; keeping the third for herself she proffered it up.

"Cheers."

"Cheers," Thomasine replied doubtfully watching the tiny bubbles leap from the top of the glass "I'm not sure I should, I don't normally!"

"Ah yes," Bea exclaimed softly "only fifteen, don't worry, things were a lot more liberal in the twenties and it is only a taste."

Thomasine took a little sip, the bubbles tickled her nose and the taste made her tongue curl, she was not sure how anyone could enjoy drink masses of this.

"Should she really be drinking and driving?" She whispered as Cara steered with one hand whilst sipping from her glass with the other.

"Well like I said, things were a lot more liberal in the twenties." Bea smiled. Thomasine took another sip of her drink and Bea offered a top-up; she felt it would have been impolite to refuse, but only took half a glass.

"Do not drink that too quickly," Cara spoke, glancing to the back from her driving position "alcohol may not affect us like humans but it can still take some getting used to."

"Okay mum!" Thomasine replied jokingly, Cara raised her eyebrow.

"Do you miss her?"

"A little, maybe, it's probably not been long enough yet, but I know she won't be missing me."

"Really; are you so sure?" Cara continued to sip and watch the road but listening intently as the journey progressed; Thomasine gazed out the window as explained.

Thomasine was sitting at her usual table of four nearest the door. She liked it here because the shape of the room meant that she could not be seen clearly by either the teacher or most of the rest of the class. The six Venetian blinds in the first floor corner classroom are down and they were watching a video that had something to do with the making of America. It was a tiresome program about how the early pioneers had suffered so greatly; as yet there had been nothing about the suffering of the indigenous population.

Suddenly the school secretary was at the door, should one stand at this point? No one is too sure, there is an uncomfortable silence then Mr Rundle the History teacher is across the room; talking to her in whispers. She leaves a moment later and Thomasine was invited outside, there are mutterings amongst the class and she begins to gather her clutter before being told to leave it, apparently she will not be gone long.

Outside Mr Rundle told her that he wants her to look after a first year class for twenty minutes or so, he did not offer an explanation why and although Thomasine has doubts she knows that he knows she has a half-ambition to teach so she nods and goes along; hoping that this will be good practise she goes next door and 'baby- sits'. There was a little noise but there were no real problems.

Forty-five minutes later class ends and as no one came to relieve her she lets them go and returned to her own classroom; everyone was gone of course though her own things are left untouched and Mr Rundle was wiping the board clean ready for the next class after break. He did not thank her but asked how she got on. She answered positively and reiterated her desire to one day become a teacher. Mr Rundle then spent the next five minutes explaining to her in great detail about how teachers are overworked and underpaid, apparently teaching was not now the job that it once was. Then he took her along a different path, by asking her if she has ever considered work in the financial sector. She had not, banks and offices were really not her thing, but he pointed out a poster on the notice board advertising a meeting that very afternoon once classes were finished hosted by a national bank for jobs with good pay and prospects; he advised her to attend and she did.

It was half-five and dark by the time she arrived home, her mother was not happy, though not it turned out at Thomasine. She was rushing from kitchen, to dinning room, to bedroom in an attempt to get Toni's dinner cooked and get ready for a night out. Apparently her father had only recently called and told her of the invite to his boss's house for dinner; they would be late and Thomasine must forage for her own food. Thomasine attempted to explain why she was late, but her mother hadn't even noticed and barely acknowledged her as she spoke of her future plans.

"The lot of a middle child is often not a happy one," Cara responded from the front "I wonder if your elder sister ever felt similarly when you came along?"

Thomasine considered this and yes maybe she was being a little judgemental. It probably hadn't been that important that she had talked to her mother the moment she had got in and truthfully she could not really see herself working in a bank. The people always seemed dead bored, especially the girls made up like dolls, eye candy for disgruntled customers.

"It wasn't just the one occasion; there were other times, lots of other times."

"I understand, I was not judging, just playing devil's advocate."

Thomasine caught her eye in the rear-view mirror and smiled. She realised that Cara was making her think about things carefully and try to see different points of view; still she felt a little hard done by.

They travelled for about thirty minutes still not seeing another soul and as Cara drove, Bea explained a little more about the upcoming party. It was being held at the home of Conservative MP Sir John Leftfield, his wife and their daughter; it was for her the party was being thrown, a kind of combined twenty-first birthday and engagement party to the son of a Rear- Admiral whose name was double barrelled and escaped Thomasine's memory as she started to imagine the scene that she would see. The fabulous clothes and jewels, the men and women acting out fantasies that she held deep within her; polite conversation, delicate flirting and salacious musings in the wings of some sprawling manor, hidden away from the horrors of the 'real' world. How she would love to find herself in a situation that would double as one of Vettriano's paintings; strange how truth sometimes mirrors dreams.

Thomasine stared at the stars until she felt sick; rarely had she seen them so clearly. Well it was understandable, living as she did in town with the ceaseless orange glow that fought the night for the benefit of drunks and the lost, those who were forced to travel the streets at night. It was a point she could never quite comprehend in her head. There were so few people about at night and the few cars that were out all had lights on…so why exactly was there this need to swamp the world in a dull orange glow?

The road narrowed and the car slowed, Thomasine looked through the windscreen to see other headlights ahead, then suddenly they were gone, there was a road leading away from the route they travelled, the gateway to Melcombe Hall, or so the plaque on the open gate stated. The other car was just in front having stopped inside the gates; it was old like theirs but open topped and inside, illuminated by the headlights was a man shiny hair and a black tuxedo and a long-haired blonde in skimpy dress, with what appeared to be a whole fox draped about her shoulders. They started up again as they approached and with a wave the man shot off at some speed.

Cara followed at a more considered pace driving for ages through immaculately manicured fields framed with trees that looked staged their shape was so perfect. Thomasine was convinced she saw at least a dozen deer, their eyes flashing reflectors as headlights caught them.

Finally they reached a steep drop and down in the valley below the lights from a grand house illuminated the night. Slowly they edged down the valley, the road stayed narrow and mostly straight but the drop to the left of the car was most severe. Thomasine wondered why Cara did not drive faster; it was not like she was going to die or anything even if they did have an accident; then again she thought about the car…if there was an accident was that immortal too?

They pulled onto the front lawn, which judging by the forty or so cars parked at random angles was the nominated car-park.

"Everyone must be drunk already. The last time I saw parking as random as this was Christmas eve at the supermarket!" Thomasine muttered as she studied the scene.

"Possibly," Cara replied as she parked under a tree someway from the house or anyone else "parking was often like this even on good days, don't be surprised to find butlers squashed into the ground under many a fashionable wheel!"

"Why do I get the feeling that's not a joke?" Thomasine asked rhetorically, Cara just smiled and turned the engine off as the first spot of rain fell on the windscreen. Within seconds the rain started falling a little harder, then quickly much.

"That should keep everyone indoors." Thomasine heard Bea mutter to herself as she watched the rain dribbling down the car windows. Several figures could just be seen in the gloom running from bushes into the house, giggling and shouting as they went with bottles of champagne in hand. Bea collected up the glasses and returned them to their proper home and Cara turned to speak to Thomasine.

"Okay, nervous?"

"A little," Tom replied truthfully, "but excited as well."

"Good, never mind that you will not know anyone but us, hardly anyone ever knows anyone except by reputation at these things."

They started walking to the front door, Thomasine was surprised that they did not rush more to avoid the rain, maybe it was unladylike, but then again, they were not really getting wet at all. Sure the rain was falling, she could see it, smell it, but none fell on any of them. They paused by the impressive marble portico and Cara explained.

"There has been a house here for over six hundred years, although up until the 1790 rebuild it was a much more traditionally manor house." She tapped one of the huge marble columns and pointed to the two wings sprawling out from the centre. "See, money doesn't always accompany good taste." Thomasine looked at her puzzled, to her it was just another grand house and surely everyone aspired to live in them. "Bit to open plan for me; I like things a little more cosy…these places can be a bugger to keep warm in winter!" Thomasine smiled at Cara's practicality. "They'll probably not talk much too you, on account of your young age," she frowned and seemed far off for a moment "though there are always lascivious wolves lurking; don't be controversial, just go with the flow."

Thomasine thought about this for a moment; then voiced what she felt.

"This isn't just a theme party is it? This really happened once, so as time travel is out something bad must happen tonight; am I right?"

"Maybe." Was the only reply that came.

The scenes that then followed would fill Thomasine's thoughts and dreams for years to come, yet whenever she tried to remember any one particular event or face her memory often got confused. Faces would blur and become unreal, maybe that was the problem, the surrealism of the whole event, or maybe just the horror of it.

She remembered the interior of the house quite well. Through fine double doors they had flowed into a wide hallway, off which a series of rooms on both sides were filled to bursting with people, which when the house was stuffed full of antiques and paintings was kind of an odd thing to witness. It made her realise that people actually lived in these houses, rather than just visited them for a few hours in the summer.

Bea vanished from their company only to return minutes later with more champagne, seconds later she was gone again, to dance; she said which was happening everywhere, for every room had a gramophone, all mostly playing the same kind of jazzy music Thomasine had never heard except on television or in films.

Cara led Thomasine through the various rooms on the ground floor of the house, no one approached or talked to them, few even noticed. Not that they were invisible, it was something more than that to Thomasine, like they were being deliberately ignored, but she could not understand why. She voiced this concern to Cara but she just shrugged and told her that was just the way it was, that these people were mainly professional party people spending their families accumulated wealth on fun, too them they were nobodies, at least until someone introduced them.

Their wandering led them up onto the first floor where Cara continued to point out various people; mostly they were the offspring of MPs, landed gentry and business leaders. Thomasine was beginning to hate this place and these people. They were so false with their accents and outrageously exaggerated actions. They talked of the world as though they were barely a part of it, though they certainly seemed to feel above it. Finally their wandering led them to the second floor where the rooms had changed from being large and formal to smaller private boudoirs.

"Are you sure we are allowed up here?" Thomasine asked.

"Of course, we cannot see everything unless we look!" Cara smiled innocently. Raised voices were coming from somewhere out of sight, doors were slammed and feet pounded the heavily carpeted floors. "Perfect timing."

Cara muttered as she made her way to a door, beaconed Thomasine to join her, then opened the door softly and stepped inside.

The room was a huge bedroom, but the décor shocked Thomasine; it was totally at odds with everything else she had seen in the house. Cara was one step ahead of her and shook her head in disgust.

"Goodness, Futurism, one would never have expected this from outside."

The bed took up at least a third of the large room. It was white save for its black marble head and footboards, which were highly polished like gravestones; each corner was topped with an erotic statue that stood on raised white marble panels whilst two black neon tubes zigzagged their way above the headboard to provide light. Next to this was a black marble dressing-table, with a white marble top and a huge cone shaped mirror that whilst only being four feet wide at the bottom, rose at least ten foot up the wall. The large double windows were a hotchpotch of variously shaded geometric cuts of glass and this design was repeated about the room, through strangely formed chairs and coat hangers and the most bizarre lamps of white cubes of glass on black stalks.

"Are you sure this is the right place?" Thomasine whispered into Cara's ear.

"Hmm, Futurism in the Domestic Sphere," a voice spoke from beside them, Bea had returned "yet another European export Britain could have well done without."

Suddenly a door on the far side of the room burst open and in stormed a young woman in a floaty saffron flapper dress. She slammed the door shut behind her, but it was quickly reopened as two men with slicked hair, sweating brows and moustached faces stormed in, followed again by two women, both in flapper dresses, one deep red the other emerald green. Thomasine remembered to breathe again as the three of them were ignored as they watched on as the new arrivals began, or rather continued, a mass argument.

The first young women to enter flung herself onto the bed face down as the other four argued. One of them men grabbed her by the back of her neck and shouted angrily at her in, what Thomasine believed was Italian. The woman's response was to first utter an exaggerated cry then swipe out with her fingers, her wickedly manicured nails raking his face, drawing from him blood and slightly effeminate high-pitched screams. The other man guffawed loudly, whilst the two women stopped arguing long enough to rush to the wounded man's side. The man spat blood and Italian swear words and punched the other; he stumbled and bumped into one of the other women. She fell smashing her head on the dressing table. Thomasine went to step forward but Bea's hand was on her shoulder instantly.

There was a momentary pause, then the fallen woman was forgotten and the two men fought as did the two women. Ornaments were thrown and the neon tubes smashed, as was something else, something worse, for the taint of gas filled the air. The fighters seemed not too notice but the three girls had and Cara ordered them to leave. Running on automatic Thomasine followed Bea down the stairs and back through the house, the smell of gas rose about them, but no one else seemed to realise what was happening. Thomasine thought to call out a warning, but something inside said it was too late and they were outside looking back at the house.

There was a smash of glass as Thomasine watched in horror as the first women to have entered the bedroom came flying through the geometric glass window head first, her eyes staring as the ground approached fast, her face scarred from the jagged glass. She landed with a soft thump on the ground and appeared to move, was she actually okay? No, she did not rise. Briefly Thomasine thought she saw the figure of a man sobbing at the window, had he pushed or tried to prevent her fall? Then the building fell.

A blue orb of light instantly sprung from the very core and just for an instant Thomasine thought she had x-ray vision as she could see through the eerily beautiful glow and along the wings right into the interior of the building, then it was gone, replaced by an explosion of hot thunder, screams and flames, a wave of released emotion, of hopes and dreams remembered for a fraction of a second washed through her.

Thomasine ran across the lawn to where the women lay broken amongst shards of coloured glass arriving just in time to see the women blinking her last through bloody tears; then she faded into the past. The heat of fire instantly abated, but Thomasine's skin itched from the heat, she turned to find Bea and Cara at her side looking up at the decades old ruins of the portico virtually swallowed by ivy and the less than magnificent building that now stood nearby; the Manor Park Golf Club. Cara held out her hand and helped Thomasine to her feet, she offered a pristine ivory coloured handkerchief, which Thomasine accepted and wiped her reddening eyes; she desperately hoped not to cry.

"We should go now." Said Cara.

"Okay, I'll drive?" Bea offered as she walked to the car. Thomasine held onto Cara's arm as they walked back to the car slowly.

"There was nothing we could have done was there? Don't answer that I know I'm being silly." Thomasine stifled the tears she felt building.

"No, you are acting the same as anyone else would have in a similar situation."

"Such tragedy!" Sobbed Thomasine.

"So much death; one does sometimes wonder why. Before the accident you felt nothing for the people, except maybe a little resentment?"

"True, but the explosion seems a little much to resolve my distaste for their lethargy and hopelessness."

They got into the back of the Rolls-Royce, which was now rather neatly parked on the 18th green and Bea drove them away.

No sooner had Thomasine reassumed her seat she was asleep. She did not intend to, she was trying to remember the faces of all those at the party; but she couldn't. The seat was soft and comforting and reminded her of her bed in the inn and just for a moment that was where she found herself. Sitting with her feet on the floor she began to lean backwards and by the time her back touched the soft covers she was gone, aware that she was asleep, though not exactly where she was.

"So what do you think; is she going to make it?" Bea asked.

Cara looked across at the sleeping girl at her side and considered her reply. She had wanted Thomasine to see the true horrors of the world in which they lived, the world of the living and the dead and she had responded well so far. She was not afraid to show her feelings and this was expected from a teenager, yet she was showing a remarkable maturity in accepting everything she had seen and done.

"I think so," she smiled catching Bea's eyes in the mirror "she is about to sample her possible future in the otherworld and I do not think she will like it there." Cara looked at Thomasine and gently patted her knee.

In her sleep and yes Thomasine knew she was asleep, she was working in a supermarket filling its shelves with brightly coloured packets of biscuits. Although there were no windows to see the outside world and despite the gloomy orange glow of the gently buzzing lights above she knew that it was late in the night, perhaps two or three in the morning.

She was holding a cardboard box in her left hand whilst putting the last of a long succession out. When she had finished she stepped back and admired her handiwork. It was a perfect vision to her and she felt a strange sensation of satisfaction, yet also a nagging loss of something, that maybe she could have achieved more. She looked carefully at the aisle, but no, there was not a thing wrong here. Every packet was facing forward and all types built to exactly the same height. Every shelf had the correct label, in the correct place; but still she was not satisfied.

Then the strangest thing happened. Feeling slightly dizzy and a little light-headed for a moment she watched. As if by some unseen hand she was lifted from the aisle and set down in the next. Here the shelves were virtually empty but there were eight square wooden pallets laden with large boxes of crisps just waiting for someone to put them in their place, and this she did.

She would work an aisle to perfection and then be lifted to the next. So many aisles, yet sometimes the work she did was strong and visible in her mind, at others she knew not what she was doing. In the pet food aisle she watched as the images of cats and dogs leapt from their various tins and sat at her feet waiting for her to feed them dried biscuit treats or throw some of the many pet-toys for them to play with; but she never did, for that would have made her aisle untidy. Besides they all ran away when the sound of whinnying horses began emanating from many of the tins.

In the tinned vegetable isle she was horrified to discover that amongst the three pallets of stock provided for her there were only two types of products; a cheap supermarket own brand of chopped tomato's and Heinz baked beans, multi-packs of course. But still she triumphed in her task.

Eventually she reached the last aisle before the chilled section and she knew that she would travel no further. Standing by the rotisserie, which smelt of grease and burnt chicken entrails as it was being cleaned, Thomasine noticed a huge set of doors in the wall of the store. They were fifteen feet high and at least six feet wide, when she pushed upon the door on the left it glided open easily. A bright light hit her right in the eye.

The glare of the light refused to subside and she was forced to look away, meanwhile the stench of warm cheese and ham melted into the thick stale air and lapped about her, turning her stomach close to the point of release. She steadied herself and stepped inside, the door gliding shut silently behind her.

On her left where two walk-in chillers, their doors firmly shut, whilst on her left a rough wooden fence had been assembled. Stretching from the top of this fence at an upwards angle ran thick planks of wood draped with thin polythene sheets. The source of light was identified as coming from an industrial sized arc-lamp at the end of this surreal corridor, whilst from above fell a sprinkling of dust and the sounds of workmen.

Along the edge of the wooden fence there were numerous metal tables stacked with catering cutting equipment and piles of sliced cheeses and meats; all were soft and smelt terrible as they were in various stages of decay.

She moved to the first of the chiller doors and slid it to one side on its rollers. Pulling the thin purple plastic stripping aside she enjoyed the coolness of the air and looked inside to see four girls, their ages ranging from teens to forties, all were eating chunks of cheese from a communal paper plate. They looked at her in unison, Thomasine felt her breath stall as she looked into their eyes, devoid of colour, so blank and lifeless at odds to their overtly made up faces and perfectly coiffured hair, neatly bundled under barely visible nets beneath starched white hats, their uniforms positively glowing under the soft ultraviolet lights. They were surprised at having been disturbed.

The eldest looking of the four held forth the paper plate and offered a welcoming smile, mirrored an instant later by her three colleagues. Thomasine found it easy to refuse and took a step back, allowing the plastic curtain to fall back into place. As she slid the door closed her last view was of the four returning to their munching. She moved to the next door.

She slid the door aside as she had done the other but this time the interior was swathed in pure darkness; no light, not even from the powerful arc-lamp dared pass through the plastic curtain. Thomasine stepped inside letting the blackness enveloped her; the air warm and muggy touched her exposed skin and made her want to scratch, refusing to do so bought a perverse kind of enjoyment.

The door behind her slid shut softly and she waited, for she knew that this was transition only and surely, yes, the air about her stirred and dropped a degree or five and the blackness gave way to the orange glow of streetlamp as she once again found herself on a suburban street, although this time it was most definitely night. She stood under the single streetlamp and waited, watching the darkness and the houses about her, not one of the many houses had a single light visible.

After five minutes she heard the sound of a motorcar rumbling somewhere nearby and then as if by magic she saw headlights approach from her left. The car was old and red and seemingly not in any great hurry to get to wherever it was going. As it neared it slowed slightly and Thomasine was able to see the driver, a woman of about forty years with short, blondish hair and thick rimmed glasses. As she passed she threw something from her open window and it landed at Thomasine's feet; she bent to pick it up as the woman increased speed and drove away.

Thomasine examined the item in her hand; it was a paperback book with a stripped black and red cover. There was no author but the title was clear enough, it read 'All about Thomasine'.

With hands slightly shaking she flicked quickly through the pages and examined the text, it didn't take long. There was just a single word repeated over and over again on every single page, 'me', even in the place of the page number was a miniature 'me'. She dropped the book and watched as it landed silently, then horror of horrors the words slipped from the pages onto the pavement like transfers from a sheet immersed in water until they had all collected into a black pool and all became illegible; but what did it mean?

With a start Thomasine awoke, just as the Rolls stopped outside *The Sailor's Harvest*. She looked at Cara who was just turning from conversation with Bea and spoke softly through the lifting sleepiness.

"I think we need to talk."

Cara nodded.

Eleven
Having 'The Talk'

Five minutes later Cara and Thomasine were sitting in comfy leather porter chairs opposite a pleasantly glowing fire. There were no lights on anywhere inside the inn. When they had arrived back there were candles burning in wall-sconces but Bea had extinguished them before saying goodnight and disappearing upstairs. The fire had been on its last embers, but a skilled turn from Cara's hands had soon bought it back to life.

They were sharing a comfortable five minute silence as they sipped small glasses of bourbon and cola; Thomasine wanted to refuse anymore alcohol at first, but gave in when she realised that Cara was only offering it to pacify her nerves as she mulled the various questions in her head; it was certainly working, or maybe it was just the fire making her so warm and willing to speak.

"I have been having the strangest dreams recently," Thomasine frowned and thought that through again. "Well that is to say that whilst everything has been a little odd recently my dreams when I sleep seem so...real."

"We call them Violet Hours," Cara replied, her eyes momentarily miles away. "We all have them; even humans to some degree are susceptible to their effects. They are the mind's way of reasoning and adjusting to new ideas...to reach a final understanding. I do understand how disorientating they can be; the things you see and do...the experiences sometimes real, yet not necessarily so."

"Violet Hours," Thomasine repeated "I like that. They have been amazing just recently, so detailed and long, I seem to remember everything."

"Yes, its like that James Bond theme tune, you know the one for *You Only Live Twice, one life for yourself and one for your dreams.*"

Thomasine was surprised by her pop culture reference.

"I can't see you watching James Bond, it just doesn't seem right."

"No, no to be fair I gave them all a try and I distinctly remember seeing it on August the 18th, 1971...it was on in a complete fleapit in Stockholm; I was in the area and had a free evening." She sipped at her drink. "Of course I would have seen it when it first came out in the sixties, but there was just so much to see and do back then."

Thomasine shook her head and smiled.

"You must have seen and done so much, don't you...and please do not take this the wrong way, but don't you ever get bored."

"Never!" Came the instant reply. "On the contrary, there is just never enough time it seems. There is a whole world out there; billions of lives happening simultaneously, the possibilities are endless. I have travelled the world a dozen times and each of those times it has been different. I sailed the oceans in the best and worst of times, learnt to fly a Sopworth Camel and seen too many wars."

"So how long have you actually been a vampyre then?"

"I suppose since my life began, I never knew my mother for she died giving birth and was buried a long way from where I grew up."

"I'm sorry, I didn't mean to pry." Thomasine stoked her hair nervously.

"Do not be silly, it is perfectly all right, besides given the age of even the youngest of our group everyone's mothers have passed on."

"So it's not like on TV then, being a vampyre, I mean you don't get turned and some demon takes over your body and you always remain as you were when bitten."

"Goodness no!" Cara smiled broadly "the power of television to corrupt facts into a distorted amalgam of falsehood truly never ceases to amaze."

"And the whole blood thing, you know killing, do I have to do all that?"

"We do not kill anymore, well not as a general rule, though there are of course always exceptions; sometimes needs must."

"And the blood?" Thomasine pushed cautiously.

"Mostly fictitious."

"Mostly?" Thomasine repeated wondering when her time might come.

"Well, each to their own." A playful smile rose on Cara's lips.

"So if I become a vampyre, I won't always be the same age as I am now, interesting." Thomasine muttered more to herself than Cara.

"Back when I first started to change I had no-one to talk to. My father had moved to England upon my birth and we lived in a huge empty mansion in Sussex, which was actually a lovely upbringing and I will never complain. My father feared what was going to happen and attempted to protect me and though we never really talked about it, I know he always did his best for me; eventually though I ran away."

Thomasine perked up at this.

"Really!" *Just like me*, she thought to herself.

Cara nodded and continued her tale.

"Of course back in 1818 it was highly unusual for a young woman to run away, especially if she had a privileged background, but my father knew what I was attempting to run from and tried everything he could to stop me, though not in a malicious way, no, he truly believed he was doing what was best for me. Fortunately I managed to evade him, I met the man who would later become my fiancé and we travelled across Europe."

"That sounds so romantic, running away together; when did you know that he was the one for you?"

"At the time it took a day, but I suppose looking back I knew the instant I stepped onto that train. He was running too, though only as a way of trying to find direction in his life. One of the biggest problems I was facing was that so many people just didn't notice me; it's a vampyre thing. We exist of the world and interact with it, usually at our own choosing; but he noticed me, he helped and guided me through the transition for the better part of four years until he died, taken by my own stupidity and lack of foresight."

Thomasine's eyes grew wide at this revelation.

"So vampyre's can die then?" She pondered out loud.

"He was not a vampyre. Okay, edited highlights version?" She leant forward in her chair and placed the now empty glass next to Thomasine's, who nodded eager to hear all.

"As I took control of my power I built a small group of friends about me, we who were vampyre traded death for power and he was part of this. I was planning for the time when we would break our ties with Death and gain control over our own destinies. However before I could act Death struck first, taking my man away from me; but we survived. A pact was made and ten years ago it came to fruition. We bargained our immortality on the single decision of a reincarnated man, my fiancé. He was given another chance at life and when the time was right we had one week to persuade him to join our way of life. If he refused we lost everything we had, everything, but as you can see he accepted and now we are free."

"It must have been an easy decision for him to make, I mean if he loved you and all."

"Well it was not really that straightforward, he had after all no memories of the past, save for the few gentle nudges we gave him; we had to be so careful. I mean imagine how you might feel if someone just popped out in front of you on the street and said 'hello I am your 180 year old vampyre ex-fiancé and I want you back'?"

"Well, I might be a tad sceptical I must admit." Thomasine smiled. "So in all that 180 years of waiting was there ever another?"

"No." Came the instant reply; Cara looked her straight in the eye.

"Never?"

"Never. What is 180 years of waiting to us? Well maybe about nine tenths of my life so far, but in the greater scheme of things it is nothing. Obviously I wish he had been there and seen all the things I did, but we have the rest of our lives together now and we try to visit the past as often as possible."

"A story with a happy ending?"

"As yours will be I am sure."

"I had all these ideas in my head about what vampyre's might be like, I was so wrong."

"Not so much." Cara assured her.

They sat in silence for another five minutes before mutually agreeing that they should return to their rooms and continue the discussion later. As they walked up the tight stairway Thomasine could barely keep her eyes open, amazed at how quickly the need for sleep had stalked up on her.

The phone rang. He paced his way along the cool marble corridor and picked up the bakelite receiver; instinctively he knew who it would be even before he heard the soft voice.

"What can you see?" She asked.

He looked about him and smiling coyly described what he saw.

"There are cabinets, two by two filled with all manner of taxidermy, interspersed with tall arched windows and delicate plasterwork. The evening breeze is blowing the netting against the night and if I look down from the landing I see a seat of learning."

"Go to the window and tell me more."

He paced gently to the window and pulled the netting about him so he could see clearly; even though he had seen the scene so many times before, it never tired him and he could have described it in his sleep.

"I am on a hill, not too high, just enough to appreciate the blueness of the lake and glinting lights from the castle at the furthest reaches; even from here I can smell the lavender."

"Can you see the moon?"

"No, to cloudy, there maybe a storm later, but I can feel it near."

"Ah, Italy…are you alone?"

"No one else was up for it, so yes. How are things?" He asked.

"Very good, I'm in bed; we have only just got back from the party."

"I wish I was with you."

"So do I; you could come over for a while."

"I'd like that very much, but I do not want to be a distraction for you right now."

"Hmm, that is true; I must not overload Thomasine now, especially as we are so near to completion."

"How long?"

"Just a few more days then I'll be back…why are you still up anyway, it's so late, even later there?"

"My head is to full of ideas to sleep, I'll give it a little longer."

"You were supposed to say that you could not sleep without me by your side!" She scolded light-heartedly.

"I know."

She smiled at his voice and pictured him in her head.

"What are you wearing?" She enquired.

"The blue silk dressing gown and you?"

"Nothing…take of the gown."

"Okay." He replied; Cara shut her eyes and placed her free hand on her stomach, instinctively many miles away he did the same.

"Now close your eyes." She whispered.

Twelve
Shopping

Thomasine woke to find herself lying on top of the sheets; bathed in bright sunlight she wore just a simple silk chemise. She was so relaxed that when she came to check the mantle clock she was surprised to find it before ten; she had only reached bed just before six. Getting off the bed she moved to the window and gazed out across a town at peace with itself. She could hear the sounds of life, cars in the street, footsteps, a deep rumbling laughter that surely came from an ancient portly butcher or wizened grocer and birds calling upon the breeze; but thoughts of the previous night were still in her mind. She remembered Mr Morphus on the beach and the events at the Hall; where they real? Then she remembered the conversation with Cara.

She washed quickly in the ceramic bowl and dried herself with a warm soft cotton towels that had been lying on the back of a chair in direct sunlight, it smelt of freshly cut roses. *Was there no problem a soft cotton towel could not solve*, she wondered as she crossed to the wardrobe to find clothes. There were plenty to choose from, but it was the outfit from the train that won the day again. It was hanging on the inside of the door, freshly cleaned and ready to go. She was pleasantly surprised to discover that it only took ten minutes to fasten up, though her arms did ache for a while afterwards.

Thomasine left her room and gently tapped on the respective doors of Cara and Bea's rooms; there was no one home so she moved downstairs. She found Cara in the main lounge of the inn, 'Utopia' in hand, sipping tea from a delicate china cup; she was dressed simply in white blouse and floor length midnight-blue pencil skirt. As Thomasine walked cautiously in, Cara put down the book carefully marking the page with a thin strip of black silk and offered tea and breakfast. Thomasine refused the food but accepted the tea and as she took a chair by an ancient table as Cara poured.

"Did you sleep well?" Cara asked.

"Yes, very thank you. Incredible really when you consider that it was for only about four hours."

Cara finished pouring and smiled.

"Or even twenty-eight." Thomasine looked more than a little surprised. "You have slept for more than a day, but that is not unusual given your age, alcohol and the events of the night before."

"Oh yes, how could I forget?"

"You must not, you should never try to pick and choose memories to keep or forget. Everything one sees or does is a unique experience perceived by an individual in a single unique way. These memories define us; they guide us, good or bad one must remember."

"So what if I choose to walk away from all of this and return to a normal life?"

"If that is what you choose so be it."

"No I'm not saying that exactly, but I might, do you think I would remember everything that has happened. Would the events change me; how would I feel?"

Cara sipped more tea and appeared to mull these questions over.

"Maybe, if you choose to let them, if you want them too."

"Has anyone you have chosen ever decided not to go with you, what happened to them?"

"No, no-one."

Thomasine picked up her tea and held it before taking a big gulp. "I think I might be your first failure!"

Cara shook her head.

"I said the other night that I doubted that and I still hold that opinion. We all have our own places to find in the world and no matter what type of life you choose to live I am sure it will be right for you. I am positive you will find your role through us. That does not mean you will spend forever at my side, or with any one of my companions; you may well find you want to do your own thing. We will always be there for you and of course we are able to help and guide you as best we can. I told you before that there is no fixed guide for this life, no ancient text that holds all the answers. I like to think that it makes things more fun."

Thomasine smiled at this and continued to drink her tea as the front door opened and in walked Bea in beige jodhpurs and tweed jacket. She arrived with smiles and good mornings and a big hug for Thomasine.

"Ready?" She asked, Cara nodded and put down her cup.

"For what?" Thomasine asked, desperately hoping that she was going included.

"Busy day ahead for us I am afraid," Cara replied rising from her chair. "Of course if you would rather stay…?"

"No chance!" She replied and finished her tea with gusto.

Cara grabbed her jacket and they moved outside into the beautifully warm late-summer morning. Just outside the inn entrance was a huge long car, all soft curves, deep dark blue paint and shining chrome. She recognised the cat on the front but not the model, though Thomasine did voice her approval. Cara took the drivers seat again and told her that it was her fiancé's Jaguar 420G, a present she had given him for his birthday a few years ago; one that he had lent her because it really was such a pleasure to drive.

The ride in the car was so smooth and quiet that if it had not been for the buildings they passed Thomasine might not have believed they were even moving at all. Cara drove the car back through the narrow streets of the town then out into the countryside, though in the opposite direction to the way that they had travelled the previous night. They drove through for an hour before entering another town.

Cara parked the car on the road next to a dusty field that had probably seen better days as a football pitch; the rusty and tilting goalposts were a dead giveaway. A group of scouts and guides were preparing a party in the field, stalls were being assembled and pathetic attempts at bunting hoisted randomly on several trees. The sun was directly above them as they began their walk.

Opposite the field there were a number of prefab bungalows, all looked tired, with overrun unappealing gardens; there were few other souls on the street, and Thomasine wondered what on earth they were doing in this place.

At first none of the three spoke much as they walked and together they made their way from the field down to a crossroads where a large old church, complete with jumbled necropolis sat. Thomasine could hear voices coming from within and when she looked she could see groups of people being led through the maze of graves, occasionally stopping. A figure, who appeared to be leading the group, would then talk for a moment before moving on again.

"What's going on in there?" Thomasine asked the others.

"Graveyard and mediaeval church tours," Cara responded, as she stopped to look at the church. "Once a month they open to the public and give them a guide for a little money. The church and cemetery are no longer used in the manner they were intended so the money is useful to prevent further deterioration."

"Would you like to join in?" Asked Bea

Thomasine thought about it for a moment.

"Maybe later if we get chance, though I bet you could probably tell me more about it than any guide."

"Possibly," Bea replied "but you know what the problem with these organised tours is?"

"What?"

"They usually keep out all the good stuff!" She smiled and Thomasine smiled back.

At the crossroads they turned left and started along a road which must have been the high street. Thomasine was surprised at suddenly how busy it was; she had assumed that this place was going to be a sleepy little affair; how wrong she was.

There were lots of people milling about; so many nationalities with probably more than a dozen different languages being spoken. Thomasine gazed about her as the pavements were filled almost too overflowing and remembered the other night.

"Cara," she spoke softly, gently pulling on the sleeve of her jacket. Cara stopped and turned her big brown eyes showing nothing but friendship and openness. "Nothing bad is going to happen to these people is it?"

"I don't think so," she paused and was about to ask why Thomasine should think such a thing when it dawned on her as to why she had asked. "Well not today anyway." She winked at Bea who was just behind Thomasine stifling a smile of her own at Cara's wicked humour. Fortunately Thomasine realised what was going on and breathed a huge sigh of relief, though reddening a little once more.

There were lots of funky boutiques and shops selling retro clothing; some even still had their original 1960s frontage. Further up the street some of the building where really old, it did not take a genius to tell Victorian from vulgar. It was in front of a particularly fantastic three story building complete with cathedral like windows and proud stone carving that they stopped. Thomasine believed it might have once been a theatre, it felt that it should have been and on the pavement outside was a sandwich board advertising an 'Electric Market'. They decided to enter.

Up a step and under the cast iron portico they found the interior walls of the entrance covered in peeling red paint and thick grime. Five tall steps took punters from street level down into the interior and onwards into the gloom and deep sub-base noise that rumbled from an as yet undiscovered source through the walls. Down here what carpet was laid appeared thin and sticky and little more than a patchwork of different styles, whilst the walls were covered with posters for rock acts and cabaret shows from a bygone era. What once might have been a ticket office was now boarded and strung with florescent tubes of blue and yellow and yet one could still see traces of intricate woodcarving poking out here and there.

Opposite there was a stall selling rack upon rack of old clothing, Thomasine chanced a glance as they passed and was sure she saw fur coats move on their own. Pausing she looked at the man sitting slumped with his stock, he wore a skinny fit white shirt and the tightest leather trousers possible, they might have suited him, if they had not ended at his calf rather than his ankle. He wore a full length coat of fur, though someone had strategically shaved swirling crop-circles all over the surface and they matched those in his shorn black hair. She was not sure if he was awake or not, he did not move and his eyes were hidden behind yellow and black sun glasses, something that was definitely not needed in this gloom. She was bought back to her sense by a gentle touch on the shoulder.

"Seen something you like?" Bea asked softly surveying the stall. Thomasine shook her head.

"Fur; not really my thing."

Quickly they hurried after Cara who stood just past the stall at a set of multiple doors ready to enter the thumping bass filled place within.

Inside was a world Thomasine had only ever dreamt about. The doors opened into a large hall and inside over seemingly every inch of space the most marvellous market sprawled. There were stalls selling clothing, footwear, jewellery, books, magazines and just about anything else that fitted in with the Goth ethos. There was even a stall offering crypt tours of that nearby cemetery and another selling coffins made from wicker and cardboard; rather unnervingly in between these two was another selling small memento's, in the form of rings and bracelets, of the dead made from their own hair. Thomasine was fascinated but also just a little disgusted; still they were all doing a roaring trade. Bea saw her looking and sidled up to her, whispering, though possibly shouting into her ear as they had to stand close together to be heard.

"That is pretty gross."

Thomasine nodded an agreement and shouted back.

"I know, do you think they take the hair before or after death…and do they ask first?"

"Probably not," Bea smiled "especially if they're already dead!"

Thomasine shook her head and mock shivered.

"Well I would not want to be the person who has to gather up the hair."

"Me neither, especially as not all the hair comes from the scalp!"

Thomasine turned to Bea who was looking most sincerely at her.

"Now THAT, really is disgusting." They both laughed.

The people manning or maybe womaning the stalls were mostly dressed for the part in clothes of black and dyed hair either black or scarily bright seemed to be popular; as was body piercing. There was a large crowd which they mingled with easily and progressed slowly about occasionally stopping to look at particularly interesting items.

Thomasine found that many of the people working the stalls were uncomfortably pleasant, constantly reaching out and trying to pull her into trying something on, be it a coat or piece of jewellery, she refused them all. She found it odd, maybe just because in the last few days she had gotten used to not being noticed by anyone and being able to do her own thing; she was not sure she could ever go back to this way of life.

As they continued to wander the sounds of thumping music changed to ever more manic tunes, in the farthest corner of this place was a DJ booth and the head of the incumbent occupant could be seen bouncing ever more feverously to his tunes. Talking to one another was growing more difficult, so after another ten minutes they decided that it was time to leave.

Back on the street, ears ringing slightly they paused for recollections opposite a shoe shop. Bea commented on the fantastic plastic boots with their twelve inch built up soles in the window.

"Cool market," Thomasine rubbed her ears "little bit high in volume, but some wacky stuff."

"It is usually a nightclub, though once a month they open through the day and gather to sell their wares. I actually have not been here for a few years now and I must say standards have dropped a little."

"I liked it," Thomasine added, not wanting to be unappreciative.

"I've waited for years to go to a place like that, I think?" She frowned and was lost in thought for a moment. Thomasine was feeling something she did not expect; disappointment.

"But?" Cara probed gently.

"It's funny though that when I thought about wanting to go to a cool Goth market like that and hang with all the people I did kind of have a plan of what it would be like, what I would buy and what I would do."

"If there is something you want, we can go back and get it." Cara offered.

"But that's it, the thing I can't quite put my finger on...there isn't anything that I actually want back there, I mean I loved every ear-splitting minute and the people too are friendly...but it's all just!" She waved her hands, seeking help in finishing her sentence.

"Ephemeral?" Bea offered, and then thought again seeing as Thomasine stood blank-faced "stuff?"

"Yes, I think that's it, it's just 'stuff', it doesn't really matter. Everyone looks and acts the same...like everyone trying to be alternative and different from one another yet they all end up the same; does that make sense?"

Bea and Cara exchanged a look before Cara moved over and put her arm about her shoulders.

"Don't worry, the feelings you have at the moment do eventually reconcile themselves."

"What do you mean, I'm fine honest." Thomasine tried to bluff, but secretly she was angry that they had so easily seen through her emotions.

"You see only the pointlessness of people's lives, their insidious desires to mate unchecked, to buy without regard for needs and wants."

"So for me, us, what is there?" Thomasine asked.

She looked at Bea, but she just smiled and shrugged, then at Cara who had released her, she also smiled.

"We cannot ever tell if we have had an enjoyable journey until we arrive at our destination, I can offer you the choice of two lives, but no guarantees either way. You have a role to play with us; I have seen your potential."

Thomasine looked back to the market. Three girls had just emerged from within with plastic bags full of clothing and other treasures. They were so happy in their world, unaware of the bigger one within and about it and she knew where she wanted to be. She looked at her own clothes, at Bea and Cara and remembered how she had felt over the last few days; she was sure where her path lay, now if only she could travel along it.

Cara smiled broadly and Bea appeared to let loose a long held breath.

"Good." Was Cara's only response and they moved onwards.

For another ten minutes they walked and the high street continued to offer up the same kind of shopping treats. The more they walked the further the street seemed to continue, yet when Thomasine looked behind her she could still see where they had started from; the street was relentless and she wondered if there would ever be an end.

Thomasine knew that there was definitely somewhere they had to be soon though no one was letting on exactly where it was. Then suddenly they stopped; the end of the road still not in sight. Thomasine looked about her expectantly, but could not see anything of particular interest leaping out at her.

"Can you feel anything here?" Cara asked; her eyes on Thomasine so as to not give anything away.

"No," she replied shaking her head.

"Concentrate on what is unusual here."

Thomasine did as requested and then there was something, a pull deep within her, something similar to the feeling she had when she first been alone on the beach and unsure what her next step might have been.

"Is it this?" She asked focusing her eyes on the wall behind Cara.

Built between an estate agents and a charity shop was an undistinguished door. It was aluminium with frosted glass so no one could see through and obviously had not been opened for a long time because there were cobwebs everywhere.

Instinctively Thomasine reached for it and found to her surprise that it moved easily. Giving the door a cautious shove it swung open and revealed another set of doors hung from a much older black iron arch. The doors were wooden and had rotted at the bottom but they were also hanging slightly open; beyond them steep steps rose up into darkness. Cara stepped forward and pushed them further apart.

"After you?" She offered to Thomasine who looked doubtful.

"Where does this go?" She asked her nose twitching at the musty air.

"This used to be a fire exit for the St Tomas Arcade; well I guess that it still is, though no one comes here anymore."

"No one but us," replied Thomasine "why don't we use the proper entrance?" She placed her foot on the first stone step and began to climb.

"The entrance is gone, lost and blocked by one of these shops, it is strange how something can be in use for so long, it was closed in 1983 after ninety-nine years of use and yet here it is just forgotten." Cara explained.

"So how come you know about it; did you used to come here?"

"No I do not recall ever having visited; you know there are doors like this in every town, on nearly every high street."

Thomasine stopped walking and turned back to Cara.

"Seriously?"

"Oh yes, just look between the shops because they are always there; doors to places above, below, between and behind. People see them, pass them everyday and accept them, unaware that maybe no one has been through for years; all manner of secrets just waiting to be explored."

Thirteen steps led up to a stone arched corridor. There once must have been at least a dozen shops here, but now everything was closed. Paint peeled from the walls and dirt and muck gathered in piles strewn across the black and white tiled floor and rain had obviously got inside for there was a general smell of damp and neglect.

Cara pointed down to the left.

"Over there, see where the corridor ends in wood and scaffolding?" Thomasine nodded. "That was the entrance; it must have been quite grand."

"What is that awful smell?" Queried Bea. "It smells like rotting lamb or something."

"Hmm, kebabs I think." Replied Thomasine.

"Maybe, I'm still going with the something." They both giggled.

They continued down the corridor until they reached another flight of stone steps once again leading upwards to a higher balcony level. At the top there was a choice of directions; left and right into darkness or straight on towards a dim and distant glow. Fortunately once they had all arrived at the balcony Cara led them straight onwards.

They walked dark corridors in virtual silence, only occasionally was Thomasine aware of her own footfalls and when she considered that they were quite near the high street and so many other shops she was surprised just how quiet it was. Eventually they stopped as the path they followed passed through the wall of the building and out into the open; here it overlooked an open courtyard; they were a good two stories up.

The only way onwards was across a narrow concrete bridge. It was worn and stained orange where the concrete had broken away and the steel inside had been exposed to the elements. This in turn led to the wall opposite, where there was no opening, just two spiral staircases which were the only access down; the three girls looked down into the courtyard.

It was roughly thirty foot square, concrete floored and directly under the bridge there was a giant round concrete plant tub, though there was only distressed looking dirt and a few weeds inside; then Thomasine noticed a dark alcove in one of the walls.

To the right of the bridge, recessed into the yellowing concrete wall, was a large rectangular opening complete with what appeared to be a pay booth. Though the letters that once adorned the wall were now gone their shadows remained and softly they proclaimed COSMOPOLITAN. The doors of the place were largely black with streaks of yellow placed across them giving the image of a half setting sun, with the booth stuck in the middle the two doors either side were both marked 'Entrance'. Pinned about the alcove where the box-office sat empty were tatty posters for films that Thomasine had never seen; most of the titles were in French, but she did recognise the name on each; Jean Rollin. He was a French film producer who specialised in strange vampire films, she had heard of him, but unfortunately never seen any of his work. Was this a strange cinema dedicated to his work? It looked kind of abandoned, well it was hardly accessible from the direction they had come and as far as Thomasine could make out there was no other way into the courtyard below.

"Have you been here before then?" Thomasine asked looking at each of the others in turn; both girls shook their heads in silent response.

"No one has been here for years." Cara virtually whispered, never taking her eyes of the scene.

"No one alive that is!" Added Bea, her eyes darting quickly from the courtyard to Thomasine then back again.

The three girls walked across the bridge with Thomasine and Cara taking the spiral staircase on the right, whilst Bea took the one on the left. They wound their way down to the floor but Bea failed to emerge. Cara seemed not to notice, instead concentrating on the cinema.

"Bea's gone, did she go back?" Asked Thomasine innocently.

"I do not think so," Cara turned raising her eyebrow slightly before whispering conspiratorially "stairs do things like that to people sometimes!"

Thomasine looked horrified, but Cara simply smiled and gave her a little hug then reassured her that Bea simply had other things to do.

Thomasine looked about her excitedly and noticed that once they were on solid ground again that there really were no other ways in here. There was not even a single window overlooking them from any of the buildings that made the four walls. It hit her suddenly that if the bridge was to collapse and the cinema was not open there might be no way out of here! But why should that happen? She could not quite shake the sense of paranoia and the feeling that she was being watched, no more than that examined; like when the dog walkers marched across the all too public playing fields when there was a games lesson going on. All the girls knew that those old men never put in the effort except when there were short skirts and tight tops on show.

Collecting herself together she focused on the cinema and noticed a girl standing with her back to them, her face nearly pressed against the door. She was shorter than Thomasine and dressed in what appeared to be a black school uniform; a very similar uniform to the one that she herself would normally be expected to wear. The girls' long dark hair was scrapped tightly back in a long tail that fell well down her back.

"Okay, I saw that film," announced Thomasine in a whisper.

Cara remained silent and focused on the girl. Thomasine had just summed up the nerve to step forward to speak to the girl when the door clicked open wide enough to allow the girl entry and in she went; the door remained open and Thomasine stepped forward. She had not planned to and for a while afterwards she could not explain why she did; she just felt that it was the right path to follow; the pull tickled within her again and she thought about the reasons why she walked with Cara and Bea when she first met them. She had just known instinctively that it was the right thing to do and that something life changing was about to happen.

"You do not have to go," Cara offered gently "only if you want to."

Thomasine nodded but did not turn.

"I know, but I actually think I want to, and besides that girl did and for some reason I cannot fathom I know I must not let her go alone." She took another step towards the door. "And besides I don't want to fail this test."

"There is no test, just what we want to do."

"If I go through this door will I come out again?"

"There are other ways out!"

"Alive?" Thomasine smiled nervously.

"I just know we will be seeing each other again soon; as do you."

Thomasine straightened her shoulders and pulled an imaginary hair from her cheek. "Right!" She said firmly and stepped inside. "Coming; ready or not!" She murmured quietly. Upon entry the door shut immediately and silently behind her.

Cara stood in the courtyard, the sun beating down directly. She could feel the long removed presence of all those that had once come here and she knew that the last few days had gone as planned. Now all alone Cara checked a hitherto unseen delicate gold watch that had been tucked up her sleeve.

"Hmm, should make it to Italy just in time for tea." She muttered quietly.

Turning she made her way back to the spiral stairs. If there had been anyone else present they would have seen the smile on her face and in her eyes. She started to climb but never emerged at the top; she did, after all, have somewhere else to be.

Thirteen
Snakes & ladders

Inside was not what Thomasine expected. It was not a cinema at all just a single huge room and with the door now invisible in the wall it was really more of a box. It was virtually dark, like twilight in a curtained bedroom. Thomasine shivered and wondered if any of the shadows were ready to reach out and nip at her flesh. It took a moment for her eyes to fully adjust before she could just make out the furthest reaches of the room, which were about ten feet wide, twenty deep and at least thirty high.

There was no sign of the girl but Thomasine could make out a series of steps directly opposite and further to her right was the source of the meagre amount of light. She moved to investigate and saw that the whole 'wall' here was just a single sheet of smoked glass. Looking out she saw that somehow she was standing on approximately the third floor of a building overlooking a high-street.

"Thomasine," a voice whispered from everywhere, she turned to face the dark room but there was nothing; just a feeling of being intensely examined again.

"Thomasine," again a voice whispered. She strained her eyes and right at the top of the stairs, she could just make out what appeared to be a thin figure. However the shadows being such as they were meant that she could make out little else save for the hideously unnatural glowing green eyes.

The figure started gliding down the stairs towards her and as it came she began to see it more clearly. He, Thomasine was assuming because it looked slightly more masculine than feminine, was at least seven feet tall with slicked back hair, pale skin and no facial features whatsoever, save for those evil eyes that pierced the darkness. He was gaunt, his smart black mourning suit sat uncomfortably loose on his frame and he beaconed to her with evil looking sharp talons rather than fingers; Thomasine edged back to where the door had been. *Vampyre*; was Thomasine's primary thought. Was this what vampyre's truly looked like? Surely Cara would not have lied to her? No; she staunchly refused to believe that. This creature, no matter what it was, might have been convincing in a film but she was not about to believe it. This was not something she might become.

He was talking again, though because he had no mouth the words seemed to come from somewhere else in the room directly into the depths of her mind.

"So in boxes you put all the sections of your so called life and here in this box you go and end up." He was now barely five feet away and Thomasine might not have showed it but she was worried. "You know I have never liked pond-skaters; nasty little things walking on water, just who do they think they are? You don't happen to have any on your person do you?" He asked. Thomasine shuddered, her skin creeping, but somehow she managed to keep it together.

"Nothing to say? Come along Thomasine you have reasoned everything else out over the last few days; tell me what you're thinking."

"Yeah, like that's ever going to happen!" She replied looking about her for something akin to an escape route. He took a step nearer her.

"Excellent, so why come in here?" Thomasine responded with silence; unperturbed he continued. "Is it because you thought Cara wanted you too? I don't think so, maybe it was to see a film; like that would ever change your life...maybe to save the girl, she went upstairs, you were wondering weren't you? Though I don't think she wants rescuing."

"Who are you?" Thomasine found herself asking.

"Good question; though much too late!" He leapt at her talons raking the air emitting high-pitched singing sounds as they did. Nimbly she sprang to the right and once more they stood a few feet apart. "Ooh, slippery!" He whispered.

Thomasine was angry more than scared, why was she letting him get too her? She reminded herself that she had something to do.

"That wasn't very friendly was it? Why can't we just talk, you know maybe become friends; go for a long walk...*over a short cliff!*" She whispered the last part still look for a means of escape.

"I bet you say that to all the boys...or is it girls?" He lunged again; once more Thomasine sensed it coming and dodged until she found herself back in front of the smoked glass window. The stairs were in view right in front of her; she glanced at them quickly, not wanting to take her eyes of him for too long.

"Think you can make it?" He asked teasingly, nodding to the stairs as he did, inviting her to try.

"If I want to I will, you can't stop me." She spat back angrily.

"Tut, tut; did your parents never tell you that there's no such word as can't?"

Thomasine looked at him dumfounded.

"What now you are bringing me up on pronunciation!"

"Tell me Thomasine have you finished blaming everyone else for your life?"

"I'm very happy where I am thank you."

"Oh, could have fooled me!"

"Frequently and as pleasant as this little chat has been, I do have other things to do today."

"But what about me, how are you going to stop me?" His eyes widened as he realised what he had just said.

"And what makes you think I want to? I don't know you, love you or hate you. I feel nothing for you…I don't know why, that's just the way it is!"

"I have been in here for fifteen years, I could get out and do terrible things; I'm quite capable and then it would be your fault entirely!"

She looked incredulously back at him.

"Look, I have to go up these steps, are you going to get in my way?"

He took a step backwards.

"It's not always all about you Thomasine."

Before her eyes his claws retracted back into his hands and reformed into fingers whilst his whole body started to change. He shortened and facial features developed, but Thomasine did not get a good look for with a final cursory glance he turned his back on her and walked to where the door had been. It reopened and he stepped through into sunlight, a man; the door immediately shut and vanishing again behind him.

Should she go rushing over? Thomasine considered it but then opted for the stairs. Taking them carefully she found herself at one end of a narrow corridor. It was ill-lit but she could see that there were five doors; one straight ahead and two on either side, all were slightly ajar.

She tried the first on the left, then its' opposite and so on past the first three. All were identical being about six feet square with unfurnished wooden floorboards and pockmarked plasterboard walls; the only light source in each came from a narrow slit window high on the wall, which would have been far to dirty to see through even if they had not been so high. Thomasine stopped at the forth door, the soft sound of sobbing was most definitely audible. She pushed the door open and found it as before except for the addition of a narrow iron bedstead with a girl sat upon it.

"Hi," Thomasine gave a little wave, but the girl was not looking at her, instead her head was buried in her hands "can I join you in your moping?"

The girl cried louder and Thomasine decided it would be best just to sit with her for a while and maybe she could get some information out of her.

It took an hour to get her to stop crying but eventually she relented, though getting her to take her head out of her hands proved to be a trickier.

"So, you going to tell me your name?" Thomasine had told the other girl hers ages ago but there had been no acknowledgement.

"Toni." Was the softest of reply. Thomasine barely heard.

"Sorry, did you say Toni?" The girl nodded, head still in hands.

"Toni." She repeated.

"I have a younger sister called Toni…" then the realisation suddenly dawned on Thomasine. But no, Cara had said this was not a test, it must be just a coincidence; she pushed the girl away a little. "You're not going to remove your hands and show me that you look like my sister are you?" There was no response, so Thomasine gave her a little nudge. "Oi, don't give me this psycho-bull-crap like there's some great moral dilemma to be resolved here; I won't believe it!"

The little girl finally raised her head and looked at her a little confused. Thomasine felt her heart race madly, but fortunately the girl was not her sister and was most definitely of Asian extraction.

She spoke perfect English and told Thomasine that she was worried that she might never escape this place. She was all wide-eyed and pitiful; it just annoyed Thomasine even more when still she would not explain how she got here.

"Right!" Thomasine mustered raising herself from the bed. "Bored now and I am going through that last door, coming or not?" Thomasine took a step to the door and looked back; the girl was gone. "Oh, very bloody clever," she practically screamed to the room in general "the next person I meet get's tagged."

Thomasine pushed open the final door and found herself in a small attic-like opening facing a wobbly looking narrow wooden ladder. She started to climb, first up one ladder to a landing, then another, then a third; all the time the walls were narrowing inwards. Finally she made her way up a fourth and this came up through the floor into the centre of a rectangular room. There were no windows just the overall sense of being in an attic, light came from a single unfettered light bulb.

"Hoorah she made it!" Thomasine knew that voice from somewhere and turned to see two familiar figures sitting opposite one another at a glass and aluminium table, complete with four matching chairs. The figure with his back to her did not turn; instead he raised a smoked glass of tea and toasted her.

"Congrats and all that, Champion of Snake's and Ladders...care for some tea?"

"And toast!" Offered the other. "Must have toast now, freely given to be enjoyed with tea."

Thomasine looked at them, a slight smile forming on her lips and she took her seat at the table where toast and tea waited.

"Hmm, thank you, but I can only stay a moment; I do have people to meet and places to see."

They both smiled, "Of course" they jointly muttered before tucking back into their toast and Thomasine noticed a door in the wall.

Epilogue

Far away under a baking Mediterranean sky a blue Jaguar purred its way up the gently curving roads of the valley and into the driveway of her summer home. Cara looked into the rear view mirror and watched as the dust clouds she created settled amongst the olive groves and parked in front of the house.

Stepping out she glanced up seeing her man sitting on one of the terraces. He wore a white silk shirt open to the waist and dark blue pants. He was surrounded by papers and books, but he still found time to look up and wave. She blushed; she always blushed when he looked. Even after such little time away from him it was still a thrill to be back.

Cara started towards the door and was met by Bea in a slight summer dress woven from cotton that was such a fine weave that it looked as though it might have been spun by spiders. Bea smiled and it was returned.

"How are the preparations for dinner?" Cara asked, although fully aware that Bea was a demon in the kitchen and would never let her down.

"Perfect of course, though you will have to wait to find out what it is."

"Sounds exciting."

"It will be." Bea looked behind Cara to the car and noticed that she was alone. "How many placing's will there be?"

Cara smiled broadly.

"Tonight, there will be twenty-one."

Can't See Shadows, Lest they want to be Seen

Can't See Shadows, Lest they want to be Seen
Beginning

Picture the greyest day in suburbia, the dankest day to darken your door this or any winter and you can begin to imagine the drabness of this place. Sometimes the approach is manna from heaven; but this is rare. Where the sea meets land and one catches the vista from afar…such a picture; however much of the time it is hell; a hotchpotch of differing ideas heaped, one upon another. Today is such a day. Even now you can see the grey terraced houses, row upon row, occasionally breaking into a rudimentary cul-de-sac or one-way street, the monotony flattered by the myriad of seemingly identical middle-class cars that spill from driveways onto pavements so frequently that those walking are summarily forced onto the roads. Even today, during the school holiday, the roads groaned and sighed as an impossible volume passed through the narrowest of passages; another Cornish town awoke and went to work…another stalled birth, how progress chokes us as we allow it to shape our path.

Yet even amongst the dimmest of possibilities there must be the faint hope of progressiveness and here in Cornwall, despite initial appearances, this nation is nothing if not resilient…the future and the strange things it might bring had do better than be complacent or fare less than well. Even the darkest evil is afraid of something, often the simplest thing that brings horror back to its roots and negating it; that something lies hidden…waiting.

Everything dies, so everything has something to lose; well… nearly everything.

There was a gentle thump of footsteps up the stairs, then a brief pause followed by gentle knocking at her door. She had pushed the slim brass bolt through its latch when she arrived a few hours ago, she was not sure why, no one had ever entered uninvited before. Maybe it was because it had been so long since she had inhabited this place, that it seemed wrong, almost as if she should not be here, maybe she was the intruder and the lock was better suited to keeping her within and not anyone else out. Either way she was grateful.

"Letter for you Thomasine…um, sorry if I woke you but I thought I heard you moving earlier. Would you like me to leave it outside?"

Thomasine had hoped to avoid her father who should have left for work at least ten minutes ago. She had been awake since arriving and it was now ten minutes to seven and she had decided to lay on the bed in silence and listen to Chris Moyles on her DAB radio for as long as possible; it had been a while since her last listen but the show still sounded the same...she was happy.

"You haven't gotten into any trouble have you?" He asked, clearly not about to just leave the letter outside the door. The postman had been unusually early today and handed dad the letters as he left the house rather than putting them through the letterbox; strange though that dad had simply not left them on the sofa for mum to sift through, he continued speaking to her. "Only the writing on the envelope is much too smart to be from one of your friends."

Thomasine was off the bed in an instant and unlocking the door threw it open, her hand out ready to take the letter. Her father looked her up and down a frown growing on his rotund features.

"Do you sleep in that thing?" Thomasine looked down at the only item of clothing she wore; an extra-large, blue Blur t-shirt circa *There's no other way*, the well worn image of a baby just about visible despite it being as old as she was.

"Not always." She answered truthfully, before adding with a cheeky grin as she realised how much of her leg it was showing and how she would never have dared be so revealing a few months ago; even in front of her parents. "Why; too short?"

"No, but if you need a new nightie and you're too embarrassed to go into town I'm sure mum can get you one..."

Thomasine rolled her eyes but realised her fathers' genuine concern so answered sensibly rather than sarcastically.

"I have three nighties already, thanks, this is more comfortable." She spied the letter in his hand. "For me?"

"Hmm, yes..." her father held the letter up and looked again at the writing "are you sure you're not in trouble?"

"It's heartening to know that you think of me so highly." She rolled her eyes again and waggled her fingers impatiently.

"I don't mean it to...it's just that...you know? Quality envelope, posh writing, by a female unless I'm mistaken and definitely someone older; they don't teach kids to write at school like that anymore; mind you, this style even predates my days if I'm being honest." Momentarily his eyes seemed miles away; but then he handed over the envelope and Thomasine took it eagerly; there was something more than a letter inside. She glanced quickly at the writing; it was from whom she had hoped.

"You're not wrong," she agreed "home education; that is definitely the way forward…you should think about that for Toni, might turn her into a genius!"

"One genius in the family is enough for me and your mother." Her father raised his hands in mock surrender and half-smiled; he moved across the landing toward the stairs then suddenly stopped. "From one of your teachers I suppose?" He nodded at the envelope in her hands.

"Kind of," Thomasine agreed "more of a friend than a pedagogue but I am learning loads." She smiled at her father who seemed a little perplexed by her words. She made a mental note to try and be more 'her' and shut the bedroom door without bothering to lock it; returning to the warmth of her bed Thomasine gathered the duvet about her to read the latest news from her friend.

One
Gathering

The phone had been ringing for six minutes and forty seven seconds without letup. Darren was impressed; whoever was on the other end of the line was displaying some serious commitment. He sat in the attic flicking through back issues of *Kerrang* in his ripped jeans and unwashed *NIN* t-shirt when the monotonous ringing had first tickled his ears. He had ignored it for the first two minutes, one particular picture of Hayley from *Paramore* was more than holding his attention, became more frustrated by the second two minutes, and seriously puzzled by the end of the third two minutes; now he was lying on the floor of the attic, magazine abandoned, with head sticking through the entrance high above the landing.

He checked his watch, seven minutes and two, three, four…*silence*. He rolled over and scrambled back to the thin mattress and sleeping bag…*now where had Hayley got to?* The phone began to ring again. Immediately Darren looked at his watch and started counting the seconds.

Four-hundred and twenty four of the longest seconds later the ringing ceased with Darren once again lying prostrate on the floor, his head dangling over the landing. *Surely there has to be a fault on the line* he tried to convince himself; probably one of those stupid automated cold-calling machines old people were always moaning about on the news. Deciding that all the effort used moving back and forth from his bed was deserving of refreshment he grabbed hold of the steps and lowered himself down.

In the dinning room he began rooting around at the back of the cocktail cabinet as the phone began ringing; he glanced at his watch, *14:32:04…this should end at 14:39:08*, he decided and continued shoving bottles of wine and tonic water aside so he could get to the good stuff hidden at the back. Finally he tracked down the bottle of Bacardi he had watched his dad tuck away in the cabinet twelve months ago when they had done last years pre-Christmas shop. He knew that his dad had a dodgy back and so tended to grab whatever was nearest the front of the cabinet whenever he wanted a drink. It had been clever of Darren to note this and within five minutes of the bottle of Bacardi, and a bottle of Smirnoff, being put into storage he had pushed them right to the most inaccessible place at the back and hidden their presence with a random selection of other wine bottles and mixers. Dad had duly forgotten them.

The Smirnoff had lasted until May and now he was on the Bacardi. He withdrew the bottle and looked at the thumbnail nicks on the label indicating the numerous tasting he had made…*not much left* now he realised. He swirled the clear contents around at the bottom of the bottle; *not much left…sod it, might as well have it all.*

The contents of the bottle, once in one of his dad's pint glasses, were more than he had anticipated; just over a quarter pint, *oh well!* He dumped the bottle in the green recycling bag in the kitchen and filled the glass up with cola from the fridge, he took a long gulp…the phone had stopped ringing. Darren checked his watch expecting it to read 14:39:08 but it was more than two minutes shy. Armed with a new curiosity, fuelled by the immediate light headedness of the alcohol, he made his way back through the dinning room and into the ground floor extension where the phone sat next to the settee.

He stood by the armchair for a couple of minutes, waiting for the phone to ring and occasionally sipping the drink. Noticing the most recent copy of *NME* on the pile of papers by his dad's chair Darren slipped into the comfy leather seat and began flicking through it amazed at the number of shots of the *Long Blondes* and *Blood Red Shoes* and wondered why he hadn't paid more attention to this issue when he read it last week. Suddenly he heard the front door being shut; as he jumped in panic he accidentally nudged the now half-filled glass from the arm of the chair…then the phone started ringing.

His mother stuck her head around the door.

"Oh, didn't expect to see you down here…you going to answer that?"

"Um…yeah," Darren quickly looked over the side of the chair to see where the glass had gone "just getting it" he muttered. He reached for the phone and noticed the glass half buried in the waste paper basket, upside down of course, the brown sticky contents somehow managing to have found an escape route through the bottom. Ignoring it for now he grabbed the phone; he didn't recognise the voice.

"You're a hard boy to get hold off aren't you Darren!"

"Erm, yeah," Darren saw his mother still standing in the doorway and was desperate not to have her come over so he decided to act as though he knew the speaker. "Sorry mate, sidetracked in the roof."

"It's not a problem…I would have kept on ringing; you are going to be here tonight aren't you?"

A chill ran down Darren's back, although his mother had moved into the kitchen he knew her ears would still be tuned in *mothers can do that!*

"I'm not sure." He answered although what he really wanted to say was no.

"You must." The voice was slightly familiar yet such was the way the words where spoken Darren couldn't tell what sex they belonged to or put a face to it.

"It's not that easy," Darren tried to argue; the voice cut him off.

"You have everything you need; I cannot see a reason why you should not do what you need to."

"I'm not really invited."

"That's hardly surprising is it? You need to have friends to be invited to parties." Darren remained silent and the voice spoke again. "It's time to change that, I know what they say about you…even Mathew and David, your supposed best friends. So here's your invite, be there and do what you have to."

The phone clicked off, Darren just looked puzzled at it for a moment.

"Who was that?" Asked his mother who had sidled up to him unnoticed during the conversation.

"Just a friend."

His mother crossed to the television and flicked it on, she turned and with her mother 'super vision' she noticed the growing brown stain on the carpet.

"What's that?"

"I spilt my cola." Darren half lied.

"Why haven't you mopped it up then?"

"The phone rang…I was about to!"

"I'll do it." She muttered as she went to fetch a damp cloth and a towel from the kitchen. Darren looked at the glass and fairly certain she wouldn't notice the illicit Bacardi mixed with it he ran off back into the attic.

**

Tony pulled his pride and joy, a rather tired 1989, white MG Maestro Turbo to a stop-start halt at the roundabout by McDonalds. He patted the slightly sticky steering wheel absentmindedly with his hands encased in black driving gloves and contemplated; he realised she had seen better days, but she rarely let him down, accept when it rained, and was resolved to 'do her up' when he had the money. The roads were as busy as he anticipated they where going to be just before five on a Friday evening.

Leaning against the wooden fence a group of teenagers where demolishing their takeaways and dropping the litter on the floor; Tony kept his eyes forward and tried to look inconspicuous. Suddenly one of the boys was pointing at him, Tony felt nervous he hoped they wouldn't recognise him because he didn't have time to waste. A thumping baseline caught his ears from the right and as the car that had been there moved forward a lowered hatchback, in canary yellow with blacked out windows, sprang into view. The horn of the car behind him bailed out as his momentary loss of concentration meant he had missed the gap in the traffic; he glared in the mirror, but as it was so dark it was a wasted gesture.

The kids at the side of the road where gawping at the hatchback, which revved it's engine angrily as it waited impatiently to launch itself onwards; they weren't looking at his car at all. *Stupid kids, impressed by a flash paint job, bet its bark is worse than its bite.* Tony gripped the wheel tightly, wringing his hands angrily and watched the traffic for gaps; a half-gap appeared and he struck the accelerator firmly with his foot. Tyres span madly on the damp tarmac as four thousand plus revs exploded after a turbo lagged delay that shot him between two cars with barely inches to spare.

He struggled to stop the rear of the car swapping places with the front as he swung around the tight corner and onto the Mevagissey road. Somewhere underneath something mechanical groaned its disapproval at suddenly having to work so hard and as the car regained its balance the weight of the equipment on the back seat shifted and a heavy, leather-bound case nudged into the back of his head. Tony slowed the car and pushed the case back into position, *have to be more careful,* he patted the steering wheel; *still showed those young idiots.* The engine gave a little splutter and the steering wheel vibrated oddly for a second; fortunately a brightly lit building to his right loomed through the night.

The house had fairy lights hanging over the front door, windows and along the guttering. Tony turned the car off the main road and along the driveway, down through the gate and then onwards; where after ten feet she promptly died. All the electrics had switched off; there was nothing, no headlights, no emergency warning flashes from the dashboard and unfortunately no power steering. Unceremoniously he ground to a halt just slightly off the main path so any other cars would still be able to pass. Tony checked his watch, still just before five so at least he was on time. *Ah but your car is dead,* a voice at the back of his head whispered; *yeah but five grand after tonight should fix it* he reasoned.

Tony thought quietly for a moment about what he should do and stepped out of the car. He noted the soft ground on which he had stopped and it confirmed that he was going to need a hand; there was no way he was going to lug all that equipment up to the house on his own. He looked towards the house and saw several figures moving through the doorway; with a final look at his beloved car he strode off purposefully.

"Hey; anybody able to give us a hand for a minute?" Tony had been standing just inside the front door for thirty seconds without seeing anyone when suddenly two girls had walked into the main room from somewhere out back. The air was filled with the delicious smell of fish and chips.

"Why, what's up?" A girl with long black hair asked.

"Car's conked out on the driveway, could do with a hand to either push her down here or a hand to unload."

"Oh, what you got?" The girl asked.

"Music equipment, I'm the DJ."

"Right, sorry it's my brother, Rob, you want," she nodded towards the backroom "he's back there…the one who looks like Mr Bump!" The girls shared a private chuckle and walked off and up the stairs.

Tony strode across the room checking out the lights and speakers someone had already fitted, sticking his head into the next room he saw three boys and another girl seated around a table laden with cans of beer and open bags of fish and chips.

"Hey, its Tony isn't it?" The youngest of the three boys was up in an instant, his hand planted straight into Tony's.

"Yeah, hi…you're?"

"Ian, hi…you looking for…"

"Rob," Tony smiled welcomingly as he identified the boy he wanted, his head swathed in a thick crepe bandage; letting go of Ian's hand he stepped forward to speak to him. Rob looked up at the mention of his name, his eyes were red and puffy and generally he looked tired; he didn't offer his hand to shake.

"What's up?" He asked sharply.

Tony kept the smile on his face.

"Need a hand to shift the stuff from my car." Rob looked at the other bloke and the girl; both just frowned and continued eating.

"I'll help Tony," Tony turned to see Ian bouncing enthusiastically at his side, "I don't mind." Tony nodded and let his smile drop *bloody kids* he pondered.

"There you go," said Rob turning back to his dinner "all sorted."

**

Parked just around the corner from *The Ship* at Pentewan Joel sat in his lowered, white 207 tapping the steering wheel in anticipation. A few stray tourists made their way into the inn out of the cold and he turned the stereo off so as to not attract any unwanted attention. He checked his watch by leaning forward so that the streetlamp would illuminate it; 20:24. A gentle hand tapped on the passenger glass, then a familiar face peered in; flicking a switch on the dashboard released the lock and the door was pulled open, the courtesy light remained off.

"Hey Joel." Joel responded with a quite useless nod in the darkness. "Ladies first." The familiar male voice added. A hand reached in and pulled the leaver allowing the seat to lean forward and two figures poured themselves into the back of the car. Once they were inside, the seat was repositioned and a third figure took the front passenger seat. Joel looked across at his childhood friend and business partner Michael who was similarly dressed to himself in black Reebok bottoms and matching hooded top. In the back sat Mark and Stacy; Joel had only met them once before because neither had gone to his previous school or his current college, but Michael said he had know them for years, although previous to the last two weeks he had never mentioned them before.

"Everybody got their supplies?" Joel asked. Mark tilted his baseball cap back and pulled a prepared rollup from his inner pocket and lit it; he took a long drag and passed it to Stacy. "Oh yeah!" Mark responded.

"Oi, that better not be our merchandise." Said Michael. Mark shook his head and pulled a transparent packet from his inner pocket and waggled it about showing a selection of pills, wraps and small cellophane wrapped lumps. Stacy undid the top button of her polo shirt and put her hand into her bra, pulling out an identical packet to Mark; she offered the rollup forward and Joel eagerly took it.

"Did you get mine?" Joel asked; Stacy kept her hand held out from handing over the rollup and made the international sign for money with her fingers. "Proper little business woman aren't you!" Joel commented as he reached into his tracksuit bottoms and pulled out £60 which he placed into her palm; immediately the money vanished into her bra to be replaced with a packet identical to the previous two. She handed it to Joel who took it and pressed it to his nose. "Hmm, still warm!"

"You'll more than triple your investment with that." She clicked her fingers at Michael and he was ready with his own money. "There you go my dear." The money disappeared into her underwear and was once again replaced with a transparent packet. Michael took it and examined it closely, sniffing it. "Ah, still showering in lavender." He jabbed Joel in the shoulder. "To look at you'd think she had great tits for her size."

"Get stuffed!" Was her response from the back seat.

"But it's all drugs and money."

"Anything more than a handful is a waste." Stacy pointed out.

"And if it's too small to fit in your hand?" Joel asked, playing along with Michael.

"Will fit in your mouth!" Laughed Mark; Stacy responded with a quick, painful slap to his cheek.

"Well you know what they say?" Stacy replied. "Small hands small c…"

"Alright children," Michael placated "they're always like this…nervous exhaustion!"

"Whatever," Joel cranked the ignition and the car burst into life "know where we're going?"

"I know the perfect spot to park" Michael nodded "and we'll stroll right on in."

**

"Thanks." Jenna muttered to the driver as she hopped of the single decked bus. Standing on the grass bank as it chugged off in a cloud of diesel smoke she glanced up and down the road making sure the way was clear before crossing to the footpath on the other side of the road. For a moment she paused and looked through the dark trees that lined the road and saw a building illuminated deep within. *That must be the place* she thought to herself and started to walk along the path in hopefully the direction of the entrance.

She had asked the bus driver to drop her at the Whitehouse, but he had just looked at her funny; *hell if he didn't know where it was how was a girl from Tresillian?* She remembered her boyfriend telling her it was just before London Apprentice, so had asked for the stop before. Jenna had been unwilling to go to this party right from the start, she being at college in Truro meant that she knew virtually none of her boyfriend's friends and when he had told her to make her own way there as he was 'otherwise engaged', that had virtually been the last straw. Now glad that she had opted to wear jeans and a jumper under her three-quarter length coat as protection from the cold she sighed inwardly and carried on walking.

Jenna's mobile rang, it was buried in her handbag so she barely heard it but when she removed it from the bag the funky *McFly* ringtone seemed a little incongruous in the night.

"Hey Tim." Jenna spoke brightly.

"Hey babe, where you at?" Tim's tone was harsh, *was she running late?* She looked at the clock on the mobile, *no, still not due to meet for three minutes.*

"I'm about twenty metres from you!" She chose to ignore his harshness and when he turned to look at her from the end of the driveway she waved…he didn't, instead he just rung off and pocketed his phone. Jenna frowned to herself and tucked her own phone away and prepared herself for the worse. Worse was what it seemed, Tim set off down the driveway before greeting her properly, not even a kiss. Jenna stopped and watched, dragging imaginary stray hair back into position behind her left ear; he stopped after ten paces and turned.

"Come on…don't want to be late." He called before walking off.

"Don't keep him waiting," a voice whispered. Jenna whipped her head around but couldn't see the source; hoping that maybe it was just her subconscious talking she bit her lip and noticed a bus coming down the road. Fighting every urge not to hold out her arm and hail the bus she trotted after her boyfriend, catching up with him before he got too far away.

**

It was getting to the point of darkness in the attic. Darren had painted his light bulbs dark blue with glass paint stolen from his sisters' room; which had seemed like a good idea at the time. Unfortunately they had quickly started to give off a truly awful smell every time they got warm; still the effect given out from the smothered lighting was pretty impressive and so much safer than draping length of silk from the ceiling beams over candles had proved in their last house! He had drawn the single curtain across the window as soon as it was dark enough to need the light; he knew that the old couple opposite peered in whenever they could.

He looked at the kit he had placed on his mattress and at the rucksack he planned to use to carry it…there was no way it was all going to fit.

**

Harry believed in arriving on time, so much so that when his mates had discussed going to the party and Harry had heard them say it started at 18.00 he took that to mean they should all meet at that time; they hadn't. Harry only lived a mile down the road on the edge of St Austell so had walked, but when he arrived at 18.00 dead he found himself virtually alone. There were maybe a dozen or so people in the house, a few blokes working on the sound system, a few more sorting out the booze and some girls hanging out in a room that would make a really nice kitchen when it was completed.

No one had spoken to him; in fact he was sure they were talking about him whenever he was out of earshot. He felt for his mobile to see if any of his mates had text him…shame it wasn't in his pocket. *What should I do?* He wondered silently as he tried to weigh up his options; there weren't many but basically they summed up as; throw yourself into conversation and act like you own the place, leave now and hang around outside like an idiot for everyone else to arrive, leave and go home and miss what was promised to be the party of the year or finally hide in the toilet until more people arrived.

"Gotta hide boy…gotta hide away till more people arrive and you can hide amongst them."

Simple choice he agreed. When he was sure the few people present were no longer looking he slipped up the stairs and followed the hand drawn signs to the toilets.

Two

Readying

Sitting at the ASDA bus stop Carly, Sandy and Alison waited with four trolleys filled with a mixture of alcohol and nibbles.

"What time is Rob getting here with the van?" Alison asked impatiently as she pulled at her scrapped back, bleached blond hair.

"Half twelve is what he said," replied Carly rolling her eyes and turning to stare at her friend "told you three times; you being deliberately forgetful or just plain thick?"

"Wet, anyway." Chipped in Sandy pulling the collar tighter around her neck in a vain attempt to stop the gentle rain running down her neck; she too had her bleached blonde hair scrapped tightly back and was aware that it was causing the rain to run in channels down her neck and back.

"That ain't my fault." Carly argued shaking the rain from her long black hair.

"Never said it was, we could go back to the café and get some shelter."

"Then he won't see us and he'll just drive on."

"What and miss out on all this booze!" Alison frowned. "Don't think even he's that stupid."

"True; still nearly. Fucking horny though." Sandy smirked at Alison.

Carly gave them both a playful slap on the shoulder.

"Don't say stuff like that about my brother...you know it fucking freaks me out."

"Here he is." Sandy pointed to the small white van pulling into the 'Taxi and Bus Only' stop. Alison was up like a shot and pulled her white jeans down a little to her hip and her knickers up, so a good inch of green lace was on show.

"How long you been wearing posh pants?" Asked Carly as she scrunched up her nose in disgust.

"Since I went to Plymouth last Thursday." Alison ran her little finger under the elastic and gave them twang. "Boys think green underwear is sophisticated."

"Some boys might, my brother would just think green underwear was a few more days wear away from its monthly clean!"

Sandy burst out laughing but Alison was unperturbed; she poked her tongue out at her friends and rushed to great Rob with a big toothy grin on her face.

**

Darren looked at the tightly packed holdall on his bed and nodded, *that looks mighty sweet* he told himself. He took the coarse canvas handle in his hand and steadied himself *this is gonna look so cool*; with a quick pull he hoisted it over his shoulder before promptly collapsing onto the bed as the unexpected weight caused him to overbalance...and he had already left half of what he had intended to take out of the bag.

**

Standing preening in the mirror was one of David's favourite pastimes, *if you looked as good as me you would to,* was the only response anyone who questioned him ever got. He tensed his shoulders so the muscles bulged, then tightened his abs and posed with one of his signature scowling/one eyebrow raised/half-frowns he was famous amongst his friends for. He checked his just brushed teeth for the final time and pulled his mobile out from the dressing gown pocket. The clock on the front said 18.35; David flicked it open and ran through his contact list: Alison, Cathy, Ems, Fran, Hannah, Hazel, Jenna, Jenny G, Jenny M, Josephine, Marla, Rachel, Rebecca, Sophie...and the list went on; he flicked the mobile closed and fixed himself with a cheesy grin in the mirror *which of you is going to get lucky tonight then?*

Back in his bedroom David hung his dressing gown on the back of the door and started to dress. As he did his mind wandered back to last year and the twelve Christmas parties he had attended; how his liver had suffered. Pausing between putting on boxers and socks he opened the top draw on the bedside cabinet and pulled out a red leather photo album and began flicking through the images. Looking at them he saw lots of smiling faces, kissed cheeks and hugs aplenty...this year was definitely going to be *the* year.

**

It had taken a while but finally Tony had the system banging the way he liked, he looked up at the growing crowd of onlookers nodding their heads along with the rhythm and smiled as he played with the revolving vinyl; *yeah this is gonna be a messy one.* He turned to the over enthusiastic teenage boy who had been hanging around him since he arrived, Ian, he thought he said his name was and nodded for him to come over.

Ian had been a fan of Tony 'Nimble Fingers' Tonkin since first hearing a bootlegged mix tape his older brother Rob had acquired several years ago. Unfortunately being only fourteen, and looking it, he had never been able to see him live, until now. When he had heard his brother and his friends discussing this crazy Christmas party and the rumour that local legend 'Nimble Fingers' would play, Ian badgered his brother all week to let him come along.

"Just going for a leak," Tony pointed at a CD multi-changer under the twin decks "make sure decks keep running…if it stops, press this." He pointed at a button and Ian nodded to confirm he understood.

"No worries Tony mate; I got yer back." Ian rushed over, fearing that Tony had forgotten him once all the stuff had been bought in from the car and the music levels had started to rise. *Looking after the Nimble decks, what an honour* he told himself. Tony moved off towards the steps with a wave at two cute girls and a smile on his face; *he's laughing at you…thinks you're just another stupid kid dazzled by his glowing star.* Ian shook off the doubts and continued to nod his head to the beat…now which button did Tony say to press if the music stopped?

Tony bounced up the bare wooden stairs, around a couple who stared blankly as he winked at them and onto the first floor of the building, pausing once at the top. The sign on the wall pointed right so he followed along one corridor until he came to a dead end. He passed half a dozen rooms, all open and sparsely furnished with roughly made beds, but no obvious toilet.

"Little boy lost." Whispered a voice from somewhere near.

"Someone up here?" He called. *"Someone who knows where the toilet is hopefully!"* He added under his breath.

"Little boy lost." The voice repeated just as quietly, only this time Tony was able to locate the source as coming from the last room passed on his left.

The door was a stripped pine affair with four central panels of planking that looked like they were a second hand fit thanks to the large splits that ran through them. Although the door was six inches ajar he decided to peer through one of the cracks first; he was unable to see anyone so decided to push the door open.

Cautiously he looked for a light switch, which there was, he flicked it and half expected it not to work, but it did and a rather kitsch wooden chandelier sprang into life. Stepping into the room made him shiver; the atmosphere in the room was moist and slightly cold, probably because this room was apparently the toilet. On the wall to his right was a single washbasin with a tall mirror fixed to the wall behind it, whilst opposite a thick brown corduroy curtain was nailed to the wall, presumably across a window.

The actual toilets were against the wall at the far end of the room. Five cubicles had been formed from a wooden frame fronted with sickly coloured doors; they reminded him of a 1970s council estate. Three of the doors where a dark mouldy green, one was a dark blue, almost black and the final was a bleak washed out saffron; *maybe they had been recycled from a council estate*. All of the doors where slightly ajar except for the saffron and all where marked with crudely drawn chalk images of male and female genitalia, *beats stick figures* he mused, except for the closed door, which had a wheel chair drawn on it. To be fair it did look slightly wider; the disability commission would be proud.

He started walking towards one of the empty cubicles.

"Little boy lost."

Tony stopped, the voice had come from his right, not any of the cubicles…*but how could that be*, the only things to his right was the washbasin and mirror. He looked at the mirror; it was covered in condensation, presumably because someone had just run warm water to wash their hands; however there was only one tap and when he touched it all he could feel was icy coldness.

Despite the cold damp air in the room sweat suddenly dripped from his forehead, *too many early shandies*, he told himself as he turned the tap and placed his hand under the cool water before dabbing it onto his face. Worried that he might have messed his hair he wiped the mirror, at first the condensation refused to shift but he persevered.

"What the…?" He muttered for instead of his own face looking back in the half-cleared mirror he was instead saw the back of someone's head. His stomach somersaulted as an uneasy sickness welled up inside; feeling suddenly vulnerable his eyes shifted to the door, *no one there*, then back to his left and the toilets, doors still as before, four slightly open, one shut. As his head moved with his eyes, he noticed movement in the mirror.

That's weird? As he moved his head, the head in the mirror also moved. *Hang on a minute*, the more he looked the more the back of the head seemed familiar;

but how? Slowly Tony raised his hand to his left ear, his movement being matched in the mirror, he wiggled his ring finger just to be sure and the light glinted off the gold band. *Must be some trick to this* he pondered chancing a quick glance over his shoulder, nothing obvious to see, no cameras or anything, smiling and nodding at the clever trick he was reminded by his bladder to continue onto the toilet when he looked again at the mirror; the image had changed.

"Little boy lost."

Tony's blood ran cold and he barely heard the voice this time. In the mirror he saw his shoulders covered in blood pouring from a wound above his left ear. Automatically he raised his fingers to see if it was true; they were inches away when everything went black.

**

Thomasine had read the letter from Cara and was now huddled under her duvet holding the long, narrow, powder blue tissue wrapped object in her fingers that had accompanied the letter; she contemplated moving. Cara's words had been well chosen to provoke her to thought. Six months ago she would have dismissed instantly any thought of what she was about to do; in fact, no, that really wasn't fair she decided. She probably would not have seen the possibilities in what the night might bring, but she would not run away if the chance had come.

From the top drawer of the unit next to her bed she pulled out her mobile phone, it was covered in a thin layer of dust; well it had been six months since last used. "You better still have power." She muttered as she flipped it open, to her delight it was fully powered. Scrolling through her contacts Thomasine located Tracy and mused as she pressed green; *hope this doesn't give her a heart attack.*

**

"So...do you want to go in?" Graeme looked across at Hannah, his girlfriend of three months.

"Do you?" She smiled back in that pleasant non-committal way he had come to love.

"Only if you do." He was not sure who had suggested coming here in the first place, but if it was him had she felt compelled to come? He didn't want to be the kind of boyfriend who did that.

"I only came 'cos you said you wanted to go." She looked at him and realised that he might take that the wrong way. "Not that I didn't want to."

"No, I thought you might want to, so I said I did…but if you don't want to?" He noticed the slight look of disappointment in her eyes and vowed to try and make amends.

"I wouldn't have said anything if you hadn't asked…but I am happy to go in." She smiled positively and hoped he wouldn't be put off.

"We could go somewhere else if you prefer?" *That's it* he thought *let her decide.*

"I don't mind." Hannah unbuckled her seatbelt and patted him on the leg. "Whatever you'd rather do."

**

Thomasine was a bundle of nerves as she waited for her friend to pick up; it took just three rings for Tracy to answer, her light, chirpy voice a half-forgotten memory awoken.

"Hey Thomasine, what on earth you doing up this time of the morning?"

"Um, well actually I'm not technically up, just sprawling under a lovely warm duvet…you know how it is."

"Cow!" Tracy responded sarcastically.

"I'm just trying to plot out the day; what you up to?"

"Oh are you! Well unfortunately my day's all sorted what with work and everything."

"You're working now?" Thomasine frowned and hoped her friend would not make a big thing of her mistake.

"Only for the last five months…come one Thom, don't tell me that amazing brain of yours has forgotten all about the joys of weekends at Asboland I've been regaling you with."

"Guess so…must be all the exam pressure. Supermarkets; who needs them?"

"Everybody it seems…it's supposed to be a two week holiday, yet every bloody teacher seems to think it's an opportunity to dump extra coursework on us?"

"No Christmas spirit, that's their problem," laughed Thomasine.

"But not mine, not tonight, you gonna make it?"

"That's why I'm calling; what time you planning on getting down there?"

"Jacca's picking me up straight from work; we'll probably eat *en route*, so I guess eightish."

"Oh yeah, what exactly will you be eating?" Thomasine found herself speaking without thinking, for a few moments she was back in the café on the corner of Brassy Road lost in girly chat.

"Thomasine!" Tracy scolded, but then added with a giggle. "I'm sure I don't know what you mean."

"How's he working out?" Thomasine asked trying to getting more information out of her friend.

"He's cool…it's only been a couple of weeks…I don't want to rush…though he does look so fit in and out of his *Vans*…tight muscles from neck to ankle."

"There's an image I don't need at this hour of the morning! Here was I thinking I might have got you two all wrong; should I buy a hat?"

"Steady…no actually…maybe you're right, better be a sunhat, Jacca was saying last night he was looking forward to seeing me in my bikini on an Ozzy beach! I gave him a demo in my bedroom." She giggled. "Cheeky boy said he preferred it on the floor to my body!"

"Tracy, really!" Thomasine tried to sound stern and failed, months may have passed and she might have moved on immensely, but it seemed her friends had developed too. "You're unstoppable."

"I know…Jacca says the same." Tracy laughed out loud. "You know I was telling him about you and I think he wants to hook you up with one of his friends."

"Erm no thanks." Thomasine said decisively.

"Come on Thom, could be fun for you. Get a boy with a stomach like a washboard to play with!"

"Okay fine."

"Serious?"

"Oh yeah…I'll make sure I bring my dirty laundry!"

"Ooh! Your barbed tongue cuts me to shreds."

Both girls giggled.

"Actually no, maybe I could rip all his clothes off, lay him on my bed…and play him like a glockenspiel!"

Tracy snorted a laugh.

"Thom! Shut up will you…I'll be thinking of that next time I get Jacca naked."

"Sorry." She tapped her fingers on the phone and made bonging sounds with her mouth as if she was playing the instrument.

"Enough…you'll meet him tonight."

"Okay look, better let you get to work; I'll see you after eight, but hey, no blind dates."

They said goodbyes and rang off. Thomasine flopped back on her bed and giggled to herself and she recalled their conversation but as she did something caught her on the neck. She turned to see the letter from Cara gently tickling her flesh and immediately regained control of herself…time to go to work herself. Thomasine suddenly remembered the tissue wrapped present; there was something hard yet floppy inside. Gently she unwrapped the gift and was rather delighted to discover that tucked within the folds of the powder blue tissue was a beautiful black necklace; holding it carefully in her hands she studied it carefully. The necklace chain was formed from delicate beads of jet, some round, others oval, but all perfectly balanced, smooth and slightly warm as she ran them through her fingers. Centrepiece of the necklace was a large jet oval, carved with what looked like the face of an old woman above a single word *Helios*. This was surrounded in three thin jet bands held a millimetre apart from one another by five small silver supports.

Pulling off the covers she opened the wardrobe and looked at the clothes within; on one side those from the past and the other a selection she had bought with her when she arrived last night. For old times sake she quickly ran through her old clothes and was impressed, there were a few items she might still wear; then she began going through her new collection…*something Christmassy;* she pondered…*ah perfect.*

**

Sally looked at Ann and rolled her eyes as her other friends Katie and Marla continued to listen on enthusiastically. For the last ten minutes the four girls combined quiet late lunch and photo project meeting had been interrupted by the loathsome and slightly dribbling Kevin, his mate with the lazy eyes Dwain and their dumb, repetitive attempts to persuade the four of them that they had to come to this magnificent party they were helping organise on Friday night.

"So how come the booze is gonna be free?" Marla asked; she was all up for a Friday night out that didn't involve going to their regular haunts, especially if it was not going to cost her any money. She remained clearly oblivious to Sally's attempts to draw the conversation back to the work at hand.

"Don't really know." Kevin looked a little like a startled ferret at her question with his greasy unwashed hair and small furtive eyes; surely the mere offer of a party from him should have been enough for them to be eating out of his hand. He stopped speaking for a moment and appeared to rock unsteadily on his toes as he thought out a response.

"Ah, it's 'cos this girl is having a celebratory birthday come Christmas thing…big welcome home thing after spending the year down under, or in Spain, or somewhere else that's hot." He appeared to forget what he was trying to say so Sally tried to help him out of frustration.

"But you don't know who?"

"Not exactly." Kevin smiled at Sally. As he was standing and she was sitting he was able to get a great view of her boobs; she noticed his not very subtle look and shuddered slightly to herself, discretely hitching her vest up a little.

"But you're asking people if they want to go. Won't she be annoyed if hundreds of people turn up and she doesn't any of them?" Marla had visions of appearing on television in one of the 'Teens Trash House' headlines.

"No, no, no she asked her mates to ask their mates to ask other mates to come along. She used to go to this college before she went to university…knows loads of people."

"Where did you say it was again?" Katie asked.

"The Whitehouse, down along Pentewan Road." The girls all exchanged puzzled looks, their minds instantly full of images of the American seat of power.

"How long you lived in S'nozzle?" Kevin questioned; the fact that he had been drinking already obvious as his Cornishness seeped out through his slurred speech.

"If you mean St. Austell? All our lives." Sally pointed out, the other girls agreed.

"Ah Sally and you've lived in my heart that long too." Sally made a face like she had just sat on a hedgehog but Kevin simply continued. "You *must* know The Whitehouse then." He was met with continued blank looks from each girl so Dwain felt obliged to chip in.

"It's before London Apprentice…just on the right, in a field."

"Hang on, I think I know where you mean," Marla closed her eyes as if she was thinking; she opened them and scowled at the boys. "That place! That run down old farmhouse…you can't have a party there."

"Why not?" Dwain asked frowning like a scolded child; in his mind you could have a party anywhere.

"'Cos it's a ruin or something and it's not in a field, it's in the middle of giant marsh." Marla exclaimed.

"Ah, well this girl's dad has just got permission to redevelop the site into this B&B and restaurant spa thing so party now before the decorators move in…they were shifting a lorry load of soil and gravel up there last weekend to make the ground easier to work on."

"And there's free booze?" Ann asked sceptically.

"That's why we're going!" Kevin slapped Dwain on the shoulder and laughed enthusiastically, bordering on manically.

"And the music…supposed to be some top DJ playing." Added Dwain.

"So you gotta be there, yeah?"

"Yeah!" Sally agreed obviously sarcastically to all bar the two boys; Ann chuckled to herself.

"Excellent," said Kevin rubbing his hands together "come on mate plenty more people to invite."

Dwain raised his hand in silent goodbye and he and Kevin moved off into the college refectory to find more women to invite.

"You know," said Kevin as they walked "I think that Sally fancies me."

"She's all yours mate…after she's had me!"

Three

Arriving

Joel followed the Pentewan road toward St Austell until they reached London Apprentice; once through the village he had begun building up speed again but Michael ordered him to slow. They were barely nudging thirty and had been overtaken by an impatient Robin Reliant when Michael pointed to a gate.

"Just here. Pull up and I'll get it open…oh and cut the lights."

"Cut 'em? There's no streetlight, how the hell are we going to see where we're going?" Joel exclaimed, Stacy tittered from the back "Stop it" she murmured as Mark chuckled amorously. Evidently someone knew where they where going in the dark.

"Hmm good point," Michael agreed "cut back to sidelights…that'll do."

Joel did as instructed and shortly they were on the other side. Michael shut the gate after them and rejoined the car.

"Right carry on" he ordered.

"Where are we?" Joel queried as he leant forward in the car to try and look at the buildings that surrounded the car; the sidelights only showing the way forward.

"This is my Uncle Dillon's farm…drive on."

"Why are we doing this in the dark?" Joel asked as he guided the car across the yard and round behind several barns.

"Well we don't really get on…family shit y'know, go right at this junction and follow the path."

Joel guided the car cautiously past a series of fields until a large house illuminated with an aura of light and booming music emerged from the night. The car was parked in a copse of trees near a tall stone wall and an adjoining gate to the next field where the party was taking place.

"Right this'll do," Michael cautiously looked in each direction to make sure there was no one watching "the car will be safe here in case the party gets crashed and we need to make a quiet exit."

"Is that likely?" Joel asked his attention momentarily distracted as Stacy let out a little moan.

"Not likely," Michael flicked on the courtesy light and both boys turned to see a surprised Mark trying desperately to remove his hand from inside Stacy's trousers "it's good to be prepared though."

"You need a…hand there mate?" Joel asked with a laugh.

"You wish," Mark replied "just got me jacket stuck, come on babe make yerself useful."

Stacy grabbed his arm and pulled it, freeing it with a loud comedy rip; unfortunately a substantial strip of sports top remained attached to her zip.

"Shit…my mum will go ape, this thing ain't even paid for yet." He held his arm up so everyone could see the inner lining hanging free.

"Serious, your mum actually pays for things?" Michael enquired. "I thought she just nicked them from down ASDA."

"Shut up, that's just a rumour that was never proved."

Joel and Michael exchanged a knowing look and shake of the head whilst almost pretending not to look at Stacy who sat legs open with her trousers unzipped as she attempted to remove the offending material.

"We could just leave them here." Joel reasoned.

"They'd just bugger up your suspension with their shagging."

"Got it!" Stacy waved the material now free from here zip and handed it to Mark who was already taking off the damaged jacket. "Fuck it!" She muttered. "Well done idiot, the bloody zip's had it."

The two boys in the front tried not to laugh.

"Can't you just go in your pants and pretend your Sienna Miller?" Michael asked. "I mean with your model looks you'd be a ringer for her."

"Not wearing any."

"Oh yeah, so I see." Michael couldn't resist a look, Joel could.

"Hang on a sec," Joel leant over to the glove box and after a quick rummage revealed a small plastic packet with three small brass safety pins in. "Any good?"

"Hmm, I like a man who comes prepared with a packet of three," Stacy winked provocatively and took the packet before addressing Mark and Michael, who both had eyes wandering into places they shouldn't. "And you two, eyes front."

Five minutes later they were out of the car and ready to sell. They had all opted to leave their jackets in the car to make themselves look more casual.

Michael decided that they should split into couples with Stacy and Mark going in first, with Joel and himself following in five minutes. Unfortunately the gate had proved to be padlocked shut so they had to vault over, or in Stacy's case, be manhandled over. As Mark and Stacy walked off he had tried to put his arm over shoulder and been met with a resounding slap and several choice words; the two watching boys just shook their heads, sat on the bonnet and waited.

**

The four girls looked at the parked car.

"Seems alright to me." Marla decided.

"That because you've already drunk half a bottle of scotch and you're pissed." Sally told her.

"She's right," Ann agreed and began walking towards her car "maybe I should just straighten it a little."

Ann had been trying to back the car into a gap between two others but had hit a muddy spot and only succeeded in burying the back wheels deeper the more she manoeuvred.

"I think you'll only make it worse," Sally frowned "if that's possible."

"Oh cheers!" Ann remarked sarcastically.

"No problem…besides it's as straight as any other."

Ann looked at the other two dozen cars and had to admit that parking was a bit of a free-for-all.

"Yeah…I suppose," she admitted.

"And, as it's stuck it's not like anyone will be able to nick it!" Marla added as the girls started walking towards the house. "Still, looks like the party's already started so let's get in before Kevin's too pissed to snog you."

"Eurgh…gross!" Sally shivered. "There's no way his lips will be coming anywhere near me."

"I don't think it's his lips you have to worry about!" Marla continued to playfully tease.

"Stop it! You're really starting to gross me out."

"You're right of course…he's much more a hand straight down your trousers kinda bloke!"

"Your trousers maybe!" Sally countered.

"Nah, nobody's gonna get in." Katie quipped, just dodging a light-hearted swing from Marla.

"Not without a crowbar anyway." Sally added.

"Its fine," Marla replied speeding up to pull slightly away from the other three "can't upset me."

As they entered the house Ann took one final glance at her car; something whispered in her ear, or was it the voice of reason in her head? *"You should check your lights".* Her friends had walked into some other people they knew from college and were already downing their first drinks; *"Flat battery".* Ann looked again, she could just see the bonnet of her Ka and yes it did look like she had left the headlights on…or was it just the reflection from the house…she'd have to check.

**

"Penny for them?"

Thomasine sparked into life at the voice; she adjusted her position in the armchair where she had slumped gazing at the vast open fireplace and took firm hold of the glass of port that was on the verge of toppling off the arm. She turned to see Cara leaning against the frame of the door. Dressed from riding in jodhpurs and a simple white shirt she stepped into the room, poured herself a glass of port and offered the decanter to Thomasine, who shook her head, then took a seat next to Thomasine. Cara took a sip and allowed the huge leather chair to mould itself to her shape, her pale features mellowed by the light of the fire.

"Good ride?" Thomasine asked, grateful for the company as she had been on the verge of sleep.

"Fabulous, the air is so fresh in the fields tonight."

"Where's Steven? He didn't fall again did he?"

Cara chuckled slightly, before putting her fingers over her lips to excuse herself. "I shouldn't laugh, no, he offered to clean the horses down; Ellis is helping him."

For a few moments they sipped their drinks in silence, much as they had done on more than one occasion in recent months. Thomasine knew that Cara was allowing her time to ready herself before opening up to her, it was just that on this occasion, what was going through Thomasine's mind was hard to broach without offending Cara. Cara broke the silence first.

"You know the best thing about this time of year is the opportunity to have a super party with your friends…and family."

"So what have you planned?" Thomasine turned to face her smiling, knowing that she now regarded Cara and her companions as her true family and friends.

"I'm not sure yet…I think Steven has something up his sleeve…as it is your first Christmas with us why don't you choose where we have it?"

"Really?" Thomasine blushed at the possibilities; never had the opportunity to choose anything about a Christmas party presented itself to her before. "I wouldn't want to force others to do something just because I wanted to."

"Not at all, I think it would be perfect…Cornwall?"

"You read my mind." Thomasine smiled inside, amazed at how Cara always made difficult subjects easy to face.

"Well Steven and I have a little errand to run near Polperro on Christmas Day…"

"Anything I might do to help?"

"I am afraid this is something we must do mostly alone, although Bea has a small role to play in Falmouth."

Thomasine frowned, surely after all they had been through this year they would spend Christmas together.

"Oh, but a party won't be the same without you three?"

"We will still gather and have a jolly good time on Christmas Day, we will not be away too long. I hear there is to be a party near St Austell on the twenty-third…maybe some of your friends will be there?"

Thomasine frowned and looked carefully at Cara, who kept her face expressionless.

"Are you suggesting I go back to my old life?"

"No," Cara replied with a gentle smile and a conspiratorial wink "but you could just visit, maybe check up on your family…you have been thinking of them."

"Does it show?" Thomasine laughed nervously.

"We all do."

"But…that's gone?"

"If there is one thing you must have realised over the last six months is that nothing is impossible to us."

"It might be nice just to visit, for a day…so long as I can come back." Thomasine heart was racing and inside her mind was in turmoil, filling with possibilities. The last six months had been the most enjoyable and challenging of her life, but she could not deny that the time of year had bought thoughts of her old existence. She sat forward in her chair and regarded Cara carefully; she had never lied to her before so what she said had to be true.

"Absolutely, it is good to keep all things in perspective…and if a party you happened to be at, just happened to be held in a house with a three hundred year chequered history of murder and intrigue," Cara paused and gave Thomasine a sublime smile that filled her with positive energy "then it must absolutely be investigated."

Thomasine got out of her chair and crossed to Cara, giving her a big hug.

"I have no doubts about you," Cara smiled once released from Thomasine's embrace "so neither should you."

"Thank you."

"There is no need for that."

"I'd better get myself prepared…if that's even possible."

"Everything will be fine," Cara playfully rolled her eyes "just try not to have too much fun."

"I'll try!" Thomasine chuckled as she left the room.

"Everything okay?"

Twenty minutes had passed since Thomasine had left the room and now the fire was on its dying embers. Steven stepped into the room and gently shut the stout oak door behind him.

"All is well," Cara looked up as her fiancé entered the room. He bent over and kissed her lightly on the forehead.

"Shall I top that up for you?" He nodded to the nearly empty glass in her fingers.

"Thank you, no…I'm ready for bed." Steven moved to the table and poured himself a half inch into a glass before turning back to Cara; he found her gazing off into a distant corner. Her shirt was now unbuttoned to the navel and opened to a barely decent degree revealing her pale, perfect skin; her jodhpurs were also unbuttoned allowing him to see hints of green lace beneath. Slowly she turned her head and casually watched him as he downed the liquid in one. "And you?"

**

Rob pushed the front door open with his foot and shouted.

"Oi, Bob, where are you? There's beer to be unloaded...BOB!"

From somewhere upstairs a door shut and there was the sound of footsteps. Rob dropped the case of beer into a small room they had elected as store and made space for the girls to each put down their loads.

"So where is he?" Carly asked.

"I heard him upstairs; he's probably been at the whiskey already and had to sleep it off."

"Nope," said Bob as he stepped out from the kitchen "it wasn't me."

"Yeah right, I heard a door bang and steps."

"I know it's been happening on and off since you left."

"Well have you checked? There might be someone up there, or is it a ghost?"

"On my own?"

"Chicken." Sandy laughed.

"If you like," Bob shrugged his shoulders. "I don't like this place, I've been saying for years this place is nasty."

"Well if your dad has another property available for your sisters surprise party tonight you should have told us!" Rob looked at him with a raised eyebrow. "Thought not...now give us a hand to unload the motor."

Five minutes later and the van was empty. They all stood in what they thought had once been the main room for it was certainly the largest on this floor.

Sean Barnecott, Bob's father, was a builder and decorator who had been inexplicably drawn to the Whitehouse ever since he was a little boy growing up on a farm near Polgooth. Fortunately fate dealt him a kind hand and just as he reached a point in his life when his business was booming the Whitehouse had come onto the open market for the first time ever; or so the papers reported. Sean hadn't been the only person to see the potential of the property, but a few greased palms later the property was his; planning consent for a B&B and

175

restaurant had followed a similar process and building would commence on the second of January ready for the first Easter visitors.

The Whitehouse had been built in three phases, each enlarging on the previous. The central portion of the house had a cellar, which was now full of rubbish cleared from the rest of the house, two large rooms, a kitchen and a pantry on the lower floor and steps leading up to a corridor with six rooms on the first floor. To this were three extensions, one on either side with another at the back of the property. The southerly extension offered another eight rooms on the first floor and three small rooms on the ground. On the northern side the extension was virtually a separate house only accessible from the ground floor; in this part there were two large rooms on the ground floor and three smaller rooms above. The extension at the back had one large room and two further small stores. There was also an accessible attic space full of stuff which really needed sorting.

Getting everything ready had taken weeks of planning but it had been worth it. The lower floor was kitted out with a DJ booth, a large 'dance floor' and speakers threaded throughout the ground floor. Each room had a table set with booze and snacks and there were plenty of sofa's, chairs, bean bags and throws scattered around. To make the bare plaster walls more exciting posters of bands, events, even adverts for places like the Eden Project and the National Maritime Museum Cornwall had been appropriated from various sources and pinned haphazardly everywhere; only the ceiling with its cracked plasterwork and visible beams showed the age and poor state of the house. The benefit of having a father in the property game and a habit of rarely throwing anything out meant they had a small barn of furniture to use. Even upstairs they put beds in many of the rooms; after all, you never know who might get lucky.

Unfortunately the Whitehouse had never had an indoor toilet, let alone bath or shower, so Sean had built temporary units; at least the kitchen was serviceable after a lot of cleaning and the gas powered barbeque was going to be a winner when it was fired up.

As with all great ideas, the party at the Whitehouse had come about through nefarious means. Sometimes these means are serendipitous, others the result of meticulous planning, decades of work and studious endeavour…in the case of this party that means was simply alcohol.

For Sandy and Alison what promised to be a dull wet Tuesday at college working on their personal projects was broken by the sudden announcement that cameras were to be gathered for an unscheduled fieldtrip. Unfortunately the ripple of excitement that flooded the room was shirt lived. From the college they had trudged, not quite hand in hand as once they might have at infant school; still the looks, snide comments and flicked cigarette butts from those at play in the Poltair school playground meant they kept their heads down.

The tour around St Austell brewery had been fairly interesting, especially when the dizzy blonde tour guide had taken the wrong turn between the mash tuns and the copper, but when they had returned to the visitor centre at the end of the tour they had been denied the chance to sample any of the companies fine ales because only three out of the ten students had bought suitable identification. Fortunately it was quite and the dizzy blonde had been left to manage on her own; it wasn't hard for Sandy to distract her with questions whilst Alison helped herself to a bottle of '125' rum from behind the counter in the shop.

Meeting up with Rob, Bob and Carly that evening in the *Brit* they had supplement their lagers with splashes of rum and what started with a throw-away comment about Bob's father's growing empire rapidly developed into promises that had been regretted two days later, once the hangover had finally cleared. Still, Bob's dad had surprisingly said yes and two months of preparation finally had a result.

"Okay…what's this?" Sandy held up the half empty whiskey bottle.

"That wasn't me." Bob raised his hands defensively.

"Yeah right, we all know you practically run on the stuff." Rob shook his head, just as he thought, *knew it was daft to leave him alone with the booze.*

"Swear, smell my breath if you want!" He took a step towards Sandy, who raised her arms to keep him back; the closing of a door on the floor above was followed by the sound of footsteps. Everyone looked at Bob, who had visibly paled, but he was looking at his watch.

"Seven minutes." He whispered to himself. "Every seven minutes."

"What you muttering about?" Said Rob as he glanced up.

"Every seven minutes, well just a little over actually, I told you it's been happening since you left."

"And you haven't even gone and had a look? Jesus, I would've, could be anyone up there." Carly looked at her brother.

"I'll go," he looked at Bob "and you'll come with; ladies you stay at the bottom of the stairs."

"Is that wise? Maybe we just call the police." Sandy reasoned.

"They won't come without proof," Alison spoke "and beside do we really want them here?" She looked at the others and no one argued. "They'll only ask awkward questions."

"Come on we're wasting time." Rob started toward the front door. "Just gonna get Willie from the car."

"Why've I got to go first?" Bob whined as Rob nudged him up the stairs with his aluminium baseball bat.

"So that if anyone jumps out on you, I can hit 'em."

"Yeah, but I'll be the one that gets jumped on."

"Don't worry; I'll hit 'em before they do too much damage to you."

"Be careful," Carly shouted up the stairs.

"Shut up idiot," Rob scolded his sister.

Slowly the boys reached the landing, but were unsure as to which way they should turn. Bob pointed out that it was only about another minute before the door and steps should be heard again so they opted to move slightly down the corridor to their left and wait.

"Still think we should call the police," muttered Sandy.

"Be ready to," Carly looked surprised when the other girls turned to look at her. "Didn't want to mention it before but this place has been freaking me out at times too."

"You never said nothing," Alison frowned "you teasing?"

"Just get your phone ready."

**

Tony's head was spinning, in fact he couldn't be one hundred percent sure, but he felt his whole body was going around and around in circles; although not necessarily at the same speed as his head. *What was he doing? Where the bloody hell was he?* He tried to remember and slowly as he swung gently in darkness his mind drifted away.

The call came at the end of a bad weekend. Saturday night had seen the first gig Tony had been booked for in four weeks and what an unmitigated disaster it turned out to be. From start to finish everything had gone downhill, forgetting to bring half his set list, CD player not working, beer thrown by the wedding guests from before the cake was even cut…and all for £250. Sunday had been a day of hangover relaxation, still he wouldn't have to worry about that for much longer. No money meant no more booze, he might not be very good at doing his own accounts, but even he knew the basics of finance. His melancholy was broken by 'Get the party started' bursting from his mobile; he didn't recognise the number but opted to answer anyway.

"Hello," said a softly spoken male voice.

"Hello."

"Have you had the opportunity to consider my offer?"

Tony screwed up his forehead; he didn't recognise the voice and couldn't remember any recent offers…save for that wedding, which had been booked three months ago.

"I'm sorry, you are?"

"Forgive me, Tony, I made an offer of work to you."

"I'm sorry, I haven't received anything…if you don't mind me asking, who are you?"

"The letter is probably just tucked behind the curtain by your front door."

"Letter?"

"I posted it myself this morning. Why don't you go and see."

Tony kept the mobile to his ear as he wandered down the stars; sure enough behind the curtain was an ivory coloured envelope. There was nothing written on the front, but the paper was heavy and felt thicker, maybe even old and not at all like modern paper. Tony opened the envelope and pulled out the letter; it had been exquisitely written in ornate copperplate writing, a few of the words struck an instant chord in his mind, 'entertain', 'ten hours work', '£5000' and 'Whitehouse' being amongst them.

"Well, do I trust you find the terms agreeable?"

Tony was flummoxed, the offer was equal highest to his best ever pay day; there had to be catch.

"The offer seems very fair Mr…" the voice at the other end still refused to rise to his probing and Tony was not going to risk pushing it. "Are there any special requests?"

"No, just come and do what you do…but do make sure you turn up on time."

"That sounds fine to me."

"And payment will be met on the night…I believe in cash for services provided; I trust this suits you too?"

"Very much so," immediately Tony was seeing how he could deprive the Taxman of a sizeable percentage. "I'll be there at five to set up."

"Agreed. Don't let me down."

"I won't…wait! The Whitehouse, I'm not sure I know where that is?"

"I am sure you have not forgotten."

Tony racked his brains and tried to think of all the bars and clubs he had played; it shouldn't have taken that long but the voice on the other end of the phone was impatient.

"You played here as a child; the last time when you were eight if I remember." Tony tried to remember but nothing came to him. "Never mind," the voice continued "I am sure it will all come back to you later."

"Um, okay…till the twenty-third then."

"Until then."

The phone went dead and Tony put it into his pocket and sat on the stairs reading the letter again and again to make sure he hadn't missed anything in the excitement.

Tony continued to swing in darkness; he really wanted to stop now. He was sure his eyes were open but still he couldn't see; he wanted to call out, but his mouth would not work and all he felt now was an ever increasing sickness. From somewhere nearby something was stinking, a rotting moistness filled the air and it wasn't helping his stomach…although he was starting to get the faintest hints of recognition then the voice came again.

"Little boy lost!"

**

Harry kept his ear to the door of the makeshift toilet. He'd been in here for an age but could not tell how long for his watch had annoyingly stopped working and was still telling him that it was six; it continued to tick and the second hand still rotated, yet strangely neither the minute or hour hand would join in. He had only heard one other person enter; they hadn't used any of the toilets and left shortly after.

He sat back down on the unused toilet. *"You should stay just a little longer"* a voice whispered in his ear; he turned sharply. "Weird", he muttered, it had actually felt like there was someone in here with him.

"Stay with me and I can spare you the embarrassment of your friends not turning up". Harry's brain was sending out the same impulses as the voice, so much so that they had become inseparable and the doubts grew.

"Bet they never intended coming here at all...in fact they're probably all down at McDonald's now laughing at you."

"Bastards," Harry shook his head as he wondered how he could get out of this place without looking anymore the fool. "Bet they think they're so fucking clever."

"Soon be more people, then you can sneak away without being seen; nobody laughing at you here."

"Just a bit longer," He agreed unaware that he was now becoming fully engaged with the voice in his head and his hands had become so tightly clasped together that the nails on his fingers were now starting to dig into his flesh allowing thin trickles of blood to flow down his arms.

**

Emily stood in front of the full length mirror in her bedroom and wondered if she was making the right choice. Not just in terms of dress, no that looked quite fabulous, a cream kaftan with rolled up sleeves and beads of jet sown around the hem. Admiring her black patent stiletto heels she flicked her ginger bobbed hair and glanced sideways sexily, her green eyes highlighted with hints of black and powder blue. *Hot* she told herself *so why you single?*

She threw herself down on her bed and gently slapped herself on the forehead.

"Come on Emily, stop being a twat." She stood back in front of the mirror. "Right you look fab, available, not desperate, brain..." she moved nearer the mirror and looked herself in the eye. "Stop being negative and you will meet someone...nice."

Her phone rang from somewhere on the bed, Emily dived in amongst the white cotton sheets and found it.

"Rose, hi, sorry I've been an age haven't I?"

"Barely twenty minutes since I last called to say I was outside waiting," Rose gave an audible sigh. "Come on honey, I'm sure you're going to outshine us as usual."

"Yeah, come on Ems," another slightly more distant voice spoke "I'm wearing a mini on her leather seats and it's making my bum go wrinkly."

Emily pulled back the curtain and waved at her friends Rose and Fiona; Rose beeped the car horn in response.

"Just coming;" Emily turned off the phone and tucked it into her handbag, checked herself in the mirror again and left.

Four
Scaring

About six and half minutes had passed when Rob put his fingers to his lips, shushed Bob and beckoned him over.

"This'll get the girls hopping." He reached out for the nearest door handle.

"Don't do it Rob," Bob warned.

"Shut up and get in here," Rob opened the door and ushered his friend inside. Shaking his head Bob did as instructed.

Inside the room was a single bed, two steel legged chairs with yellow Formica seats and backs and a small wooden table. Rob slammed the door as loudly as he could then started stomping on the bare floorboards chuckling to himself.

"Come on Bob," he encouraged "get those feet moving."

Bob did as instructed but not quite as violently as Rob who decided to stop banging with his feet but instead started hitting things with the baseball bat, shouting, screaming and yelling. Bob stopped stomping and shook his head.

"Rob! Rob, stop it you'll break…" There was a crack as the table gave into age and the pummelling it was being given. Rob was in the midst of a particularly violent series of smashes and as the table gave way the bat continued right through and into the floorboards. Having gone further than he anticipated Rob suddenly found himself overbalancing and crashed down on top of the broken furniture; he was laughing madly to himself as Bob helped him back up.

"That should get 'em going," seemingly ignoring his slip he picked up the baseball bat and left the room, Bob was in no way about to stay so quickly followed him.

The boys made their way back down the stairs but the girls were not to be seen; the boys stood at the bottom of the stairs and called out.

"Idiot," said Bob "bet you scared them off." Rob just shrugged his shoulders. Suddenly the most inhuman scream either had heard before screeched out from behind them making both jump.

"You fucking idiots," Carly bounced up to them, "think we're dumb enough to fall for that moronic performance."

"Yeah," added Alison "what you kill up there?"

"He killed a table, oh and made a hole in the floor."

"It was just meant to be a laugh," Rob looked around the room "where's Sandy?"

"I thought she was with you?" Carly asked Alison.

"Nope, thought she went and hid with you."

"No...Sandy, Sandy where are you?"

"Um, think she's over here." Bob waved everyone over to the table laden with cans of beer. Behind it sat Sandy, the stain of tears on her face, her mobile pressed tightly to her ear.

"You didn't do anything daft did you?" Rob asked, Sandy just looked up with big eyes and bit her lip.

Set in a field behind a hedge on the opposite side of the road to the Whitehouse, Thomasine sat on the dilapidated tractor and watched the house. She had spotted the rusting wreck with its front right wheel missing and buried up to its rear axle in thick mud when she arrived; even though it had not moved for nearly two decades, when she had run her hand along the engine cover she could sense the ferocious rumble buried somewhere deep within just waiting for a kind, skilled hand to remind it how. She had hauled herself up onto the cracked black leather seat and rocked slightly with the little life that remained in the springs. Although unaffected by the cool dampness of the air she pulled the white cotton maxi coat about her, fixed the large round fastener at the waist and tucked her chin under the collar.

The Whitehouse was at the end of a dirt driveway almost a quarter of a mile back from the main road. Stone gateposts supported a modern wooden frame; for years chained and with a sign declaring this to be private property, now it hung open. Trees surrounded the Whitehouse from behind and on both sides, whilst in front there were several large bushes and marshy grass with large pools of water; inches deep that splattered with the gently falling rain. There where signs that clearing had begun for there was a huge pile of branches and tree trunks. However from the outside the house looked like it had not been touched for years, well not by a friendly hand. The windows remained boarded up and a stack of metal mesh fencing had been dropped on a gravel patch to the left of the main building, ready to seal of the house once building work commenced; slightly gregariously a small blue Mirror dinghy had been dumped in a hedge next to the heap.

Thomasine watched them come and go with their van; she was going to need to get into the house and rather wanted to do it without anyone else there; not that they would notice her, unless she wanted them too. From the St Austell direction the sound of a siren could just be heard and it was heading this way.

"I thought you were being attacked!" Cried Sandy.

"It's not her fault," Alison backed her up. "I probably would have done the same."

"Can't we cancel it?" Rob asked rather pointlessly.

"Can anyone hear a siren?" Bob asked.

"Fuck it," Rob threw his baseball bat out of the room and into the kitchen where it clattered against the stone sink then rattled to the floor. "Right, leave this to me…I'll explain it was just a stupid girl getting jittery and it'll be fine."

He looked at the others for any counter argument; none was forthcoming and he started to walk toward the front door. Suddenly there was a quick, sharp snap from the ceiling above and without further warning a broken beam swung down silently catching Rob smack dead-centre to the back of his head. It sent him, with rather comic appearance, sprawling forward onto the floor. Immediately his friends were at his side, dodging the slightly swaying beam and helping him turn over.

"Stay put, idiot, that's a fucking cut and a half you got there," Carly held her brother firmly as she pulled out a tissue to try and step the blood, in seconds it was soaked. "Get your shirt off and give it here," she order Bob who was reluctant to oblige and much more interested in what Rob was pointing at.

Rob stared, not speaking, but wide eyed with fear as he pointed at the hole in the ceiling he had made and from where the beam had fallen…his friends saw nothing; Rob for his part was dumbstruck with terror, why couldn't they see?

**

It was after five and Darren was not having much fun in the library. He'd been here since half past nine and was now so bored and tired if his legs had not ached so much he might have got up to try and get the blood flowing back in them. He was trying to research his next Music Technology essay, which was due in within the week; two thousand words might not sound like much and it shouldn't have been, for Music Tech was his favourite subject, but for some reason his heart just wasn't in it. He kind of had an outline plan in his head and he could probably muster up the wordage needed, *yeah*, he agreed with himself time to get a kebab and go home.

He was tucking his books and papers into his backpack when he heard two girls in conversation enter the library from the stairs behind him at the far end of the room. The girls walked slowly through the library and as they reached his position turned down the aisle, stopping after walking another couple of yards. He recognised them instantly, Sally and her friend Ann. He had vaguely known Sally since they where eleven having been at Poltair School with her; although in all that time he could not really remember ever having talked to her as she tended to hang out with her girlfriends during break time and in class had always been in higher sets.

Ann was new to the area and only joined them at college so Darren didn't know her at all, although he wanted to. Sally was pretty, but achingly thin and quite lacking in the breast department, whereas Ann had no such worries being blonde, perma-tanned and with curves to die for. She liked to wear tight black jeans and a white blouse which as far as the boys were concerned was always done up just one tantalisingly button too much. Mathew, David and he had talked about her at length, fantasising about what she must have been like at school; what fun PE must have been with her in the class. David even claimed that he had seen her down Porthpean beach back in the summer wearing the skimpiest of bikinis; he might have been believed if he hadn't gone on to spin a tale about her getting undressed under a towel, which just happened to slip at a crucial moment.

Darren started taking books back out of his bag as he listened in on their conversation.

"Yeah okay, it could be cool," Sally frowned and huffed as she took a book from the shelf, looked at the cover then pushed it back in a different place. "What do those librarians get paid for?"

"Telling us to shush I think," Ann answered "so anyway this party, Friday night Katie says she'll be around Marla's by six, I'll pick you up at half six, go get them and allowing for the usual inevitable delays we should be at the Whitehouse by half seven easy."

"Sounds like a plan, you think it'll be busy?"

"I asked Jim if he knew about it and he said yeah...seems like everyone at college does."

"And they're gonna let everybody in?" Sally looked sceptically at her friend.

"Should be a real mix," Katie agreed.

"Could be a recipe for disaster."

"Be like every other Friday night round here then!" They both sighed. "But seriously should be fun and a good chance to meet some different people; everywhere we go it's always the same faces you see."

"Fine!" Sally pulled another book out, before again replacing it in a different place. "Now you're saying you don't want to go with me?"

"That's not what I mean and you know it...I meant new lads."

"Hmm, sexy strange types who might lead you into naughtiness?"

"Exactly." Katie agreed.

"Like him maybe?" Sally nodded to her right where Darren was sitting, apparently lost in his notes. "You don't know him, but he could be your Mr Right, ready to take you on a thrilling voyage of sexual adventure and you don't even have to leave the building!"

Katie glanced over her shoulder; she recognised him from around college but didn't know his name. He was one of those weird *metal* types that hung out mostly in the music rooms and rarely seemed to talk to anyone, even their own friends.

"He might be, hang on I'll go and ask for you." Katie turned and took a step towards Darren, immediately Sally had her hand on Katie's belt and stopped her moving; Katie turned smiling. "What? Would you rather him or Kevin?"

"Oh well," Sally grinned "lesbianism it is then! This is rubbish."

"Can't find what you're looking for?"

"Don't start that again, but yes."

"I thought you wanted a book on Earnest Hemmingway?"

"Yeah, and?"

"So why are we standing in the American topography section?"

"Cos he was American!"

"Let's try fiction and maybe autobiography." Katie smiled at her friend.

"Okay, there's nothing here anyway."

As they moved off Darren repacked his bag and left the library. The moment he was clear of the building his phone was out and he was calling Mathew to find out what he knew about this party.

**

Although it was only just past seven, the party already seemed to be in good swing as multicoloured lights flashed away from inside the house. Tim took the lead as they entered and began scanning the room for his friends; although she was hiding it well Jenna was as nervous as hell. It was all very well trying to mentally prepare herself for a party where she knew no one, but now all her mind could do was try to think of excuses to get her out; how shorter time could she stay here before leaving without appearing rude? There were at least thirty people in this room alone and they were split into six distinct little groups, each hanging onto their own fragment of floor space. The music was thumping away nicely in a poppy-dance kind of way, which was cool with Jenna for at least she recognised the tune.

Tim nodded at a group of three blokes over on the far side of the room by what appeared to be a makeshift bar and two of them nodded back; Jenna thought she might have met one of them before, but couldn't be sure. Her boyfriend slipped out of his light brown Ted Baker jacket revealing the white FCUK shirt she had bought him for his birthday just over a month ago; he handed her the jacket revealing another new watch, she believed that probably made it seven for the year...he had a weakness.

"Do me a favour babe; put my coat in the cloakroom when you do yours." Jenna took the coat and without waiting for a response Tim was off across the room with a huge cry of "Johnny" as he approached his friends.

"Better do as he says."

Jenna whipped her head around to see who had whispered in her ear; though once again she found herself on her own. A couple of girls in bright pink Converse T-shirts and black jeans giggled from a settee to her right and covered their faces as they pretended they weren't talking about her; suddenly she felt like everyone in the room was looking at her. She turned away from the girls and found a stranger standing in front of her.

"Ah, someone else looking for the cloakroom." This girl who had suddenly appeared was slightly shorter than her, but then as Jenna was just a couple of inches short of six foot, many girls where. The girl had blonde shoulder length hair, sparkling blue eyes and a welcoming smile. Dressed in a full length Cardin maxi coat Jenna suddenly found herself easing slightly; she didn't know why but it was strange the way that as soon as this girl had appeared it felt like every other person in the room had stopped paying her any attention.

"Two coats? Interesting look, not sure it's really for me though."

"It's my boyfriends," Jenna explained "I'm just going to hang it up for him."

"And they say chivalry is dead," the girl frowned and Jenna blushed a little. "I remember when time was a boy would have considered it an honour to take a lady's coat…oh, I'm Thomasine by the way; through here I think." Thomasine pointed through a door to another room and they started to walk.

"Jenna," Jenna introduced herself "and there's no way you can remember a time of chivalry."

Thomasine smiled at Jenna and winked.

"Well maybe I read about it in a book or something; but there are definitely still a few gentlemen out there."

"Tim's okay…" Jenna left her sentence unfinished as she tried to think of positive things to say about him. Thomasine pretended not to notice her hesitation.

"Here we go," they had moved from the first room, through another, down a short corridor and now stood outside a room filled with rack upon rack of empty coat-hangers. Thomasine made a point of looking all around her. "Really the service here is terrible," Jenna smiled and looked into the room which was really a stretched broom cupboard with a thinly carpeted floor, bare walls and no windows; the only light came from a single bare bulb in the ceiling, which slightly obtusely was, an energy saving model.

"Do you think we just help ourselves?" Jenna asked.

"Might as well, better not leave any valuables though, just in case."

Thomasine walked in first handing Jenna a couple of hangers she grabbed from a rail. Hanging her coat up Jenna watched and couldn't help but be a little envious. Thomasine wore a knee length dress of purple paisley, shaped to her figure it plunged at the front to her navel but was tied with a matching string just below her bust which helped accentuate her shape further; on her feet she wore paisley boots in gold and green with laces up either side.

"That dress is fab," Jenna admitted, cursing her hips for never being able to wear such a dress herself. "Is it vintage?"

"Thank you yes, Ungaro."

"The fit is perfect it could have been made for you." Thomasine just smiled softly. "I wish I wore something more glam now, that's the trouble with these things you never know what everyone is going to wear."

"I shouldn't worry about it, with the mix of people I've seen here already anything goes tonight."

"That's a relief, jeans and jumper seems a bit boring now."

"Bet you're warm though…and besides look at Kate Middleton, she can wear it and the future king wants a bit of her."

"Some people can get away with it."

"And those that can't can always fake it," Thomasine smiled and looked Jenna up and down. "It's the girl that makes the person not the clothes."

"Easier said when one looks as hot as you." Jenna sighed and subconsciously ran her hands down her hips and tried to heave her breasts a little more perkily; Thomasine just shrugged.

"And did your man say anything bad about your attire tonight.

"No," Jenna agreed "but then he didn't say anything positive."

"Hmm, tough one…is that normal?"

"Pretty much," Jenna giggled slightly, surprised that she was being so open about her relationship with someone she didn't know.

"Only one thing for it then," Thomasine shook her head, looking Jenna in the eye and smiling.

"Oh yeah?"

"Yup…time to trade him in for a better model!" Jenna flushed and looked away; Thomasine gave a little giggle. "Come on better get back out there before he wonders where you've wandered off to."

**

It had been fifteen minutes since the engine had been turned off, the windscreen had begun to steam up and Graeme realised that there was only one track left on the CD before it would come to an end and their pretence of enjoying the music before having to make a decision would be at an end. He reached for the chamois to clear the screen just as Hannah was doing the same; as their hands brushed they both apologised and pulled their hands back.

Hannah unwound her window an inch and the heavy sounds of bass trickled in with the fresh air. The twinkling lights of the house were visible through the trees a little over a hundred yards away; Graeme having decided to park a reasonable distance away so they could get away easier. Hannah also realised that the CD was coming to an end and she had been watching the various groups of people arriving. Neither Graeme nor Hannah was sure if they were going to know anyone else there; both having heard about the party only last night when they were sitting in the Plume of Feathers in Porthscatho with friends during the 'curry and quiz' night.

Hannah giggled as the memory of Graeme and his over spiced beef masala suddenly filled his mind; how could anyone go so red and still hold a gentlemanly demeanour.

"What?" Graeme asked as she put her hand over her mouth.

"Nothing," she smiled.

"No go on," he insisted.

"Just remembering last night," she tried to stop her lips from breaking into a wide smile.

"Oh," Graeme shook his head "you really don't need to remind me...there are parts of my body that will take months before they get over that."

"I really don't want to know which parts." Hannah giggled and looked out of her window.

"You might not get much choice." Graeme admitted as he wound down his window.

"Maybe we should get out then." Hannah suggested.

"Yeah...maybe."

**

"Come on," Ann yelled through the open car window. She had pulled up in front of Sally's house in Boscoppa fifteen minutes late to find Sally on the doorstep, cigarette in one hand and mobile phone pressed to her ear in the other. Sally waved, turned off her phone and tottered up the path to greet her friend. She was on four inch stilettos, under black leggings, a blue and orange striped mini dress all topped off with a vibrant pink cardigan.

"Hiya," she screeched as she grabbed for the door handle. However in her rush for the door she must have failed to get a proper grip, for just as she was pulling back her fingers slipped and all Ann saw was her friend suddenly disappearing as she stumbled backwards landing with a cute squeal on her bottom. "Ow, my arse," was the first thing Ann heard.

"You getting in or what," Ann asked as she desperately tried not to laugh.

"Did I say OW?" Sally asked as she suddenly appeared in the open window, leaning in.

"Yeah, now get in and stop flashing at the old boy."

Sally looked to her left and saw her neighbour watching her open mouthed.

"Hi Mr P, you have a nice evening." She called out.

"How much have you had so far?" Ann asked as Sally finally managed to negotiate her way into the vehicle.

"Just a couple…"

"Of bottles!" Ann asked as she pulled away, Sally giggled in response.

"Don't be silly, got a whole night to go yet."

"Yeah, don't want to make it to easy for Kevin do you?" Sally gave her what she though was a playful slap, but in reality almost caused Ann to veer of the road. "Ow…cow!" Sally just giggled again.

"Now you know how my arse feels."

"It'll feel worse in a minute when I get out and kick it all the way to Marla's!"

Up the road in Penwithick Marla and Katie were kicking back on Katie's bed watching Eyes Wide Shut; two empty bottles of *Chenin Blanc* lay discarded on the floor and now they had progressed to drinking directly from a litre bottle of vodka.

"Watch, watch here," Marla exclaimed "watch how he walks a set path and the camera is low down and right in front of him."

Katie did as instructed, though found herself squinting slightly as her vision has started to blur. "Still doesn't prove your point."

"I tell you that bloke is tiny…he's walking along a built up platform so those girls on either side don't tower over him." She wrestled the bottle from Marla and took a couple of gulps.

"He's not really my thing anymore." Marla admitted

"No? I thought you had Top Gun practically on loop on your DVD player."

"Nah binned it; it was getting worn in places."

"You want to be careful," Katie looked at Marla's groin and tutted, "you'll ware it out before it's even seen a boy."

"Katie! You're so basic."

"Just telling the truth, this is boring, want to watch something else?"

"Yeah; a horror...your brother got Dog Soldiers? That Sean Pertwee does it for me."

"Ooh, don't know, I'll go see." Katie hopped off the bed to try and track down her brother. She returned five minutes later with the film in her hand to find Marla on the phone. She waited just outside the door and listened in for a moment before entering.

"...yeah, I know.........I have everything I need............we'll be there soon........."

Marla turned off the phone and Katie walked in.

"Was that Sally and Ann?"

"Nah, just someone at the party asking if we were coming along." Marla tucked the phone into her pocket and drank from the bottle for at least ten seconds nearly finishing it.

"Oh...who?"

"No one special," Marla smiled coyly holding the bottle to her chest.

"What, or rather who you hiding?" Katie held out her hand for the bottle and allowed Marla to play her game.

"Secret," Marla handed the bottle to Katie "you'll have to wait and see."

"Yeah alright...but if he's hot he better have a mate."

Marla's phone started ringing again; she flipped it open and listened then gave Katie the thumbs up. "Yea...two minutes...we'll be outside."

Katie dropped the film on her bed and finished the bottle.

"Ooh, all gone...what we gonna do now?" Marla asked.

"Resort to our back up supply." Katie opened the top drawer of her bedside cabinet and from underneath her diary and mismatched socks she produced a half bottle of scotch.

"My favourite brand; how did you know?"

"You don't think mixing this with vodka and wine will make us puke do you?"

"Don't know...lets find out!"

**

Thomasine watched the police car pull along the driveway and park next to the white van in front of the house. The female police officer inside stepped out and was immediately confronted by two of the girls who came running from the house. The girls talked rapidly whilst the policewoman listened carefully keeping her hand on her radio as if about to make a call. After two minutes of talking the policewoman began nodding and followed the girls into the house; Thomasine slipped off the tractor, which silently sighed sadly as its consciousness was once again disconnected from another living soul and through the small gap in the hedge so she was standing on the pavement directly opposite the long entrance to the house.

Less than a minute later the policewoman reappeared and made a call on her radio. Thirty seconds later the two girls followed along with a third and the two lads; one of whom was seemed to have the others shirt wrapped around his head. Thomasine frowned, *an accident* she pondered *or something more sinister.* The injured man was helped into the back of the police car and joined by a girl with long black hair; after exchanging words with the remaining three, the policewoman got into her car and eased it back along the driveway.

Thomasine looked carefully at the passengers as the car drove towards her and then waited to turn onto the road; both passengers looked to be in their late teens, the girl was helping hold the shirt to the boys head and although she was ten feet away blood could clearly be seen. The car turned left then immediately right at the first turning, following a country lane that would take them quickly to the hospital at Duporth. Thomasine turned her attention back to the house and the remaining three who stood talking by their van.

She smiled and checked both ways before crossing, whispering to herself as she crossed. "Let's see what the game is."

Five
Talking

Thomasine had barely passed the gate when her eyes were attracted to a small building hiding between two silver birch trees; smothered in ivy and brambles it was slowly losing the battle with the undergrowth. Stepping from the path she noted that this field was actually a good three foot lower than the road; carefully she made her way across the marshy grass and stood looking at the pillbox.

It was not large, Thomasine walked around it for as far as the foliage would allow and estimated it to be about eight foot by six and certainly no more than five feet in height. On the side facing the road it was much too overgrown to see the opening where the soldiers would have kept a careful watch and waited with their guns at the ready, but on the side nearest the house there was an opening where the door would have once hung. Holding back the bramble with the sleeve of her coat she peered inside; it looked damp and empty, except for the rotting remains of leaves, crisp bags and food cartons which always seemed to gather in these places having either been dumped here or blown in on the wind. She stepped inside and cautiously a step down because the floor was actually dug below ground level to make its position a surprise for the enemy and allowed the bramble to fall back across the door.

Thomasine remembered history lessons at school that had told her about the build up to D-Day and how there had been American and Canadian camps built in various places in Cornwall. Running her hands along the cool concrete walls she peered through the thin slit choked with ivy and could just see through to the road; suddenly a rich musky scent of an aftershave from a bygone era filled the little box.

"They never came," a rich, male, American accent announced. Keeping her whole body in place, slowly Thomasine turned her head and looked at the figure that had suddenly appeared at her side. He was handsome, clean shaven and dressed smartly in a grey uniform, with his hair slicked back she noticed that he was slightly hunched so as not bang his head on the ceiling. He continued to look out of the slit, apparently ignoring the fact that as it was so choked he could surely hardly see a thing.

"The Germans?" Thomasine asked keeping her voice calm and level, not that she was scared of him, in fact it was rather the opposite; she did not want to scare him away. The figure shook his head gently.

"No Miss, the Nazi's never had a chance of getting near this island once we came onboard."

"Then who never came?"

The figure turned and looked at her and almost whispered. "My mates, that's who."

She pursed her lips and remained calm, trying to think of the best questions to ask, *what would Cara do?*

"When did your friends...leave you?"

"Hard to say really, we were stationed at a camp on the Beacon down in Falmouth, great town, so friendly and welcoming...then I got this order to bring some supplies down to our boys stationed up at Duporth...it was only supposed to be one day down, stay overnight then drive back."

"But you never made it back did you?" The figure shook his head and returned his gaze to the road.

"Been here since that night...it looked like a nice place, don't get me wrong the camp at Falmouth was a great place to be, but at the end of the day it was still living in a tin can. It was gonna be a real break to stay in a nice old house in the countryside...so different to home...so green and...damp!" Thomasine smiled and let out a small giggle, the soldier smiled back. "You know some of the boys talked about staying on after the war. A few even got married to local girls."

"Home being...Texas...I'm guessing from your accent?"

"Damn right Miss, born and raised in Mockley..." His voice trailed off and Thomasine was worried that he might vanish as instantly as he appeared and she was sure he had lots more to tell her.

"Do you remember the date of your...death?"

"Of course; do you?" He turned back to Thomasine and looked her up and down again; Thomasine simply looked back her face calm, although inside her mind was doing somersaults. "There's something...not quite right about you."

"I prefer *different*," Thomasine interrupted "not quite right makes me sound slightly weird."

"Something different about you," he frowned as he appeared to be thinking. "Yeah, I prefer that," he tapped his teeth with his fingernails "June 4 1944; that's when it happened."

"Just before D-Day; all your friends would have left the country within days."

"I know...I just kinda thought maybe someone would've asked questions, noticed me missing and come looking."

"They might have, if any of them survived." She looked out of the corner of her eye at him wondering how he would take that comment.

"Probably thought I'd done a bunk with one of the local floosies, those Cornish girls were right goers," he blushed and grimaced "no offence."

"None taken," she reassured him "so what happened in the house."

"Don't know, I never made it to the house...I got mine as I walked up the path." He pointed out the door to a spot where a large puddle of water had gathered, "just about there in fact."

"About there?"

"Well, I wasn't really paying much attention at the time, someone was killing me."

"And you've been in this box ever since?"

"Not allowed out, he won't let me."

"Who?" Thomasine asked intrigued, thinking she might be getting to the nub of the problem, but the soldier just looked at her as if she was daft.

"Don't know."

"But you said *he won't let me.*"

"Ah, I never actually seen, but he feels like a he, just like when you walked in, *you* felt like a female, *he* feels like a bloke."

Thomasine hoped *you felt like a female* didn't mean what it sounded like and wondered who *he* was and why *he* was doing what he did.

"Sorry I'm not really helping very much am I?"

"These things are never easy," Thomasine agreed "sorry I can't stick around longer, but you know, things to do."

"Parties to go too."

"How did..."

"I've been watching; I'm surprised they've got so far with their plans without more accidents."

"You saw that then...the bloke with the head wound?"

"They tell me people who come to this place are always having accidents…hey I mean, look at me." He smiled broadly "that was certainly one hell of an accident." Thomasine looked him straight in his big blue eyes and was about to seize on what he had just said, he anticipated and raised his hand. "Don't even ask…there's evil here that predates the house, but it's very comfortable and not wanting to move out…then again it's never met anyone like you before has it?" He chuckled to himself and Thomasine took a step towards the door.

"So you got a name?"

"Yep, Anderson, Lieutenant James Anderson…Jimmy too many a friend and foe…good luck Thomasine, I'll be rooting for you; we're all rooting for you." She stepped past him and turned to give a final look, ask one final question, but he was gone.

**

An hour into the party found Stacy and Mark drug light and cash heavy. Having decided to leave the ground floor for Michael and Joel, well it was too well lit to really do business well; they had begun trading near the toilets. At this early stage of the party people were not yet having to queue but careful eye contact and the right words let the punters know what they where about; word had quickly spread that 'traders' were in the house and mostly customers had come to them.

After ten minutes they began working their way along the corridor, casually stepping into one of the rooms to sell in private; they both realised that the police were a threat, but at these kind of parties rival sellers where usually more troublesome. The selling had gone without any trouble so far and as usual with her flirty eyes and slightly visible breast Stacy had sold her stash first and as usual she kept watch for Mark as he bumbled his way through, making a little less profit on every sale than she had but still doing alright.

By her reckoning Mark was down to his last two pills and was haggling with a girl dressed in a flirty schoolgirl outfit of black mini skirt, with fishnets of course and white blouse, unbuttoned to reveal a black lacy bra. The fit was slightly too perfect for her petit body and her obviously over made up young face made her look like the thirteen year old she probably was.

"Such a sweet treat…gonna be a tasty bit for a famished hog later." Stacy shivered as the voice whispered through her head; she turned and looked over her shoulder half expecting some leering bloke to be looking down her top. There was no one there, but the voice entered her head again. *"And once your friend had sweetened her still further…oh how we're gonna enjoy her screams."*

The moral minority in her brain sparked into action and Stacy stepped forward between Mark and the girl, who had revealed her name to be Diana; they were haggling over a pound difference in the price of a pill.

"Leave it Mark."

"Hey, chill honey…we're cool…the girl's got the cash." He smiled at the girl and she battered her badly applied false eyelashes in response.

"That's not the point," Stacy struggled not to appear as annoyed as she suddenly felt. "Just leave it and let's move on."

"Come on," the girl interrupted, her voice tinged with concern at the possibility of not getting what she wanted and all of her thirteen years. "I got a fiver, that's a fair price."

"Indeed it is," said Mark taking the money and replacing it with a small white pill "a fair deal all round."

"Cool!" The teenager announced and began to walk off.

"Not cool," said Stacy grabbing the girl by the arm "give him back the pill."

"Ow! And no way," the girl tried to break free but Stacy held on. "D'ya know how hard these are to get hold of."

"Yeah, come on Stace…chill out." Mark held up his hands and tried to step between the girls but Stacy was having none of it; she was hardly listening to them.

"Don't interfere girl…I'll make you hurt…like you did before."

"How old are you?" Stacy demanded, pushing the voice from her head.

"Does it matter? Can you let me go now?"

"Yeah, does it matter?" Mark added; he was worried about what had suddenly come over Stacy, having never seen her like this before.

"Yeah it matters!" Stacy spat, "how old, fourteen? Thirteen? Twelve?"

"No!" The girl replied indignantly.

"Where are your mates?" Stacy demanded.

"What?"

"Who's gonna look after you if you get sick?"

"They're around."

"Can you trust them not to take advantage of you when you can't control your body?"

"Stace stop it…you're freaking her out." Mark placed his hand on Stacy's shoulder but she shook it off.

"Okay…tenner says I buy that pill off you."

"Serious?" The girl looked sceptically at the pill; she hadn't realised buying drugs was this much of a palaver.

"Do brown bear's shit in the woods?" The girl scrunched up her nose and looked at Stacy as if she was even more of a freak.

"That would be a yes." Mark said.

"Fine," the girl held the pill up and Stacy whipped it away and replaced it with a ten pound note in a feat of slight of hand that a master magician would have been proud of. The girl looked at the money and then at Mark.

"Don't even think about it!" Stacy ordered, Mark gave her his 'I was doing nothing look'.

"Weirdo," the girl shouted as she ran off back down the hall towards the staircase.

"Okay!" Mark turned on the spot several times trying to come to terms with what just happened; he thought he knew Stacy pretty well, but she had never acted like this before. "So she probably was a little under sixteen…but hey…we're hardly selling legal stuff here!" He shouted the last words as his anger broke out; Stacy had other things to hear.

"They'll still taste her…she'll not leave this house without losing her innocence."

"I think that's already lost." Stacy whispered to herself.

"What…was that an apology?" Mark shouted.

"I like you," the voice chuckled *"I'm gonna save you to last…or thereabouts!"*

"Stacy, Stacy…you apologising to me?" Stacy turned to face Mark, who took a step towards her, calming down a little as he looked at her flushed face. "Baby, what was that……OW!" He recoiled as she slapped him harder than anyone had ever hit him before.

"You stupid fucking prick," she kept her voice low which only added to the menace she suddenly prevailed. "Have you no idea what might happen to a girl that young in a place like this?"

"It's her choice……OW!" Mark held his face as Stacy's hand once again struck his face, this time even harder.

"Idiot…it's not always a girls' choice what happens to her." Stacy looked about over her shoulder and wondered if that voice would return; it didn't. "Just 'cos she's naïve, does not give her the right to become a victim."

"She'll only go and buy her fix from someone else…probably twice as much now she's made a profit from us." Mark whined.

"Maybe," Stacy held out her palm with the pill in the centre "but if anything does, we won't be culpable." She dropped the pill to the floor and crushed it under her foot.

"Oh, just by being here you're culpable…too late to bring your morals when you've run dry."

"Never," Stacy whispered.

"Hey, I hear you guys might have some fun?" Stacy turned to see a bloke in his late teens or early twenties standing just behind her. He was dressed typically in easy trousers and a white FCUK shirt that looked fresh off the shelf. "Maybe I got the wrong people…sorry." He started to back away.

"Not at all friend got just what you need." Mark responded, immediately forgetting the last two minutes.

"I need a drink." Stacy announced holding her forehead as she started to sweat; she left Mark standing on the upper landing, his face red from the slaps, but still in business.

**

Jenna was starting to realise just how similar men and women are when it comes to spreading gossip. Since returning with Thomasine, who had moved on immediately with the promise to return, Jenna had been forced to listen in as Tim and his friends chatted away in ever increasing voices. Raking through the love lives of people she did not know from Tim's work and college bored her and the conversation only grew louder and cruder when several more couples joined in. Jenna vaguely recognised some, a couple of Tim's male friends made polite conversation as did several of their girlfriends.

As the minutes ticked slowly onwards Jenna found herself inexplicably drawn slightly away from the group, with every new arrival Jenna took a step further back, giving them space to mingle with their friends and her the chance to get further away; it was very clear that most people here where simply trying to get drunk as quickly as possible.

Jenna continued to sip from a bottle of something called Fursty Ferret which had been thrust into her hand upon returning from the cloakroom. It had tasted okay when she first started it about thirty minutes ago, now though the half that was left was getting warm in her restless fingers and she could have recited every word from the label with her eyes shut as she had read it so frequently.

Suddenly the music switched off and all conversation suddenly seemed incredibly loud. Virtually everyone in the room turned to look at the DJ booth; the young guy behind the decks looked crestfallen and was reddening like crazy. Some girls at the back of the room began jeering; other people joined in and from somewhere an empty beer can flew, it bounced off one of the two stacks of speakers and rebounded into the back of the poor guys head, even Jenna stifled a giggle as he turned around perplexed. The guy appeared to duck down under the decks and whatever he did seemed to do the trick as suddenly the music kicked back in…a loud cheer went up and this time two beer cans flew through the air; both crashed harmlessly into the wall then onto the floor. The guy reappeared from under the decks and held up his hands, then instantly got back bouncing with the beat of the music.

Jenna took another sip of warm beer and looked for Tim who had disappeared from sight. She scanned the room quickly and found him standing at the bottom of the stairs talking to Johnny in whispers, he held out his hand and showed Tim something small and white and nodded up the stairs. Intuition must have taken hold for suddenly Tim looked up and straight at her, he said something to Johnny who also looked over, then slinked off back to the group; he slipped the pill into his mouth as he went and winked at her as she was already moving across the room.

"Tim," he stopped as he was just about to start up the stairs "where you going?"

"Just up to the, er, loo…won't be a sec." He smiled without making eye contact.

"What was Johnny showing you?"

"Nothing," he lied

"A pill, I saw." Jenna tried to make eye contact although now Tim was looking up the stair and had taken another step.

"Probably just something for a headache," he turned to face her "go and enjoy the party, I'll only be a min."

"I don't know anyone," she glanced quickly over her shoulder wishing that Thomasine was near. "We could leave and have a private party back at yours." She smiled sweetly and hoped he would get the message.

"Look, you won't get to know anyone unless you mix." He took a step towards her, "Johnny and the others already think your odd; try talking a bit more."

"What?" Jenna flushed *how dare he say that.* Tim smiled and turned, walking off up the stairs in that cock-sure way she found so annoying.

"Looks like someone should take that bottle away from you before you stick it somewhere even a doctor would fear to go." Jenna turned upon hearing the familiar, friendly voice and let out a huge huff of frustration. "Want to swap for one of these?" Thomasine held up two pint glasses of something red and fizzy, ice-cubes chinked merrily in the mix.

"What is it?" She put the beer down on the floor against the wall and took one of the glasses with a thank you.

"Cherryade and peach schnapps," Thomasine smiled and took a sip of her glass "there's a time and a place for beer...now is not it."

"Ooh, that's good," Jenna responded as she sipped the drink, the bubbles bouncing off her nose.

"Where's your boy gone?" Thomasine asked innocently over the top of her glass as she continued to sip.

"Oh, to buy a pill I expect;" Jenna shrugged and looked as resigned as she sounded "idiot that he is."

"Told you, you should have got rid of him," Jenna didn't say anything, simply continued to half-smile and sipped the drink again. "Right, well I've been having a wander and there are definitely some people you need to meet." She slipped her free arm through Jenna's.

"I should wait...really." She looked up the stairs hoping her man would see sense and come back down with an apology not a fix.

"Probably should," Thomasine gave her a little tug "still never mind!" Sharing a giggle the two girls moved off into the party.

**

"Why don't you want to play?" Tony continued to swing gently, the voice of a young boy had been silent for five minutes; at least now he was saying

something different to 'little boy lost'. *"It's been so many years; you never said you'd be gone for that long...where have you been hiding?"*

A gentle breeze slipped through wherever Tony was hanging. The breeze was warm and scented with honeysuckle and something...fruity. Tony's mind was in turmoil, he couldn't say for sure what it was but it somehow reminded him of a childhood sweet whose name he couldn't remember.

**

Marla, Katie and Sally had ploughed straight on into the party without a second thought and were now with a large group of friends talking, drinking and generally bouncing about to the tunes echoing all around them. Only Sally had noticed that Ann was no longer with them; she tried pointing this out to Katie but she was too busy getting yet another drink and there was no point asking Marla because she was already rubbing her bottom up against Nick, a handsome sort who's list of conquest was as allegedly long as his appendage.

Sally could feel the effects of the alcohol on her feet already, she liked it of course, that slightly unsteady giddiness that makes her feel like she was going to fall down yet still dance like crazy; with the good tunes and almost nightclub lighting Sally was nearly ready to let herself go...not until she had found Ann though.

"Sally, good to see you," she had almost made it back to the front door when Kevin had suddenly loomed into view; she had tried the old duck and cover manoeuvre with a boy and girl who where entering but Kevin had been too alert. "Where's your friend...Annie?" He had his hand on her hip, not too grabby and as he didn't try to plant a kiss on her she allowed him to keep it there.

"She's gone to check on the car," Sally explained, Kevin looked puzzled; as if anyone would want to leave a party to check on a *car*.

"Why, is she worried someone might steal it?"

"She just wanted to straighten it, or park it somewhere it won't get bogged down."

"She pissed?"

"No! Least I don't think...she's just a bit anal about these things."

"Well if you're going out, I'd better go to."

"What, to protect me from any nasties out there?"

"No, you're so pissed you might need guiding back in!"

Ann had stepped out of the house and towards her car; it certainly did look like the headlights were still on. Outside the air was chilly and there was occasional drizzle in the air so she wasn't surprised that the only other people out here seemed to be people parking cars before moving on inside. Ann looked over her shoulder at the party and momentarily wished that she hadn't come alone and felt happier when she neared her car; the lights where on.

"Dangerous in the house tonight."

Ann stopped walking and shivered, cautiously casting a quick glance over her shoulder. The voice sounded as though someone was whispering in her ear, she shrugged and tried to act more nonchalant than she felt for the benefit of anyone that might be watching.

Opening the car, she had a quick peek over the front seats to check no one was hiding in the back before leaning in and turning of the lights.

"Safer in here."

Ann slammed the door in fright and four lads passing by looked at her, slowing their walking pace and exchanged laughed comments. Ann took a step away from the car and turned to the house.

"Hey Miss," Ann turned to see two guys in tight jeans and even tighter shirts, both were in their early twenties "you left your lights on." The taller and blonder of the two smiled as he passed and Ann flushed, momentarily lost for words.

"Um...cheers, always doing that," she turned to her car and sure enough somehow the lights were still on. Checking to make sure the guys had moved on Ann took a step back towards her car. "So now you've embarrassed me in front of some hot blokes! Anything else you want to do to piss me off?"

"Safer in there."

Once more Ann flinched; this time the whispered voice had been matched by a breath on her neck.

"Okay so now I'm talking to my car...AND IT'S TALKING BACK!" She slapped herself on the forehead and looked about to make sure no one was watching her talk to herself, or her car; looking in she saw that the lights were off. "Weird," she muttered.

"Hey Annie," Kevin's voice cut through the silence and Ann turned to find Kevin stumbling towards her with Sally a few feet behind. "Your car okay?"

"Yeah fine," Ann tucked the keys in her pocket.

"Did you leave the lights on?" Sally asked, she shivered slightly and her lips trembled.

"Yeah, but I got them."

"Great," Sally bounced up and down on the spot "now let's go back inside before this cold sobers me up."

"Agreed," said Kevin.

"You cold?" Ann asked looking at his thick jumper over t-shirt combination.

"No, getting sober!" He mock shivered, "brr, now let's get inside before no amount of alcohol can ever revive us.

"Okay," Ann strode purposefully towards the house in front of them. "Hey Kevin, is Dwain here?"

"Yeah, keeping the beers cold."

"Good," she smiled suggestively at him over her shoulder "so nice to have a man around in case I need him to help with the car later."

"Ouch," winced Kevin holding an imagined wound to his heart. "Sally, Sally...you'll have to help!" He grabbed for her in the dark and managed to grab a hint of arse cheek.

"Oi, cheeky!" Sally slapped his hand away and sped up to overtake Ann into the house with Kevin in hot pursuit.

"Hey, steady you two," Ann laughed "there's hours to go yet." Just as she was about to cross the threshold into the house Ann was buzzed once more by whispered words.

"Dangerous in this house tonight."

**

Darren watched the white car, and when he referred to it as a 'car' he was happy to admit that he had no idea what make or model it was, come to a halt on the driveway and a shortish, balding man hop out. Darren had been skirting through the shadows since prising open the boards over a storeroom window and had nearly escaped the house without being seen when the car's light-beams had cut right through him; he didn't think he had been seen, but he buried himself in the damp undergrowth to be sure.

He watched the man walk down the path towards the house constantly looking back at his car as he walked. Darren decided that he looked dodgy, why else would someone be so preoccupied with their car? Fortunately he wasted no time in entering the house. After waiting five minutes to be sure nothing else was coming down the driveway Darren raised himself up to his knees, then after carefully looking all around, he crouched and sprinted along the driveway, not straightening up fully until he was back on the main road.

A car zoomed past at a ridiculous speed making him jump and feel incredibly conspicuous; he started the walk towards town and pulled his khaki military surplus jacket tightly about his thin frame and was annoyed to find it dripping with water. This was a problem. He stopped walking and looked down at his coat and trousers and although they where both dark, the trousers being black combats, they showed obvious signs of having been ducked into the wet undergrowth.

Darren considered his options, everything was in place at the house, his tools ready in places where he thought best to put them and now he was hungry; and thirsty. McDonalds was a ten minute walk away and the half bottle of Bacardi felt like it was burning a hole in his pocket; he could drink that neat, but he'd rather have a coke and a cheeseburger to wash it down. Deciding that it was dark enough to cover his dirty state he nonchalantly pulled his sunglasses from an inner pocket, slipped them onto his face and pressed on down the road.

From a crack through the tiles in the roof Thomasine watched the young boy leave under cover of darkness and after everything she had seen in the last few hours she feared; not just for him, but also everyone else that was coming to this place tonight.

**

A little earlier Thomasine continued to walk along the driveway having just left the pillbox and as she walked she studied her surroundings. The grounds where fairly level although massively overgrown, only twenty yards or so around the actual house had been flattened; the ground was boggy thanks to all the resent rain but at least you could see where you where walking. As she reached the house she saw that the driveway continued on past the house, around the back and off up the hill backing onto the house; this road was more overgrown than the rest of the driveway but there were deep tracks in the mud that indicated something had gone up there recently. Thomasine stopped for a moment and noticed ruins on the hill, a short stumpy chimney and at least one supporting wall, the visible remnants of Cornish past.

Promising to take a closer look at the ruins if she got chance later Thomasine reached the front door and cautiously looked inside; there where no people in the room, but there was blood on the bare wooden floorboards and a six foot beam hug down vertically from the ceiling. Suddenly voices were raised from another room and then a girl with bleached blonde hair entered this front room, she was carrying a washing up bowl and water slopped over the side as she walked. Quickly following her was another girl, similarly dressed in just jeans and vest top and a slightly bemused looking man. Thomasine lingered in the doorway and listened.

"Look just give me five minutes." Said the first girl to emerge, she dropped down to the floor by the blood and began mopping it up with a cloth rinsed in the washing up bowl. The other two exchanged glances and looked nervously at the hole in the ceiling. It wasn't a particularly large hole, but the beam hanging down was certainly a hefty piece of work.

"I told him not to fuck around; said there was something weird about this place."

"Shut up Bob," the girl on the floor answered without looking up. "Alison can you go and get me some kitchen towel?" She asked the other girl, who was looking at the beam.

"Rob was lucky he wasn't killed, that looks heavy."

"Good job someone called the police then wasn't it?"

"Rob was hopping," said Bob.

"Well he shouldn't have gone round smashing the place up should he," quipped the girl on the floor "you getting that towel?"

"What towel?" Asked Alison was seemed preoccupied with adjusting her knickers so they remained an even height over the waistband of her white jeans.

"Do I have to do every fuckin' thing?"

"Calm down Sandy," Bob held out his hands, "everything'll get sorted."

"Only if I do it myself!" Sandy spat back giving Alison daggers.

"Don't look at me like that," Alison stropped out of the room, emerging seconds later with the kitchen roll. She threw it at Sandy who caught it just as it seemed it would hit her in the midriff. "Well don't say thank you then!" Sandy just gave her a 'look' and carried on wiping the floor; Alison stepped toward her and pushed her firmly on the shoulder. "Oi, say thank you," again Sandy just gave her a 'look', then suddenly the girls were in heap on the floor, punching, pulling hair and screaming obscenities with Bob hopping around them trying to pull them apart.

Thomasine was shocked at how quickly people could come to blows; she stepped into the room, around the writhing group and grabbed hold of the end of the beam which was at about waist height. She tested it for weight, it was certainly sturdy, but it seemed it was held in place by only a couple of nails at the other end. Giving it a sharp twist ripped the nails free and beam crashed to the floor; Thomasine let her end go and the beam bounced on the floor inches from the girls' heads.

As quickly as the fight had begun, it stopped, the girls scrambled to their feet helped by Bob, hair was pushed back into place and clothes tidied. They looked at the beam and the ceiling, none of them saying a thing. A muffled mobile phone started ringing out *Get the Party Started*; Alison dug it out of her jeans pocket.

"It's Carly," she said looking at the screen. She flipped it open and listened.

"How's Rob?" Bob whispered; Alison raised her hand to shush him.

"Yeah, okay we'll be right over." She closed the phone. "He's fine, probably knocked some sense into him…though Carly says he was doing this dying swan act till this pretty nurse came to clean him up."

"Typical," said Sandy rolling her eyes.

"Yeah, apparently he even invited her tonight."

"We still going on?" Bob asked.

"Of course," Alison looked at the beam "we've come this far, invited so many people." She pursed her lips and kicked the beam gently with her foot, "have to stick you somewhere out of the way though…right let's go pick 'em up."

Leaving the bowl of bloodied water on the floor the three left, shutting and locking the door behind them; Thomasine looked about her and shivered momentarily, the house was silent, not a creak could be heard.

Six
Telling

Thomasine wandered around the house for nearly half an hour but so far all she could see was that it was just as it appeared to be a big, old, empty house. Well not completely empty, obviously it was kitted out for a major party with oceans of booze, acres of food, places to sit and relax, a burgeoning music system, toilets and even bedrooms…evidently they were preparing for *every* eventuality.

Thomasine had reached the end of the corridor on the first floor when she heard the soft but unmistakable sound of footsteps. Standing still she listened closely, her mind attempting to pinpoint exactly where the steps were coming from; it was difficult because whoever was taking the steps was being exceedingly cautious, taking just a couple of steps at a time, stopping, then taking several more…slowly…but ever so definitely…creeping up on her.

"Aveeseenen?" Thomasine sensed a human presence just before it spoke, *not a ghost* she realised; from his voice she anticipated a boy, probably around six years old; she was correct.

"Aveeseenen?" The boy repeated; Thomasine turned and saw that he was an angelic looking child with bright sparkling blue eyes, light blonde hair and a dirty, pale face. His pink lips were parted as if still halfway through a question revealing straight white teeth; he looked her up and down quizzically, a slight frown forming on his face as he apparently struggled to sum her up. He wore a filthy, once white loose cotton open-necked shirt and ripped brown trousers, held up with a piece of cord tied in a loose knot at the front.

"Have I seen what?" She asked, bending to her knee so she was nearer his height.

"Gwalather!" He responded and continued to look at her as if she was quite mad.

"What's a *Gwalather*?" Thomasine struggled with the pronunciation. Although she was a Cornish girl her accent was never as broad as this small chap, she hoped…*still maybe that's how I sounded to Cara when we first met*, she pondered.

"Badunman," the boy explained.

"A bad man," Thomasine repeated to herself, the boy continued to look at her as if she was quite daft for not knowing. "What's your name?" She asked, the boy scowled at the question; an idea sprang into her mind, it seemed a bit silly *but why not give it a go.* Putting on her thickest, most over the top Cornish accent she repeated the question. "Gotun-name avee?" She cringed inwardly and knew her friends would smile when she recanted the story to them later.

"Tom," the boy said.

"Hey I'm a Thom too," she smiled and held out her hand for the boy to shake "well Thomasine…actually and I've never liked being called Thom…still!" The boy continued to eye her with suspicion and refused to offer his own hand forward, instead balling up his tiny fists and clamping them firmly to his hips.

Thomasine was struggling to think about how best to get information out of him when she sensed that there was something else coming. The boy must have realised too because his eyes suddenly grew terribly wide and instead of looking at her he began looking through and about her. She quickly looked over her shoulder, saw there was nothing, and then back at the boy.

"Gwalather," he said again in little more than a whisper and without hesitation he ran into the first bedroom on his right. Thomasine quickly followed and watched with sympathy as he pulled up the duvet on the bed and dived under it, pulling it tightly over his body. She smiled a little and remembered how until only a couple of years ago she had been unable to sleep at night without burying herself under the sheets leaving only a tiny space exposed so she could breathe.

"Hmm," she whispered to herself "just because you can't see the evil thing, doesn't stop it from being able to get you."

Thomasine waited a moment to see if anything was going to happen, when nothing did she decided to try and talk to Tom again. She tried to lift the duvet but the boy was holding it tightly in place; for a moment she let go.

"Okay fine, be like that." She waited a second then grabbed the duvet and yanked it firmly into the air; the boy gave a little squeal and rolled over onto his stomach hiding his face, she reached out to pat him on the back but the moment she made contact everything changed.

Thomasine had moved location; she was still in a bedroom, just not the same one; this one being larger and better furnished. She stood in the corner and held her breath. In front of her was a large metal four poster bed, richly covered in clean white covers embroidered with floral patterns in gold and green, clean copper coloured hangings dripped from the upper supports; an old man lay back, covers tucked under his chin, his head almost disappearing into the vast softness of the pillows.

Tom was on his knees at the edge of the bed, eyes closed he appeared to be praying; to his right a woman in a simple skirt and shawl was fussing over a bowl of water. A tall thin man in his late thirties or early forties walked into the room; facially he was similar to the old man on the bed.

"Don't worry grandfather," said Tom "we won't let anything happen to you." Thomasine was surprised that Tom could speak so properly, however she wasn't about to get much time to dwell on the subject…a dark presence was gathering in the shadows and slowly spreading out about them.

The grandfather let out the most fearful scream of terror making everyone, including Thomasine jump, momentarily he had sat forward, now though he slumped back, the spark of life utterly extinguished. A gathering stain of blood appeared through the sheets from around his middle. Tom lifted the sheets, tears in his eyes; underneath the old man lay in the bed in a nightshirt and there was what appeared to be a knife wound near the top of his groin.

"But it's only a single cut," Tom muttered as he slumped over the body.

The room cooled as Thomasine found herself back in the first bedroom, alone she sat on the bed. Her brow was aching, then she realised that she was frowning. Easing her facial muscles she thought about what she had just seen; it was darker now and at a guess she would have said that at least a couple of hours had passed. She drummed her fingers absent-mindedly on her lips as she thought. The sounds of people moving about downstairs could be heard; obviously the people from earlier had returned and were continuing with the party prep.

Something metallic dropped to the floor in the hallway outside the bedroom and a voice cursed softly; Thomasine remained seated on the bed and a figure appeared in the doorway.

Darren looked into the bedroom, *no one here, good*; it was the last room on this level and perfect place to leave a weapon as he wouldn't get confused about where he left it. There were not many hiding places, the bed really was the only option; carefully he moved across and lifted the mattress; weird, it was much heavier than it looked.

Thomasine watched the boy approach her, he was probably only about sixteen, but with his full length khaki jacket, black combats and chunky boots he could have passed for older. He was coming straight at her, although of course she knew he would not see her; now he was bending at her knee, was he going to propose? Quickly she hitched up her coat and skirt and moved her legs just as the boy reached out for the mattress; she pushed herself backwards as he struggled to lift the mattress and watched with horror as from a black holdall draped over his shoulder he produced a six-inch stiletto blade with an ornate silver handled; he looked at it lovingly for a moment before tucking it safely out of sight and allowed the mattress to cover it.

Darren did a quick mental check and reminded himself where the knives where hidden so far; he pulled the holdall into view, had a quick look inside then moved on.

Thomasine watched him leave and was up in an instant; she lifted the mattress with ease and took the knife, it was quite beautifully made and balanced perfectly on her fingers. She looked for a place to put it safely, unfortunately there was really nowhere else; even the window was boarded up, so she couldn't throw it out the building. She looked up and smiled. Holding the knife firmly she threw it directly upwards where it stuck firmly up to its hilt in a thick oak beam. Pleased she had neutralised that one weapon she was suddenly worried about how many others the boy may have planted, so quickly hurried after him.

For the next twenty minutes Thomasine followed Darren around, removing the weapons as he hid them; under beds or chairs, behind loose skirting boards and even beneath the floor in one case. There were two survival knives, three morning stars, two flat throwing knives, a replica Walther PPK filled with blanks, an expanding baton, two tins of lighter fluid and matches, a flick knife and knuckle duster. His bag must have been nearly empty and he seemed relatively happy with what he had achieved; Thomasine just shook her head and wondered on the mentality of a teenager to do such a thing…what did he hope to achieve?

Finally he pulled out one last weapon, an ornate battle axe with a thick wooden shaft tied criss-crossed with strips of leather. Thomasine watched him holding the weapon; god she was so embarrassed as he wafted it around like some grotesque phallic symbol. There was nowhere they had been so far that he could hide it; he paced up and down the corridor checking each room to see if a new hiding place had appeared, it hadn't.

Darren jumped as he heard footsteps approaching up the stairs from below, *shit what do I do with this?* He wondered looking between the axe and the stairs.

"Hide it up here." A voice from somewhere whispered; Darren turned in the direction the voice had come and saw a panel in the roof at the end of the corridor; *of course the attic.* He ducked into a bedroom as a figure emerged into the corridor; fortunately they walked in the opposite direction towards the toilets. Once he was sure he was not about to be discovered he grabbed a chair and dragged it into the corridor and used it to reach up, pushing the panel to one side was easy, then he levered himself up and shut himself in. Thomasine watched all this in silence. She pushed the chair back into the bedroom so it would not be discovered out of place and waited.

She could hear him moving upstairs; two minutes later the panel was pulled open again and the boy peered down. He didn't seem bothered about the chair having been moved; he simply lowered himself down as if he was at home and disappeared off down the corridor.

Thomasine let him go, his final weapon was all she was interested in for now; she closed her eyes and the next step along the corridor took her instantly into the roof.

She opened her eyes and allowed them to quickly adjust to the blackness. The attic had been fitted out as another room with proper floorboards and panelling on the lower portion of the room, all manner of junk littered the space and she wondered how she might ever find the weapon up here; maybe she should just leave it as surely no one could hope to find it in the dark. However she realised that was really not a practical option just in case.

It was dusty in the attic and smelt of old man, wood and lacquer; Thomasine began moving methodically about, looking in boxes and behind stacked chairs and various other furnishings; she wished the light was better and she had more time for she could tell from the vibrations given off by the objects she was handling that some of them were really beautiful old things with fantastic stories to tell.

"Aveeseenen?" Tom was sitting on an old three-legged stool in the corner of the attic; draped in shadows Thomasine could barely see him. He looked at her hopefully.

"I don't suppose you saw where he put it?" She asked, not expecting much of a response but the boy pointed to a wardrobe on the other side of the room. Thomasine walked over and was relieved to find the axe propped up inside. She held it in her hands for a moment and wondered what to do with it; finally she decided to move it to the opposite side of the room and hid it behind a pile of old paintings and mirrors. Okay it didn't put it out of action, but the chances of anyone finding it where greatly reduced.

Tom had been watching her all this time and once she was done she faced him and thanked him; he beamed a white smile and held out his hand as if for Thomasine to shake it. Surprised she took a step forward and was about to take it when she noticed the young boy looking over her shoulder at something.

"What is it?" She asked.

"Cain telly," the boy whispered his eyes getting wider as the smile faded; he retracted his hand.

"What do you mean," Thomasine asked "tell me and I might be able to help."

"Gwalather," the boy said in an even quieter whisper. Thomasine blinked, but that fraction of a second was enough for the boy to simply vanish...still she wasn't alone though.

She sensed the old man's approach, he came accompanied by the smell of brandy and expensive tobacco; she turned on the spot slowly and recognised him in an instant as the man from the four poster bed she had seen not long ago. He looked through her to where the boy had been; then, realising there was only Thomasine he focused on her.

"Izze gone?" Thomasine nodded; the old man frowned and muttered something incomprehensible to her. He began to turn away from her.

"Wait, are you Gwalather?"

"Iz whatee callsee."

"Right, think that's a yes." Thomasine was glad when he stopped walking and turned to look at her

"Nawn Gwalather diddy?" He asked. She studied his face, it was lined with age and the hair was wild, grey and wispy, yet still the eyes shone with a pure blueness that seemed to penetrate through the darkness.

"Err...no," Thomasine responded; her knowledge of the Cornish language was nowhere near that well advanced to understand properly.

"Baddun, Gwalather izza baddun," he offered an apologetic smile.

"Oh," she looked at the old man and how he was dressed in the flowing white nightshirt she had seen him wearing in bed; though thankfully without the blood stain. Thomasine knew never to judge by appearance, yet her senses told her that on this occasion she could.

"Seenengain." He muttered with a sad shake of his head and once more Thomasine was transported back to the other bedroom.

Again Thomasine stood in the corner, Tom knelt on the floor and a woman was fussing on the other side of the room; Gwalather lay on the bed. The door opened and the man came in again, only this time it seemed slightly different to her; rather than walk in, his movements seemed false...almost as if he was floating in, or pulled into the room as if on wheels; a disjointed memory that a child might remember the event as.

"Don't worry grandfather," said Tom "we won't let anything happen to you."

As previously a dark presence began gathering in the room, seemingly imperceptible to all but her.

Gwalather let out the most fearful scream of terror making everyone present except Thomasine jump, momentarily he had sat forward, now though he slumped back, the spark of life extinguished once more. A gathering stain of blood appeared through the sheets from around his middle. Tom lifted the sheets, tears in his eyes; underneath the old man lay in a nightshirt in the bed, there was a knife wound near the top of his groin.

"But it's only a single cut," Tom muttered as he slumped over the body and Thomasine watched as the knife fell from the young boys hand to the floor; he knocked it under the bed out of sight with his knee.

The presence in the room grew ever more oppressive, like being in an oven it smothered everything with a sense of warmth and stifling stillness or treacle covering water a sickly sweet layer separating two states of reality. Suddenly Thomasine was no longer standing in the corner of the room, instead she found herself on her knees in the place where Tom had been moments earlier. She could feel the heaviness of an evil presence stalking up her back, holding her down, feeling for places to grip hold of. As she knelt she slowly leant forward and the presence itself started to tilt, slowly over stepping its grip, the sensation off oppression was slipping away.

Without warning it gave out the most terrifying huge guttural growl, like a tiger cornered it grabbed hold of her or was it Tom and as it did so the whole body flexed with power, rage and tension.

The oppression vanished as Thomasine found herself back in the coolness of the attic; Gwalather still stood before her. For a moment she acted as though she was alone, looking through a crack in the tiles she watched a car approach and Darren leaving under the cover of shadows.

"Seenen eh?" He asked.

"Yes I saw," Thomasine looked upon the old man and saw slowly through the layers that make up a person, the wrinkles, the clothes, the smell; that which Gwalather was revealed himself...a kindly old man, father of a generation. He bent towards the pile of paintings stacked against the inside of the roof and carefully pulled them apart; he stopped and looked up at Thomasine and beckoned for her to come over.

"See?"

Thomasine stepped forward and looked down at the painting he was showing her; it showed The Whitehouse standing proud in its former glory, a large engine house on the hill behind it.

"Your house; your mine?" Thomasine asked and Gwalather nodded.

"One 'ere, one in King's Wood," he shook his head as he muttered something incomprehensible. Thomasine watched and waited as he continued to look through the paintings; finally he stopped and he lifted the penultimate frame from the floor. It was much smaller than the others and he seemed to strain as he had to bend further to pick it up; Thomasine moved forward and helped him gently lift it and Gwalather seemed genuinely pleased. It was only about eight by twelve inches in size and depicted two children, a boy and a girl; both in their preteens she judged.

"Is this the boy?" She asked pointing at the male.

"No, t'is Gwalather," he replied a puzzled expression on his face, he was obviously confused "Gwalather," he pointed at the boy "Morvoren," he said pointing at the girl."

Thomasine began racking her brains, that name was familiar. Frowning as she thought hard, Gwalather remained mesmerised by the painting. Suddenly it came back to her, it was only last year that they had been studying Cornish legends at school; Morvoren...maid of the sea.

"Mermaid," she whispered; Gwalather suddenly seemed embarrassed and tucked the painting back into the pile whilst continuing to mutter. "Wait," Thomasine put her hand on his shoulder and he went rigid. "Who was she, Tom's sister?" Gwalather nodded, "an unusual name," Thomasine continued, the old man looked at her carefully, then at the hand on his shoulder; Thomasine kept it there to show that she held no fear and was there to help "but Morvoren wasn't her first name was it?" Gwalather shook his head. After a moments pause he shuffled across to the far corner of the attic, Thomasine followed and watched as he slowly lowered himself onto all fours and lifted part of the floorboards; inserting his long arm into the space he pulled forth a red leather bound book and after a moments thought handed it to Thomasine.

She took it carefully and noted the strange drawing of an evil looking gnomish figure on the cover, naked, but holding a cloak and waving a short, thick stick it grinned mischievously at her. She turned the book over and looked at the spine, it was written in Cornish. Remembering back to the first day she met Cara and Bea and their visit to the Library of Lost Books she waited a moment and slowly the words changed shape and the title revealed itself; *Cornish Romances & Drolls: Tales of the Wild & lost West.*

Holding the book carefully in the palm of her left hand she allowed it to fall open gently on its own on the pages that had been visited the most, two seemed to be the answer; *55: How to Become a Witch* and *79: The Dead Hand.*

Gwalather was watching her, he bit his lips but his eyes were shinning; quickly she scanned through the other titles, of which there where over one hundred, grouped into differing subjects. Thomasine looked up at him and nodded an agreement. "So homework eh; guess I don't have to long though do I?" Gwalather didn't say anything at first but slowly a half smile spread across his lips; he pointed at the book "King's Wood," he whispered and nodded as his body mysteriously faded into the shadows.

Thomasine's mind raced, but she was calm and held the book firmly. The two passages in the book were not especially long and within a minute she had memorised the text; she considered leaving the book here in the attic, but realised that it might come in handy later and she was sure Gwalather would not mind her taking it; she tucked the book into a surprisingly capacious pocket on the inside of her coat. She nodded to herself, yes there was a problem here; that problem had a solution…and she, and this book, might be it.

Seven
Finding

In one of the smaller downstairs rooms David was holding court in front of his friends with ease, but the contents of his stomach with difficulty. In an attempt to keep his stomach as flat as possible for the party he had tried to keep his food intake to a minimum, unfortunately the single half bowl of breakfast cereal, without milk, he had eaten for breakfast had worn of by mid afternoon and by the time he had finished dressing he was positively famished again. He had tried to suppress the hunger with a quadruple whiskey in a pint glass and been hoping to top it up with cola from the fridge; but there was none. Eventually he found a single can in a cupboard under a bag of birdseed; both belonged to his sister. Despite the cola being warm he poured it into the pint glass; it barely filled it three-quarters full. As he had stood in the kitchen trying to digest the warm sticky liquid he had given in to temptation and made himself three slices of toast, margarine on all plus jam on one. It had seemed like a good idea at the time.

Another can of scrumpy had passed his way, he thought it might have been his third or forth, but couldn't be sure. He took the sunglasses off his nose and put them back into pocket, hanging them via the arm from his front trouser pocket on his teal chinos so everyone would still see them; well they had cost a lot of money. He flopped down onto the green velour sofa between Dean and Steve who each moved slightly to give him room and took a long gulp from the cold drink in his hand and contemplated the various brown shadings that made up his new brogues.

A minute or many may have passed until David realised that people where still talking around him but he was not focusing in on any one particular conversation. Adrian was bringing two four-packs of cans in his direction and a number of people were moving through the room. The music seemed sometimes very loud but at other time most distant and every now and again someone in the group would recognise a favourite tune and break into some raucous singing, everyone else would smile and laugh.

He watched as people entered the room and passed by in groups of two or three; occasionally they were even girls, he tried to make eye contact with a few but none seemed interested; *must be the company he was keeping.*

Marla and Katie had moved away from the group of friends they had greeted upon arrival in the main room; they were just the same people they usually hung out with on a Friday, and now they were on a mission to check out any new talent. As they slowly disentangled themselves from their friends they spotted a handsome, well groomed chap hanging around the entrance to one of the side rooms; he spotted them looking over and winked.

"Do you spy what I spy?" Marla asked.

"What the stud by the door? "Her friend confirmed. "Think he's got any friends?"

"So long as they're not girls."

"Oh, I thought you might be out to experiment."

"Urgh, please," Marla gave her a friendly shove with her free hand "think it's gonna take more than that to give a girl satisfaction tonight!"

"Right, let's find us some...*satisfaction* then," Katie giggled.

The guy they were watching moved back into the other room so they crossed the main room and looked inside the next room. There were several groups of people in here. Just to one side seven likely looking lads were camped around a green sofa, on the far side of the room four Goth girls were sprawled, glowering on bean bags by a small portable heater, on the other side of the room two girls sat chatting together on a purple chaise lounge and finally, in the middle of the room a mixed group of boys and girls standing around a table laden with snacks and booze.

The can of cider had somehow managed to empty itself, he crushed it and it groaned with a rather satisfying metallic sigh, Steve cheered at his friends' prowess and patted his biceps. David grinned to his other friends who cheered as he tossed the empty can away over his shoulder forgetting that the sofa was placed against a wall. A second after it left his hand it had bounced back of the wall and clunked into the back of his head. Marla and Katie started laughing.

"Did you see that?" Katie asked the glass of vodka and orange in her hand dripping as she shook so much.

"To right, look at him trying to work out what just happened."

The bloke on his right noticed them giggling and tapped David on the shoulder, he looked up and realised what they must have seen. Although more than slightly embarrassed he rose to his feet and took a huge bow. Both girls started applauding and moved over to join the boys.

Thomasine left the house and found herself stopping as she neared the pillbox. Although her eyes adjusted quickly in darkness, the gloom and covering of damp foliage actually made the pillbox look like any other lump in the countryside. She only knew the box was there because she caught a whiff of Jimmy's aftershave on the breeze and when she stopped and looked across she saw a tiny glowing ember that could surely only be the tell tale sign of a lit cigarette. Cautiously she stepped across the sodden grass and stood in the open doorway; Jimmy looked her up and down a puzzled look on his face.

"I'd offer you in to get out of the rain, but it doesn't seem to affect you."

"That's just the way it is with us."

"I miss the rain…boy, never thought I'd here myself say something like that."

Thomasine smiled.

"Because you never come out of the box?"

Jimmy nodded.

"Still at least I don't miss the cold and damp," he took a drag on his cigarette "and this place definitely has damp related issues. Don't you miss the rain?"

"No," Thomasine shook her head "we still feel the elements, they just don't affect us like they did."

"Handy," he muttered "how'd it go in the house then?"

"When we talked before you said *he* wouldn't let you out, do you know who *he* is?" She asked, avoiding his question for the moment. Jimmy shook his head. "You've never seen *him*?" Again Jimmy shook his head and took another drag on the cigarette.

"Sorry, not much help am I?"

"It doesn't matter, I'll work it out…I have to ask, but where the hell do you get your supply of those?" She pointed at his hand.

"What this?" He waved the cigarette. "Ah the benefits of being dead," he removed a full packet of cigarettes from his top pocket "like a Texan oil field; never runs dry."

"Lucky boy…and it's not like cancer will ever get you…"

"What's that?"

"Nothing."

"So where you off to now? You're gonna miss the party."

"I'll be back!" Thomasine smiled, though the reference was completely wasted on a man dead for more than sixty years. "I would never miss this party for the world."

**

"Do you think they know those guys?" Jenna asked between sips of her drink.

"What, more than twenty seconds ago?" Thomasine replied with a wry smile.

"Uh huh."

"Nope…but I don't think it will take them long before they exchange intimate details." Thomasine and Jenna watched as the two girls practically threw themselves on the guys they had spied from the doorway. "And if that one doesn't hitch the straps up on her dress a little I think we'll all be getting to know her intimate details!"

Jenna laughed lightly; then sighed.

"What's up?"

"Thinking."

"About your boy, we can go and find him, if you want?"

"Nah just admiring your necklace, it looks old."

"I think it is, it certainly feels old," She held it in her fingers then offered it to Jenna so she could touch it. "Someone told me Phoenician, but I think the writing on it is Greek."

"Yeah, think it means sun or something…I wonder who the young girl was…jet's a mourning jewel isn't it."

"I believe so, but you know this crazy world of ours, what's death to one is life to another!"

"Uh oh, way to heavy for me!" Jenna smiled and let the necklace go.

"Sure you don't want to find your man?"

"We could, I expect he'll be off his head with his mates."

"You shouldn't have come."

"I know, I had reservations, but I ignored that little voice…"

"Never ignore the little voices; they got me where I am today," Thomasine smiled sincerely at Jenna.

"So you not here with anyone; no friends…or boyfriend?"

"Nope, might be meeting up with a mate and her boyfriend later, if they turn up, but I got a feeling they won't make it."

"That's a shame, so you don't know anyone here either?"

"This is true," Thomasine smiled and winked conspiratorially "but that often makes for the best parties."

"I don't mind parties when I know the people."

"Evenings in with the girls?"

"Yeah, that kind of thing…or just something with couples; we had a great Bollywood themed party in late August at a friend's parent's house in the countryside that was such a fab weekend."

"Sari's and jewels everywhere?"

"Oh yeah, and we rigged up all these sheets on the outside of the house to create this kind of tent effect, which was beautiful when it was lit with all these globes filled with candles."

"Hmm, it does sound idyllic." Thomasine agreed.

"It was…right up to the point John, a friend's boyfriend decided to leap out of a first floor window and slide down on one of the sheets."

"Don't tell me not fixed up properly?"

"Nah, I just recon he was too heavy; there was a lot of blood…"

There often is at parties, Thomasine thought to herself. "Was he okay?"

"Once he was patched up, certainly sobered him up quickly," Jenna smiled half-heartedly at Thomasine. "I'm not bringing you down am I?"

"Never, I love a good party and this one has every chance of shaping up into a memorable one."

"I take it you don't live with your parents then?"

"Moved out six months ago and in with friends," Thomasine nodded "best thing that's ever happened to me."

"Student house is it? I can't wait to get to uni and away from *the family unit.*"

"Well, it is a kind of education, but none of us is at university; my best friend Cara spends a lot of her time travelling, and has been kind enough to take me under her wing and let me tag along. But when we are all together there's always lots of fun to be had." Thomasine leaned across to Jenna, "Want to place a game; guaranteed to make you smile?"

"Go on then, what?"

"Toothless vegetables!"

"Pardon!"

"Toothless vegetables...don't tell me you've never played?" Jenna shook her head "such a sheltered upbringing." Thomasine smiled slightly shaking her head.

"I dread asking, but how do you play?"

"Easy. We take it in turns to name either a fruit or a vegetable without showing the teeth, no repetition, first to stutter, show teeth or laugh is the loser...ready?"

"No!" Jenna smiled.

"Good; banana!" Thomasine started the game.

"Carrot!"

"Pea!"

"Pear!"

"Sprout!" Jenna hesitated and her mouth broke into a wide smile; "loser!"

"Damn that's difficult," Jenna admitted.

"Wait until you've had a few more to drink...then it's *bloody* difficult!"

Exaggerated laughing drew their attention to the group of boys and girls by the sofa. The boys appeared to be having a drinking competition in pairs, trying to down whole cans of cider whilst the girls gyrated on their laps; there was much spurting of fizzy liquid from facial orifices. "Fancy going on a little wander; maybe recharge the glasses and see who else is out and about?"

"If you can show me where I can get another one of these then certainly," Jenna replied holding up her empty glass. Another round of laughter broke out on the sofa as this round of the competition had apparently been won by a large chap in an England football shirt and light brown tracksuit bottoms; he rose to his feet and lifted his arms in mock salute and crushed his empty can before tossing it across the room where it landed at the feet of one of the Goth girls. "Although we could just stay and watch the show." She added.

"It is tempting, but I have a feeling it's just going to descend into a pseudo-lap dancing extravaganza; and I don't think either of us need to see that." The Goth girls collected themselves up and shuffled out of the room to stifled giggles from those involved in the drinking competition. The victor in the England top let out a huge belch as the final girl passed him, she looked at him with a look of disdain, but didn't say anything; the group of boys cheered loudly. *"Geve us onys drinken er we go henne!"* Thomasine whispered, staring at the chap for the briefest moment.

The guy turned to face his friends, his arms still raised a smile of success on his face; suddenly the little group fell silent, then several seconds later the girls both looked at one another, covered their mouths and started tittering to themselves.

"Ah mate…you dirty bugger, you gotta learn to control yourself." Winced one of his mates as he looked away. The big guy looked down at his groin and turned away in shame from his mates, giving Thomasine and Jenna a perfect view of the ever widening wet patch that grew there. He was turning rapidly redder and looked for an exit; seconds later he charged from the room.

Jenna was slightly lost for words; she looked at Thomasine who simply responded with a raised eyebrow.

"Wander?" Thomasine asked, not in the slightest surprised at what had just happened.

"Agreed, let's go wander."

Thomasine stood and helped Jenna rise from the surprisingly comfy chaise lounge, her knees wobbled slightly as she straightened.

"Dead legs?"

"Either that or that lovely drink is having the desired effect."

"Not too much, I trust?"

"I know when to stop," Jenna smiled as she let Thomasine slip her arm through hers "unlike some people!"

"Certainly not time to stop…plenty more to happen tonight."

Together the girls made their way back into the main body of the house and the ever burgeoning party atmosphere.

**

Within ten minutes of leaving Jimmy in his pillbox Thomasine was closing in on King's Wood; she could have got here quicker but she wanted to feel her way forward. From the main road leading through London Apprentice Thomasine branched off onto a compacted gravel cycle path that ran alongside the river, deep under the canopy of deciduous trees; the moon flicked on and off through cracks in empty branches and rain laden clouds. Although she had never walked here before she found her way with such ease; King's Wood, spread across a hill as it was, throbbed in the night with the blood red hue of a land disturbed.

Thomasine stopped where the path forked into three. One ran over the river via a narrow wooden bridge and appeared to double back toward London Apprentice. The path on this side continued to follow the flow of the river, eventually ending at Pentewan, whilst a third path was blocked with a new wooden gate. Leaning on the gate she looked into the woods; there was such silence. Through the occasional moonlight individual trees became visible and through it all the blood red shapes danced, deep in the heart. From her pocket Thomasine produced the book Gwalather had given here and quickly reread the passages. Confident that she was doing the best thing she moved forward.

She passed through the gate, being careful to shut it after her and looked at her options. Ahead one path led straight up the hill, stooping to the ground she felt the odd surface…concrete, cut with grooves *strange* she pondered. The narrow path was walled with moss covered stone, layered in a very Cornish way…they reeked of metal and oil; the stench of progress. This roadway was much younger than the rest of the wood; *Second World War* she decided. There was a sign that declared 'Unsuitable for Motors' and in her mind she pictured how the land might lie and the positioning of the most vibrant red hue and chose another path instead.

The main path was wide, flat and rutted with gouges cast from horse hoofs and Land Rover tyres; sticking close to one side or the other was obviously the safest way of making her way forward. The path wound about the hill on a level plain. To her right the hillside plunged downwards sharply and was thickly covered with trees and bushes and because it was lower she could see out for miles over the countryside…although as it was so dark it was hardly a great view…at least the land here was at peace. It was black, but she could sense the movement of life, animals living in their space, it was at complete contrast to what was happening on her left; she started walking again.

Thomasine kept a wary eye out, but pressed on. To her left the land rose as sharply as it fell to her right; that was where the similarities ended. Although it was dark there were patches of red everywhere, they seeped and swirled around trees and through bushes and hung in patches like early morning storm clouds captured within the slight grasp of elderly fingers; but although it signified disturbance, it did not indicate any malice. Still there was nothing to indicate life here. After five minutes the path started to turn anti-clockwise and began to get steeper; a separate path broke away downwards and turned back so that it would lead into the lower, darker woods, but that was not where she needed to be.

As the path she followed grew ever steeper Thomasine began passing through patches of the blood red hue; as she did she allowed her hands to run through them, they felt warm, though slightly coarse, like running fine sand straight from a summers' beach through her fingers. Suddenly the ground levelled out and Thomasine found herself standing on a small plateau; the moon obligingly blossomed and Thomasine was awarded with a beautiful view from the top of King's Wood out across the countryside to where she thought she could just make out the sea at Pentewan. The stars twinkled intermittently as the clouds steamed across the sky in unison like some manic line dancing contest.

"T'is beautiful," startled by the soft voice Thomasine turned to face the speaker, a girl of barely 10 years. "I never tire of the view…it changes every night."

"It is most impressive," Thomasine replied as she studied the little girl. She wore a simple cream dress with dark stockings underneath. Her face was pale, her hair wild about her head, whilst her eyes sparkled the palest blue. "Does it look this beautiful during daytime?"

"Can't remember," the girl shrugged "not seen it like that for an age; have to stay in."

"Why's that then?" Thomasine knelt down slightly to be nearer eye level with the little girl; the girl smiled and seemed resigned to the facts.

"Morvoren says the sun makes you age and that if I never go out in it I can live forever."

Thomasine smiled outwardly but inside was frowning.

"Well I'm sure that Morvoren wouldn't mind if you came out every now and again and saw the sun."

The little girl shook her head and looked deadly serious as she replied.

"Morvoren says that vampyre's can never see the sunlight, lest they age."

Thomasine paused for thought. The girl was dead, Thomasine understood that, although apparently the girl did not; but, someone, this Morvoren, had told her that she was a vampyre…*why*…the question screamed in her mind. Thomasine knew the truth, though felt that now was not the time to tell it, instead she smiled and rose to her natural height.

"So what's your name then?"

"Tegen," the girl replied brightly, with a warm smile revealing sparkling white teeth.

"That's beautiful, I'm Thomasine. Well Morvoren sounds like a most interesting person, is she about; I think I should like to meet with her?" The girl shook her head and kicked at an invisible stone with her foot. "Do you live near here?" Thomasine asked.

**

"He looks dodgy."

"Who, him?" Thomasine replied to Jenna as they stood at the bottom of the stairs.

"Yeah that guy with the khaki jacket I mean, come on, it's not that cold in here."

"He was here earlier and acting strange then." Thomasine agreed, watching as he slunk in through the open doorway, looked watchfully all around before moving across the room to a table that groaned with alcohol.

"Do you think we should warn someone?"

"Like who? Look around, unless it involves them I don't think anyone is going to be that bothered about what happens tonight." Thomasine wondered how long it would take for him to begin whatever he had planned, *it won't be yet* she decided *he hasn't been told what to do.* Darren grabbed a can of super strong lager from the table and immediately popped it open; taking a sip he moved away from the table as others approached and tucked himself in a dark corner near the DJ.

A girl dressed in something akin to a schoolgirl outfit bounced across the room hotly pursued by a bloke with wild eyes, a big smile revealing Hollywood teeth and a tie around his head. "Sorry," she yelled with a giggle as she bumped into Jenna; she didn't stop; her attempt to get away from the bloke with the tie was much more important.

"See what you mean," Jenna said rubbing her arm.

"You okay?"

"Fine," she looked at her empty glass "where did you get this from?"

"You sure you don't want to look for your boy now?"

"He'll wait," Jenna smiled "besides there are so many other fun things going on."

Thomasine smiled and slipped her arm through Jenna's and led her off to the kitchen.

Tegen led Thomasine across the plateau and into the very heart of King's Wood. As they walked the blood red hue became denser but separated to allow them through, closing up tightly again as soon as they had passed. Finally Tegen stopped at what appeared to be a particularly dark wooded area; she pointed into it and Thomasine watched in amazement as the thick fog emanated from its murky centre.

"Is this home?" Thomasine asked; the girl shook her head.

"Not home, but where I've been for some time," she replied obtusely "see." She let Thomasine's hand go and encouraged her with a nod to step forward.

Thomasine took several cautious steps forward towards the centre of the red melee; raising her hands in front of her because it was so dark in the centre she was immediately glad she did when suddenly out of the darkness loomed a stone wall. Thomasine looked over her shoulder to see if Tegen was still with her, she was although she was hugging herself; turning back to face the wall Thomasine slowly began walking around it to find out just how large it was.

The wall was encapsulated with the knotted grasp of moss covered trees, ancient holly bushes and smothering ivy. Thomasine worked her way along the wall for about ten feet before the wall turned sharply to the left; continuing to follow the wall, it turned twice more before she found herself back at the starting point; there was something odd about the building. Thomasine knew how a building should feel and this one definitely didn't feel right. She couldn't tell exactly why, probably because the anomaly was far below them; there was something and possible more than one thing that should not be there.

Tegen was still standing a few feet away looking wary, but when she saw Thomasine remerge she seemed to perk up and took a step forward, her arms out in front of her welcoming Thomasine back.

Thomasine took the hands and stepped a few feet away from the building, momentarily she turned to look back at it, then at Tegen.

"An engine house?"

"Wheal Thomas," Tegen replied "shut down by the men in 1842."

"Which men?" Thomasine asked watching Tegen bite her lip before replying "the miners?"

Tegen nodded.

"Why?" The little girl looked up at Thomasine, shapes silently forming on her lips; Thomasine understood them and filled in the words for her. "The dead hand."

**

"Cheers," said Jenna as she touched glasses with Thomasine, she sipped a little of the drink "that is mighty fine."

"Cheers, yes it certainly hits the spot." For a moment they stood quietly in the kitchen with only the beat of the music to accompany their thoughts. "This your kind of music?" Thomasine asked as she noticed Jenna slowly moving her head in time with the tune.

"Not really, I prefer something you can sing along with."

"Ah, karaoke queen are you?"

"No," Jenna blushed "definitely not, unless there's champagne, I like dance music just not all the time."

"Certainly seems popular here," both girls looked out into the main hall and noticed more people than ever "the DJ's doing a good job."

"Apparently he's quite well known, once had a show on the radio and everything."

"Really? Thomasine looked surprised, "he looks a little...young."

"I thought that!" Said Jenna. Four girls entered the kitchen three of them obviously the worse for drink and Thomasine decided it was time to move on.

"Come on, let's wander.

Stacy stood on the final step and looked around; she hoped she might see Joel or Mathew.

"Hey babe, wait up," gasped Mark breathlessly, the fifteen yards he had just jogged the most exercise he had undertaken since leaving school "I didn't mean to upset you." He put his hand on Stacey's shoulder but she stiffened and shrugged it off.

"Don't" she hissed.

"Okay, whatever," Mark tucked his hands in his pockets, "come on babe, let's get a drink and chill...no more business tonight." Stacey turned and looked at him frowning. "Seriously, I got nothing...promise you." He gave her his puppy dog eyes.

"Okay, okay get me frigging drink before I change my mind."

"Straight this way my lovely," he waived at a bloke with a bandaged head chatting to a blonde haired girl guarding a table set with dozens of bottles of different spirits. "Hi Rob, do us a couple of large vodka's would you mate," the bloke nodded whilst the girl gave Mark and Stacey a filthy look; Mark was oblivious, intent only on the drink although Stacey noticed. The bandaged bloke set up a couple of plastic tumblers and began pouring.

"What happened to your bonce mate?" Mark started to reach out to touch Rob's bandaged but he pulled out of the way.

"Did it tidying up mate, got a bit enthusiastic…that enough for you?"

"Stace, that okay?" Stacey nodded.

"Plenty ta."

"Want anything in it?" The girl asked.

"Orange, if you got it," Stacey replied "or coke."

The girl grabbed a carton of orange juice and topped up one of the glasses.

"And you?"

"Coke," Mark replied "this is a banging night man; you should do this every year."

"Way too much like hassle mate and besides in days the builders move in and all this will change."

"Too bad, too bad," Mark mused looking around and noting the every growing throng of people filling the house. "Good turn out and totally banging music."

"Yeah, don't know who arranged it…getting some famous bloke to play here, dad I guess, trying to do his bit."

"I don't recognise him," said Stacey.

"No, you won't," the blonde girl replied looking across at the young kid behind the decks "that's Ian, Rob's brother…the DJ's gone missing."

"Oh, didn't know you had a brother," said Mark.

"So where's the DJ?" Stacey asked; the girl smiled and shrugged.

"Dunno, weird huh?"

**

Tegen cocked her head slightly and looked surprised that Thomasine knew the words she hadn't said; Thomasine noted this but felt compelled to press on if she was going to find out anything.

"The ghostly hand of the miner that continues to travel the mines after the death of the man," Tegen shook her head, but her eyes told the truth. "What was his name and why was he so unpopular?"

"Don't know what you mean," Tegen muttered sheepishly.

"The dead hand usually belongs to a pariah, you said the men closed this mine...why...to prevent him coming back?" Thomasine paused and then the possibilities dawned on her. "Or was there something else down there?"

Tegen wore a look of complete and utter horror upon her face. "What do you know about that?" Before Thomasine could answer Tegen was running in the opposite direction; Thomasine sucked in a wary sigh, vanished from the night and appeared again in Tegen's path an instant later. Tegen thudded to an immediate halt.

"It's impolite to ask a question then run away before an answer is given," she chastised. Tegen pushed away from Thomasine and ran back in the direction she had just come from; once more Thomasine moved instantly and was back standing by the engine house as Tegen arrived. Determined not to be chasing about King's Wood all night Thomasine made sure she grabbed hold of Tegen's arm before she could attempt to disappear again.

The moment their flesh touched the landscape changed; the blood red hue collapsed to the floor as if someone had cut invisible strings, the sky suddenly cracked into an open full moon, most of the trees about them where but samplings and the mighty engine house stood stoutly in front of them. To the side of the engine house a group of two dozen miners huddled and talked in whispers; from out of the woods a small figure appeared, in a simple cream dress it was a slightly younger Tegen. Upon spying this other version of herself Tegen slipped her hand into Thomasine's; in return she clasped it tightly. The Tegen from the woods skipped her way towards the engine house, the men fell notably silent as she neared and several doffed caps as she wafted right passed them towards a building attached to the engine house.

The door marked 'Foreman' was opened from inside and Tegen walked in; the door shutting the instant after. Some men swore, whilst others crossed themselves; Thomasine continued to hold Tegen's hand firmly and was about to stride over to the Foreman's room but Tegen held her back.

"Don't, she makes me do bad things."

"Morvoren?"

Tegen nodded. "But how can I see the past?"

Thomasine smiled briefly at Tegen and squeezed her hand. "I need you to be truthful and honest; can you do that?" One of the miners stepped forward from the group, he looked back to his comrades for a moment, then straightening his cap upon his head he reached for the door and banged upon it with a meaty fist.

"I will," Tegen whispered as the door was flung open and a man, presumably the Foreman stepped out. His face was slightly red and he was hitching his trousers straight.

"Were short for 'e night," said the miner. The Foreman looked sceptically at him and then at the group of miners mustered near the entrance to the engine house.

"Where be John, Tom and Peter, he asked.

"Not shown, they..." the miner paused as the Tegen who had entered the Foreman's office appeared with her face streaked in tears; she gave them a cursory glance and waltzed off back into the woods. From within the folds of his coat the miner produced a short lead bar and raised it above his head. "T'is more than honest man care bare!" He bellowed as he bought the bar down across the Foreman's face; the man, completely taken by surprise, let out a low groan and slumped to the floor, dazed but certainly not dead.

"This is a year before I was left here," Tegen whispered.

The other miners moved forward and gathered around the downed Foreman. They exchanged hushed words and then a decision was made; four of the men hoisted him by his limbs and together they moved towards the engine house.

"I watched as they took him below from behind those trees," Tegen pointed off to the left and Thomasine could just see the hint of a cream dress tucked in amongst the trees. "They were only gone thirty minutes; Mr Trembeth was never seen again...alive that is...they were protecting me."

"No, they thought they were protecting themselves," Thomasine corrected, she gave Tegen a reassuring smile "and what did Morvoren think of their actions?"

"She was so terribly, terribly angry."

"Why?"

"'Cos she hadn't finished with him."

King's Wood returned to darkness and the blood red hue once again rose from the ground and continued the seemingly never ending flow from somewhere deep below ground.

"How long after that night before the dead hand was first seen?"

"There were rumours of a rock-fall with days; the first sighting came a week later."

"A rock-fall could hide many a misdemeanour."

"There was a single shaft down which then branched into three, each of these split further down twice, all suffered sightings."

"The ghostly hand carrying the candle," Thomasine confirmed "with no way of escape." Tegen nodded.

"Never saw it myself though."

"Tell me more about Morvoren." Thomasine asked.

"Well, I don't remember much," her eyes focused on a memory buried long ago "but I think it started at Pentewan. My grandfather and father used to come here six days a week and more often than not my brother and I would accompany them; my brother I suppose was heir to all this so that is only right and proper, me, well I preferred the beach. I used to go down there on my own, see the fishermen coming and going, whilst the landlady at *The Ship* would always try and feed me up. One day I was walking on the beach near the cliff when I heard the most beautiful singing...so light, so joyful...can you ever imagine?" Thomasine shook her head.

"Go on," she urged.

"I started to dance, I couldn't help myself, I felt like I danced from dusk till dawn; certainly when I stopped the whole beach was covered in my footprints thousands and thousands. I was exhausted but the voice continued, although it stopped singing and instead it began whispering kindly words, such soft beautiful words compelling me to go forth and find it...it came from the sea. I took myself onwards, not caring that my stockings, shoes and dress were quickly waterlogged, I had to find that voice. The water reached my mouth, yet still the voice wanted me to go further, I couldn't breath," her voice suddenly became more urgent "*I was gasping for breath...choking on the cold, briny...*" Thomasine squeezed her hand and Tegen regained control, "sweet, sweet taste."

"You okay?" Thomasine asked; Tegen nodded.

"Years since I remembered that…I awoke some time later on the beach and went home but every once in a while I would hear that singing and find myself dancing, dancing in all manner of places, before finally one day I came up here and danced and Morvoren left me." She began crying softly.

"You poor thing," Thomasine sympathised, putting her arm around her "don't worry, I'll soon see this at an end."

"I'd like that;" Tegen wiped tears off her face "I've been here so long now I want to go home."

"To The Whitehouse?"

Tegen nodded. "But it's not possible, Morvoren says…"

"Morvoren said what exactly?"

"That these ancient paths would bind me here."

"It's never simple is it?" Thomasine smiled as she tried to unravel the words. "Ah," she exclaimed "what if Morvoren meant that you could never leave on a path you had already travelled; an ancient path if you will? What if there was a much younger path that she did not know about?"

"But I could not risk being seen to leave and there are no other paths here."

Thomasine smiled broadly, her blue eyes twinkled as she remembered the concrete path, and the pieces of the puzzle in her mind began clicking into place. Absentmindedly she fondled the necklace.

"We'll just see about that!"

Eight
Meeting

Emily was pulling shapes on the floor; with Rose and Fiona at her side doing likewise...people surrounded them, moving to the rhythmic beats, lost in worlds made of notes...talking about her.

The track was familiar; no words, but the tune was known from a hundred daytime radio stations; silently she hummed the words to herself "..........*is it a monster?*" *Monster*, that's what they where saying, as she danced and moved awkwardly...obviously out of time with the music and the others about her. She pulled shapes and pretended she was beautiful...*monster* was what they thought.

"Hide your face you abomination!" Emily looked over her shoulder as the words thundered into her ears. *"Take yourself away from their eyes; they're so horrified at the sight of you."*

"What's up?" Fiona asked, leaning across to shout in her friends' ear.

"Nothing; why?" Emily replied.

"Cos you look like someone just walked over your grave...you want a drink?" Emily stopped dancing for a moment and her friends slowed their movements, but did not stop. Thoughts flashed through her head how to silence that voice, or should she? Maybe it was right and she should hide.

"Emily; you going for a drink?" Rose asked as she continued to shake to the beat.

"Urm, yeah," what you want?" Emily replied her mind half lost in thought of hiding away and half of alcohol to drown out the voice.

"Bring me beer!" Rose giggled; Fiona trumped her approval and both let their dancing pick up speed as Emily began to fade from the dance floor. Stepping away from her friends her place immediately swallowed by the mass of bodies that seemed to grow minute upon minute into the centre of the room. She had something to do...oh yeah, get some beer...she turned and headed for the table in the corner of the room, her mind swimming with thoughts... now why was she hiding?

"Cos you're a monster!" The words penetrated her skin and sunk within the second and third layers of epidermis as she picked up ice-cold cans.

"What?" Emily squirmed as the word seeped out through her lips quite unintentionally and she shuddered felling slightly dirty; "Ow" she yelped as someone knocked her to the ground.

"Sorry miss, my elephantine feet;" a muscular hand laced across her bottom and then around her waist, pulling her upright "are you okay? I haven't hurt you?"

She was momentarily lost for words, then grabbed the hem of her dress and yanked it down as is it had ridden up far to near her waist revealing major hints of the pink lace beneath...*god he was hot...god hope he didn't notice...but maybe hope he did...and liked it!*

He backed away from her slightly and gave the impression of not noticing as she straightened her dress.

"Hey." He said

"Hey." She replied.

"Urm, three cans of ale and only one of you...now some might say that's an addiction!"

"Or just a carry-out service," Emily replied, her face flushing just as much as his. "And HEY, you've got a four pack so don't be so judgemental."

"Yeah, well I'm a bloke...I can handle it!"

"And I can't"

"No, no, no...didn't mean that," he seemed genuinely scared that he had offended her.

"Only teasing," she whispered.

"Me too," tucking the beer into his left armpit he offered his hand forward "The name's Tim...and I'm an idiot."

"Emily...likewise," she narrowed her eyes and tried to look menacingly at him "so why you knocking me over?"

"Really didn't mean that, honestly I slipped on a wet patch, it's these shoes," he lifted his right off the floor and showed her the sole of his shoe "see? Their first outing; knew I should have roughed them up a bit before."

"This is true...hasn't your girlfriend ever told you that?"

"Erm, no...single actually."

"Oh, cool...you here with friends?"

"Yeah there's a few people I know knocking around," Tim moved a little closer so they could lower their voices a little "needed a break though; and you?"

"Yeah, friends on the dance floor; gotta give the legs a rest though."

"You have very nice legs," he replied smiling "from what I've seen." Emily opened her mouth in mock shock and Tim held up his hands, "still teasing!"

"You better be," she smiled and wagged her finger *he was awfully cute!*

"You fancy sampling a couple of these somewhere a little quieter?" He waved a beer at her. Emily glanced over the dance floor at her friends, but they were not to be seen. "But if you have to get back to your friends it doesn't matter."

"No way!" Emily replied, hopefully not to eagerly. "Where?"

"Through here, it's quieter back here."

Jenna and Thomasine were out of earshot of the conversation.

"Kumquat," said Thomasine; Jenna pursed her lips.

"Gooseberry perhaps."

"Saw your teeth." Thomasine replied; then waited a few seconds for Jenna's mind to rest. "They might just be friends," Jenna quickly glanced at Thomasine with a *'you don't believe that do you'* look on her face.

"No...he's on the pull."

"Don't be so sure," Thomasine tried to offer the benefit of the doubt; Jenna pushed out a deep breath.

"She's pretty, slim, red-headed, pale skinned and just flashed her, *pink*, knickers at him." Jenna rolled her eyes back as if what she had said was enough but Thomasine looked her in the eye and ground her jaw.

"Unintentionally," Thomasine moved closer to Jenna so she could whisper in her ears; the words she didn't say loaded and just as important as those she did. "He did nearly flatten her."

Jenna caught her breath before she responded, the memory of the night she and Tim had first met instantly in her mind; no matter how hard she tried to suppress it *gullible* someone whispered from somewhere. "Yeah he does that; thought it was just me."

"What where you wearing?" Thomasine probed.

"A way to short emerald green velvet mini-dress...and matching briefs." Jenna reluctantly admitted.

"Really; what decade was that in" Thomasine laughed, "the seventies?"

"It looked good in the shop," Jenna defended "I was with some friends...spending way too much money and I though it would work."

"Obviously did!"

"Yeah; I guess."

"Probably went well with your eyes," Thomasine replied; Jenna frowned.

"If only I'd know how devious he was."

"Serious? The old, knock you down to get in your knickers plan. Does that actually work?"

"One of his friends let it slip, better than a chat-up line apparently…worked on me."

"Blimey, I'll have to remember that. The next time I see a guy I fancy I won't bother with small talk, I'll just pummel him to the ground and see what underpants he's wearing!" Jenna let out an involuntarily half-hearted giggle.

"Don't, it's not funny."

"It's the past."

"You make it sound like we're talking about someone I don't know."

Thomasine made a show of straightening her dress and necklace, her mind a rush of how to tell a girl she should move on…but Jenna already knew that.

"She looks like a nice girl; shall we go and rescue her?"

"No point," Jenna turned to Thomasine with a look of resignation on her face. "If he has taken a pill and he's mixing it with beer he'll be asleep in ten minutes…trust me I know."

"How are you still dating this bloke?"

"Easier than breaking up I guess."

"Okay, tell you what. Let's give it five," Thomasine gave Jenna a lovely evil smile "then we pounce!"

**

"You know we've been here for thirty minutes." Hannah glanced quickly across at Graeme; his right hand had been running rings around the steering wheel for an age. She made a show of looking out of her window whilst her right hand slipped onto his left thigh; then across onto his groin.

"We'll give it a little longer!" He replied, both hands holding onto the steering wheel as his zip was pulled down.

"Okay," Hannah replied, quickly making eye contact with him; then looking away innocently…her right hand anything but.

**

Emily noticed his eyes beginning to glaze, *knew it was too good to be true; I really am that boring* she told herself. The beer in his hand rested upon his knee but his fingers holding the can in place where losing their grip. Everything had been fine five minutes ago. Tim had led her through to a room that had only a dozen or so people in and they had taken seats on a funky burgundy velour sofa…well it was burgundy in the patches that were not stained with something…icky. He'd complemented her on her dress and her legs again; which she made sure to keep sensibly crossed…no more knicker flashing tonight she decided! They had barely begun the conversation when he started to drift, *no* she decided *it's not me…bet he's a druggie!*

His eyes shut and *god…he was snoring*, his fingers slipped from the can and she reluctantly decided to remove it from his knee and place it on the floor before it fell there.

"You where right," Emily turned, startled by the voice that suddenly materialised in her ear; she found Thomasine leaning over her shoulder, her eyes focused on Tim "he's well gone." Emily blushed beautifully and tried to persuade some words to come out of her mouth. Thomasine moved around Emily and waved her hands in front of Tim's face; as it provoked no reaction she poked him with one finger and he slowly flopped over to one side on the sofa.

"Told you," said Jenna who stepped up next to Emily.

"Are you his friends?" Emily asked her mind full of all manner of possibilities of how Tim might know these two attractive girls; her worst fears where to be realised.

"Jenna's his girlfriend," Thomasine explained.

"Ex," Jenna interrupted and looked at Thomasine who raised a questioning eyebrow. "The best way to revenge a wrong is by forgiving it."

"Ex-girlfriend," Thomasine grinned brightly at Emily "never met him myself" she mused.

"Urm…he said he was single." Emily was again lost for words. *Stupid girl* she chastised silently *made a twat of yourself…again.*

"He is now," Jenna gently put her hand on Emily's shoulder, she flinched slightly.

"I promise I didn't know he had a girlfriend," Emily smiled meekly.

"Apparently neither did he!" Thomasine frowned giving him another poke; a wicked thought sprang into her mind. "Anyone got a lippy? We could have some fun here." Jenna shook her head but Emily rummaged in her handbag and produced a well-used stick. "Oh yes, liking that…can I borrow it?"

Thomasine asked; Emily nodded, glad that so far these girls appeared not to be angry...last thing she needed was to get into a fight. Thomasine took the stick, "Love the colour, Saint Rouge goes well with your complexion; oh and hi, I'm Thomasine."

"Emily," she relied blushing further at the compliment "what are you writing?"

"Well, now he's single and on the prowl," Thomasine turned to the other girls and gave a conspiratorial wink "we must do everything to help...by letting every one know!" She began writing on his forehead; a minute later she was done and stepped back to admire her work. Emily let out a little giggle, and continued to blush, she looked across at Jenna; who just rolled her eyes and tried to pretend that she wasn't smiling either.

Jenna had known that her relationship with Tim was on the rocks for weeks, she just hadn't had the guts to accept it until tonight. She knew that it was slightly weird, the way that Thomasine seemed to radiate a confidence that had somehow tapped straight into her and like some intravenous drip was feeding her, helping to guide her; she should probably have been angry with Emily for going off with her boyfriend, but she wasn't.

When she looked at this slight girl she saw her great shyness, the blushes and the loss for words; despite her beauty this girl was lost; how could she be angry? She and Emily where so alike; just as Thomasine had been a support to her when she was alone, Emily was in a similar position.

"Right," Thomasine announced "three single girls at party."

"Are you just going to leave him like that?" Emily asked, "it is slightly naughty."

"Yep," Thomasine handed back the lipstick "unless you want to wait until he sobers up?"

"No way!" Emily replied sharply in disgust...some guy knocks you down to get in your pants! How horrible is that she thought. Quickly she looked up to Jenna, this guy's *former* girlfriend and hoped she hadn't upset her. Jenna just looked back and without saying a word seemed to understand how she felt; shrugging her shoulders and waving at her ex goodbye.

"Brill! Right I've made a decision," Thomasine announced "if it's the last thing I do tonight I'm going to find you both decent blokes." Jenna and Emily looked at each other; but Thomasine just smiled broadly the plan in her mind forming as she spoke. "You know, girls that stick together, make a pretty potent force."

**

He was wearing a tight white t-shirt and sky blue shorts; the August sun baked down on his four year old body and he was blissfully happy. Tony was in a field, running madly after his sister and two other girls, Heidi and Sarah daughters of a friend of their mothers; they were all older and faster than him and he had lost absolute sight of them around the last sty; but he could still hear their panting and girlish laughter always constantly slightly ahead. He charged across the open, dodging dried cow pats as he went and towards a bushy area where he was sure he would catch up.

The path thinned down to little more than a rabbit run but Tony charged onwards before coming to an instant stop as the barbed wire strung across the path dug deeply into his thighs; rabbits might be able to cross this path between fields, humans could not. He bent over in pain and momentum, his hands grabbing the floor to support him as the sharp rusty steel bit deep into his flesh; stifling a yelp he gripped the thin tufts of grass and noticed the mass of rabbit droppings inches from his face; he tried and succeeded in not crying.

Within seconds the pain began to subside and Tony looked at his legs to see the damage, he had visions of blood pouring profusely down his legs but thankfully only a single barb had caught on each leg. He stayed this way for a couple of minutes wondering if anyone would come to his aid and how many droppings a single rabbit could produce in a day. An Elephant Hawk moth with its olive-green and pink colouring zipped across in front of him; there must be willow herb or bed straw nearby; the heady scent of honeysuckle flooded his nostrils. His back was starting to ache and he decided that as the pain in his legs was not too bad he should try and move, so gripping the grass firmly he pushed back and straightened himself.

Stepping away from the barbs allowed the blood to flow a little freer, it ran in trickles past his knees and headed towards his sandals so he wiped at the blood with his hands, it was sticky and thick and smeared beautifully. For several minutes he was lost in this game, watching as the blood emerged from the tiny tares in his skin, allowing it to run for a moment, then, just at it was growing in confidence that it might make it past his knees, he would cruelly 'kill' it by smearing into the mass of its fellow drips.

He grew bored as the game came to an end; scabs began forming and the trickles of blood that did emerge where too slow for his patience. Tony looked at his legs and hands, they were a mass of clotted blood, dried smears of various shades of red, rapidly turning almost brown; 'how much of this stuff can I lose before it became vital?' He pondered.

"Are you going to die?" A voice asked. Tony turned to face the voice and found himself looking at a boy a little taller with blonde hair and bright blue eyes.

"Don't think so," Tony replied looking down again at his legs. The blood had stopped flowing, though they certainly looked a right state. "Don't think I lost enough blood."

"You should get clean; blood can attract all sorts of nasty creature."

"Like what?" Tony asked sceptically.

"Like rats and vampyres...and mermaids." Tony looked at the other boy as if he didn't understand the words; he didn't.

"What's a rat?"

"A huge, hungry beast that stalks the countryside feasting on weak and dying animals...scenting out the blood, they stalk and rip their prey to shreds without mercy!"

"But I'm not an animal, I'm a boy."

"Makes no difference to a rat, nor a vampyre."

"What's that?"

"A vampyre? A disgusting pale beast that stalks the night feasting on anything with fresh blood flowing in its veins." Tony didn't really understand what was being said, and to be honest the way the boy was speaking was slightly scary.

"I think I better go now."

"Come to my house and get clean; it's not far and then you'll be safe."

"What was the other thing you said?"

"Rats, vampyres and..."

"Tony! Tony!" The voice of his mother was urgent and cut across whatever the other boy might have had to say. "Tony for goodness sake what's happened to your legs?"

"Caught them on that mum." Tony pointed at the barbed wire.

"Oh you poor little man," his mother immediately produced a tissue from her pocket and was applying saliva to it; she knelt down and began to dab and the bedabbled mess on his legs. As she went to work his mother's friend appeared from behind her as did her daughters and also his sister...none of them came close. "What where you thinking?" His mother directed the question to his sister.

"Nothing to do with me!" She scowled.

"You shouldn't have been running."

"I didn't run this way." She scowled again.

"Still!" Realising that her supply of tissue and saliva would run out before the job was done, she changed tack. "Have one of these and we'll go back to the car." She handed Tony a packet of Spangles. "I was saving them" she looked at him and gave him a soft smile, "but I guess now is as good a time as any to open them.

As they walked back to his mother's friend's aqua-blue Datsun he put one of the fruity boiled delights into his mouth and carefully folding the top over the remaining sweets he offered them back to his mother; but she refused to take them, instead insisting that he tuck them into a pocket off his shorts for later...he promised to make them last. As they walked Tony suddenly remembered that he had forgotten about the boy; he looked quickly over his shoulder but the boy was not in sight...but as they reached the road and the place where the car was parked he briefly glanced a large white house tucked away in the fields...he hadn't noticed that before.

That was the smell, Spangles, that smell and the taste suddenly filling his senses in the most realistic manner; he ran his tongue around the inside of his mouth for a clear minute to be sure there was not one tucked away between tooth and gum.

"Do you remember what that other thing was?" The voice asked. *"Mermaids!"*

**

Kevin put his ear to the door. "I think I can hear someone breathing; heavy breathing," he looked to the girls a smirk on his face "or maybe more than one!"

Sally and Ann exchanged a look *didn't he ever think of anything but sex?* The end cubicle with an off-green door opened and a Goth boy slunk out without making eye-contact.

"Here you are m'lady," Kevin held the door open for Sally who looked in with crinkled nose "well?"

"Okay, okay I'm going; Ann, make sure he doesn't listen."

"As if I would," he gave a crossed his arms and took a disgusted stance "don't you know I'm a gentleman."

"No; a gentleman would get more drinks for the ladies."

"Have them lined up for you when you come down," he uncrossed his arms and leant into the cubicle. "Kiss to remember you by?"

"Ha!" Sally slammed the door in his face. "And no listening!" She yelled through the door.

Harry stood up and slammed his hands into the walls that confined him; he felt something at the tips of his senses, heard something, someone different to the voice that had been tormenting him, so he hit out again...*there it* *was…*pain…*ahh*; the sweet sensation of realism. His mind began to focus and to drift back to reality; the reality of the toilet. My god, how his head spun, like he had drunk two bottles of whiskey or more.

"You alright in there mate?" The different male voice came through the door again. "Sounds like your stuck or something."

"Urm, yeah," Harry's through was dry and croaked "just taken a little sleepy."

"Take it easy on the booze then mate," a voice from the cubicle next to his spoke through the wall "you've been burbling away like a deranged tramp since I got here…there's a whole lotta party still to be had.

"Right, cheers." Harry was glad the cubicle hid his blushes…*how to get out?*

The toilets on either side flushed virtually simultaneously and the people left; no one took their place. Finally the people in the other cubicles left and he was alone.

"Okay…so my hiding place is discovered; time to leave this place…*legs wake up!*" Harry whacked his legs; he'd been sitting on this toilet for far too long…then he noticed the trickles of blood running down his arms, *how did that happen?* He wondered.

**

It had only taken them half an hour to collect Rob from the hospital; Bob had driven the van up the short distance with Alison at his side and Sandy rolling around the back; no one had wanted to remain on their own in the house this time. When they arrived they found Rob and Carly sitting in silence on a wooden bench outside the entrance, they where both smoking and apparently not talking; both starred off into the distance as the van pulled up in front of them. To be fair on Rob he probably had a reason to be miserable. His head was swathed in white bandage and the paleness of his skin, presumably through shock, revealed huge bags under his eyes.

"Is he supposed to be smoking?" Bob asked.

"Don't think I've ever seen him smoke before," Alison replied; Sandy leaned forward from the back of the car to peer out.

"Not usually whilst his sister's around anyway."

"Aye," Bob agreed with Sandy's comment and explained to a puzzled looking Alison "grandfather and three uncles, so far, died from lung cancer; all smoked."

"So their not supposed too," Sandy added "'cos their dad would probably throw them both out if he knew."

"Thought he'd be in a better mood than this after getting all patched up, "Bob pressed the horn, Carly and Rob looked up "but it looks like Mr Bump has turned into Mr Grumpy! OW!" Sandy slapped him on the back of his head.

"Shut and don't be a twat."

"Alright, shit, look their coming over; make some space in the back there." He looked at Alison. "And you; can't expect the wounded to bounce around the back."

Alison did as requested, muttering under her breath as she went. With the three girls in the back and the two boys in the front the journey home was undertaken at a snails pace, partly because Bob didn't want to thrash Rob's car and partly because the police car that had visited them earlier had left the hospital at the same time and had been following them; fortunately it continued along the main road when they pulled off into the Whitehouse. As they made their way along the driveway, Bob noticed that Rob was clenching his fists so tightly together that the knuckles where glowing as white as the bandage around his head.

"There's someone by the front door," said Carly from the back of the car. She pointed between the boys to the house.

"Looks like your brother," said Bob "it is."

"What's he doing here?" Rob turned to his sister in the back and winced as he brain bounced in protest. "Suppose you told him about what happened?"

"Nope, you told him to get to the house about mid-afternoon didn't you?"

"Don't remember that," said Rob turning back to face front, the car arrived, stopped and Ian bounced over the car.

"Is he here yet?" He asked excitedly.

"Who?" Rob asked getting out of the car.

"Tony of course," he seemed genuinely shocked no one else was excited about Tony "and what the fuck's happened to your head?"

"Don't ask?" Carly replied as she emerged from the back of the car.

"Just did!" He replied indignantly before noticing Sandy; he'd had a thing for Sandy for a while now. He managed a quick 'hi' and about a second's eye contact before having to look away and claming up with embarrassment.

Alison unlocked the front door and they all moved back into the house; Rob the only person to hesitate. As she entered Sandy picked up the bowl of bloodied water, the floor was well on its way to drying and Bob picked up one end of the wooden beam. He called for Ian to give him a hand. What was going unsaid in the room was making Ian's brain do somersaults, but he was able to pretty much put two and two together. He did as asked and together with Bob they took the beam back through the front door and out around the house where they stowed it safe, flat on the ground where hopefully it would do no more damage.

"Wait," Ian stopped Bob before he had chance to head back into the house "is everything alright?"

"If you mean is the party still on, then yes; is everything ok? Then I don't know." Bob looked about him as if someone might be eavesdropping. "Come on we've still got some things to sort out then you can go drive down Holmbush and get us all some chips."

"Serious?" Ian beamed. "Wait, I got that little issue with the license...and insurance."

"Well don't have an accident," Bob started to make his way towards the house "I intend to be too drunk to care by then anyway!"

**

"So what do you do then?" Marla asked David; she been bouncing on the lap of the guy sitting next to him but as he had got up to go to the loo she decided to move on.

"What?" *This music is getting louder*, he moved closer to Marla, his hands working from her wait to her bottom; she didn't seem to object.

"I said what do you do?" She smiled and noticed his eyes glancing at her cleavage; he was seriously cute and smelt nice so she decided to let him continue.

"Student in Truro; off to Oxford come August." He neglected to tell her he meant Brookes.

"Really? Cute and clever; fancy a dance?"

"Sure baby." David lurched to his feet pulling Marla up by the hand; she flopped into his arms dramatically and squeezed the muscles in his upper arms.

"Hmm, strong," she purred, ignoring Katie's shaking head as she watched her play with the boy. "Come on she giggled." Leading the way into the throng of people occupying the dance floor.

Sally and Ann arrived at the bottom of the stairs just in time to see Marla dragging a boy onto the floor.

"Hope she's got protection," said Sally.

"It's him that's gonna need the protection!" Ann replied, "I wonder where Katie is."

"Marla came from that direction so let's have a look around."

"Don't you want to wait for Kevin?" Ann teased.

"If he wants it, he'll have to work for it."

"Too late," Ann pointed at Kevin heading towards them by taking the most direct route from the far corner of the room; straight across the dance floor. "And he's bought you cake!"

"Alright ladies?" Kevin bounced his way over to them two bottles of lager held by their necks in one hand and a small paper plate with cake and a handful of nibbles in the other. He handed a bottle of lager to each girl then just stood there looking at the girls expectantly. "They got a table with a few bits on; I thought you might want to take the edge of that drink."

Ann looked at the two fairy cakes and handful of nuts and crisps and smiled politely. "M'mm looks yummy, but unfortunately I have to be…somewhere, so I'll leave you two to…enjoy your nibbles." She had noticed that Kevin didn't have a beer for himself so she pressed hers into his hand. He smiled his manic smile.

"Alright, have fun!" He offered the plate to Sally and as Ann walked away she glanced over and noticed Sally giving her a glare; although to be fair she was shoving a crisp into her mouth as she did.

Nine

Learning

"Is it me or does this place seem to be getting bigger?" Jenna asked.

"It's not you, but this place isn't getting bigger, just emptier," Thomasine explained "well emptier in here! If any one else tries to start dancing in that room it will probably explode."

Thomasine, Jenna and Emily had made their way to a room on the ground floor at the furthest end of the building away from the DJ; however thanks to the music's volume and it being piped through speakers into numerous other rooms it permeated even here. The door to this room was shut; Thomasine tried the handle it was stiff, *have to wary that doesn't become permanently stuck* she mused, but she was able to open it carefully, just in case it was a place they should not go. At first glance the room appeared devoid of life although there was a small old portable television sitting precariously on an aspidistra stand, three large brown velour corduroy sofas, a huge pile of bean bags and on the far wall a boarded up door that by Thomasine's calculation would lead outside. One of the brown sofas had been pushed to within four feet of the television; its back was to the door so although the three girls could see the black and white images on the screen they couldn't see who was watching them.

"Go away!" Said a voice.

"Yeah and shut the door," said another. A head appeared over the top of the sofa and scowled at the intruders; the boy looked at the three girls for a second then ducked back down again; words were muttered out of sight before a second, different head appeared for a second then once again disappeared. Further words could be heard being exchanged between the two boys; Jenna and Emily looked at Thomasine who just shrugged.

"Well I think it's the perfect place to chill away from all that racket." Thomasine decided.

"If we're not intruding," said Jenna.

"Not intruding," the two boys appeared in unison, leaning over the back of the sofa. The one on the right had a trimmed moustache and beard, soft blue eyes and hair that was squashed flat on one side, as if he had been leaning against something for a little too long; he was wearing a black *Pop Will Eat Itself* t-shirt. The other bloke had straggly shoulder length hair, a trimmed goatee and appeared to be wearing a shirt made from the remains of a Hessian sack; he raised his hand in welcome.

"Sorry thought you were some of those chavs coming back to take the piss again."

"But you're not;" said the other "so come in...s'cuse the mess."

Thomasine stepped forward and her companions followed. The two blokes had made a home of the enormous sofa that was certainly suitable for at least four people; however as there had only been two of them they had filled the gaps with cushions, bags of crisps and bottles of beer. There were two other half-opened cases of beer where their feet had been resting. They hurriedly began tidying and within a minute had made the place more habitable.

"You sure we're not intruding," Emily asked half hoping they might say yes.

"Not at all; well," said the guy in the black T-shirt "no more than us anyway!"

"Yeah rubbish party, way too many people" added the other guy "and we found this way retro seventies telly and a whole night of *Blake's 7*!" For a moment there was silence. "I'm Trevor; this piece of hippy trash is Marmalade."

Hellos were exchanged between the group and the boys invited the girls to sit.

"Apparently I was named after someone in this programme;" Jenna said, taking a seat her eyes watching the small black and white screen "but I've never seen it before."

"Really," asked Trevor he sat next to her, putting a beer in her hand and clinked it with his own as he did "parents called you Blake...that's a mean thing to do."

"Idiot," replied Marmalade "she looks more like a Trillian."

"Wasn't that a character in Hitchhikers Guide?" Said Emily, she blushed beautifully and looked to Thomasine for help as she realised what a geek that comment made her look. "I could be mistaken," she added meekly. Thomasine hid a giggle behind her hand.

"You're totally right," said Marmalade his eyes wide with amazement. He was impressed; a cute girl who knew science fiction...*wow*.

"It's Jenna actually." Jenna sipped the beer; which had a lighter taste than the beer she had earlier and was really rather nice.

"Jenna would have been my next guess," Trevor replied "and she's a totally cool pirate."

"Mine too," added Marmalade, he handed Emily a beer and together they sat down on the sofa so only Thomasine was standing.

"Pull up a bean bag and join us Thomasine," Emily offered swallowing a mouthful of the beer "this beer is rather good." Suddenly the sound of a distant crash came from below them.

"Weird that's the third time!" Remarked Marmalade.

"Really?" Said Thomasine intrigued.

"Yeah, we reckon it's like that film...you know...the one in the desert with the big underground snakes?" Trevor and Marmalade exchanged looks; neither of them could remember the name of the film.

"You mean *Tremors*," said Emily "and they were called *Graboids*." Marmalade turned and looked at her with a huge grin on his face.

"Outstanding!" He said as they clinked beers together causing the beer to slosh about and froth up out of the top of the bottle; a little dribbled down the side of the bottle and onto her cream kaftan but before it had chance to soak in Marmalade was dabbing at it with his baggy shirt.

Jenna leaned forward in her seat and peered across at Emily; she was still blushing but smiled back and seemed a little less ashamed; Jenna mouthed the word *geek* at her and Emily just nodded and covered her eyes in mock shame.

"Three times?" Asked Thomasine.

"Yeah, like someone trashing furniture." Trevor replied.

Thomasine moved around the room, casting her eyes over everything making sure that this room was safe; when she was sure that it was she moved to the sofa and whispered in Jenna's ear that she would be back shortly. Jenna nodded and watched her leave then turned back to the small screen; Trevor had a jumbo bag of salt and vinegar squares and was offering her some.

Thomasine took a final glance as she left the room; she could just see the tops of their heads, Trevor, Jenna, Marmalade and Emily. Closing the door she tested the mechanism; still nice and stiff. She twisted the handle until it came free in her hand; no one was going to get through that door again tonight.

Harry flushed the blood-soaked toilet paper down the pan and took another deep breath. Each arm was indented with five, blood-filled, slug-shaped gouges; almost as if leaches had been ripped form his skin, their task to remove foul tempered blood unfinished. He looked at his nails; they had no significant length, but each was filled on the underside with blood and loose skin *how on earth could that happen?*

"*Ah,*" a voice whispered through the wall of the next cubicle "*but girls like scars, think they make a man, a man!*" Harry watched the gouges slowly fill with blood once more; he remembered how a shaving cut can be stemmed with tissue so after wiping the blood away once more he tore large squares from the roll of paper and placed them over each mark. "*Feels good doesn't it?*" The voice continued; Harry grunted in the affirmative. "*The way the tissue fills with blood, goes clotted and sticks as you pull it from the skin; so...nice.*" Harry pulled the tissue away from the bloody tears in his skin; it had mingled with the short, thick hairs on his arm and tugged and tingled pleasurably as it was removed. He closed his eyes and let out a low moan.

Katie was feeling a little left out as she stood alone, though surrounded by other people. With Marla off dancing somewhere out of sight, no doubt grinding provocatively against her new found toy and not having seen her other friends for what seemed like a good couple of hours it suddenly dawned on her that she didn't actually know anyone else here. Maybe it was the alcohol talking; but she felt terribly vulnerable.

"*Who do you think's gonna be the first to have you now?*" The quick, spiky voice spat the words so quietly Katie couldn't tell exactly from where they had come. Lads talked in groups of two's or three's in different parts of the room; she shivered and jumped slightly as the next words seemed to slip like fingers through her hair and around her neck. "*He's handsome, him...the one in the white shirt...think it's gonna be him?*" Katie slowly allowed her eyes to wander across the room; she didn't want to make it look to obvious that she was looking at anyone. She sipped her drink; he looked ok.

"*Don't they always?*" The voice whispered again from just behind her; it started in her left ear and then moved across to the right; she could feel the breath cross her neck as it did. How did it know what she was thinking? "*It's always the handsome, gentile ones that are the most dangerous.*" Katie sipped at her drink again but found it empty. Suddenly she felt another pang of vulnerability; standing alone at a party was one thing, but trying to do it without a drink was impossible. The guy in the white shirt suddenly caught her eye; Katie looked away...too late, he smiled at her and began moving in.

"I thought Harry would've been here by now," Dominick showed his watch to Brian who nodded and swallowed more beer. "He's never normally this late."

"Yep, maybe he's pulled already." Brian swallowed more beer and looked across at Dominick who looked stupefied. "Okay, so not likely…but looking at some of the skirt in here you'd have to be a real lemon not to get any."

"Not a lemon, a Harry!"

"So what you want to do; leave?" Brian asked. "You know we got to be in Exeter for the football tomorrow; I don't want to be out late."

"True," Dominick noticed that both of their beers were nearly dry. "Tell you what let's get a couple more, have a little look-see and then go."

"Cool."

Darren finished the first can of strong beer and closed his eyes; he was feeling good. His head bounced along to the music and for a moment he could have been anywhere.

"Darren," a voice broke bought him back to reality. "Mate, wondered when you'd get here!" Darren opened his eyes and saw Mathew standing slightly unsteadily in front of him; he landed one of his meaty paws on Darren's shoulder making him drop his empty can. "Sorry mate, here have mine!"

"Get rid of this oaf." The voice whispered.

"Nah, its' fine mate…was empty." Darren explained; Mathew seemed relieved that he wouldn't have to give up his beer.

"Time to do your job boy."

"You seen David anywhere?" Mathew asked; Darren shook his head and leant forward, beckoning conspiratorially for Mathew to do the same.

"But I did see Ann looking well hot."

"Really," Mathew smiled "how long ago?"

"About five mins, she was over there." Darren pointed to the far corner nearest the entrance. "I think she might have had an argument with Sally."

"Really, what makes you say that?"

"Looked like she needed cheering up."

"Ah, needs a little festive cheer," from his pocket Mathew produced some rather squashed mistletoe "and I'm just the man. Catch you later."

Darren watched him go… *now didn't he have something to do?*

"Hi," the guy in the white shirt smiled; the music was loud and he leaned in so he didn't have to shout so loudly. "I'm Kieran; couldn't help but notice you being abandoned by your friend."

"She's only gone for a minute," Katie answered quickly; she tried to peer over his shoulder to see if Marla was coming back yet but this guy was even taller up close.

"Just a quickie eh?" He laughed; Katie tried to back away slightly, but the wall was right behind her.

"Don't let him trap you in a corner little girl!" Katie shivered and fondled her left ear as the voice tickled it as it passed.

"You cold? I'd offer you my jacket...if I was wearing one."

"Oh that's just the start of what he can offer to give...wait till he asks you to go somewhere else."

"Do you want to go somewhere warmer?"

"No, really I'm fine." She thought she heard Marla but couldn't see her; trying to move to the right her feet caught on handbag and she stumbled slightly."

"Whoa, steady girl!" Trying to be a gentleman Kieran caught her before she fell unfortunately as he did his hand brushed her breast.

"It starts..." The spiteful voice shrieked touching just the nerve it intended in Katie's mind. She reacted through instinct, kneeing him in the groin...or would have done if she had not been so drunk she couldn't aim straight or hard. Instead her knee banged harmlessly into his thigh and appeared to onlookers as more of a nervous twitch. *"You deserve everything you're gonna get tonight...pathetic...little...bitch..."* Katie started to cry.

"Honey, what's wrong?" Katie looked up through reddening, eye shadow streaked eyes at Marla.

"What's all this then mate?" Kieran looked across at David who had returned with Marla; he shrugged and made the 'she's had too much to drink' arm gesture.

"I don't feel well." Katie muttered as she wiped her eyes, Marla stopped her so as to prevent her from completely ruining her makeup. She looked up at the two boys and rolled her eyes. David stooped and helped Katie stand up, Marla put her arm around her allowing Katie to rest her head on her shoulder.

"Come on, let's go to the bathroom and sort out that slap." Marla instructed; Katie nodded. Kieran and David watched them go.

"Scary moment for you there I'll bet!" David joked.

"I'll say," Kieran let out a big sigh and looked at his friend. "How come you came back so quick, I thought you were well in there?"

"Me too," David shook his head, "it was weird, like someone flicked a switch in her. One minute she's got her hands on my balls, next she says she's got to go get her handbag!"

"That's women for you!"

"Aye," David agreed "least you can trust that." He pointed to the beer and both men smiled.

"You're going to have stop." Graeme muttered, his hand moving to cover hers.

"You sure?" Hannah asked.

"Yeah, for now," He leant across, kissed her and cupped her left breast gently "but only until we get…"

"Home!" Hannah smiled removing her hand; Graeme turned the ignition and the car came to life.

"Oh yeah!"

**

Jimmy watched the ever increasing number of cars join the mass parked in front of the Whitehouse. Despite having been stuck in a pillbox for more than sixty years Jimmy recognised that the world was now a very different place to the one that he had died in; whilst he couldn't leave, he could see. Motor vehicles had changed shape, new style buildings had sprung up, just in view, over the road; people wore different clothing and the air tasted so much worse…he might have been dead, but that didn't mean that he was out of touch with the world. Perhaps it was this that suddenly caused him so much agitation.

Someone punched him in the stomach, or might as well have for that was how he felt as he doubled over; his left hand clasped himself whilst his right stabled himself against the wall. The feeling subsided slightly and Jimmy pulled himself upright to the door and looked out as a small car passed, *four female occupants…one of them…SHIT…no; it couldn't be…could it?*

Jimmy strained against the power that kept him captive. After the initial first few years of frustration he came to a level of resignation; now that was all gone.

"You gotta let me out!" He bellowed to anyone who might listen. "I won't let this be!" He raised his fist as if he could bash his way out and then, just for a moment an image of Thomasine popped into his head.

He lowered his fist and pursed his lips, thinking. She was different...*how*...he pondered; *well, cute and nice figure*...hey only fifteen...*yeah but so much older really.* He slapped himself about the head and tried to tell the argumentative parts of his brain to work together rather than against. *Because she's calm*...calm...calm! Where'd that ever get anyone in life...*but not death*...oh!

His nose twitched, *strange, smells like aftershave*...and not mine! A gentle hand rested on his shoulder and Jimmy, despite already being dead, nearly died of fright.

"Gently lad; t'is blood you recognise in that car."

Jimmy watched the car as it made several attempt to find a suitable spot to park. He looked up at the old man who continued to hold him; the old man returned his gaze and half-smiled-nodded.

"Kept you safe here; but now the pull is too strong."

"Kept me safe? Wait you mean you where the one who's been keeping me in here?" Jimmy was having a moment of revelation and struggling to control his emotions.

"Kept you from her touch...she killed you once," he shook his head and looked down "don't let it be forever!" Jimmy flinched at this comment, *what was forever?* "Tonight everything changes. The girl needs your help."

"Who?"

"The girl who came here dressed in shadows," the old man said exasperatedly.

"You mean Thomasine?"

"Aye, she wears shadows like lace...first help your blood if you wish." He released his grip from Jimmy's shoulder. "Remember, though the living have no sight of you...don't mean you can't save a soul."

"Wait, wait," said Jimmy trying desperately to get his head around everything; he sucked in a deep breath and looked at the door. "I got tons of questions..." the old man shrugged "which I guess are best left for later!" Jimmy said with a sigh; the old man grasped his hand.

"Whatever you feel and do, don't enter the house till you're called...she'll be busy with all these souls to feast on; but as soon as you enter she'll know." The old man's eyes where pleading and Jimmy began to understand the nature of the evil in the house; the old man faded from view.

"Damn, never even gave a name!" Jimmy muttered as he stepped outside the pillbox for the first time in his death

**

The novelty of sticking and removing tissue paper to his body was gone; it was hardly any fun when there was no blood flowing. Harry didn't know what to do, he was tired and wanted a drink, not just alcohol, anything would do to quench the thirst that seemed not to just fill his mouth but his whole body.

"What you need is more blood," the voice told him.

"Where I'm gonna get that from?" He whispered so no other person in this place would hear.

"You got more to give?"

"Yeah, but how?" Harry wondered.

"Your belt."

"My belt?" Harry didn't understand but as quietly as possible he undid it anyway, slowly unlooping it from his belt until he held it in his hands. He looked at the buckle which was simple and shone with faux chrome lightness.

"Break it..." the voice ordered.

Harry tried to snap it in his fingers but after several minutes of effort he realised that he just couldn't do it; he looked about for something to help...*ah, the bolt on the door.*

"No joy?" Dominick asked as he was reunited with his friend having split up to search the party.

"No mate," Brian agreed "I really think he's actually stood us up."

"First time for everything I guess!"

"Aye, I even tried his mobile." Brian stood to one side to allow a couple of lads to pass on their way to the toilets.

"Hey, we're not that desperate," his friend chastised. "Let's bale."

"Ok. Just gotta take a leak first."

"Sounds like a plan to me." Dominick agreed.

"You wanna go outside?" Kevin asked with his usual enthusiasm; he and Sally where slowly being squeezed together as the crowd in front of the DJ continued to grow. They hadn't spoken for some time, speaking was difficult it was so noisy without shouting in each others ears.

"What?"

"Outside; you and me?"

"Why?"

"Fresh air; a bit of space...you know?"

Ordinarily Sally would have probably said no; however maybe it was the alcohol, maybe it was that the umpteenth person had just stepped on her foot, but she found herself agreeing and steadily they made their way to the door. Once outside Kevin told her to wait a moment whilst he nipped back in for something; he emerged a minute later with something tucked under his shirt, but refused to say what.

"Come on over here," Kevin pointed into the darkness away from the house.

"What you hiding there?" Sally asked; trotting after him intrigued.

"Something to make this more fun," he stopped and was looking for something. "Come on, I saw you earlier; aha!" He dived off into the bushes and emerged a second later dragging something large. "Give us hand Sal!"

Sally looked unconvinced as Kevin dragged the small boat out.

"What is that?" Kevin stopped pulling, looked at her and opened his arms and was about to say *it's a boat*. "I know it's a boat! What do we want with it?

"Thought we'd go for a romantic sail."

"I'm not dragging that all the way to the sea; it's bloody miles away!"

"Nah, they got a lake...saw it when I arrived."

"Really?"

"Yeah, besides...where best to enjoy this..." he whipped out the bottle he had hidden under his shirt "champagne!"

"Serious?" Sally smiled eyeing the bottle.

"I ain't got no glasses though; have to drink straight from the bottle."

"No problem!" Said Sally as she grabbed the boat and helped Kevin drag it towards the 'lake'.

It was really busy downstairs and Joel had found the going easy; he was very happy with the nights work and kept on patting his trousers pockets to reassure him that they where full of money. He smiled outwardly however this was relaxed as Michael approached; he didn't look at all happy. "What's up; you not sold out?"

"No…I mean yeah," Michael was definitely agitated. "Just seen an ex."

Joel smiled, *was that all?* "An ex-girlfriend…"

"Business partner," Michael interrupted "so to speak." Joel didn't understand and Michael was cool with that; *if he knew half the shit…* "I gotta go find Mark; he'll need to be warned."

"Okay, okay…I saw him and Stacey through there about twenty minutes ago; they're probably on the booze by now." Michael nodded.

"Right, stick with us…just in case." *In case what?* Joel wondered, he wasn't about to fight anyone.

Stacey was sitting cross-legged on a stack of beer cases, her head bounced along to the rhythms coming through the speakers. She was feeling much more relaxed; the music was uplifting, she'd given up on the orange juice and just concentrated on the vodka. She'd done about three-quarters of a bottle, a pub-sized bottle that had already been started; the label was on upside down…that had certainly confused her at first. Mark was nearby talking to a couple of lads by a table near the kitchen; she watched him occasionally, she was feeling horny…but she didn't want him; no, she wanted something new. She had one button of her polo top undone so she undid the other two.

Michael loomed into view and went straight up to Mark and was greeted with an unreturned high-five; they began talking; Stacey couldn't hear what was being said, so long as it didn't involve her, she didn't much care.

"Hey, Joel!" She beckoned him over, having to shout despite him being only just out of reach. She leant forward to welcome him with a big hug making sure that she pressed right against him…he had strong arms and a bigger, more manly chest than Mark. She rocked unsteadily as Joel eagerly hugged her, uncrossing her legs she placed one either side of him as he stood in front of her. "Drink?" She lifted the bottle and Joel nodded; she went to pour then noticed that Joel didn't have a glass. Looking to her left she spied an open packet of plastic tumblers on the floor behind her; she raised a finger to say 'wait' to Joel and leaned back to try and get them…she would've tumbled off had Joel not grabbed her hips and held her steady; she locked her legs onto his. Grabbing the packet Stacey pulled herself upright and resettled, making sure that she bumped forward on her bottom to get a more comfortable position and that in doing so their groin's briefly touched.

Joel took the packet of tumblers from Stacey and took one out; he figured she was pretty drunk but he wasn't going to complain. She poured him about half a pint, despite him saying stop several times earlier, she concentrated on not spilling a drop and making sure that Joel could see right down her top. Once the drink was poured she looked up at him taking his eye.

"Label's on upside down; isn't that weird?" She pointed out; Joel nodded.

"Yeah," he wasn't really paying attention to the bottle because Stacey was gently rubbing her legs against him to the beat of the music and she did have very pert breasts. "Probably been nicked from some pub."

"Ah well, their loss, our gain." Stacey looked across at Michael and Mark who were both gesticulating at one another. She reached up for Joel and pulled him in closer on the pretext of whispering in his ear; their cheeks touched and neither made any effort to separate. "What's the problem?"

She smells so good, Joel took a deep breath. "Some sort of problem with an ex-business partner."

"Oi, mate, gotta go" Mark suddenly separated himself from Michael and leaned into Joel's ear. "Meet you at the car in twenty; right!"

Joel was still enraptured by Stacey's perfume and touch; he turned and nodded without truly listening to the words spoken…pure vodka works quickly on an empty stomach. Mark and Michael disappeared off into the crowd and Stacey continued to hold onto Joel.

"Tony, why won't you talk to me? Last time you were much more talkative."

The voice had changed from being just a suggestion, a hint at the edge of his conscience to something tangible; a real voice he could focus on. Someone grabbed hold of Tony's shoulder and pushed and he felt himself spinning; it was then that he finally realised that he was actually hanging upside down.

BANG…BANG, BANG, BANG…BANG; somewhere, someone was desperate to get in…and for a moment even the voice that taunted him was silent.

"So how old you?" Trevor asked as he offered Jenna an open bag of salted potato hoops.

"What a question to ask a lady!" She placed her hand into he bag and withdrew a small handful of crisps.

"Not asking a lady," Trevor took a breath; something in the deepest recess of his mind told him *DON'T SAY THAT*, Jenna didn't react, but that in her hand may have suffered; quickly he switched tract and hoped he hadn't ruined things before they got started. "Umm, just asking for, you know…continuity."

"Born April seventy-eight." She turned to him and smiled ignoring his little slip; he did have the most innocent eyes.

"Cool; totally named in the height of season one."

"Probably," Jenna smiled. All the crisps in her hand where gone…the beer accentuated her thirst; should she try and take more? Trevor offered the bag. "I shouldn't." she muttered as she straightened her jeans in the vain hope her hips would be less noticed.

"What? Your boyfriend giving you a hard time over your figure?"

"No, single actually."

"Really? Cool. Cos you look cool."

"Should probably eat less of these," she said as she took another small handful. "Less on the hips!"

"You gotta good shape," Trevor replied as he watched the screen. "Oh, she is totally dead this episode!" All three of the others looked briefly at him; Trevor was oblivious. "No…you look fine…I…" He said briefly casting a look in Jenna's direction; in a fraction of a second his eyes wandered from the screen and across Jenna's face, down over her breasts to her hips. Despite there being no flesh on show… he was captivated. He looked up and Jenna was looking at him; both of their mouth's twitched in half-smiles.

Ten
Confronting

As soon as Ann was out of Sally's sight she began thinking about her car; the same nagging thought that maybe she had better check again was bouncing around her brain. She knew the car was overdue for a service perhaps that was why it was playing up and that this was probably its little way of getting her attention; once outside she dodged through the clouds generated by at least a dozen smokers and headed towards her car.

Jimmy sat on the bonnet of Ann's car and wondered what he should do. He had realised that this night was going to be different as soon the build up for the party had begun and as soon as he met Thomasine he started to wonder; however he had been totally unprepared for what he would see and feel *it was completely new to him.* The girl in that car, *this car...my blood...how come?* He'd known it even before Gwalather had confirmed his thoughts, he just hadn't quite got his head around how it was possible; he had a fairly shrewd idea but that would have to wait until he could make sure she came to no harm.

Once released by Gwalather, Jimmy had chased after the car and caught up with it as the passengers where disembarking. He whispered to her and for a moment he thought he made a connection; then she went into the party anyway. But he kept trying and before long she came back. However once again he was thwarted as couldn't seem to stay concentrating on him for long enough, *kids, why can't they focus,* and he thought his opportunity gone once Ann's friends had turned up and she had gone back into the house with them; yet he wouldn't give up.

Ann tried to spy he car amongst the mass of vehicles, there where loads more than there had been the last time she came out; vaguely she wandered in what she thought was the right direction. Jimmy felt her coming before he spotted her, *could be your last chance Jimmy boy,* he told himself, *don't screw this up.* Fiddling around with the lights had got her back in the car before; well it might work again.

"Bloody lights," Ann muttered under her breath as she noticed that her headlights were still on. "I'm gonna have a flat battery at this rate." She opened the car and tweaked the light stalk but the switch was off, therefore the lights should have been as well.

"Safer in here," Jimmy whispered in her ear. "Why don't you shut the door?" After a second that seemed like an eternity Ann got in the car, she shut the door and addressed the steering wheel.

"Why are you playing up…hmmm? I know you need a service; I promise to get it done next week, just don't let me down tonight." The lights switched off and Ann patted the steering wheel. "That's my girl." She tried to open the door, it wouldn't budge; must've pressed the central locking button on the key fob she thought, but pressing that made no difference. Realisation hit her and Ann considered banging her head on the steering wheel; then decided against it just in case the airbag went off, settling instead to throw her hands up in frustration she was well and truly trapped.

Jimmy watched her from outside the car; he could feel his blood flowing in her veins and reminiscence of how this was possible filled his mind.

Darren slowly worked his way through the throng on the makeshift dance-floor and headed toward the stairs; no one was paying him any attention *more fool them* he thought; *I'll make them remember me.* Casually he walked up the stairs, pausing for a moment he looked down over the crowd.

"Take a look boy," the voice whispered *"this ends now."*

Darren continued up the stairs and turned left into the first room; it was empty. He stood in the centre of the room for a moment and tried to remember where he had put the weapon in this room.

Michael led Mark as they worked their way through the crowd; suddenly he came to a halt.

"What," Mark asked "you seen him?"

"Yeah, just ahead…think he might have spotted me."

"Shit!" Mark looked for a way out. "Come in here." Together they headed through into the annex where there were loads of people dancing. Keeping close to the wall Mark now led into what he hoped would be a direction with an exit at the end; up ahead he saw a door. "Damn, it' locked."

"Let me try," Michael ordered "and keep an eye out."

Michael crouched in front of the door whilst Mark stood next to him and tried not to look conspicuous. Fortunately the room was quite dark and packed with people moving so no one seemed to be paying them any attention and also blocking them from being spotted. His eyes wandered and to his left there was a sofa pushed up against the wall every now and then the crowd would break slightly and he could see who was on it, he thought he recognised one of them and he was right, it was the schoolgirl he had nearly sold too earlier. She was having her face snogged off by some lucky bloke.

"Got it," Michael announced, pushing the door open he peered into darkness. "Don't think it leads outside but a place to hide for a while could be useful." The two lads disappeared behind the door, Mark shutting it with a final look at the school girl who was now underneath the bloke. "Careful," Michael warned as he turned on the small laser torch he kept attached to his house keys. "Stairs down."

Pushing the boat off into the 'lake' Kevin leapt in and grabbed the bottle.

"Allow me my lady." Kevin removed the foil and cage, then let the cork loose into the sky accompanied by a little whoop of pleasure from Sally. He offered the bottle with a smile and Sally took it; taking a swig the liquid foamed into her mouth and out, she giggled and looked at the label, hoping to see Moet or something similar.

"Here, this isn't champagne."

"Yeah it is!"

"Says Cava on the label."

"Well, that's Spanish for champagne isn't it?"

"Okay, tastes alright anyway."

"Excellent. Pass it over then!"

"Are we actually going anywhere?"

Darren was getting annoyed; he couldn't find the weapon he had left here. There where no loose floor or skirting boards, so it definitely wasn't behind them…and they where the last place he could think of looking in the room. The bed had been first; he was certain that there should have been something under the mattress. He sat down on the bed and frowned, the beer and vodka he had drunk where clouding his memory as to what was where and the voice came back.

"Wasting time, move on to the next room." Darren could feel a headache brewing and he was starting to feel uncomfortably warm; he slipped out of his coat and left it on the bed as he moved back into the corridor and on to the next room.

The buckle had snapped easily when twisted on the bolt and now Harry had plenty of blood. As he sat on the toilet he raised his right arm over his head and enjoyed the tickling sensation as the blood trickled downwards; then as it neared his clothing he lowered his arm down so the blood would have to flow back on itself. So far he had done it four times and he was sure his arm was getting lighter.

"Looks like someone's a little worse for wear!" Brian had stopped walking just in time to avoid Darren as he emerged into the corridor; Darren didn't even notice as he was too focused on the job in hand. Brian turned to Dominick who stood right behind him.

"Whatever, there's a lot of that going on; come on the bog's over here."

They entered the room with the toilets and joined a mixed-sex queue of a dozen people.

Tim was having the strangest dream about eating toast…a lot of toast; he didn't like toast. He was sitting at a table in his old school canteen surrounded by his old school friends, who where all as he remembered ten years ago, even though he was older. From somewhere the silence of the canteen was broken by an unknown voice.

"Well he's kinda cute," said a distant voice.

"Yeah, but you wouldn't, would you?" Said another.

"Nah," the first voice agreed "not if that's true." Both girls giggled.

"And I'm definitely not having someone likely to dribble all over me!"

"That is so not a good look!" Both girls giggled again. "Hey quick, I think he's waking."

Tim opened his eyes gently, his head was aching as was his neck and back; this was hardly surprising as he found himself at an awkward angle sprawled on a sofa hugging, ever so tightly, a lime green cushion. He looked at the cushion and then up at the two girls watching him; they didn't come into focus terribly well.

"Look at those eyes," one of them screeched with a laugh. "That is one tripped out boy."

Tim smiled and tried to introduce himself; unfortunately to the girls what came out was no more than a garbled jumble of syllables and they quickly disappeared into the crowd laughing. Tim didn't understand and he wasn't one-hundred percent sure where he was, actually he wasn't even one-hundred percent sure who he was, but he fairly sure that he had some friends somewhere nearby. He tried to move but at the moment his body wasn't ready to move; *just rest a little bit* he thought to himself and promptly fell back to sleep.

Thomasine stood in one corner of the cellar allowing not only her eyes to adjust to the darkness but to also take in properly what they were witnessing. The cellar was a vast space, with a dozen or so rustic stone pillars supporting the floor above and huge alcoves in the walls at either end; there were windows high on the wall opposite allowing a little half-light through, but mostly what little light there was, filtered through the cracks from the rooms above. Rotting wooden beer and wine crates where stacked in heaps everywhere; many where smashed as the small figure dancing in the centre of the room was growing every more agitated.

"Tony, why won't you talk to me? Last time you were much more talkative." The small figure gave the person hanging upside down from the ceiling a shove that belied its size and the figure spun madly. Thomasine was resisting the urge to step forward and intervene...now was not the time. Something began banging on wood somewhere nearby; the small figure stopped its dancing and listened and Thomasine recognised it as Tom; the banging repeated, from a door across the cellar. *Now's the time; whilst he's distracted* Thomasine decided, stepping forward from the shadows the banging repeated itself again but before Thomasine could reach the boy he turned to face her.

"You," he looked confused for a minute, not just at spying Thomasine, but more like a little boy who suddenly didn't know where he was. "You," he refocused and just for a moment in the poor light Thomasine was sure that his face changed from that of a young boy, to that of a woman, accompanied by the unmistakable smell of the sea. "Should not have returned, my warning to you was an over kindness I shall not offer again."

Something banged upon the door for the fourth time and this time whatever it was, was coming through. Tom reached out to the figure hanging and as his hand touched it burst into the most intense supernatural flames Thomasine had ever seen; taken aback by the sudden ferocity of light both she and Tom both recoiled although Tom appeared even more shocked at what had happened than she was. Thomasine focused and willed the fire out; as instantly as it had begun it was gone. Fortunately the figure seemed not to be in any worse condition than they already where so Thomasine turned her attention to Tom.

He looked at his hands perplexed; his face appeared to flex and change shape, as if there was more than one face trying to show itself, then he looked up at her.

"Please stop her singing..." His face changed shape again and once more for the briefest moment Thomasine smelt the sea and thought she saw a woman. "Save one then, plenty more." Tom's voice had changed into something altogether more spiteful but before Thomasine was able to say anything Tom backed away into the corner of the cellar and vanished.

The figure hanging groaned and Thomasine could see that in addition to being tied he was gagged and blind-folded; there was blood at the back of his head, but otherwise he was none the worse for wear; she had quelled the supernatural flames before they could harm his very real flesh. She felt the two boys fall into the cellar so left them to deal with him whilst she sought answers elsewhere.

Stacey watched Joel watching her. Occasionally he made eye contact for a second, then closed his eyes or diverted them away towards the DJ who was banging out ever more manic tunes; he had kept his hands on her hips and she kept him close between her legs. *Now or never* she thought.

Joel was very comfortable, but at the same time was worried about his friends. He knew that Michael had a tendency to walk a tightrope between right and wrong, and all to often fall off, but he had seen genuinely worried by whoever he had seen; still, with Stacy holding him with her legs and the music so banging, why worry too much? Stacey was wriggling about, pulling away slightly and then pulling back close.

"Hey," she pulled his head down nearer hers and pressing something into his left hand whispered into his ear. "You wanna go back to the car and play?" Joel looked at the contents of his hand; seeing three brass safety pins, he looked Stacey in the eye and a smile formed on her lips.

His head was aching and the thumping music wasn't helping; Rob was sitting at the kitchen table with Alison, both nursing cans of beer when Carly and Bob came bouncing in.

"Hey, we're not disturbing the lovebirds are we?" Bob asked and was met with withering looks from both of those seated. "God, someone die or something?"

"His head hurts," Alison replied "so will yours if you ask anymore stupid questions!"

"Alright, calm down" Carly placated, "anybody want a beer?" Everyone said yes and once new cans where opened all seemed more relaxed.

"You seen your brother?" Bob asked Rob and Carly knowing full well they hadn't ventured out much further than the kitchen since the party had begun.

"Nope," Bob replied "what's he done?"

"Nothing more than keeping the party going!" Bob smiled. "That DJ is still nowhere to be seen."

"He's probably upstairs with some bit of skirt," Rob cautiously looked upwards at the ceiling.

"You want to go look?" Bob asked innocently.

"NO!" Rob snapped back.

"Okay, okay, come on Carly let's go mix."

Once Rob and Carly had left Alison waited in silence. She noticed that the veins in Rob's neck were quite pronounced, his firm grip on the can was whitening his knuckles and occasionally he would break off staring straight in front to glance at the ceiling.

Carly grabbed Bob by the arm once they were outside the kitchen.

"He's not right!"

"That's hardly surprising is it?" Bob reasoned, he was worried about Rob too; but what he could he do? "He's had half his brains knocked out," he shrugged.

"I know he still seems well on edge though; I thought he was going to explode when you suggested going upstairs."

"Aye, me to; glad he said no though…this place is still giving me the creeps even though it's so full of people."

"Come on, you two where just fooling about earlier…weren't you?"

"Rob was; I wasn't." Bob smiled, Carly frowned. "Something shit's going to happen here tonight…I just know it."

Darren had checked in every room; there where no weapons to be found and he couldn't understand it all. There where too many people milling about to make it look too obvious that he was looking for something. The voice constantly drove him on to search the next room, but now he was at the end of the corridor; the only way was up!

Thomasine emerged into the attic from the shadows, it was just as she remembered although this time Gwalather was already here; he stood in the furthest corner from her, his back to her; he was holding something and sobbing gently.

"Gwalather," she said softly so as not to spook the old man "tell me about Tegen and the mine." Gwalather turned, his eyes were red and he shook as he spoke.

"Tegen?" He asked quizzically, looking first at Thomasine and then at the small portrait of the two children in his hands. Thomasine looked at the painting and saw the familiar images looking back.

"Your grandchildren?" Gwalather confirmed with a nod. "You said that the boy was you, Gwalather before; what did you mean?" Gwalather shrugged and gently touched the face of the girl. "Her name was Tegen wasn't it?"

"T'was my fault."

"You shouldn't blame yourself, Morvoren is really to blame."

"But I bought here, I built the mine."

"How did that attract her?" Thomasine asked wondering what a mermaid would want with a mine. Then she thought about the miners. "What did you put into the mine?"

"They told me not too, but the stone was so cheap and we needed to strengthen." Gwalather looked most apologetic. Thomasine thought back to the book and the chapter on how to become a witch...*a Logan stone!*

"We found tin aplenty, but the rock was inconsistent and the first deaths came within months...we needed to strengthen, properly, the main shaft to the surface and the works..."

"So you used a Logan stone." Thomasine finished, Gwalather nodded.

"I didn't know Tegen was taken by Morvoren until she danced upon the stone, then it was too late and Morvoren moved onto Tom; Tegen was lost forever."

"Maybe," Thomasine replied "so the problem is Tom?" Gwalather nodded frowning.

"Won't be easy, but remember you have allies."

"Right, bettergogitten!" Thomasine was about to leave when she heard someone scrambling their way into the attic through the hatch.

Darren had grabbed a chair and pulled himself with ease into the roof; he was rather surprised to find himself face to face with a very pretty girl.

"Hello," said Thomasine "can I help?"

"I...don't know?" Darren was confused; the voice in his head had gone and he couldn't remember why, or exactly where he was. He looked around the room but it was too dark to see much, besides the girl did look rather sexy, *don't think that* he told himself *it'll just make you tongue-tied.*

"You don't know?" Thomasine crossed her arms as she noticed him eyeing her up. "Why are you up here...Darren?"

"How'd you know my name?" He asked surprised, then probably thought that maybe she knew him from college.

"Because that's the name on your gravestone." Thomasine whispered seductively as she took a step forward; Darren noticeably whitened. "Why are you up here?" She repeated.

"'Cos the voice said I had too."

"What voice?"

"I dunno!" He took a step back because she was still slowly coming towards him. "What do you mean my name on a gravestone?"

"You don't know what voice," Thomasine asked, ignoring his question "yet you still do as it says!"

"I don't understand."

"You came here for the weapon you hid here earlier." Thomasine explained bluntly; for a moment Darren looked blankly at her, then his brain obviously clicked in. He began shaking his head and sweating; Thomasine was now within touching distance and she honestly believed that he was about to cry.

"The voice said I had too; that it would make everything alright." He continued stepping back towards the hole in the floor.

"You're a fool," Thomasine reached out and grabbed hold of the waistband of his trousers just as his first foot stepped over the opening and he was a fraction of a second from tumbling backwards to the floor below. "But that doesn't mean you have to die tonight!" She allowed him to precariously hang backwards over the drop; one foot safe, one dangling uselessly, his hands reaching out in front of him trying to find something to hold onto. With a quick tug she pulled him back into the attic so he could once again place both feet safely on something solid, his legs were visibly shaking as he realised how close he had come to death. "Get out of this house now," she jabbed his chest with her finger "don't come back ever…do you understand?"

"Yeah," Darren wiped away tears feeling very stupid to be crying in front of a girl.

"You've been used," Thomasine said as she watched Darren lower himself out of the attic. *"And you're not the only one!"*

Eleven
Fighting

This is well easy, Ian told himself, *and bloody good fun.* Tony had been gone for ages and to be honest Ian hadn't even thought about him for hours. There where two massive boxes of records to work through and tons of CDs; he could keep going until tomorrow morning easily. His hands where a blur, fuelled by alcohol and whispered words as the music cautiously gathered pace and volume and the crowd in front of him grew as more and more became intoxicated with the beats.

"Hey," Thomasine popped her head over the back of the sofa between Jenna and Marmalade; she noted the comfortable atmosphere growing between the couples and was pleased that what she had hoped would happen, was. "Sorry to disturb you…"

"That's cool," said Marmalade "you coming to join us?"

"Maybe later, I just wondered if I could borrow your mp3 player?"

"Sure, if you want; the music out there not to your taste?" He picked up the music player from the table wiping off the splashes of beer on his sleeve. "Sorry the earphones are a bit old school, I just can't get those in ear ones to stay…in."

"Me neither," agreed Emily "and I'm sure they're no good for your hearing long term. You okay out there on your own?"

Thomasine put the phones to her ear and turned the player on.

"No I'm good at the moment thanks; I'll come and join you later." The music blared out. "Wow, what is that?"

"Pop Will Eat Itself, *the looks or the lifestyle.*" Marmalade smiled. "A classic."

"Hmm, loud anyway, does this thing go up to eleven or something?"

"Pardon?"

"I'll take that as a yes." Thomasine stepped away and looked at Emily and Jenna and was pleased to see them relaxed and happy. *Now how do I find Tom?*

Marla held the compact mirror in front of Katie as she dabbed the wet tissue around her eyes. The only sink in the toilet was in constant use and offered no privacy so once they had some wet tissue Marla had taken her friend into the far corner away from the toilets and was helping her sort her makeup.

"You okay?" Marla asked.

"Yeah, just came over a bit funny…must've been a dodgy bottle of vodka."
Katie smiled. "How'd they look?" She blinked her eyes.

"Cool, red must suit you!"

"Ooh, cow!"

"Shut the door!" Michael whispered as he shone the torch around the cellar.
"I don't think we were spotted."

"Well let's not stick around to find out; there has to be another way out of
here." Both lads stopped as something let out a low moan. "Haunted?"
Michael asked, wafting the torch across Mark.

"Don't point that thing at me, the sound came from over there!"

"Oh, right." They moved carefully across the cellar, the torch guiding them
to a man-sized bundle hanging from the ceiling. "Do you think that's what I
think it is?" The figure groaned again and tried to move. "Hang on! Give us a
hand mate."

Together the two lads lifted the figure from the hook attached to the chain
around its ankles and lowered it to the floor; slowly they undid the gag, blindfold
and restraints and a rather pale and weary looking man peered up at them.

Thomasine was getting annoyed now. Tracking Tom was easy, despite this
place being full of people she could sense him easily; the only problem was he
wouldn't stop around for very long. Constantly he would flit in and out of
rooms, she could keep this up forever and knew that she would get him
eventually, however time was pressing…she needed a hand.

Ann was lying back on the reclined seat, wrapped in a blanket grabbed from
the backseat she had turned on the radio. Annoyingly the only station that had
reception was one playing *Hits from the Movies*; unfortunately all those movies had
been made between 1925 and 1945, still there was something soothing about
them and she turned the radio down a little but not off. Jimmy was sitting on
the bonnet listening to the tunes and watching the house, his head a mass of
unanswered questions but he was ready for action and revenge.

In his mind he heard Thomasine's thoughts regarding Tom and he smiled.
With a final look back at his granddaughter he entered the house more than sixty
years after he had first tried.

"You alright there mate?" Mark asked the man they had released from bondage; the man eyed them suspiciously.

"Steady," said Michael "don't know what's been going on down here but I swear it's got nothing to do with us."

"Yeah, we only just arrived," agreed Mark.

"Where am I?" The rescued man asked.

"In the cellar," Michael explained helping the man to his feet. "You okay...you want us to call an ambulance or something?"

"I'm fine," the bloke replied as he listened to the music coming from above. "Sounds like quite some party."

"Yeah, the Dj's tearing it up good and proper...you sure you're gonna be okay; there's blood on your back?"

"I'll live...and I'm the DJ." Tony knew who was responsible for this; now he was going to get revenge on Ian.

Thomasine was coming down the stairs just as Jimmy was coming up them; he had lots of questions and hoped that she would have answers.

"Hey," remarked Thomasine "you seen a little guy about this tall;" she put her hand to waist height "looks angelic but will kill you as soon as look at you?" She smiled brightly and Jimmy shook his head.

"What you need me to do?"

"We need to box him in; get him in a corner."

"Okay, I can do that...Thomasine, was he responsible for...me...?"

"For killing you? No, it's what's in him we want."

"How we gonna get him?"

"I can sense him, and follow him, but he knows as I approach. The plan is to make him run towards you."

"And I can keep him trapped whilst you?"

"Whilst I put these on him," Thomasine showed Jimmy the headphones. "There!" Jimmy turned and just caught sight of a small boy wending his way through the dance floor crowd; Thomasine was already in pursuit.

"I'm on it." Jimmy dived down the stairs, but instead of following Thomasine he worked his way around the edge of the room.

The floor heaved with people oblivious to the chase taking place amongst them. Tom sensed Thomasine and kept ducking and diving through legs and around handbags until he reached the far side of the room. He ran down the short corridor towards the cloakroom before coming to a sudden halt as a figure emerged from amongst the various coats and grabbed him; Tom struggled like crazy, but whoever held him was just too strong and persistent.

"Get off!" The young boy yelled as he struggled.

"Not likely," Jimmy replied "you gotta date with a friend."

Thomasine trotted into the corridor and was pleased to see Tom captured; she had the headphones on him in an instant, turned the mp3 player on to full and Tom stopped struggling, his eyes and face showing no emotion. As the music blared into his ears he stood statuesque, Thomasine signalled for Jimmy to let go which he did and came to stand at her side.

"What the hell is that?" Jimmy asked pointing at the small black box in Thomasine's hand.

"Think of it as a very portable gramophone," Thomasine explained.

"Hey," Jimmy frowned watching as Tom stood like a zombie. "I'm not that old!"

"Sorry," Thomasine smiled.

"No need; it's like a radio isn't it? What's it doing to him?"

"Yeah, kinda like a radio; but you can choose what you listen to." She looked at the scrolling display and showed it to Jimmy; the track was *Get the girl + Kill the baddies*.

"Prophetic," he muttered.

"Hopefully it's blocking out the mermaid's singing," she explained. "That way we can break her out and sort this."

"Right," Jimmy agreed nodding but looking blankly at Tom. "What mermaid?" He looked at Thomasine for answers but before she could offer any she nodded towards Tom.

"This one!"

Tom's face was twisted and distorted and his body shook as if thousands of volts passed through it; the thick briny smell of the sea rose throughout the corridor and Jimmy thought he might be sick such was its intensity. Thomasine watched Tom's face intently, it continued to flex and change, but the image of a woman was becoming more frequent; suddenly there was an intense crack of bright blue light centred on Tom and Morvoren was released causing Tom to collapse backwards to the floor of the cloakroom and Thomasine to drop the music player.

Thomasine and Jimmy looked on. Morvoren was in her twenties, or so she appeared to their eyes, with a pretty, pale face though her eyes, lips and cheekbones were shadowed in blue tones as was her black hair. Her slim upper body was wrapped in a figure-hugging dark brown bodice made from a strange material that held a dull shine like weed freshly dredged from the sea; it was fastened up the front with silver buckles that sparkled and the material ran along her arms so that only the tips of her pale fingers could be seen. Underneath this she wore a billowing blue, multi-layered miniskirt that rolled and shivered like waves on a sunlit day; it would have come to well above knee height…if she had knees or indeed legs. Morvoren floated three feet off the ground her eyes closed; her hands raised either side of her head as if in surrender, her blue skirt continued swaying like waves around an island.

"I thought when stories said mermaid's had no legs…" Jimmy started to say.

"Yeah, I know," Thomasine didn't take her eyes off Morvoren "myth and reality…can't trust either."

"Look at the boy!"

Tom sat up and looked about him, he looked confused for a second, tears began to form in his eyes and then he simply flopped lifeless backwards to the floor; instantly his body crumbled to dust as years of death finally caught up. Morvoren's eyes flicked open revealing black irises swirling in pools of emerald green.

"You shouldn't be here," Thomasine warned her "you belong in the sea, not on land."

"Is that your considered opinion?" Morvoren's voice was strangely soothing, rising and falling in sweet tones she continued. "You have no idea what it's like to live in the sea…so cold…so dark, so salty and boring. There's no music down there."

"Really; what about dolphins and whales, don't they sing?" Jimmy asked.

"Ignorant human life underwater…feeling the breath forced from your body, suffocating you without the relief of death, having to rise to breathe your polluted air every seven minutes or die; you've no idea what that's like."

"Like everything you thought was real, then it turned out it wasn't…then yeah," Thomasine disagreed "probably do."

"I came creeping from undersea, draped in greens and browns of undersea…the weeds; you call it seaweed, like it's something of yours, something you understand."

"I think she's nuts," Jimmy commented "she's just talking like a crazy."

"Hard to say really," Thomasine shrugged "never met a mermaid before…maybe this is normal."

"I guess; so what do we do with her?"

"We need to break her final connection, before she does anymore harm."

"Is it me, or is it getting warmer?" Jimmy asked; both he and Thomasine slowly turned to look at Morvoren; her hands were placed on the walls on either side of the corridor; rich blue fire swirled from her touch and was cheerfully ploughing its way through the ancient building. Before Thomasine had chance to suppress it Morvoren was moving, knocking both her and Jimmy aside.

"You okay?" Thomasine asked as she was instantly back on her feet and helping Jimmy to his.

"Yeah…" screams could be heard coming through from the dance floor; they looked at one another.

"We need to stop her before her singing takes everyone over." Thomasine explained.

"How we gonna stop her? You got any weapons; I mean what sort of weapons do you need to stop a mermaid? Do we just cover her in batter and threaten her with some boiling oil!"

"I got this." Thomasine showed him the necklace and Jimmy looked at it closely.

"Hmm, think I prefer my idea."

"Trust me; this will make her very unhappy." More screams could be heard and the two of them charged off in pursuit of Morvoren.

Rob was sick of the noise coming from the main room, *should've left the kitchen door on so I could have shut it* he mused. But now the sounds coming through was different; whoops of ecstasy turned to screams of terror; he got off his chair and stomped out into the main room to demand everyone should shut up. Unfortunately as he stepped out of the kitchen he did so straight into the arms of Morvoren. Perhaps all the alcohol he had consumed made him burn quicker, he certainly didn't scream.

Brian nudged Dominick as the door to the 'disabled' toilet slowly swung open a few inches. "Look, free toilet."

"No one's come out," the door opened a few more inches. "Maybe they need a hand." Dominick walked to the door and gently pushed it. "You alright? You need a...fucking hell!" He backed away slightly.

"What!" Brian hurried over to his friend and looked inside the toilet. Inside he saw Harry, he recognised the face; it would take a pathologist to identify the rest. His body had been ripped to shreds, blood and viscera covered nearly every possible inch of wall; a small piece of metal fell from Harry's hand to the floor and he half-smiled as he breathed his last.

Katie screamed, curiosity had got the better of her and she had to see what was going on; Marla grabbed her and made her look away. Brian was on his mobile, but couldn't get a signal other people began screaming outside the toilets and suddenly the door to the corridor was thrown open and a burning figure tumbled through making everyone in the room jump.

Several people ran over and thrashed at the flames with jackets, but the fire was irascible, simply setting fire to the clothing which was quickly discarded but it was clear that there was no immediate escape from the room and the fire was spreading. The corduroy curtains were ripped from the walls revealing not windows, but heavy chipboard panels screwed into place instead of glass; without tools or a miracle escape was going to be impossible.

Mark and Michael helped Tony to the stairs, he grumbled and groaned as he went but to the two lads he seemed determined.

"Leave him," Mark ordered. "We can't go back up that way." Michael looked at Tony who had to support himself against the wall as he opened the door.

"Can't just let him go alone, look at him; he might fall and hurt himself."

"Suit yourself...can you smell burning?" Mark asked looking about. "Probably from a boiler I guess."

Michael went across and helped Tony to the door, he cast a quick look back into the cellar to see if his friend had changed his mind, but he was off with the mini torch trying to find another exit. Slowly making their way up the stairs the smell of something burning definitely touched their nostrils.

"Steady mate," Michael waited halfway up the stairs at Tony faltered for a moment. "You sure you're ready for this? It was pretty banging party when we left...might be a bit...noisy."

"Thanks for the warning," Tony tried to smile "but I am a DJ."

"Right, yeah forgot you said…" he continued up the stairs and reached for the door handle; it burnt his fingers. "Ow!"

"What's up?"

"Bloody thing's red hot."

"Let me," Tony finished the last of the stairs and grabbed the handle, he flinched as the searing heat bit into his fingers; but not enough to stop him wrenching it and throwing the door open…the fiery heat swept into the corridor encouraging flame to charge forth in its wake.

Michael instinctively took a step back however Tony was determined; putting an arm in front of his face he jumped through the flames with only one target in his mind. Michael could see through the flames that Tony was through safely and moving on into the room; it was strange for despite the flames, he was sure he saw people continuing to dance. He called back down the stairs for Mark, but hearing nothing in reply he too made up his mind…he would never see his friend alive again. Shielding his face he dived forward hoping to land on something soft.

Morvoren spun through the house like a whirling dervish touching whatever she willed; fires sprung up in dozens of places, yet still people danced. Thomasine and Jimmy plunged in amongst them hoping to drive her away; it was working. Whenever she came face to face with one of them she turned ninety degrees and continued, every time it was the same, as if it was programmed into her very psyche. Working this to their advantage they guided her towards the back corridor and forced the spinning mermaid down the corridor towards where Emily, Jenna, Trevor and Marmalade were chilling; all four jumped as Morvoren banged against the jammed door, her escape route barred as Thomasine and Jimmy closed in from the other direction.

"Jesus," Trevor cried "someone wants to get in here hellishly badly!" All four of them turned around on the sofa to see if anyone was going to come through, of course they didn't know that thanks to Thomasine no one could.

"I'll go see who it is," said Jenna as the banging came again "it could be important."

"Wait!" Said Emily. "It's never safe to do that on your own; it's always how they get you in films."

Jenna paused and looked concerned for a moment, then smiled. "You…I'm not that gullible."

"Well, you never know" Emily added, "just thinking about your safety."

"She's right," said Marmalade nodding "trust the sci-fi queen on this." Something banged against the door again. "But it could just be someone wanting their TV back!"

"Don't let them in" Trevor remarked, "the next episode is brilliant."

"I'd better see," Jenna was inches away from touching the door when she heard Thomasine shouting.

"Don't open it!" She and Jimmy blocked the corridor so Morvoren had nowhere to 'run'. "Remember, girls that stick together, make a pretty potent force." She called out and could just hear Jenna replying *okay*.

"What now?" Jimmy quite reasonably asked as he watched Morvoren spread her fire onto the door.

"We need to get her up to the attic; then the three of us can finish this."

"Okay; how?"

"By thought."

"I can't do that" Jimmy sheepishly admitted. "I mean I noticed you can…"

"What kind of ghost are you anyway?" Thomasine jibed playfully.

"A not very experienced one," he agreed. "Hey sixty plus years trapped in one small concrete box…it feels good just to walk anywhere!"

"Trust me on this" Thomasine smiled, "it's as easy as thinking."

"I'm not sure I want you to see what I'm thinking," he raised an eyebrow provocatively.

"Hey, eyes on the prize soldier!"

"Yes ma'am!" He readied himself. "Say when…"

"Now!"

Tony stumbled through the crowds aiming straight for Ian, murder on his mind; he never made it. As the crowd bounced and burnt to the tunes Tony's unsteady footing was taken from him and he ended up crashing to his knees a few feet short. He tried to stand but every time another body knocked into him and put him back down again and every time getting up got a little harder…until it was just too much.

"It's gone quiet" Jenna put an ear to the door "Thomasine; are you okay?"

"That looks like smoke" said Emily pointing at the bottom of the door.

"And smells like it," agreed Trevor. "What do we do?"

"We need to block it out," Jenna replied "we need towels of some sort of material soaked in water...that'll block it."

"Can't we just open it?" Marmalade asked; the other three just looked at him and shook their heads.

"Think people," Jenna raised her voice. "Quick!"

Everyone looked about for suitable material; Emily caught Marmalade looking at her dress...she crossed her arms, raised a quizzical eyebrow and gave him a 'don't even think it' look; he blushed and smiled.

"Rumbled," he muttered as he looked away and began taking off his own shirt. "Hey Trev, come on get yours off." Trevor reluctantly did as asked.

"We need liquid" said Emily blushing as she tried not to look at Marmalade's trim figure or his boxers which where visible over his low-slung trousers.

"Gotta be beer," Jenna got Trevor to hold his shirt out and she poured beer over it.

"What a waste..." Trevor remarked.

"Don't worry; the t-shirt can always be washed," Jenna assured him.

"Nah, got two more identical...beer!"

"Do you think that's enough?" Emily asked Marmalade as she did the same to his top.

"Hope so; we've only got a few bottles left!" Marmalade smiled what he hoped was a reassuring smile.

"Better save that then," said Emily "just in case we have to use this dress." She flicked her eyes up to his.

"Promise to look away," he smiled.

Jenna stuffed the two sodden tops around the base of the door and everyone moved to the far side of the room to see if they could prise away the boards covering the blocked doorway.

Having grabbed Morvoren, Thomasine and Jimmy arrived in the attic to find Gwalather awaiting their arrival, he held out his hands and encouraged Jimmy to take his right and Thomasine his left; Thomasine and Jimmy held hands trapping Morvoren in a triangle. She bounced back and forth looking wildly about her and spitting unrecognisable words, but bound within the grasp of three she could apparently not harm she appeared powerless.

"How did you know she couldn't burn us too?" Jimmy asked.

"Well, I figured that as she's killed you once, she couldn't do it again."

"How sure were you?"

"Oh reasonably." Thomasine smiled brightly.

"How long do you think to hold me here?" Morvoren asked focusing on Gwalather. "I know you, I sense your blood on my fingers…your family was so good to me; took me in and gave me shelter." Gwalather couldn't bring himself to look upon her; which made her chuckle. "You think you've been hiding from me for all these years; well I've always known how to reach you…I enjoyed your suffering too much to grant you release." Gwalather continued to look away uttering Cornish curses gently as he did.

"Enough," Thomasine interrupted "time to let you go."

"Let me go?"

"Send you back to the sea…that is where you belong…even if you are the last of your kind."

"We are many," Morvoren bluffed but her frown gave her away.

"No, you are alone…the last of your kind; I can sense it." Thomasine looked sadly at her, "you must be so very lonely."

"Hence I lose because there are more of you?"

"Well, you are evil."

"Says you…your kind don't sit to well with them either."

"But we are never judged," Thomasine shook her head. "You don't belong here."

"I just wanted to play…it's so lonely…" Tears formed in the corner of her eyes; Thomasine let go of the two men and took the necklace off. Wasting no time she slipped it over the mermaid's neck, making sure that the image of the girl was uppermost. "Please don't make her come here," the mermaid begged.

"Too late" Thomasine whispered, "you've kept her prisoner in Kings Wood, bleeding her of life for too long…besides, she's already here."

Light emerged from the black necklace and focused itself into a spot behind Thomasine, who stood to one side and the two men disengaged hands as Tegen emerged from shadows. Thomasine held out her hand.

"Come on, don't be frightened." Tegen took her hand and stood in front of Morvoren. She looked up at the creature that had condemned her to decades of loneliness in Kings Wood; tears formed in her eyes as she gazed first upon her tormentor and then at Gwalather who smiled, mouthed words of forgiveness and reached for her. However as the curse was broken the years caught up with

Tegen and as she reached for Gwalather, as Tom had before her, she simply crumbled into dust. Gwalather lowered his head and his eyes.

Morvoren continued to sob, but as she did her appearance began to change, she paled; not just physically, her clothes also drained of colour. Unable to draw life from Tegen she could no longer retain her form on dry land and as Thomasine and Jimmy looked on in awe the mermaid's living form transformed into a beautiful pinkish-white statue, a perfect replica of the living being though now exquisitely constructed from coral and shell.

Gwalather mumbled something indecipherable and shook his head gently as he faded into shadow leaving Thomasine, Jimmy and the statue alone; from somewhere nearby sirens could be heard wailing awfully into the night. Jimmy let out a long held breath as Thomasine took the black necklace from Morvoren's neck.

"Is that all?" Jimmy asked; Thomasine nodded.

"The curse has been broken here, everyone has been released. Listen; the music's stopped." They stood in silence for a minute; all that could be heard was the sound of panicked screams and an old house burning with gentle pops and crackles.

"Should we be helping people evacuate?" Jimmy asked; his soldierly impulses immediately kicking in.

"No need," Thomasine explained looking at the statue. "Now Morvoren's influence has been removed from the music, people's survival instinct will see them safe." Thomasine ran her hand over the statue; the surface was smoother than it looked.

"You sure that's safe?" Jimmy asked.

"Yes, she's…gone" Thomasine licked her finger. "Hmm salty, like the sea."

"Let's try," offered Jimmy taking Thomasine's hand and licking her finger; he looked nonplussed.

"Well?"

"Can't taste a thing; dead remember!" Jimmy smiled.

"Men!" Thomasine snatched back her hand but smiled cheekily.

Ending

Jimmy finished pushing the statue of Morvoren into the back of the van and shut the door; he looked in at it cautiously through the glass almost expecting it to spring back to life. They had tried transporting the statue directly to the beach but for whatever reason the statue had refused to go any further than the Whitehouse grounds so they were forced to do things manually; fortunately it was incredibly light. Thomasine was watching the fire brigade bringing people out alive from the building, memories of the summer rekindled when she saw the fire engines. She was pleased to see so many people safe, however others had not been so fortunate and to the left of the house a row of at least a dozen bodies covered in blankets lay silently.

Thomasine smiled as she saw Emily and Jenna snuggling up with Trevor and Marmalade under silver blankets; they had managed to smash their way free but she didn't go over to speak...they would have forgotten her by now. She smiled again when she saw Tim, but for a different reason...he sat chatting to a female paramedic, the words Thomasine had written still on his forehead.

Elsewhere Carly and Bob where being approached by police for information; Ian sat rocking to himself under a blanket nearby, his hands badly burnt whilst Alison gently stroked his hair...Sandy was to the left of the house.

"How do you think they'll explain this?" Jimmy asked.

"Accident I'd say," Thomasine shrugged "dodgy wiring in the music system, too much alcohol in too many people in too smaller space."

"You sound like you've seen this kind of thing before."

"We could tell them a mermaid did it; but I don't think they'd believe us."

Jimmy nodded and looked over at Ann as she hugged her friends Marla and Katie as they waited for Dwain and a burly policemen to pull the small dinghy with Sally and Kevin out of the large muddy puddle where it had become beached; more policeman stood in the next field talking to two young men and a girl by a small white car almost hidden amongst a small copse of trees.

"Ready?" Thomasine asked. "Or do you want to hang around a bit longer?"

"I'm good," Jimmy replied wistfully "really good."

"So to the sea, who's going to drive?"

"Don't look at me" Jimmy held up his hands "ghost...remember."

'Well I'm only ... " Thomasine nearly said. "Good job I've been taking lessons!" Five minutes later they arrived on Pentewan beach.

"Phew and I thought riding in Jeeps was rough!" Jimmy commented, Thomasine looked at him and he did seem a little green around the edges.

"Hey you said you couldn't feel anything."

"I can feel travel sick!" He replied with a grimace.

They dragged the statue to the edge of the sea and the incoming tide began to lap at the base; like sugar in boiling tea it rapidly crumbled and within minutes there was nothing left of Morvoren except memories.

"What's to stop her coming back?" Jimmy asked.

"There are no guarantees; but if she does I'll give you a call."

"Thanks, but I'm sure you can manage without me." He looked at the necklace and the image of an old woman. "I don't suppose you can explain how you knew what to do?"

"Help from a very knowledgeable friend; so what you going to do now?" Jimmy looked off at the distant horizon. "I mean now you've found a granddaughter and all!" Jimmy smiled broadly.

"The dead and living can't live long-term together...I'm going over there," he nodded to the horizon. "But I might come and visit occasionally."

"What's over there?" Thomasine enquired.

"Normandy; my mates, fallen on the beach, still waiting." Thomasine saw that he had tears forming in his eyes and patted him on the shoulder.

"Well you better get on; you have kept them waiting rather a long time."

"Right...thanks."

"Thanks yourself...there's a lot of people alive today that have you to thank."

"And what about you Miss?"

"Ooh, Christmas...party with friends tonight."

"Another party!" Jimmy shook his head. "You must be nuts."

"Just with friends," her phone bleeped as a text message came through. "Speaking off..."

"I'll see you around Thomasine," He leant in and gave her a gentle kiss on the forehead; a smile blossomed on his lips. "I'm a bloody granddaddy!"

Thomasine giggled and waved as Jimmy faded into the morning light and after a moment she remembered to look at her phone. It said it was from Tracy; she was about to open her phone and read the message when she remembered what Jimmy had said about the dead and living…she turned the phone off; *might check it later* she thought.

Thomasine turned to get back into the car but found it buried up to its axels as the incoming tide had taken hold of it. She grabbed a stray hair from her face and pulled it behind her ear hoping that there was no one watching…*still who'd see.*

"Oops, that's not good at all." She muttered under her breath and disappeared off into the ether eager to ready herself for the forthcoming party.